THE ROYAL WEDDING HOUR

BOOK SEVEN: A GAME OF LOST SOULS

LISA SILVERTHORNE

Can a human and an angel of death live happily ever after?

Jack and Talia are about to find out.

At a romantic vineyard with old friends.

A squad of death angels. TONS of demons.

And Jack's overbearing mother.

Get ready for the wildest & craziest reality TV wedding ever!

As **Jack and Talia** recover from the battle for Heaven, the hunt continues to harvest Jack's soul.

At an isolated **Sonoma County, California winery**, Jack and Talia hide on reality television and compete in the show's wedding **games** to win a **fairytale wedding** on the live finale.

But first, they must survive Lucifer's slayer demons, hellhounds, and worst of all—**Jack's overbearing mother** in...*The Royal Wedding Hour*.

The Royal Wedding Hour

Lisa Silverthorne

Copyright © by Lisa Silverthorne

Published by ElusiveBlueFiction.com

Cover Layout Copyright © by Elusive Blue Fiction

Cover Art Copyright © by: lighthouse, koya979, danilina.olga.gmail.com, shawn_hempel, /DepositPhotos; Brusheezy.com; Obsidian Dawn

BOOKS BY LISA SILVERTHORNE

Standalones:

ISABEL'S TEARS

REDISCOVERY

LANDFALL

PACIFIC BLUE TATTOO

A Game of Lost Souls series:

THE CINDERELLA HOUR

THE PRINCE CHARMING HOUR

THE EVER AFTER HOUR

THE FALLEN HEARTS SEASON

THE RISING SPIRITS SEASON

THE ETERNAL SOULS SEASON

THE ROYAL WEDDING HOUR

Haunted Portraits Series:

BEAUTY: CAPTURED AND FRAMED

True Purple series:

RECOMBINANT, Book 1

AFTER THE FINALE OF *THE EVER AFTER HOUR*, TALIA AND JACK RECEIVED a heroes' welcome in Heaven. For defeating Lucifer's assault while most of Heaven's angels struggled to fix time on earth.

Talia knew that Jack was surprised to see the Heavens again, expecting his wings and halo to be removed back on earth—along with the seraphim powers he carried. Not even the seraphim knew how to handle a human with rare, mirrored angel powers. It had never happened before.

Even before the seraphim channeled their powers through him when they were trapped in the spire, Jack Casey had been an enigma that they hadn't reconciled yet.

Azrael said Jack's temporary wings and halo had complicated things even further.

She and Jack flew past the gleaming white Gates of Heaven where Archangel Puriel and her angels cheered them. Together, they circled around the massive, silvery-white gates and glided toward the upper reaches of Heaven. Toward the spires. Tall and delicate, they glistened with a pearly sheen beneath Parrish blue skies and Constable white clouds that scuttled past.

All around them, cherubim lined the crisp blue skies surrounding the spires, so many pairs of lustrous white wings lifted high in tribute as the cherubim hovered in formation. Some were in eagle form, others appearing as angels, winged lions, and winged oxen. They extended golden swords of Holy fire that guttered in the warm breezes scented with honeysuckle and roses.

Talia grinned, dove grey wings spread wide and caught the warm updrafts. Heaven's response to her and Jack's return made her so proud. They'd fought Lucifer and his army with everything they had that day.

When she and Jack almost lost each other.

The thought of losing him sent a cold wave washing over her heart and her human soul.

Jack glanced over at her, his silver-grey wings burned and ragged, feathers blackened and torn.

"That welcome for us?"

She nodded and held onto him as he struggled to stay aloft.

They passed parks, thoroughfares, and meeting places below—all crowded with angels now that Lucifer's threat had been quelled. They soared low as the meadows fanned out toward the grand hall of Eolowen that glimmered ahead, at Heaven's edge.

The turquoise blue skies above the shimmery white grand hall undulated with charcoal grey wings. Heaven's entire guard of death angels floated above Eolowen. Those left standing after the battle for Heaven, after Samael's treason got him imprisoned within the High House spire. The Death Angel Guard raised Eternean swords and golden shields of light to the sky.

Saluting them.

Even the Watchers below stood at attention along the terrace and in the grass, wings flexed as she and Jack flew over. They lifted their flaming bows toward the sky, lightning arrows crackling overhead like fireworks.

Getting Jack into to the grand hall was work.

He was severely injured from arming all those seraphim powers at once. Pain showed on every breathtaking feature of his face and in those sizzling, light green eyes.

He'd put on a huge front for the cameras and *The Ever After Hour's* live finale. The reality television show had almost become his show. For three seasons, he'd been the most popular contestant on it. She and Jack came in second place this season, but after the pain they went through when Lucifer froze time, she was thrilled that they even finished the competition.

Herb Rutherford, the show's director looked forlorn when she and Jack didn't win the final couple's challenge. Herb constantly said that Jack Casey was ratings gold, best thing that had ever happened to the low-budget production that Jack had propelled into the stratosphere.

She smiled, arms tight around Jack as she kept him in the air. Even his silver-grey wings dragged through the clouds, battered and frayed from the all-out war he fought against Lucifer.

Alone in the haunted woods. After Jack triggered the seraphim power that broke Lucifer's control and erased her memories.

"Can't—make it, Talia," he said with a groan, listing to his right, left wing dropped almost flat against his Navy blue Henley.

"Don't worry, lover," she said, "I've got you. And I'm never letting go again."

She held him close, still wearing her ice blue dress from the show's finale, but Jack insisted on getting out of his suit. They'd packed everything from the beach house and loaded Jack's Explorer. He drove them an hour south. Back to his apartment—in this condition. But after they arrived, he couldn't climb out of the vehicle. She'd just started to help him slide out when Muriel appeared, bearing a message.

Azrael had summoned her and Jack back to Eolowen. Back to Heaven.

Had the fixes they put in place repaired all the fractures in earth's timeline?

Right after the halo tether dragged Lucifer back to Hell, Berith saved Jack's life. Berith kept him alive after he had set off all those seraphim powers, intending to blow up Lucifer.

She shuddered. And himself.

Wincing, she remembered her memories rushing back to her from

Berith's story gem—followed by the news that Jack believed she'd lost all memory of him…the man she loved.

Berith's rare healing gifts kept Jack from dying that day, but there hadn't been time to assess his injuries. He'd barely gotten to his feet when Seraphina sent her and Jack back to earth. To reenter the timeline they'd been torn out of—to the exact moment in time and space when time froze.

To set everything right again. If only they could have reversed Lucifer's Phoenix Shift. Stopped him from regaining his wings and halo—and all those seraphim powers.

Sunlight washed across the glistening white stone walls of the grand hall. Above Eolowen, phalanxes of the death angel guard floated with shields of gold light raised and Eternean swords held high. They cheered as she half-carried Jack down the hall's long nave, above the crystal rooftop, and toward the terrace.

Where Azrael stood on his dais, soot-grey wings unfurled, hands behind his back, and a worried expression on his face. His silver-black hair blew in the soft breeze, those steely grey eyes alight with concern as she held Jack against her and landed on the terrace.

"Talia! You're back!" Azrael cried. "Report."

She smiled, holding Jack up with both arms. His wings drooped, but the left one hung limp and at an odd angle. His halo looked dim, eyelids hooded over those haunting, light green eyes. He was hurting.

After they said their goodbyes to the crew, they struggled through an emotional goodbye with Armand Gianni and Izzy Castilla, the winning couple of *The Ever After Hour*. Jack seemed subdued and sad when they climbed into his Explorer and left the Malibu beach estate behind.

At that point, Jack still acted physically fine. But it had been just an act.

After he'd pulled onto the highway, his game face slipped. She held his hand most of the way back to Los Angeles and his apartment. When he couldn't climb out of the Explorer, she knew he was hurt much worse than he'd let on and she went into action.

She sent Muriel ahead to Eolowen, letting them know she and Jack were on their way. And to make sure Berith was available. Jack desperately needed her rare healing talents.

"I didn't think we'd be returning here so soon," said Talia, still holding up Jack. "But everything on earth seemed back in place. The show's last challenge went fine. No glitches or demons showed up. The timeline appears to be fixed, sir."

At last, Azrael sighed in relief, shoulders and wings relaxing.

"We weren't sure what would happen to earth's time once the two of you reentered it," said Azrael, the corners of his mouth curving upward. "I can finally report to the seraphim that the last of Lucifer's damage has been repaired."

Talia nodded at the guard still standing at attention and honoring them. "We were a little surprised by everyone cheering for us."

"That wasn't cheering, Tal," Jack replied, his voice thin and quiet as he looked over at Azrael. "That was a heroes' welcome. Wasn't expecting that."

Azrael reached out and gently patted Jack's sleeve. "Believe me, Jack, you and Talia earned it. The guard would have mutinied if I hadn't allowed them to give you a soldier's salute. Every angel that fought Lucifer wanted to stand and honor the two of you. Heaven won the day because of the sacrifices that both of you made."

A crooked smile appeared on Jack's pallid face, blond hair disheveled and windblown. She grinned at him. Even though he was hurting, he looked so hot and sexy in those wings and faded Levi's, like he'd just rolled out of bed.

"Is Berith at the hall?" Talia asked and nodded at Jack. "He's in dire need of her rare healing abilities after almost killing himself with those seraphim powers."

"You mean after kicking Lucifer's ass," Jack snapped. "'Cause I was winning when he got yeeted back to Hell."

Azrael raised an eyebrow. "Yeeted?"

Talia just looked at Jack and then Azrael, shrugging. She had no idea what Jack was talking about—sometimes, even she needed a translator.

"Tossed back to Hell," Jack said.

Azrael shook his head. "Humans confuse me sometimes."

"Makes two of us, archangel," Jack said with a sigh and laid a hand against his head.

Up in Heaven, the damage from Jack's battle was visible now. She'd managed to disguise it from the humans and cameras with her angel of death abilities—along with their wings and halos. Her abilities made him look fine on camera and had even tricked her for a while, especially with him acting his way through the finale. That game face wasn't moving. Even when it was just him and her in the Explorer, he was still acting. Pretending he was fine.

Until he couldn't get out of the vehicle.

Seeing all the damage now alarmed her. Deep claw marks ran down the right side of his badly bruised face. In the haunted woods, he'd been bleeding from his ears, nose, and mouth when she finally reached him. Without the failsafe, the seraphim powers almost killed Jack. And so had Lucifer with his returned seraphim powers. Jack's left wing had almost been torn from his back by Lucifer.

Berith healed the immediate, mortal injuries all that power had done to Jack's body—and that Lucifer had inflicted. Without her rare healing abilities, that damage would have killed him.

She was so grateful to Berith.

She held Jack close again, running her fingers through his hair.

"Just hang on, Jack," she said in a soft voice against his left ear.

He nodded, eyes half closed.

All around them, the guard landed. Kesien, Muriel, and Anahera rushed up to them.

"You, two were amazing!" Kesien shouted, a hand on Jack's shoulder. "The way you handled Abaddon and then all those demons! It was incredible." Kesien's curls were coal black against his clear gold Eternean armor.

"Abaddon," said Azrael, eyes narrowing. "I admit that he's my current worry at this moment. Doing Lucifer's bidding."

"And the way they handled Lucifer!" Muriel cried, a grin brightening her face, dark hair bunching around her shoulders. Her grey eyes glimmered as her wings folded against her back. "Jack, you just owned him. I couldn't believe what I was seeing."

Jack shrugged. "He matched me blow for blow. But by the end, I kicked his ass because I had one thing he didn't."

Muriel's eyes widened. "What? Talia's rare powers?"

"No..." he said and bowed his head. "A death wish."

"What?" Muriel cried. "What are you talking about, Jack?"

The entire guard went quiet, watching him with a mixture of sadness and curiosity.

He wouldn't look at Talia now. "I'd completely wiped Talia's memory when I freed her from Lucifer's control. Knew I'd lost her, so I didn't care what happened to me—as long as I brought that little bitch, Lucifer down. So, I put all my seraphim powers on overload. Used the omnificence power as my fuse."

"Jack..." Azrael's face contorted and he winced. "The seraph warned me that you were going to take Lucifer down at the cost of your own life." He gripped Jack's arm. "Seraphina said that the Maker heard your prayer and sent her to intercede."

Jack looked up at him, a look of surprise on his face. "What? God heard my feeble little prayer and sent a seraph? To help me?"

The archangel nodded. "The Maker said it was a selfless prayer to the very last word. It moved the Maker. And Seraphina."

Jack stared down at his feet and those blue slip-on tennis shoes.

Talia's eyes widened and the whole guard stared at Jack with reverence. He was shocked silent. A rare event for Jack Casey.

Finally, Azrael broke the silence. "Berith is finishing some work for Pravuil in the archive. I'll call her back now. She'll come back in a hurry when she knows that you've both returned."

Jack pointed at his left wing. "So, now that my world's timeline is back to normal, what happens to me and these wings?"

The puzzled look on Azrael's face surprised Talia. He and the seraphim must have discussed this before they decided to put wings and a halo on Jack. And hide him among the guard. When Jack sacrificed himself after escaping Hell and trapped himself and Lucifer in the Garden—and Lucifer killed him.

Only Talia's rare powers, combined with the bond they shared, brought him back to her. And this time, Berith kept him from dying.

"I still need to discuss this situation with Seraphina, Jack," said Azrael. "For now, you just rest and heal. We'll have some answers soon."

"But I really want to know what's going to happen to me," he said and gazed at Talia. "And Talia." He sighed. "I don't want to lose her again, archangel."

Talia held him closer, if that was even possible. But she understood his concern.

After everything she and Jack had done to stay together, he wanted to know if it was all for nothing. She was an angel of death and he was a human actor. He'd asked her to marry him, not knowing anything about her life beyond the show.

So many challenges. She spent a lot of time on both earth and Heaven. Could she even marry him and stay at his side on earth?

After Jack lost these wings, he couldn't enter Heaven again, not without an archangel's assistance.

She had Jack hadn't had a chance to discuss any of these challenges yet.

"I'll speak to the seraphim right away, Jack and hopefully have an answer for you soon," said Azrael as his gaze moved back to her. "Talia, take Jack to his room and I'll send Berith there when she arrives."

"Thank you, sir," said Talia and half-carried Jack off the terrace.

"No, wait," said Jack, glancing from her to Azrael as he dragged his feet. "Talia, I want to know the answer to my question."

She lifted him into the air and flew through the largest opening in the crystal roof and landed in the room beside the terrace. Long, white curtains pooled on the circular room's stone floor and drenched the bed's white sheets with warm sunlight.

"We'll know soon enough, Jack," she said as she guided him over to the bed.

The room was unchanged. The bed stood against the nave wall, white sheets crisp beneath two white pillows. A white wooden chair sat along the farthest curve of the wall. Jasmine and rose water scented the air. Sunlight glimmered in rivulets of reds, golds, and purples across the warm stone floor, sparkling like confetti as she helped him onto the bed.

"I need to know right now," he insisted with a grimace.

She stacked the two pillows on top of each other and eased him back against them.

"Why right now?" she asked, leaning over him as she pulled the white quilt across his body.

"Just want to know the score, that's all," he said, arms crossing. "And I want to get a different place than that 1960 studio hellhole of mine. The lease is up, so we have a lot to talk about, Talia."

They had a lot to talk about. She smiled.

She loved hearing him say those words, especially the word, *we*. But she understood his concern. He probably felt anxious now that his hit television show had ended and Lucifer had been sent back to Hell. With his renewed fame, Jack would have his pick of film and television roles, requiring him to either show up at a studio every day or go away for weeks—or months—on location. Like they'd done for *The Cinderella Hour*.

"It's all up in the air right now, isn't it?" she said.

He nodded. "I have a bazillion job offers sitting in voice mail and on that old answering machine. Depending on where the productions are filming, I might have to go on location somewhere for months. And now that you're back in the guard, will you have to be here in Heaven most of the time?"

His sad eyes shined with worry.

"I have a lot of questions for Azrael, too," said Talia.

"We tried so hard to stay together, but will just the fact that I'm human and you're an angel make it impossible to be together?" His mouth pressed into a taut line, jaw tightening. He reached over and gripped her hand. "Just want you to know that if I've gotta walk away from being an actor, I will," he said in a quiet voice.

Her eyes grew misty. He was willing to walk away from his entire life for her.

He understood that she just couldn't walk away from being an angel of death. It wasn't a job. It was who she was. It was the reason she existed.

"I love you for that, Jack," she said and leaned over, kissing him. "But I'd hate to see you forced to walk away from the thing you love the most."

"That's you, Talia," he said with a smirk. His voice was like hot caramel, his touch like heat lightning. "You're what I love the most in my life, but I'm afraid they'll make you stay up here—someplace I can't go once these wings disappear."

Reaching up, she ran her fingers through his short, light blond hair. "We'll find a way to make it work, so don't worry about that right now, Jack," she said in a soothing voice. "Now, you just lay down and rest. As soon as Berith is back, she'll have you feeling much better."

He nodded, those hooded eyelids getting heavier as he laid his head back against the pillows.

"Can't help but worry," he muttered, his voice getting sleepy. "Kicked everything in Hell's ass to get you back. Need to know if...I'm going to...have to fight Heaven, too."

She laughed. As beaten up as he was, she loved that he was still willing to fight everything for her.

"Give Azrael time to discuss it with the seraphim, Jack. While you heal."

When she looked up, he was asleep.

The rustle of wings made her turn around. Berith. Landing in the room, Muriel and Kesien behind her.

"Talia!" Berith replied, long, dark-brown hair flowing down her back, light grey eyes wide. "I came as soon as I heard you were bringing Jack in—how is he?"

She rushed over to the bed and Talia moved out of the way as Berith peeled the white quilt off Jack's prone form.

"He's not doing well," she said. "He put on a brave front for the cameras and the show's finale, but he's been hiding a lot of damage. I don't know how he got through the live finale, acting like he was fine for the cameras and me. After the show, we drove back to Los Angeles. But he couldn't get out of his vehicle."

Berith laid her hands against his chest and summoned pale gold light at her fingertips that washed over Jack in waves. She closed her eyes, concentrating until the waves of light disappeared.

"Extensive damage," she said with a groan. "That left wing is broken in three places. He's got five broken ribs, a fractured collarbone, broken left wrist, and a fractured right knee cap. For starters. Those long gashes on the right side of his face need attention, too. I'll need all my powers to knit them back together without scarring that gorgeous face of his." Berith shook her head. "Lucifer about killed Jack again."

Talia's eyes narrowed as she studied Jack, her eyes still misty. He must have been in terrible pain this entire time. How had he stood it as long as he did?

"I thought you'd healed him after that fight with Lucifer," said Muriel, floating beside the bed.

Berith glanced up at Muriel. "The immediate, mortal wounds, yes. All my healing powers went to fixing the damage done by the seraphim powers. There wasn't anything left for his other injuries after I managed to keep his soul in his body. That took almost every drop of power I had."

"And I'm so grateful, Berith," said Talia, a hand on the redeemed angel's shoulder. "Thank you for giving him back to me."

She smiled. "It was the only gift he wanted, Talia. Broke my heart to see him like that. He thought he'd lost you forever when he lured Lucifer into the haunted woods. And he didn't care if he lived or died."

The flutter of wings brought Anahera through a portal in the crystal roof. Tall and willowy, she landed in the center of the room, short red hair windblown, grey eyes sharp.

"Talia," she said in her soft-spoken soprano voice. "one of the Watchers is reporting that someone named Herb Rutherford was trying to contact you. He thinks he called you on a phone, but the *call* got rerouted here, through the Watcher." Anahera smiled. "She pretended to be your agent."

This ought to be good, Talia thought with a chuckle. The director of *The Cinderella Hour* was calling her. She smiled. She could only imagine why.

"Why did he want to contact me?" Talia asked.

"He said he was very serious about what he said on camera at the live finale," said Anahera with a shrug. "They want to do a fourth season of the show, calling it The Royal Wedding Hour. They want you and Jack to compete with other couples for an all-expense-paid, fairytale wedding fit for royalty. Televised live to millions—he said to make sure to convey that."

She remembered the director saying something like that on camera during the live broadcast—after he proposed a rematch to Jack and Armand. Then Izzy suggested a royal wedding. Apparently, Herb did want to do another season of the show.

"He was serious?" Talia replied.

Anahera nodded. "Apparently so," she said. "They want an answer about doing another season right away. Said you stole the show when you told Jack that you would marry him. And they've been trying to call Jack's cell phone for days. The Watcher mentioned something about this Mr. Rutherford losing his mind while he waited for Jack to return his call."

She chuckled. She and Jack must have made the show's ratings skyrocket again. And she had no idea where Jack's cell phone was… probably someplace between Hell and Heaven.

"Thanks, Anahera. I'll talk to Jack when he wakes up," she said, watching Berith use her healing gifts on Jack.

"Is the kid going to be all right, Berith?" Kesien asked.

Kesien leaned his lanky six-foot-six or so frame against the wall, looking concerned. His curly, coal black hair framed his face and made his light grey eyes look so intense. He was easy-going and soft spoken. He liked Jack a lot—all the guard did. She was glad Jack was asleep and hadn't heard Kesien call him a kid.

"He's going to be laid up for a while, but I think he'll be fine," said Berith, glancing at Kesien.

"Gotta say that we all miss him in the guard," said Kesien, nodding toward the roof. "Jack always kept things lively."

Muriel laughed. "Yeah, he made patrols and other missions a lot of fun. Going to miss watching him lay waste to all those demons."

"That was an amazing thing to watch," said Kesien.

Talia squinted. "When he fought demons at the crossroads?"

"In the Middling," said Muriel. "Azrael, Kesien, Anahera, and I went after Jack when he tried to rescue you. We were sure he was going to get himself killed."

After being held captive so long in that watchtower, she wanted to cry when he broke through that window and took her in her arms. He almost got her through that window, too, but Lucifer stopped him. Jack managed to escape and Lucifer pursued him with half his demon army. She remembered the Scribe showing her that battle through the protection stone that she'd given Jack to carry.

"He almost got me out of that watchtower," said Talia, "but Lucifer interrupted him. Jack escaped through the window he'd broken and Lucifer chased him down with half an army. He was pretty masterful, wasn't he?"

Kesien nodded. "Azrael thought we were all about to be erased from existence. Then he saw Jack pounding those legions with murder marbles and other powers."

Talia laughed. Jack and his murder marbles.

"What made it amazing was the fact that Jack was human," said Muriel.

"Agreed," said Kesien.

Berith glanced up at Talia. "Give me some time with him and I'll have him back on his feet like new in a couple of days, Talia."

Talia nodded and motioned the guard out. "Let's give Berith space to work," she said and flew up and out of the room beside her squad.

She and Jack had a lot to talk about, but right now, he needed to heal. And she needed to talk to Azrael.

When she cleared the top of the roof and set down beside Muriel on the terrace, Azrael's dais that stood above Eolowen's rolling green meadows was empty.

"Where's Azrael?" she asked.

"Went to the spire," said Kesien.

"High House," Muriel added. "Said he needed to speak to Seraphina immediately about what happens to you and Jack, now that Lucifer's assault was thwarted and he's tethered in Hell."

She hoped that the seraph had some compromises in mind for her and Jack. Without those wings and halo, he couldn't enter Heaven. With hers, she could never truly be his human partner. Somehow, they had to find a way to make this work because she was never giving Jack Casey up again.

2

IT TOOK JACK A WEEK TO GET BACK ON HIS FEET. IT WAS A LOT LONGER than he'd expected, especially after Berith used her rare healing abilities on him. Even with all that rare healing, he was still hobbling around Eolowen—struggling to fly. His left wing caused him considerable pain whenever he did more than hover.

Like it or not, he was grounded for a little while.

Azrael went to High House to speak to the seraphim. He'd asked about what happened next for him and Talia, but hadn't gotten any sort of response yet. All the archangel said was that the seraphim were in council about the matter and would let him know.

One afternoon, Jack heard the archangel and Berith on the terrace, whispering. His blood chilled. About a slayer demon.

He kept his back to the wall and stood in the doorway of his room, listening. Something felt wrong here.

"Berith, I can't just blurt that out," said Azrael in a quiet voice, his back to the terrace.

His soot-grey wings twitched as he gestured toward the horizon. Azrael sounded worried.

"You're going to have to tell them, Azrael," said Berith, her tone insistent. "They have to know."

"He's not even fully recovered from the battle yet," said Azrael. "I can't just drop this on them right now, especially when Seraphina hasn't given me an answer about what to do with Jack yet. And now, you want me to say, *Hey, Jack and Talia, there's a slayer demon still after you.*"

That slayer demon. He remembered that huge, angry demon that had emerged from the Middling. The one Lucifer sent. And not just any demon either. The king of slayer demons.

He and Talia had tricked it, sending it back to Hell. Talia gave it a story gem with a tether loaded inside it. That meant this demon figured out the gem hadn't contained his soul like Lucifer wanted. That demon hadn't activated the tether either.

And unlike Lucifer, this demon wasn't stuck in Hell either.

Now that Jack no longer had seraphim powers, how in Hell would he and Talia take this thing down? Whatever its name was—he couldn't remember.

"What about talking to Pravuil about Abaddon?" Berith offered. "He was once in service to the Maker. Maybe the Scribe can help us deal with him?"

Abaddon. That was its name.

"I agree," said Azrael. "We'll discuss this with Pravuil. Abaddon spent millennia in Hell, herding souls through the Abyss. Giving Lucifer plenty of time to turn him to his cause."

Berith turned her gaze toward the hazy grey horizon beyond the edge of Eolowen's meadow. "Something made Abaddon abandon his connection to Heaven and join Lucifer. I'm certain that Lucifer has done everything in his power to get Abaddon on Jack and Talia's trail again. Since he's tethered in Hell now. It's his best way to strike back at them."

Azrael propped his hands on his hips, wings rustling. "And if I know Lucifer, he's doing everything he can to hit back at them. Especially Jack."

"Jack?"

Startled, Jack whirled around.

Talia stood behind him, long white curtains billowing around her. He grabbed his chest and exhaled sharply.

"Talia! Almost gave me a heart attack."

"Why are you eavesdropping on the archangel and Berith?"

He moved toward her, away from the threshold leading out to the terrace, and laid his hands on her arms.

"Overheard Azrael and Berith talking. They don't want to tell us that there's a slayer demon still after us. Abaddon. Remember him?"

Her luminous grey eyes got wide and she stared at him for a moment. "What? Abaddon is still after us? Wasn't he the king of the slayer demons?"

"That's the one. Remember? We tricked it into returning to Hell."

She nodded. "I remember. I slowed your heart and handed him a story gem with a tether inside it. If he's after us, then he didn't activate it. You couldn't have fought him and Lucifer both. Fighting both of them would have killed you, Jack. Fighting just Lucifer almost killed you. Again."

He sighed. He didn't need a reminder about Lucifer almost killing him. He still had nightmares about it.

"And now, I don't have those seraphim energies anymore," he said in a quiet voice, glancing out the doorway. "How are we going to fight this thing?"

"We don't," she said with a smile. "Even Abaddon isn't brave enough to walk into Heaven alone and try to kill us, Jack."

He pulled her closer, his voice falling to a whisper. "How long do you think that will last? Especially when they're about to cut me loose and take back their wings and halo. Even if I still have your mirrored powers, I'm no match for the king of slayer demons."

She frowned, her brow furrowing as she laid her hand against his cheek.

"Abaddon wouldn't hesitate to follow you back to earth," she said, worry in her voice.

Great. That's all he needed to hear. "I'm going to get evicted from my place if I have another demon fight in there."

She smirked at him. "That happen often?" she asked.

He gave her a sideways look. "Only since I met you." He let her go and began to pace. "So, how do we handle this king of slayer demons?"

She reached out and made him stop pacing, putting her arms around his neck. She leaned up and gingerly kissed his lips, a gentle nip.

"We talk to God's Scribe and find out what weaknesses Abaddon has," said Talia. "And then we take him down. Like we've done with everything from assassin demons to Lucifer himself."

Jack pulled in a hurried breath, feeling more than a little torqued over this news. He wasn't going back to Hell.

"I won't go back to Hell, Talia," he said, his voice sounding a lot more intense than he'd intended, but she had no idea how painful that experience was for him.

It was something that they hadn't talked about yet. There hadn't been time.

"You won't," she insisted, her lyric soprano voice reassuring as she kissed him again. "We will fight Abaddon like we've fought every demon chasing us, Jack."

Abaddon was probably furious at Talia now for tricking him. Making Abaddon look stupid. He had to protect her from this behemoth demon.

He sighed. "Hope you're right. But he's probably really pissed at you for tricking him. I won't let him get a shot at you either."

She looked at him funny, like there was something on her mind that she didn't want to bring up. He groaned. *Please don't be something about Lucifer.* The last thing he wanted to do was deal with that douchebag again.

"So, what's on your mind?" he asked, cupping her face in his hands. "The thing you don't want to tell me either. This must be *let's keep things from Jack* day."

She laughed. "It's nothing like that," she said, her gaze falling away from his face.

Uh, oh, that wasn't good. She wouldn't look him in the eye. That was trouble. His stomach dropped, his heart beating faster.

"Talia?" he said, serious now as he lifted her chin with two fingers.

"What's wrong?"

"Herb Rutherford contacted me," she said, still not looking at him.

"Director and creator of The Cinderella Hour?" he replied. "And the reason I met the love of my life." He leaned down and kissed her.

At last, she smiled. "He says he was serious about a rematch, Jack. Wants me to sign onto The Royal Wedding Hour. Says he's been trying to contact you for over a week and he's losing his mind because he hasn't heard from you."

Was that all? He felt the tension drain from his shoulders, wings relaxing against his back. He could breathe again.

"We're being hunted by the king of slayer demons and you're worried about the next season of the show?" He chuckled. "Thought you were going to start a conversation with either *Lucifer's free* or *it's not you, it's me.* I was getting scared."

Her luminous grey eyes sparked with anger and she glared at him. "Jack Casey, don't you even think that!"

"Figured after I lost my seraphim powers, you'd want someone more powerful," he said with a smirk.

She pulled away, arms folded against her Eternean breastplate, grey short robe rustling against her dove grey wings.

"I'm serious, Jack. We fought so hard to stay together through everything Lucifer threw at us. And again, when he assaulted Heaven. Do you think I'd just walk away from you now? After all of that?"

He ran his hand through his hair, feeling like a dick for making her feel badly. "Guess I'm afraid that after everything we went through, our responsibilities will still get in the way."

She frowned at him. "What does that mean?"

He held out his hands. He hated saying these things, but they had to deal with them. Soon.

"You're going back to being an angel of death again. Tell me I'm wrong."

Her anger cooled, the sharpness in her gaze softening. "You know it's the whole reason I exist, Jack," she said in a quiet voice, the pain sharp in that reply.

He'd known that was coming once everything with Lucifer got

resolved. It was the thing he feared most. Irreconcilable differences. A polite, legal way of saying that they were just too different as people, that they had vastly different—incompatible—interests. *It's not you, it's me.* It made his stomach churn. If she had to go back to Heaven, there was no way he could follow her without wings.

And it would break his heart into pieces.

He took her hands in his, drawing her against his chest. "I know," he said in a soft voice. "I've been afraid of this moment since I found out you were an angel of death. When they take away my wings, I can't follow you back here again." He bowed his head. "Being in Azrael's guard requires you to be here. In Eolowen." He sighed. "In Heaven. Someplace I can't follow."

"What are you saying, Jack?" she asked, her eyes welling with tears.

"I'm saying that I can quit my job, but you can't," he replied. "I'll follow you to the ends of the earth and beyond, Talia. I'm home when I'm with you, but will Heaven eventually take you away from me? Force you back here—where I can't follow?"

She threw her arms around him, holding him tight. She kissed the side of his face, her fingers tangling in his hair.

"Will you wait for me? Because I will return to earth to do my job as an angel of death."

"Until my last breath," he whispered in her ear.

"I love you so much, Jack," she said, her voice breaking as she held him tighter. "Promise me you won't give up on me. We'll find a way to make this work."

He just held her against his chest. "I'm not going anywhere," he said. "You did promise to marry me, Talia."

He felt her nod against his cheek.

"What better place to do that than Herb's Royal Wedding Hour," he said with a laugh. "It's only fitting that we get married on the show. If we win."

They met on the show. They fell in love on it and he proposed on it. It was only fair that they get married on the show—if they won the challenges.

She laughed, tears still slipping down her face and shattering against the stones. She entwined her fingers in his and turned her left hand up with his dad's wedding ring on her finger.

"You really want to?" she asked.

He nodded. "Can't think of anyone I'd rather be on a reality television show with than you, Talia. And maybe they'll pick an exotic location so we could even turn it into a honeymoon?"

"I like the sound of that," she said.

Struggling with his injuries, Jack got down on one knee and held her left hand. "Talia Smith, would you appear on The Royal Wedding Hour with me? So, we can kick Gianni and Izzy's butts and have the craziest and cheesiest wedding ever?"

She laughed. "Yes, Jack Casey," she said, "I will appear on The Royal Wedding Hour with you."

He got to his feet, still shaky and unsteady. "Since my cell phone's somewhere in Hell at the moment...demons are probably fielding my calls. Can you reply to Herb? Tell him we'd be delighted to appear on the show. Find out where and when." He leaned in close to her ear and whispered. "Maybe if we're married, I'll get some sort of spousal rights here in Heaven to come back here with you? You dudes should unionize and demand those rights."

Talia's face brightened. "I'll bring that up at our next guard training." She took hold of his face and kissed him again. "And I'll get in touch with Herb. Now, you and I need to talk to Azrael and God's Scribe about our situation with Abaddon."

Jack turned around and there stood Azrael, arms crossed, wings flat against his back. His charcoal-grey eyes looked like granite, mouth set and jaw clenched.

"So, you heard about Abaddon?" Azrael replied, silver-black hair disheveled from the air currents.

Jack nodded. "Heard you and Berith talking on the dais."

"Well, now that you know," Azrael replied, eyes narrowed, "we need to figure out a plan for dealing with him. Because he won't stop pursuing you until he's accomplished his goal—which is to destroy you both."

Jack leaned against the wall. "Guess we need to talk to the Scribe again. Find out how to deal with the king of slayer demons. Permanently." He cast a smile at Talia. "After The Royal Wedding Hour."

Azrael's eyes widened. "What? You can't do that. Alone, on earth, the two of you wouldn't stand a chance against Abaddon."

"So, you planning to let me stay in Eolowen indefinitely, archangel?" Jack asked, motioning at the doorway. "Because we both know the seraphim will have to kick me out sooner or later because I'm not an angel. What happens when I have to return to my timeline on earth anyway? Abaddon's gonna gank my ass the moment I return to my life and you know it."

"Ganked?" Azrael replied, squinting.

"Kill me," Jack snapped. "When I least expect it."

"Right," said Azrael, giving him a deep nod. "Ganked. Is that like yeeted?"

"Uh...not really," Jack replied.

Just then, Berith flew into the room from the rooftop.

"Jack's right, Azrael," she said, her feet thumping against the stone floor. "Abaddon is just waiting for Jack to return to his timeline and Talia to return to her duties as an angel of death. So, he can pick them off one by one."

Azrael sighed. "You're right. We have to address this issue. We have no choice. Berith, get Pravuil out here. We need a plan to deal with Abaddon. Since he obviously didn't activate the tether in that story gem, he's the only loose cannon that can still leave Hell. Now that Lucifer has turned him, Abaddon is a serious threat that must be handled."

"I'll contact Pravuil immediately," said Berith.

She rose into the air and flew out of a portal along the crystal rooftop.

Then a knowing look appeared on Azrael's face as he turned around to Jack and Talia. "But you know...that show will be on location again. Another isolated location. That might be our best hope of luring Abaddon out in the open and taking him down."

Talia frowned. "So, you want us to become bait?"

"If that's what it takes, I'm in," said Jack.

Bring it on. If he and Talia handled that little bitch, Lucifer, then they could handle Lucifer's mule, Abaddon.

"It would be a joint effort with the guard, Talia," said Azrael. "We'd send several squads down to earth like we did when Lucifer was hunting you."

So, they wouldn't have to face Abaddon alone. Now that he didn't have any seraphim powers, Abaddon would be a tough fight. He and Talia had the resurrect and omnificence powers, but those powers would drain him fast. Talia had only used omnificence once, but the resurrect power took a lot out of her. Omnificence would take even more. At least he wouldn't be power drunk.

"Can't tell you how glad I am to hear that," said Jack.

Azrael nodded, his gaze drifting to Talia and then back to him. "If you and Jack stayed here in Heaven, Abaddon would just wait you out. As king of the abyss, he has nothing but time and patience. He'd just wait for you to leave Heaven and ambush you. This way, we can control when and where to confront him."

Talia put her hands on her hips, that clear gold Eternean breastplate catching the sunlight in a bright gold aura.

"I like the sound of that, sir," she said. "I don't like the idea of a surprise attack by Abaddon."

"All right," said Azrael, clapping his hands together. "It's settled. Talia, as soon as you find out when and where filming will begin for this royal wedding competition, we'll gather squads together and work out a plan of action with the Scribe."

"Thank you, sir," Talia said, flexing her wings. "I'll tell the Watcher pretending to be my agent to contact Herb and get all the details. Looks like Jack and I are getting married."

He couldn't halt the grin that rolled across his face. He was getting married.

He thought about texting his sisters, but decided against it. After his mother convinced them he was a dangerous coke fiend that just wanted money from them, they blocked his number. It had been years since he'd spoken to any of them.

Besides. He'd lost his phone in Hell. Even if that *where's my damned phone* app worked, it wasn't like he could actually go into Hell and get it.

Two of his sisters, Jenna and Tara, lived in northern California near his mother. His two oldest sisters, Meredith and Whitney, still lived in Indiana. He couldn't even tell them about the show or invite them to the wedding. He hadn't spoken to any of them for years—thanks to his vindictive, overbearing mother. She owned an event planning business in northern California. Until he got his big break, she hadn't spoken to him since he was ten (when she and Dad divorced). But the moment he screwed it up, she forgot he was her son again.

Great. Dealing with Lucifer and his demons was bad enough, but they paled against dealing with his mother. There was a reason he kept most of California between him and that woman.

Talia stood in front of him, looking concerned.

"Jack?" she said, her eyes filled with worry. "You look very pale all of a sudden. Are you all right?"

He sighed, unable to hold back his apprehension. "Just realized that if I'm getting married, I'm going to have to deal with something far worse than Lucifer and Hell."

Her eyes widened and she gave Azrael a frightened look. "Worse than Lucifer?"

He nodded. "Yeah. My mother."

Azrael snorted and turned away.

Talia shook her head. "What does that mean?"

"It means that I'm going to have deal with her after she finds out about the new show. And the fact that I really did ask you to marry me. I think I'd rather just have Abaddon slay me right now."

The words overbearing and controlling were her hallmarks. And not in that laughable, family movie sense. By the time he was ten, he wasn't surprised when his folks divorced.

"I'm sure she'll be fine with it, Jack," said Talia, gripping his hand. "She's probably already watched the other shows."

And analyzed them in great, great, stupid-ridiculous detail. And just waiting to tell him why he'd chosen poorly. If she'd still been speaking to him, she'd have emailed him lengthy responses about the best women to choose during *The Cinderella Hour* (Thank God she hated texting.) She'd have rated each woman based on dozens of factors (that he didn't care about) with detailed breakdowns on the best choices. That he'd have ignored.

Even though she hadn't spoken a word to him in four years.

He had no idea what she'd think of Talia either. And as his dad used to say, that was only half the story. The other half of that story was he didn't care what that woman thought.

After the divorce, she forgot he existed and returned to California —even when his dad died two months before he turned eighteen. Didn't even check to see if he had a roof over his head or food to eat.

Until he got famous and Rachel entered his life. She loved Rachel.

He didn't know what she thought about the show—or Talia. And he didn't care either. But since it put him back on top again, his email account was probably brimming with new emails from her. Like nothing had happened between them. And since he'd been enjoying an extended holiday in Hell, he hadn't read email in quite some time.

"She loves Rachel, Talia," said Jack, shaking his head. "Because demons usually recognize each other."

Azrael chuckled and then cleared his throat.

"I'm sure she's not that bad, Jack," said Talia.

"Trust me, she's worse," he replied. "If she finds out I might be getting married on the show this season, she'll bombard me with emails, texts, and phone calls. I'd rather deal with Lucifer again than my mother."

He thought Abaddon was bad enough. Now, he might have to deal with his mother, too. He really needed to talk to Seraphina about getting those seraphim powers back. He'd need them to deal with his mother. But at least it was only from a distance. With his phone being in Hell right now.

And that made him happy. He wouldn't have to take her calls or read her texts.

He turned back to Azrael. "Archangel, think you could spare the whole guard for the show?"

Azrael turned back to him. "I'm worried that Abaddon will force me to send the whole guard."

"Not for Abaddon," he said. "For my mother. If she finds out about the show and me getting married, she'll try to barge onto the set and takeover the wedding. She won't listen to me or the bride."

This time, Azrael grinned. "I think my best angel of death will be able to handle your mother, Jack."

"Hope so," he said with a sigh. "My mother doesn't like to listen. Or take my preferences into consideration. At least she can only email me since my phone's probably still in Hell somewhere. Even then, she'll need reminding that Talia's got the final say on wedding stuff."

Talia patted her breastplate. "I'll remind her."

He laughed. Sadly, an angel of death was no match for his mother. If she found the show's location, there'd be Hell to pay. A lot more than he'd already paid during those months in Hell, dealing with Lucifer.

3

AZRAEL HOVERED IN HIS STUDY BESIDE GOD'S SCRIBE AND BERITH WITH two things on his mind. What to do about Jack Casey's wings and how to handle Abaddon, king of the slayer demons?

Sunlight streamed through the crystal rooftop and the portals along the ceiling, the air currents swirling and eddying through the small study and along Eolowen's wide hallways. The smooth, white stone walls glistened as sunlight washed over them. Even at this distance, the roses and honeysuckles along the pergola and the winding stream wafted soft floral scents throughout the grand hall. Distracting him from the complex mess of Talia and Jack's situation.

"Seraphina said the matter required a great deal of research and thought. And she would contact me soon about it."

His glass desk stood in the center of the room, the only furniture present besides the bookshelves that wound around the walls. Angel wings required lots of space. Angels had no need for chairs and benches because they didn't sit. They floated or hovered. Human books had always fascinated him like the old earth castles and fortresses. When he established Eolowen as his domain in Heaven, he had fashioned it after those romantic places and notions. With lots of bookshelves.

Pravuil shook his head, white robes fluttering as his wings flexed in the gentle breeze that whispered through the room. His short white hair framed his face and made his gold eyes burn brighter than sunlight.

"That's a polite way of saying this has never happened before and we have no clue, Azrael," said the Scribe, a hand against his chin. "And it hasn't happened before, so it's an accurate statement. If they just strip him of the wings and halo now, he becomes a fallen angel. Banishing him from Heaven. Can't do that. He's human and he has a soul."

Azrael moved toward the wall, thoughts racing as he hovered beneath a sunlit portal up to the roof. He'd been worried about this moment since they first gave Jack wings. But with so many traitors loose in Heaven and Lucifer hunting Jack, they couldn't leave him open—and vulnerable—to attack. They had to hide him. Even then, Archangel Raziel found him.

The Scribe slid around the desk and hovered beside Azrael.

"You have to admit, Azrael, none of this has been straightforward. There's never been a human with angel powers before. So, from the start, Jack's been different than any of his other human counterparts. And then there's Talia, an angel of death with a human soul. It's all wound together into a big, tangled mess, if you ask me."

"Pravuil's right," said Berith. "I don't think they're going to be able to just take Jack's wings without causing him harm."

She landed on the floor and sat down on top of the desk, facing him and the Scribe. Berith was still getting used to having wings again. After millennia of living without them, she still hadn't gotten back into old angel habits. She still walked and sat, but he expected that in time, she'd rediscover those old habits again.

"And the seraphim won't allow that," said Azrael, crossing his arms against his clear gold Eternean breastplate. His wings fluttered in the currents as he floated under the portal to the roof. "Jack's sacrificed enough, they said. Especially now that the Maker has interceded on his behalf."

"What about Talia?" Berith asked, those light grey eyes filled with concern.

She wanted to see Talia and Jack stay together like everyone else in Heaven. But there were so many challenges to overcome.

"You mean, how do we keep Talia and Jack together?" Azrael asked.

Berith nodded. "As an angel of death, will she be allowed to spend a much greater amount of time on earth? With Jack? Once he gets sent back to earth. To the life that got interrupted by Lucifer."

He'd dreaded those words since Talia started falling for the young man when she'd first been charged with saving his soul.

Sent back to the life that got interrupted.

Jack's life had been slated to end at twenty-six when Talia was tasked with saving him. And then Jack saved Talia from her bitterness toward humankind. From falling. And not one of them—not even Lucifer—expected Talia and Jack to fall in love.

The aftermath of that first wager with Lucifer had been terrible. Talia was inconsolable after being forced to leave Jack behind and Jack was obsessed with finding Talia after the show ended.

Lucifer's double or nothing wager forced him to send Talia back to earth again—back to Jack. But even before that, Talia and Jack were already deeply in love.

And he felt responsible.

He'd given Talia a human soul, let her feel love in a way that angels never felt that emotion. That love also brought Jack back from the edge. To have taken it away from him even then would have been beyond cruel.

But now? It would be unforgivable.

No, he had to find a way to ensure that Jack and Talia remained together. Part of that dilemma was dealing with Talia's duty as an angel of death. But then there was the issue of Jack being mortal. He would grow old and then leave her behind when he ascended with his eternal soul. How would Heaven reconcile those issues? They created this problem and somehow, they had to resolve it. Somehow, they had to keep these two soulmates together.

Even the Maker saw that now.

"Azrael?" Berith asked, standing in front of him now.

"Sorry," he said with a sigh. "I'm just struggling with how to resolve the issues that Talia and Jack are facing. I can't bear the thought of Talia having to watch Jack grow old and die and then lose him when his soul ascends to Heaven."

She nodded. "That's what I was just saying to Pravuil before you fell out of the conversation."

"It's a big problem," said the Scribe, floating around the desk, a hand still on his chin. "That's why angels and humans were never meant to fall in love. The logistics are a nightmare."

"Agreed, Scribe," Azrael replied, soot-grey wings shifting in the air currents. "Jack asked Talia to marry him, not knowing that she was an angel of death. But she wants to marry him more than anything. And he's willing to give up everything to stay with her." Azrael sighed. "And I mean everything. Impressive."

The Scribe nodded. "Yes, Jack Casey is a very impressive young man. Surprised everyone. I even had to rewrite passages of his Book of Life and Death because of it. As a very successful television and movie star, no one expected him to be so selfless. Paired with an angel that has made as many sacrifices as Talia has...well, they make an incredible team. And that's why we have ensure that they stay together."

Berith smiled and crossed her legs, grey robes flouncing against the glass desk, wings flexing behind her.

"Now, that's what I wanted to hear," she said. "Heaven willing to make some sacrifices on their behalf."

Azrael grinned and floated away from the wall, toward the desk. "Now, that they've impressed the Maker and enchanted the Heavens— and even the seraphim with their love story—I think everyone is committed to keeping them together. In a way that's best for Talia and Jack."

The Scribe hovered beside Berith and leaned against the desk. "My staff about lost their minds when they met Jack and Talia. They're celestial celebrities up here. Writing their love story in Jack's Book has been a task they've all begged to handle."

"Good," said Azrael, taking Berith's hand in his and gazing into her eyes. She was so beautiful with her rose-gold halo and dove grey wings restored. "I think the Heavens need more of that kind of love. Don't you?"

Berith cradled his hands against her grey robes. "I couldn't agree more, Azrael."

"All right," said Pravuil, turning away. "So, there is still much work to be done to keep Jack and Talia together, but there's Heavenly commitment to making that happen. While that's being engineered, let's talk about Abaddon."

Abaddon. Azrael a cold wind against his skin.

He let go of Berith's hands and began to move around the room, brow furrowed, wings restless. Abaddon had been an angel once, sent to oversee Hell and its abyss. All that time spent in the abyss and around Lucifer had corrupted Abaddon, turned him. Changed him into the terrifying slayer demon form he had taken.

Only Abaddon had a key to the abyss—to Hell. Now that Lucifer had turned the angel, Azrael was thankful that they had tethered Lucifer in Hell. Even with Abaddon possessing the key, Lucifer couldn't leave because of that tether.

"Abaddon has grown to hate the Heavens, Pravuil," said Berith. "Lucifer used him as his enforcer in the same way that Abaddon had been tasked by the Maker as an angel."

"But how do we stop a massively powerful cherubim-level slayer demon with the key to the abyss?" Azrael motioned toward the round terrace room. "With orders from Lucifer to kill Jack and take his soul. And now, Abaddon wants revenge on Talia for tricking him with that story gem."

The Scribe turned around, arms crossed, worry in those soft gold eyes. "At one time, Abaddon was a sort of angel of death, Azrael. Before he became God's Destroyer, he dealt out death for Heaven and now Hell, but he didn't cross over the souls of those he killed. It was very clever of Talia to trick Abaddon like that. But his former line of work qualifies him with the ability to take Jack's soul. And destroy any angels of death that cross him. I'm sure Lucifer's raged about Jack and now, Abaddon's probably furious that an angel of death and a human tricked him. He's got a real vendetta against those two."

"The question is, how can Talia and Jack defeat him," said Azrael as he floated back and forth across the room, the warm scent of honeysuckles comforting. "They won't be able to trick him back to Hell and after Lucifer was tethered, Abaddon is wise to that trap as well. What about the omnificence power?"

The Scribe paused beside Berith, arms crossed, a pensive look in his gold eyes.

"In human form, omnificence simply overpowers Jack," said Pravuil as he stared out one of the portals. "He has to focus it down to a point that he can handle it and even then, it drains him. Talia is built for such energies and she could cast it, but the damage it would cause on earth would be catastrophic. The seraphim want her to store that rare power in a protective gem to keep it safe. Using it on earth would cause devastation when it may not even stop Abaddon, so she can't use that ability."

"Besides, Abaddon can't be destroyed because he holds the key to Hell," said Azrael as he continued to float through the room, his thoughts racing.

Omnificence was too powerful for use on earth. After narrowly averting the destruction of Jack's entire world, an angel using it on earth would cause widespread devastation. Jack using it would cause damage, but not on the scale of angels or demons using it.

There had to be some way of stopping Abaddon without it.

"Very true, Azrael," said the Scribe. "Abaddon's future prevents his destruction. The Maker knows that he's been turned, but He was firm about needing Abaddon later—in darker times. So, no, he can't be destroyed yet."

Berith leaned on the desk. "We're looking at this wrong. There isn't any power that Talia or Jack could use on Abaddon because he can't be killed. They can't trick him again because he would just return. And he knows about tethering. We've got to figure out some way to distract him or get him to focus on something else."

Nodding, Azrael paused beside the desk. "I agree, Berith, but how? Most angels know so little about Abaddon. He left shortly after the Rebellion as an enforcer and never returned."

Pravuil slapped the sides of his robes. "And that's why I need to return to the archive and get all my staff researching Abaddon and this issue. The best thing we can do right now is consult the texts and writings. Somewhere in those writings is a solution. We just have to locate it."

"What about Jack and Talia in the meantime?" Berith asked.

"Good question, Berith," said Azrael, moving toward the Scribe. "They've agreed to be on the next season of that reality television show. Competing for a televised wedding. We think the isolated location can be protected once again by the guard, but Jack and Talia will be bait to draw Abaddon out. So, we can neutralize him."

The Scribe nodded as he lifted into the air toward the ceiling. "I think that can work. Give me time to research a strategy before you send them back to earth." He smiled and waved at them. "And maybe by the time they pacify Abaddon, the seraphim will have an answer to Jack and Talia's relationship woes."

"By then, they'll be married, Pravuil," Berith called, rising from the desk as the Scribe soared up and out of Azrael's study.

Married. Azrael smiled. Maybe once they were married, the seraphim would have a way for them to spend their lives—and their eternities—together?

_____

4

AFTER TWO WEEKS OF HEALING IN HEAVEN, JACK WAS ON THE MEND. Most of his broken bones and other injuries had healed, including his left wing, thanks to Berith's rare healing talents.

He felt restless, waiting to hear back from the seraphim and God's Scribe. And the new season of *The Royal Wedding Hour* would start filming soon. Talia said that one angel day equaled seven days on earth. Filming was due to start on location in April. That was about two weeks away.

He rested on his right side under the willow tree, watching the guard—and Talia—train and run drills. Things had been really quiet since Lucifer got tethered back in Hell, but even Jack knew that things wouldn't stay quiet. As long as Lucifer was still in existence, he would cause chaos.

The Scribe hadn't returned to Eolowen yet and Azrael hadn't been summoned back to High House by the seraphim. That meant nobody knew how to deal with Abaddon yet and the seraphim had no clue what to do about his wings either.

Talia flew over the willow tree, swooping low, and waved at him as she and her squad did speed drills. She was squad leader with Muriel, Anahera, Kesien, and Deemah in her squad now. He missed flying with them and he still enjoyed a good demon fight, but Azrael and Berith grounded him because of his injuries. He knew he couldn't have flown anyway with his left wing broken in three places.

Lucifer did a number on him. Again.

He'd inflicted his share of damage though. And Lucifer would never know how close he came to being blown out of existence that day in the haunted woods. If Berith hadn't stopped the seraphim powers from overloading, Lucifer would have found out in a hurry.

Of course, he wouldn't have lived through it either.

Wings fluttered overhead.

He glanced up. Berith. She landed in the grass beside him and sat down, wings folding behind her.

"How do you feel today, Jack?" she asked, studying him with those large, pale grey eyes.

"Better," he said, sitting up. He flexed both wings and they responded by unfurling to their maximum width. "See? Even the left wing's working as intended today."

She smiled. "Good, I'm glad. You were so busted up. Not sure how you got through all of that filming on earth when your timeline resumed."

"Damn good acting," he said with a smirk. "Made them think I was in the best shape of my life while they filmed that finale."

"Talia said she was amazed at how well you fooled everyone. She didn't even know until you couldn't get out of your car after driving back."

By the time he'd driven an hour back to L.A., he was spent. It was all he could do to climb into the driver's seat, but it wasn't like Talia could have driven them back. Or blink them back like a seraph. By then, the seraphim had already cut off the channeling of their power to him.

He'd have to teach her how to drive after they got married. He just hoped she didn't smite any of the L.A. drivers—like he'd wanted to many times. Having those seraphim powers would have come in handy on the 405 during rush hour.

"Had to finish the show and get us back to my place," he replied, stretching his legs out again, most of the pain gone. Most of it. "By then, I almost didn't care what happened. She had to practically carry me back up to Heaven. Wasn't going to leave me at my place either— out of her sight. Which was fine by me because after her capture, I didn't want her out of my sight either."

Grinning, Berith shifted toward him and laid her hand against his right shoulder, that gold healing light washing over him.

"Let me see what else still needs to heal, Jack," she said in a quiet voice. "And I don't expect that either of you wanted the other more than five feet away from you after what you and Talia went through."

He shook his head. "Not in this lifetime. I just hope there's a way we can really be together. You know, live a life as a married couple."

"Well, we're working on trying to make that happen, Jack, so don't worry." Berith squeezed his shoulder. "God's Scribe is researching everything in the archive to come up with some options. And a way to shut down Abaddon as well."

He sighed. Finally took care of Lucifer and inherited Luci's first lieutenant. How many others would he have to fight?

"And here I thought that Talia and I could get married without having demons attend the ceremony. Or my mother."

Berith chuckled. "Is there a problem with your mother attending?"

He shook his head. "She'll lose her mind when she sees the name of next season's show. She reads Variety. She'll be contacting me. You can bet on it. Demanding to know why I haven't introduced her to Talia." He sighed. "Because I don't want Talia to leave me."

"That bad?" Berith asked, her brow furrowed, a look of surprise in her eyes.

"Worse," he said, rubbing his forehead. "First, my mother is an overbearing control freak. It's her way or the highway—no compromises. Second, she runs an event planning company. They do weddings. I don't want her anywhere near my wedding—or telling me and Talia what to do. I'd rather deal with Abaddon than my mother, believe me."

Berith grinned. "That's quite a statement, Jack."

"I wonder if I could get Abaddon to plan the wedding and my

mother could reorganize Hell for Lucifer. That's just the punishment Luci needs."

"Jack!" Berith cried. "She can't be that bad."

He shook his head. "You have no idea, Berith." He propped his elbows on his knees. "She stopped speaking to me when Rachel left me. Said the whole thing was obviously my fault. Was the only nice thing Rachel ever did for me."

"That's terrible," said Berith, looking appalled, her eyes wide.

"She loved Rachel. Liked her a lot better than she liked me."

He sighed. The moment she read that he was doing another season of the show in *Variety*, she'd be blowing up his phone. That made him laugh. He so hoped that Lucifer found his phone in Hell and answered it. Let the King of Hell deal with her. Like he had anything better to do right now.

She'd made it clear that the drug issues were all his fault, not Rachel's. And she expected him to crawl back to Rachel and beg her to take him back. He'd told her it'd be a cold day in Hell before that happened and hung up.

His sisters understood once. They'd all four tried to get him into rehab, not realizing that he'd lost everything and couldn't afford ibuprofen much less one of those celebrity addiction recovery resorts. He'd kept those details out of all conversations though and he'd played his parts well, getting them to believe he was just fine. Until the night Rachel walked out on him. His mother hadn't spoken to him since. And as his dad used to say, that was only half the story. The other half was that he didn't *want* to speak to her either.

But she'd apparently convinced his sisters to ghost him, too. That hurt.

"Wonder if Herb's going to bring back a bunch of former contestants on the show. Like Rachel and Lare."

That thought made him a little queasy.

At the time, he didn't know it, but during *The Ever After Hour*, before Lucifer dragged him off to Hell, he learned that Rachel and Lare had sold their souls. And their contracts were up. They were both in Hell when he got there and Rachel almost killed him in one of

Lucifer's cage fights. Until he forgave her and unintentionally got her released from Hell.

"Rachel...she was the one in the cage fight, wasn't she?" Berith asked in a quiet voice.

He nodded. "Didn't think you'd remember that."

"How could I forget it, Jack?" she said, her healing light washing over his chest and arms again. "You were bleeding out and I struggled to save your life that time."

"I just hope Herb doesn't bring her back on the show," he said with a sigh. "Talia might just smite her."

"I'd enjoy seeing that," Berith replied as she let the healing light fade across his body. "The things that woman did to you were terrible."

She'd caused him a lot of physical and mental pain, especially the memories hidden underneath his blackouts. He thought it had been from all the flake, but she'd even put drugs in his drinks.

"Everything's happened so fast. Haven't had time to even process being in Hell—much less what Rachel and Lare did to me before that. For now, though, I've got much bigger worries. Like Abaddon—and getting married."

Berith smiled at him. "In that order?"

He shrugged. "So, what do you know about Abaddon?"

Abaddon was a name he'd never heard before that demon showed up in his face at the crossroads. Wanting his soul. According to Azrael's guard, he was a former angel turned slayer demon, the highest order of demons under Lucifer.

Apparently, Luci had been throwing shade at him, convincing this king of slayer demons to come kill him and take his soul.

"Abaddon was an angel once," Berith explained, her gaze intense as she studied his eyes. "He was charged by the Maker to be the keeper of the key to the abyss. The Gates of Hell. He was supposed to keep Lucifer in line, but somehow, Lucifer turned him. He's become a demon, the most powerful demon in Hell—under Lucifer."

Great. Luci sent his second in command to drag him back to Hell, so he could torture his soul for eternity. Right under Heaven's nose.

"Oh, and he can't be killed."

"Just a minor detail," Jack replied, shaking his head. "Not important at all. This slayer demon can beat me to death and take my soul to Lucifer. Oh, by the way, he can't be killed. Enjoy filming at an isolated location. Where he can end me and nobody will find my corpse for weeks."

Maybe the seraphim would just forget he was still up here and let him move into Eolowen permanently? He'd pay rent. Work for Azrael's guard. He'd just need to borrow Talia's squad for a quick move out of his apartment.

His current landlord was going to shit brimstone when he saw the hellhound claw marks on the hardwood floors. Not getting that security deposit back.

"Jack, the Scribe's been researching everything the archive has on Abaddon. Hopefully, Pravuil and his angels will locate something we can use to stop him."

Jack got up from the grass, wings extended, and leaned against the willow tree trunk. "That before or after Abaddon kills me and drags me back to Hell? If I get dragged off to Hell a second time, I won't make it out again."

Berith's wings fluttered, lifting her out of the grass and onto her feet. She laid both hands on his shoulders, her expression comforting.

"I know it's hard, but don't worry," she said. "If we overcame Lucifer, then we can overcome Abaddon, too."

"Wish I could say that Abaddon was my only worry, but I've got bigger problems—like getting married on the next season of the show."

A wedding. Either it would be an over-the-top, Hollywood-style wedding or it would be him and Talia going down to City Hall and getting married. Either way, Talia was supposed to talk to the Scribe about getting some paperwork, allowing them to get married in his timeline. Only God's Scribe could create official paperwork that would allow an angel of death to get a marriage license.

"It's a big step when you and Talia are still fighting to stay together."

He nodded. Wasn't easy marrying an angel of death—or rather living with one. And with Abaddon hunting him, he worried where the show would film this season. Talia hadn't heard back from Herb yet on where the show would be filming.

"It is," said Jack, feeling restless and unsettled. "We don't even know where the show's going to be filmed yet."

Berith shook her head. "I think Talia just found that out."

He frowned. "What? She didn't say anything to me about it."

If she'd heard back, why hadn't she told him yet? She knew he was anxious to know the location.

"Talia mentioned earlier that the show was going to film somewhere in northern California. Something about Sonoma Valley. An isolated wine vineyard near Santa Rosa."

A cold chill rushed down his spine and he flinched. No…not Sonoma. Oh, God—not Northern California! He winced.

That was the worst news yet.

"Oh, no…please tell me you heard that wrong, Berith," he replied, feeling sick now. "It can't be there. It can't."

Berith's eyes narrowed and she squinted at him. "What's wrong with that location?"

He groaned, reaching for his cell phone in his front jeans pocket. Remembering it was still in Hell—like he was about to be for the show's next season.

"My mother lives in Santa Rosa," he said with a groan. "That's the worst news I've heard since I found out Lucifer was gunning for me."

On location with his mother that close would be the death of him. Maybe he'd just let Abaddon find him instead? It would be a lot less painful.

"Calm down, Jack," said Berith, hands on his shoulders. "Maybe I heard her wrong? I'm still learning all the names of places across your world."

He turned toward the terrace where Talia and her squad trained and did speed drills with their swords and shields. Maybe it wasn't too late to back out of the show and move to Malaysia or somewhere in Europe? Someplace his mother couldn't find him and ruin his life all over again.

"If I'm on location in Santa Rosa and Talia and I win this season, my mother will try to take over the wedding, who I'm marrying, and my life. Like she controlled everything when I was a kid."

Berith gripped his shoulders. "Jack...you saved Heaven and earth. You defeated Lucifer. I think you can handle your mother."

He whirled around. "Have you met my mother?"

Berith just smiled at him. "No, but your fiancée's an angel of death, Jack. I think you've got this."

"And what about these wings and halo? Will they be visible on earth? If she—"

"Jack." Berith held his arms in a firm grip. "Breathe. No one's going to see your wings. Talia will make sure of that. Everything's going to be fine."

"Maybe I should send my mother after Abaddon?" he said. "She'll have him terrified and running back to Hell in fifteen minutes. I guarantee it."

Berith laughed. "It's going to be fine, Jack. Talk to Talia about the filming location." She motioned him toward the terrace. "Go, before you give yourself wing rash."

His eyes widened. "That's a thing?"

She shooed him with her hand. "Go."

Turning away, he lifted into the air, favoring his right wing, and flew over the willow tree. To the terrace. He landed beside Talia and her squad.

"Talia, I need a moment, please," he said as she and her squad practiced different formations, floating about ten feet above the terrace.

Talia turned toward her squad, raven black hair falling in thick waves around her shoulders. "Squad, keep working through the formations," she said to the four angels of death. "I'll be right back."

"Want to train with us, Jack?" Muriel called.

He smiled. "Nah, I'd just trip you up."

"It'd be a lot more fun with your commentary," said Kesien, nodding at him.

"The boss might smite me," he said, pointing at Talia with his thumb.

Talia had her hands on her hips now, giving him an annoyed look.

"See? She's thinking about where she could hide my body right now."

The squad laughed, but Talia didn't. She grabbed him by his Navy blue hoodie and pulled him well away from the squad.

"What's up, Jack?"

He tried not to sound annoyed, but he was surprised that she hadn't told him about the location shoot yet. "So, when were you going to tell me about The Royal Wedding Hour?"

She shook her head. "What do you mean?"

"You told Berith where we'd be on location," he said, dragging the toe of his blue Vans across the white stone terrace. "When were you planning to tell me?"

"Sorry, I got involved in training and hadn't had a chance to tell you yet."

He nodded. That didn't sound good. He'd already fallen in priority behind her squad's training and they weren't even married yet.

"I see," he said, sounding a little distant.

"Jack," she said, taking hold of his hand. "Berith was there when the Watcher delivered the information to me, so that's how she found out." She pulled him close and slid her arms around his neck. "I was planning to get you alone later and tell you everything I found out."

"Alone, huh?" he said. "Here? With forty thousand openings into my room?"

She brushed her lips across his and kissed him. "Yes, alone. Ever heard of a ward?"

At last, he smiled. "I have," he said, sliding his arms around her waist. "Why don't you demonstrate how that works? From my bed."

"*Your* bed?" she teased, grey eyes sparkling.

"Our bed?" he asked.

She kissed him again. "We'll talk about it later," she said. "But you wanted to know where the show will be on location?"

He nodded. *Please be on the east coast. In Europe. Siberia. Anywhere but northern California.*

"It's in wine country, Jack," she said in a wistful tone, the corners of her mouth lifting into a smile. "Celestial Vineyards in Sonoma County, California. The show got permission to film at a huge, historic French Chateau-like castle at the vineyard, built around 1914. It's called Le Château des Angés. Castle of Angels." Her smile widened into a grin. "Oh, Jack, it sounds incredible! Like a storybook."

He couldn't help the deep sigh that slipped out.

"What's the matter?"

He bowed his head. "Unfortunately, my mother lives in Santa Rosa. My overbearing, vindictive, control freak mother. We haven't spoken since Rachel walked out on me. If my mother could have, she'd have kept Rachel and disowned me. Again."

Talia's eyes were full of enchantment. "I'd love to meet your mother."

"I'd rather meet Abaddon in a dark alley," he said, voice rising.

She shook her head, arms still around his neck. "It can't be that bad. Can it?"

"Worse," he said, nodding as he pulled back from her and crossed his arms against his chest. "Much worse. When she reads in Variety that I'll be competing on a show titled The Royal Wedding Hour, she'll be right there at the vineyard. Trying to control me, the wedding, and she'll be furious that I haven't introduced you to her yet."

Talia shrugged. "So, introduce us."

"Talia, Angel of Death, meet my mother, Nina Westwood, Destroyer of Lives. I'm sure you'll both get along famously. Seriously, Talia, she makes Abaddon look like a concierge at the Beverly Wilshire Hotel."

Talia's squad began to snicker.

Talia gave him a questioning look. Like he was exaggerating.

"You think I'm kidding, don't you? Well, I'm not. She blamed me when Rachel walked out on me. Said it was my fault and that I needed to beg her to come back to me. I'm going to need your entire squad to keep her rampages in check. Because she will try to take over everything, trust me."

"We'll deal with it, Jack," she said and moved toward him. "Don't worry so much."

"Any word on the other contestants?" he asked.

Talia shook her head. "Jack. Relax. They aren't going to have Erica or Rachel back on the show. No one's going to shoot you or attack you."

"You forgot about my mother," he snapped. "Hey, maybe I could con her into taking down Abaddon for us? Or a couple of well-placed murder marbles—"

"Jack..."

"Guess that might get me sent to Hell, huh? But not if they met her!"

Again, the guard broke into a fit of laughter.

"Jack!"

"Was just thinking outside the box a little," he said with a shrug.

"Save that for Abaddon," said Talia. "We'll deal with your mother, too. It'll be okay, Jack."

He hoped she was right. The last person he expected to deal with on *The Royal Wedding Hour* was his mother.

5

For two weeks, Talia struggled to calm Jack's growing anxiety over dealing with his mother while Pravuil, God's Scribe and his entire staff tried to find a solution to the Abaddon problem. Without any answers, she and Jack left Heaven bound for Sonoma County, California to start filming *The Royal Wedding Hour*.

Without a plan to deal with Abaddon—or Jack's mother.

Talia, Jack, and two squads from Azrael's guard of death angels used their abilities to travel from the Heavens down to earth. They flashed across the globe to North America, spiraling toward the state of California. In a small city north of San Francisco, Jack rented a dark blue SUV and drove north into the sunny, rolling green hills of Sonoma County.

April had burst into sprouts of green leaves across the trees and green grass covered the valley. Ordered rows of grapevines rushed past on both sides as Jack drove toward a distant line of hills where the Celestial Vineyards Estate stood like the palace of Versailles.

She grinned. Like a fairytale.

She'd dreamed of being someplace like this with Jack, wearing his ring on her finger and planning a human wedding. Just like the Cinderella fairytale that Muriel told her so long ago. Especially after being Lucifer's captive with no hope of escape—like Jack had been in Hell. She'd been terrified that she'd never see Jack again. But together, they overcame Lucifer and his demon armies, fighting them and the Heavens to stay together.

Now, they were back on earth again. Fighting to stay together. And competing on another season of reality television. For a live, televised wedding. She grinned. To the love of her life.

She'd wanted to marry Jack ever since he'd gotten down on one knee and proposed during the finale of *The Prince Charming Hour*. No, since that first night in his arms by the pool. Somehow, she and Jack would make this relationship work. She couldn't believe it, but he really didn't care that she was an angel of death.

As long as they were together, they could make anything work.

Jack turned down a narrow gravel lane, the blue SUV humming, gravel popping as staked and bare rows of grapevines lined both sides of the road. The road was long and twisty, leading to a grand French chateau called the Castle of Angels. The estate was massive compared to the Beverly Hills palace and the beach estate where they'd filmed previous seasons. This estate had a hundred rooms spread across its three levels. The large limestone structure had a black slate mansard roof with two rounded tower-like features in front that resembled a castle.

Where this Cinderella hoped to finally, marry her Prince Charming.

The sprawling lawn was bright green and meticulously cut short, a rectangular concrete moat in front. Box hedges lined both sides of the moat and a large, round three-tiered fountain stood in front of the black, double French doors at the front of the mansion.

"Jack!" she cried, unable to stop staring at this magical place. "Look at it! It's like a storybook!"

Even Jack smiled now. "Storybook enough for Cinderella to marry her Prince Charming here?"

"It's everything I've ever dreamed of, Jack," she said as he leaned over, gold Ray Bans aviator sunglasses perched on his nose, and kissed her.

"Good," he said, pulling the SUV behind a silver van with an orange and grey Four Acre Studios logo on the side. "Because I want to win this thing, Talia. So, you can have the storybook wedding that you deserve."

She frowned at him. "Don't you want a storybook wedding, too?"

"I just want to call you my wife, Talia, and tell you I'm home. Everything else is just icing."

She kissed him back. "That's what I want, too," she said. "To be with you."

Jennifer Collins rushed out of the black French doors wearing a red blouse and a tan short skirt. Her dark hair was pulled back in a ponytail, red glasses on, and clipboard and cell phone in one hand.

"Talia! Jack!" she called, rushing over to the passenger side of the blue SUV as Jack shut off the engine and climbed out. "It's great to see the two of you again!"

Talia opened the door and stepped out. She wore a lavender blouse and short jean skirt. Jack had changed into an olive Henley under his favorite Navy blue hoodie, those faded Levi's hugging his leanly muscled body, and beat-up tan loafers. His blond hair looked so light against the sun-drenched estate. This place reminded her of the Heavens and the grand hall of Eolowen.

The color of his shirt and the sunshine made his light green eyes smolder as he slid off his sunglasses to greet Jennifer. But only Talia could see the reflection of Jack's pale gold halo and his silver-grey wings at his back. With a little angel magic on his shirts, she got those wings through the fabric without tearing his clothes apart.

"Oh, Herb will be just thrilled that you two are finally here. Filming starts tomorrow afternoon, but just for the orientation. So, until then, enjoy the chateau and the grounds. We've got the run of two floors and the grounds for the entire shoot. We'll get your things brought up to your suite for you. You, two must be tired after that long drive from L.A."

Jack flashed a smirk at her. "Yeah, Jennifer, we're a bit tired. Would love some time to get settled into our suite."

Being alone with Jack in this beautiful chateau was more than she'd ever dreamed of since everything went wrong at the beach estate.

"Right this way," said Jennifer, motioning toward the black French doors. The doors' frosted glass panes had little moons and stars etched in them.

Jennifer held open the doors as Jack grabbed two duffle bags out of the back seat and carried them inside.

Stunned, Talia stared up at the three-story white entryway that was all white marble with small, diamond-shaped black tiles that led to a sweeping, white marble staircase. The wide, marble stairs fanned out to a landing that split into two stairways framed with black wrought iron railings. Both sides of the staircase curved gracefully toward tapered white columns along the second-floor balcony. Above it, the third floor mirrored the second, overlooking the entryway gallery with more tapered columns and ornate, black wrought iron railings. Like a Greek temple.

She smiled. Like an archangel had designed it.

Two huge cobalt blue urns stood on both sides of the grand staircase. Each urn overflowed with pale pink English roses and fragrant pink and white lilies. An unusual sun-warmed, sweet and spicy floral scent floated through the airy foyer.

"Wow, this place is incredible," said Jack, looking up at the huge balconies overlooking the entryway gallery. "Looks like a museum."

Above, the ceiling had windows across it. Sunlight drenched the marble floor and wrought iron banisters. The white tray ceiling glistened with crown molding. A recessed alcove on the stairway's landing had a rounded arch with a marble statue of an angel with wings spread, a crescent moon and stars behind her. Her hair and robes flowed around her as if the wind had caught them and frozen them in marble.

Le Château des Angés, the Castle of Angels.

Even inside, it felt a little like the grand hall of Eolowen, especially this huge gallery where she almost expected the guard to come flying in from pale blue skies and fleecy clouds. She felt right at home here. Archangel Azrael would love this estate.

She glanced at Jack who was grinning. His head turned in every direction and he looked as enchanted by this sprawling estate as she felt.

"Right up the main stairs," said Jennifer, stepping onto the wide, midnight blue carpet runner in the center of the stairs. "You and Jack are in the Halo Suite on the second floor."

She couldn't help but grin. The Halo Suite. Couldn't have chosen a better room for her and Jack.

"It overlooks the pool, the parterre gardens, and the vineyards, of course," said Jennifer.

Jack frowned. "Uh, the what gardens?"

"Parterre," she said. "It's a French style of formal gardens that are separate but symmetrical spaces with hedged borders and flower beds that are connected by walkways."

"Sounds complicated," Jack said with a nod.

Jennifer smiled. "They are pretty elaborate and well-manicured here, but all you and Talia have to do is enjoy them thankfully. And your suite faces west, so you'll have incredible sunsets, too."

"Can't wait to share some sunsets with you, Talia," he said in a soft voice, stroking her hair.

He put his arm around her as they walked up the stairs, their footfalls echoing in layers up through the tall gallery. They followed the stairs up to the second floor. Their shoes clicked across the marble floor as Jennifer led them toward a short hallway straight ahead with black, two-paneled doors, the top panel softly arched. Above the door was a sign with a starry, midnight blue background and gold script that read, *The Halo Suite*.

Jennifer unlocked the doors and pushed them both open. Into a white marbled space with white walls and oversized windows. Like they'd just stepped back three hundred years. Or flown into Eolowen.

Shiny white marble floors glistened, intricate white crown molding on the walls pristine. The tall ceiling had two large, crystal chandeliers. The floor-to-ceiling windows overlooked a long, rectangular pool, several formal garden squares edged with box hedges that looked like a grid, and pathways leading to a large, round fountain with a gilded statue of an angel in flight in the center.

"Look at the view, Jack!" she cried, standing at one of the windows.

Beyond the bubbling fountain, stood the endless, ordered rows of grapevines in the vineyards. Rolling green meadows glimmered in the distance against a crisp blue, spring sky. At the windows, white silk curtains pooled on the marble floors.

Jack stood beside her, staring out the window. "Man, this place is massive! Can't believe they're letting us film here."

"Celestial Vineyards will get a lot of publicity as a result of the show," said Jennifer, smiling as she motioned around the room with her clipboard. "And with A-List Hollywood star, Jack Casey possibly getting married here, their wedding venue business will explode."

Talia put her arm in his and laid her head against his shoulder. "Hear that, A-List Hollywood star?"

He just laughed, shaking his head.

"I'll let you guys explore a little," said Jennifer, backing toward the doors. "We'll have dinner tonight for cast and crew in the formal dining room. But dress casual. No cameras until tomorrow. See you later."

"Thanks, Jennifer," Jack replied as Talia waved at her.

Jennifer handed them each a key and closed the doors behind her. Talia slid her key in her skirt pocket and turned left toward the bed in the open concept suite. An antiqued white and gold four-post bed stood against the wall, top draped with pale lavender silks. It had a thick lavender comforter and four lavender pillows stacked high. On either side of the bed stood two antiqued white nightstands. Against the opposite wall were two gold and white French armoires and a mirrored dresser between them.

"Think they'd just let us move in here?" Jack asked, wandering through the space. "This place is incredible."

"It reminds me so much of Eolowen," said Talia, rushing through the room, enchanted by the furniture and the view.

"A little like home, is it?" Jack asked, smiling.

The huge sitting area with two lavender sofas stood in front of those massive windows. To the right of the bed was an incredible bathroom with a huge, sunken white marble tub that stood in the center of the floor. A big circular basin with gold fixtures with a round chandelier that dripped with hundreds of teardrop-shaped crystals.

A marble vanity with gold and white cabinets and two white sinks stood on one side of the tub. An ornate, rectangular gold-framed mirror hung over each sink. On the other side of the tub, a glass-enclosed shower as large as a walk-in closet covered the wall. It had several jets, all with gold fixtures, and white marble tile with those little black diamonds. Thick lavender towels hung on gold towel racks hung on both sides of the shower.

Clustered around the sunken tub were at least three dozen ivory, flameless candles. She grinned. This tub could easily fit two people. And she couldn't wait to fill it with bubbles and Jack Casey. It was a fairytale suite and for the first time since she matched with him, she felt like a princess.

Just like Cinderella.

6

JACK AND TALIA EXPLORED THE VINEYARD'S GARDENS AND WATCHED THE sunset over the vineyards from the angel in flight fountain. The setting sun's last rays lit the storm-blue clouds magenta, washing the darkening sky in watercolor pinks and oranges. Like a Monet painting.

It was the most stunning sunset Jack could remember and seeing it with Talia made his heart race and his chest tighten.

He held her close and listened to the silence punctuated by the fountain's rushing water and chattering bird calls.

"Amazing sunset," he whispered against her ear, that raven black hair bunched around her shoulders, so silky and dark against her lavender blouse. "It leaves me speechless."

The one thing he'd missed in Heaven was that feeling of life around him, that he only felt here on earth. The bird calls and insects chirring around him made him feel like he wasn't the only living and breathing creature left. Here, he felt the rise and fall of his breath, the rush of blood through his veins, the heat mixing with the chill.

Angels breathed, but not the same way humans did. The air just sort of flowed through their bodies. It was weird. They had hearts that beat, too, but not like flesh and blood human hearts. Theirs were ethereal, beating with the flow of light and air. Like they were each one half of the same coin. He smiled. Like him and Talia.

Despite the magical feel of this vineyard, he felt a shadowy presence as the countryside darkened. Something watching them. Something dark. Calculating. Planning.

His stomach dropped. Abaddon.

Like Lucifer, Abaddon had once been a powerful angel with important work, but Abaddon's responsibilities were dark. He was the guardian of Hell's Gates and destined to smite evil humans during the end times or something like that. Lucifer's jealousy and pride turned him into a rebellious, ambitious threat, causing him and the angels that followed him to fall. But Abaddon? Dude was a loyal servant, guarding the key to Hell's Gates and keeping an eye on Lucifer.

Something happened down there. Something made Abaddon stop reporting Lucifer's schemes. Something made him stop doing his job. And transform into a demon.

Had Lucifer convinced him that he was just a number in Heaven and that in Hell, he'd be rewarded for looking the other way? Maybe Abaddon just got tired of his shit job and Luci's promises started looking really good after all that time? After millennia—something Jack couldn't even fathom.

Nevertheless, it worried him.

Lucifer was smart, but his jealousy made him easy to unhinge. Unlike Abaddon. No one knew what made this angel-turned-demon tick. Or why Abaddon became the King of Hell's enforcer.

Hell-bent on delivering his soul to Lucifer in Hell. And obsessed with making Talia pay for tricking him with that story gem.

Was this dude just feeling unappreciated somehow? Feeling alone and forgotten in Hell while the rest of the angels enjoyed time under blue skies and soft breezes?

Talia snuggled against his chest, laying her face against his neck. He cradled her against him, his fingers entwined with her long, tapered fingers. He pressed them against his lips in a gentle kiss.

The past year had been the craziest year of his life, coming on the heels of some of the worst years of his life. But tonight, it all seemed like a bad dream. Like he'd just woken up from it all and found Talia beside him. Washing away all those horrible events and images.

And she was here with him now, in his arms, like a normal couple. Thinking about how they'd spend the rest of their lives together. He knew they faced so many challenges, but he'd do whatever it took to stay with her. Still, the fact that she was immortal made him ache all over. She was eternal. She would never age. Unlike him. His soul was eternal, but she'd have to watch him age and get old. And die.

Had she even thought about that?

"Think you'll still love me when you don't recognize me anymore?" he asked, wrapping his arms tighter around her and holding her closer.

She chuckled. "What do you mean?"

"In twenty years, I'll be almost fifty," he said with a smirk. "In forty years, I'll be almost seventy. Sure you wouldn't prefer Kesien? He'll always look like that. I won't."

"Jack Casey," she snapped, reaching up and cupping his chin. "I love you. Not because you're sexy and hot and make me crazy—because you do—but because of this." She slid her hand underneath his Navy blue hoodie, underneath his olive Henley, and laid it against his heart. "This is what I fell in love with."

"My shirt?"

"Your heart, smart guy," she replied. "It's the most beautiful human heart I've ever encountered. Warm, loving. Selfless. You gave up everything for me and you're still willing to give up everything for me." She turned her face toward his and ran her fingers through his blond hair. "And your light green eyes just take my breath away."

"Me? Selfless?" He scoffed and rolled his eyes. "If I want to stay with you, I'm the one that has to make the changes."

He wasn't selfless. She couldn't exactly just give up being an angel of death. It wasn't like a job or something she chose. Besides, staying with her was the one thing he wanted most in the world. So, he had to give some things up to make it happen. That didn't make him selfless. It just made him motivated.

"You don't give yourself enough credit, Jack," she said and kissed him.

He glanced at his watch. Almost eight.

"We'd better head back inside," he said and nodded toward the narrow, concrete walkway that led to the black French doors at the back of the estate. "Dinner will start soon."

She wrapped her arms around him, holding him close as they walked between the box hedges that separated flower beds on either side. The scent of roses hung in the air as they headed along the walkway, twilight settling with a misty, otherworldly feel against the soft gold lights filling the chateau windows.

"Let's go meet our competition," he said with a crooked smile. "Besides Gianni and Izzy, that is."

"And hopefully, no demons," said Talia.

He glanced over his shoulder. Was Abaddon out there watching them right now? Waiting for his chance to strike?

Of course, Azrael's guard was out there, too. Standing watch. Waiting to engage the massive slayer demon. Without those seraphim powers, Jack couldn't do much to this slayer demon. Murder marbles would just piss Abaddon off.

Sure, he still had the omnificence and resurrect powers, but they would easily overpower him now. He might get in one good shot with them, with no guarantee of taking down a slayer demon. Just the highest-level demon in Hell underneath Luci.

Lucifer was a fallen angel, not a demon, but he'd been corrupted by his own creations. That's what Talia said, at any rate. That was why he sprouted horns, hooves, and a tail when he got unhinged or enraged. Which was most of the time. Especially when he was around Jack.

"Speaking of my mother," he said as they walked toward the French doors, the twilight sky beginning to shine with starlight. "I wonder if she's heard about the show filming out here yet. I need to tell Jennifer to block her if she shows up. And I need to get a new cell phone."

Talia chuckled. "So, she can call you?"

He laughed. "No, so I can block her calls."

"But Jack, she's still your mother," said Talia. "You should probably talk to her at some point. Tell her what you're planning and set boundaries."

He frowned. "Doesn't work, Dr. Phil, but thanks for the advice."

"Dr. Phil?" she said, looking confused.

"Forget it," he replied. "Just a stupid television reference. Seriously though, Talia. You give my mother a boundary and to her, it's a hurdle. A challenge. And for the record, counselor, she's the one that stopped talking to me. Now that my name's appearing in a good way in Variety, she'll want to reestablish contact with me. Not interested."

Talia pulled him close and rubbed his shoulder. "But she's your mother, Jack."

He sighed. Giving birth to him didn't make her his mother. It just made her the egg donor on his birth certificate.

"It's just a name on my birth certificate," he replied. "My oldest sister, Meredith was more like a mom to me than my own mother."

She'd had no interest in having a son, especially after having four daughters. He'd been little more than a curiosity to her as a kid, not fitting into the vision she had for her business empire. She was an event planner. Parties, weddings, conventions—her company did it all.

When he was ten, she packed up and moved back to California, leaving him with his dad in Indiana. Fine with him—until Dad got sick. Passed away two months before he left for college. Dad didn't own a house, so Meredith took him in, gave him a place to call home during breaks and in the summers. He lasted a year in college. A week after the spring semester ended, his college career ended. He packed everything into Dad's 1969 red Firebird convertible and headed to Los Angeles to pursue acting. He still had that car—stored in a friend's garage. He'd been within days of having to sell it before *The Cinderella Hour* happened.

"Well, maybe this show will give you a chance to reconcile with your mom?"

He shook his head as they walked past the four silver studio vans and collection of the crew's cars, including the rented blue Toyota RAV4 lined up beside the four-car garage to the right of the house.

"Talia, I'm not the one with the problem," he said, trying to hold in his anger.

His mother was the one with the problem and now that he was on top again, she'd want to reconnect with her famous son to get more traffic for her event planning business. He wasn't interested.

They walked around the concrete circle driveway that curved in front of the estate and around another fountain. This limestone fountain had a huge round basin with three tiers surrounding a carving of a crescent moon and stars. The water flowed over the moon and stars with the words, *Celestial Vineyards* carved into the fountain's limestone base. Around the chateau, he'd noticed some outbuildings on the property and a small retail shop just off the road in front of the long lane that led to the estate. Closed until summer.

He opened the door for Talia and they stepped into the entryway. He gazed up at the crystal chandeliers that hung above them in the three-story gallery. Off to the left was a white sign with a black arrow that read, *dining room*. He gripped Talia's hand and they walked down a wide hallway toward another set of black French doors with frosted glass. One of the doors was propped open.

"Ready to mingle?" he asked.

She nodded.

He paused, taking a deep breath, and pulling on his game face. He squeezed her hand and then stepped through the doorway.

Into a round, white room with chandeliers framed with white crown molding. Three large windows had burgundy silk curtains that pooled on that white and black marble floor. To the right, an antique fireplace with a white mantle crackled with fire, wood smoke hanging above the sweet, spicy scent of stargazer lilies and hint of roses from two cobalt blue urns on either side of the door.

A long, rectangular table covered in a burgundy tablecloth filled the room. It seated at least twenty people. It had a huge ceramic soup tureen in the center with delicate flowers in pink and green on top, surrounded by bouquets of fresh, pale pink roses and stargazer lilies.

"Jack! Talia!"

Armand Gianni rose to his feet at the far end of the table. His dark brown hair was a little wavy, but not a hair out of place. Like Cary Grant, his hair didn't get windblown. It just got wavy. He wore a grey suit jacket, a light blue T-shirt, and jeans. Izzy Castilla sat beside him, wearing a burnt orange cardigan over a white tank top and brown pants. Her hair was pulled into a copper-brown bun. Beside them sat Mark Banks in jeans and a green sweater, Morgan Boyer beside him wearing a pink sweater and jeans.

At the other end of the table sat Herb Rutherford, balding dark hair windblown. He wore black trousers and a tan long-sleeved shirt. Jennifer Collins sat on one side, Steve Kasinski, the other set coordinator on the other side. He wore a jean shirt and jeans, gold wire-framed glasses, dark hair framing his face and close-cropped beard. Beside Jennifer sat show host Devin Van Fossen, highlighted light brown hair cut short and parted on the side, smile freshly over-whitened.

But he fought to keep his game face intact when he saw Rachel Daniels seated beside Eric Saunders.

No, this was a bad dream.

Herb kicked her off *The Ever After Hour* after what she and Lare had done to him. She almost killed him in that cage fight in Hell.

Why would he allow her to return? Had Herb forgotten all of that?

He made eye contact with her and to his surprise, she smiled at him. It set him on edge. How in hell had she managed to talk Herb into letting her onto this iteration of the show? Before *The Ever After Hour*, she'd led Eric Saunders on throughout *The Prince Charming Hour*. Like Herb hadn't known she'd been in a relationship with Lare Dumont for years.

He sighed. Of course, he hadn't known about her relationship with Lare when she was supposedly with him.

"Looks like our last couple has arrived," said Herb, getting to his feet.

Glasses of red wine set to the right of each place setting, sparkling silverware beside gold charger plates, and white cloth napkins folded like stars at every place setting. The head of the table opposite Herb was empty along with the chair immediately to its right.

Jack frowned. Why would they keep that chair empty for him? He and Talia lost *The Ever After Hour*. That spot should have been reserved for Gianni.

Jennifer stood up from her chair and took Jack by the arm. "Here, Jack," she said, moving toward the opposite end of the table. "Your place is at the other end with Talia on your right."

"Why you putting me at the end like that?" he asked. "Shouldn't that be for Gianni and Izzy to his right?"

Gianni was still standing beside his chair near the end of the table, grinning as he motioned to the head of the table. "I wanted you to have that spot, Jack," he said, glancing at Izzy. "After all, you and Talia are the only reason this show is getting a fourth season."

"What?" said Jack as he glanced down at the empty chair. "Fans are probably screaming to see you marry Izzy Castilla, Gianni. America's favorite TV doctor."

Then his gaze drifted toward Rachel who sat halfway down the table about five places from Gianni.

"Correction. America's favorite *male* TV doctor. America's favorite female TV doctor is just down the table there."

He felt Talia tense beside him, the grip on his hand tightening.

Rachel's auburn hair was cut shorter, bobbed just above her shoulders, those smokey, too-blue eyes looking a little watery, milk-pale skin freckled and a little sunburned. Probably from all that time in Hell, he mused. She wore a lacy ivory top, a pastel pink short skirt, and matching heels. The ones he hated with the red soles that cost a fortune.

"Thank you, Jack," she said with a polite nod.

But something in her manner had changed. The malice in her eyes was gone. Replaced by an emotion he couldn't quite read. She had a masterful game face, one that had taken him in for years. He didn't know what lay beneath those too-blue eyes and expressionless face. It made him nervous though. Maybe she wasn't still trying to kill him for insurance money—after he'd inadvertently gotten her out of

Lucifer's contract? Guess he'd done a lot of damage to Luci's operation.

Then Gianni and Banks were standing beside him. Gianni pulled him into a hug, surprising him, and then Banks.

"Good to see you, Jack," said Gianni, all smiles, looking all Cary Grant, silver screen-like with his perfect dark hair and Italian good looks.

"Jack, you're looking like your amazing Hollywood self," said Banks, patting him on the back.

Gianni hugged Talia next and then Banks hugged her. "Being with Talia has improved your looks considerably, Jack," said Gianni.

"And your temperament," Banks replied.

"If you say she completes me, I'll drown you in that fountain out there," Gianni said with a chuckle.

Jack laughed. "As long as I'm with Talia, I'm home," he said, kissing her hand. "And without this show, I'd have never found her." He patted Gianni on the shoulder and then Banks. "Or either of you. So, I can't think of a better place to kick all your asses and marry the woman I love."

Everyone laughed, including Gianni and Banks.

"Unless Talia kills you first," said Gianni.

"That could happen," he said, giving her a sideways glance.

She let go of his hand and crossed her arms.

"See?" he said, nodding at her as he sat down at the end of the table. "She's wondering how far down to dig my grave in those parterre gardens."

Everyone laughed again. Except Talia. She slid into the chair to his right.

"I'd prefer to drown you in bubble bath in the suite's tub," she said and squeezed his hand. "And kisses."

"I'll die twice for that," he replied, leaning over and kissing her.

"A toast with this delicious Sonoma malbec," said Gianni as he sat down to Jack's left and picked up his glass of red wine.

Everyone picked up their wine glasses and held them in the air.

"To the cast and crew of The Royal Wedding Hour," said Gianni, all smiles as he gazed around the table. "I hope we all have another fun and challenging adventure together. And for Jack's sake, I hope it doesn't involve swords."

Everyone laughed and drank a sip of red wine. It was smooth with hints of blueberries, plums, a touch of cedar, and a little sage with an almost chocolate, mocha-like finish.

"And for Steve's sake," Jack replied, lifting his glass in the air again. "I hope no one else disappears from the terrace in the middle of a live finale."

Cast and crew laughed taking another sip of wine, especially Steve. "I will definitely drink to that, Jack!"

Talia lifted her glass next. "And may everyone at this table find their true love. And their fairytale ending."

"I'll drink to that, Talia," said Jennifer, smiling as she brought her glass to her lips.

Jack turned toward Talia and lifted his glass to her. "Done, true love," he said with a smile.

She grinned at him as he watched her over his wine glass.

"And may the most madly in love princess and prince charming win this competition and have the storybook wedding of a lifetime," said Izzy, raising her glass in a toast as well.

"Says last season's winners," Jack replied with a smirk and took a drink of his wine.

Izzy smiled and drank another sip of wine.

Herb got up from his chair as a man and a woman dressed in black pants and white tuxedo shirts carried in bottles of wine and refilled everyone's glasses. Behind them, two more staff members carried in trays of salads and gold baskets of bread, setting salads on every gold charger plate. They set a basket of bread at both ends of the table and two in the center along with white ramekins of swirled butter.

Herb stood beside his chair, addressing the room.

"Now, then, let's talk a little about the show before we enjoy this meal, compliments of Celestial Vineyards." He motioned at them. "Please, feel free to eat your salad while I talk."

Jack reached for the pepper grinder and added some fresh pepper to his dinner salad drizzled with balsamic vinaigrette dressing and lots of thick, garlicky homemade croutons. He passed the pepper grinder to Talia, but she waved him off. He started it with Gianni next.

"So, as you can see, there are four couples competing in The Royal Wedding Hour. All of you have stated that if you win, you agree to marry your partner on a live, televised fantasy wedding held here at the Celestial Vineyards Chateau following the live finale. All the couples here have found a spark together and something more. Like Armand and Izzy." He smiled. "And Jack and Talia."

"I'll drink to that," Jack announced and picked up his glass of wine that the attendant had just refilled.

Everyone laughed and drank another sip of their wine before returning to their salads as Herb motioned toward Eric and Rachel.

"Perhaps the biggest surprise couple on the show is Eric Saunders and Rachel Daniels."

Eric nodded. "Rachel and I ran into each other in January and spent hours talking. And we discovered we had a lot in common—including that spark that Herb mentioned. We've been dating ever since then and moved in together in March. So, don't be surprised to see us in your rearview mirrors."

Rachel slid her arm around Eric's shoulders and kissed him. "Yep, my life has been totally different since The Ever After Hour. And Eric was a huge part of that." Her gaze fell onto Jack. "Especially after someone's incredible act of forgiveness changed everything for me. I'm ready to make the most of it now."

Jack smiled. So, she had changed her life after he'd forgiven her, releasing her from her contract. And found someone that made her happy—now that Lare was in Hell. Had she really changed or was she just on the rebound from Lare? He hoped Rachel loved Eric. The dude deserved that much.

He lifted his glass in the air. "To Rachel and Eric."

Everyone lifted their glasses and toasted them.

"So, now that you know your competition," said Herb, setting down his glass of red wine. "Let me tell you about your challenges for the show. Each couple will compete in events that to plan a wedding. Your wedding. From food and drinks, wedding vows and venues, a fantasy dress fitting, and other surprises."

And other surprises? That sounded ominous.

"Do those other surprises involve sword fights?" Jack asked to laughter.

Herb snickered. "No, Jack. No sword fights this time."

"Good," he said, leaning back in his chair.

He'd gone through his share of surprises on this show. He'd get through it—even if one of those surprises was Abaddon.

He sighed. Or his mother.

"Each week," Herb continued, "one couple will be eliminated during the live show. At the final competition, we'll crown one couple the royal wedding winner. That couple will stay an extra two weeks, filming the wedding preparations and the events leading up to the wedding day. And the wedding itself will be filmed. But we need to know by tomorrow end of day who will stand up as your best man and maid of honor. And the names of groomsmen and bridesmaids so we can get their commitments now, in the event that you win. Jennifer will send you a link to an online form to send us that information."

Jack frowned. At the moment, he didn't have a phone. Jennifer could probably get him online with someone's laptop. Maybe he could get someone to pick up a replacement phone for him in Santa Rosa?

"So, that's the format of this season's show," said Herb, holding out his arms. "Now, everyone, please—enjoy your supper. And welcome to The Royal Wedding Hour. There's been a ton of buzz about this season, thanks to some incredibly strong off-script performances last season." He smiled at Jack. "I'm looking at you, Jack. And Talia, last season's official scene-stealer. You stole the spotlight from Jack. That took some work, Talia."

Jack laughed and leaned toward Talia, kissing her lips. "Like me, America's been waiting for you to answer my question since The Prince Charming Hour."

She held up her left hand, still wearing his ring. "And my answer hasn't changed, Jack Casey," she said and smiled at him.

"Good," he said with a nervous sigh. "If we managed to win this thing, you'd have broken mine and America's hearts if you refused to marry me."

"Tempting," she said with a smirk, "But I love you too much to break your heart."

He grinned and kissed her again. "That's a relief."

After he and the table finished their salads, attendants cleared the crisp white salad plates from the table and offered them the choice of chicken piccata or cedar-planked salmon. He and Talia chose the salmon.

In a few minutes, the attendants returned with trays, setting down white plates edged in satiny black onto the gold charger plates. The salmon looked delicious, perched on a bed of rice with a tangle of roasted vegetables. The sauce on the salmon was a mixture of sweet and savory, tasting like garlic and maple syrup.

Jack drank his second glass of wine and devoured the salmon in record time. He felt like he hadn't eaten in ages. Not like they had restaurants in Heaven. Or even food when he'd been trapped in Hell. After *SanFran Confidential*, he couldn't afford to eat out. It had been years since he'd had a nice, multi-course meal when he got cast on *The Cinderella Hour*. No, this was a nice change and he enjoyed every moment of it, especially sharing it with the love of his life and good friends like Gianni and Banks.

Dessert was a white mousse cake with fresh strawberry sauce and a rich cup of Kona coffee. Something else he hadn't enjoyed in a very long time. He listened to Gianni telling Talia how he and Izzy had moved in together in L.A. and she'd gotten the anchor spot at one of the local stations. Talia listened to Morgan describe how happy she and Banks were in their place outside of L.A. They even invited the room to a barbecue after the show had completed filming. Talia seemed calm and comfortable in this environment. She, Izzy, and Morgan talked across the table about everything from fashion to current events.

He could see a life with Talia, hanging out with these friends and living in their own place. Unless Heaven forced her back there and barred him from returning after they took back their wings. Or Abaddon killed him. He sighed. Or his mother ruined everything. And then there was Rachel—a wild card here. He had no idea if she'd taken a number and gotten in line behind Abaddon and his mother.

So many ways for all of this to go straight to Hell—literally.

But without all of those worries, he felt confident that maybe an angel of death could be happy in the City of Angels. And just maybe he and Talia could stay together—without demons or angels breaking everything for them?

It was almost eleven o'clock when the dinner ended and they got their eight A.M. set calls for tomorrow. In the formal living room. When filming started. The first interviews had been scheduled along with cast introductions and an introduction to the competition for the audience by host Devin Van Fossen. At the introduction, they'd learned what their first challenge would be for this royal wedding theme.

As he and Talia walked upstairs, Talia's hand in his, he felt a sense of calm that he hadn't felt since the night that Talia dropped out of the sky and into his arms, hurt and bleeding. When everything quickly—and literally—went to Hell. He saw his first angel that night. His first demon. And Lucifer. Things he never knew existed. And it was the night when he'd gone from struggling to locate Talia to having the whole Heavenly pantheon unload on him. He thought Talia had been different than all the other women he'd known. And then she'd gone and proved it by informing him that she was an angel of death. And that demons—and Lucifer—were after her.

But tonight, as they stepped into their private suite in this amazing French masterpiece, all of that felt like a dream he'd had. It was just him and Talia for the first time since this whole crazy whirlwind began. He put the *do not disturb* sign on the door, locked it, and took Talia in his arms.

He spun her around and kissed her. "For the first time since this whole crazy ride began, I finally have you alone and all to myself."

She grinned at him, kissing him back. Her kiss was like fireworks on the beach. Like heat lightning before a summer storm. A beach bonfire on a chilly night.

"Just you and me, Jack Casey," she said and her hot mouth covered his again, pressing kissing sips against his lips. "It's like a fairytale."

"My Cinderella...after I finally put your missing glass slipper on your foot." He shrugged out of Navy blue hoodie and pulled her against his chest.

"My Prince Charming," she said in a breathy voice between kisses. "Who fought for me to his last breath."

He picked her up in his arms and carried her over to the four-poster bed. "And I always will, Talia. As long as I draw breath."

She pushed his olive Henley up and over his head, her hands sliding over his chest as he began unbuttoning her lavender blouse. He pushed it off her shoulders and slid it down her arms, pressing his face against hers. He sipped her neck and brushed his lips across her collarbones, sliding his hands underneath her bra. He kissed her skin along her breastbone and across the tops of her small firm breasts.

She moaned, her fingers tangling in his blond hair.

Unzipping her skirt, he worked it down her hips until it joined the pile of clothing on the floor beside the bed. She unzipped his jeans, pushing them off his hips. He kicked them into the floor, hands sliding across her stomach and behind her back, fumbling to unfasten her bra.

But the sound of someone clearing their throat made him freeze.

"Please tell me that's not Muriel behind me," he said in a quiet voice.

Talia's eyes widened, her breath catching as she stared behind him. "Worse."

"Kesien?" he asked. "The archangel?"

His heart beat even faster, but the fear rushed down his spine, chilling his fingertips and making his breath hang in his throat as his heart beat into it.

"Hello, Jack Casey," said the deep, rumbling voice.

He felt his insides freeze. as the rich baritone voice floated back to him from those frenzied moments at the crossroads. Where legions of demons fought angels of death, archangels, and even cherubim as the Watchers rained down flaming arrows of lightning.

Where the biggest demon he'd ever seen stepped out of the haunted woods. Wanting to end his existence and deliver his soul to Lucifer for an eternity of torture.

"Shit," Jack said through clenched teeth as he turned around.

Abaddon.

7

ABADDON STOOD EIGHT FEET TALL, LEATHERY DEMON SKIN THE COLOR
of white ash. Chandeliers burned bright through the Halo Suite as he
moved toward them.

Talia glared at the demon, a hand on Jack's bare shoulder, pulling
him beside her as she sat up on the bed.

Abaddon's cloven hooves thumped against the marble tile, his voice
echoing through the room as Jack turned around on the bed, clad only
in a pair of blue boxer briefs that hugged his leanly muscled thighs.

Talia slid forward, an arm held out protectively in front of Jack.

"What do you want here, Abaddon?" she demanded.

"The same thing I came for at the Crossroads," he said, his voice
rumbling through the room, echoing in layers. "To kill Jack Casey and
take his soul. But you humiliated me, little angel of death, so I intend
to end you for your treachery."

"You'll try," said Talia, sliding off the bed.

"Uh, Talia—be careful," said Jack, his unsettling gaze locked on the
slayer demon.

Jack moved across the bed past her, but she pushed him behind
her, into the pillows. She had to keep him safe. He didn't have

seraphim powers now and the omnificence power could severely harm him and his world if he tried to use it.

She had to stay between Abaddon and Jack at all costs.

"Stay back," she snapped in a whisper. "It's too dangerous, Jack."

Where was Muriel and the guard? She had the omnificence power, but using it would cause severe devastation. To this chateau. To the land. To the nearby population. And that wasn't an option.

How could she keep Abaddon from killing them both right now?

"You were a powerful angel once, Abaddon," said Talia, stepping onto the cold marble tile as she faced the monstrous, ashen-white demon. "Doing the Maker's bidding, in charge of Lucifer and the abyss. You possess the key, after all. Yet, now you've reduced yourself to being Lucifer's lowly lieutenant. Nothing more than his executioner. Why? Why would you behave like a fallen angel with such responsibility and power?"

Jack crawled off the bed and stood beside her.

"Stay back, Jack," she said again.

"I'm not letting you face him alone," he snapped, standing his ground.

Abaddon's face twisted into a look of fury and he balled his huge corpulent hands into fists. "Because the Maker has forsaken me. Left me in Hell like I was just another demon. With a key to the abyss when Lucifer already had free rein of Hell. He showed me what our Maker truly thought of His angels. How he'd thrown us over for these pathetic, weak little humans."

"Getting really tired of being called little and weak," Jack said through gritted teeth.

Talia stared at the demon, unblinking and then crossed her arms. "But you are God's Destroyer. Ready to smite the wicked when it's time."

"A time that may never come," Abaddon said with a feral growl. "I've grown tired of watching over the key for a gate that has never been locked. I grew tired of being forgotten by the Maker and my own kind. By angels with half my powers and abilities. Lucifer gave

me a new purpose. A new goal. Until I am free to smite the wicked."
He pointed a large index finger at Jack. "Like Jack Casey."

"Me? Wicked?" A grimace darkened Jack's face. "You're the
dumbass that decided to work for a loser like Luci. Dude who lost his
bid to takeover Heaven. In case you missed it, dude—the good guys
won. You're on the wrong side. The dark side, dude."

"Jack! Sssssh!"

"I will destroy you, human," Abaddon said through bared, pointy
teeth. "Slowly. Painfully."

"I get that a lot from your kind, Aby. Or do you go by Aba? Like
the pop group? Bet your rendition of Dancing Queen is stunning,
Aby."

"Shut your unholy mouth, human!"

"Whoa, dude—calling Abba unholy? Bet you lose your shit when
you hear Ozzy Osbourne or Judas Priest."

"Jack!" Talia shouted.

"He started it," Jack said in a quiet voice.

She winced. Jack didn't have seraphim powers anymore and
couldn't use most of the rare powers mirrored in him because of the
devastation they would cause him and his world. Why did he insist on
poking a massive demon that could easily end him?

Abaddon growled again and rushed at Jack, but she stepped in
front of him, blocking him with her wings.

"You lied to me, little angel of death," Abaddon said, pointing at
her. "You said that you'd crossed over this foolish, little human and
given me his soul. But the stone you gave me was empty."

"Sorry, Abaddon," she said, hands on her hips now as she kept her
body and wings between Jack and the slayer demon. "Had to get you
out of the crossroads. Jack's soul is still being used and I intend to
keep him alive. Go back to Lucifer and tell him that he's not getting
Jack's soul. Now or ever."

A loud, rumbling sound echoed through the large suite. Abaddon
was laughing, she realized.

"Afraid I can't do that, little angel of death," he stared down at her
with a leering grin. "I will kill him and take his soul myself."

A brilliant flash erupted through the suite, the light almost blinding her.

Talia shielded her eyes, but Jack cried out, hands pressed against his face. He turned away, falling against the bed.

Archangel Azrael stepped out of the brilliant white light. The haunting, powerful radiance of a seraph surrounded him as he burnished a flaming sword of Holy fire in his right hand. He wore a charcoal grey robe underneath clear gold Eternean armor, breastplate glistening.

Behind him, Muriel, Anahera, Kesien, and Deemah fluttered into the room and surrounded Abaddon, gold shields of light and swords raised. They wore short grey robes underneath burnished Eternean armor.

"Sorry to disappoint you, Abaddon," said Azrael, silver-black hair blown back from his face, soot-grey wings unfurled like sails behind him as he glowed with the light of a seraph at his back. His halo burned red-gold. "Seraphina sends her regards and bids you farewell. Now."

The eight-foot tall, muscular, ashen white demon laughed with another deep rumble and surveyed the room, watching each angel surrounding him with amusement in his glowing red eyes.

"I do enjoy a challenge, archangel." He gave a stiff nod to Azrael. "Seraph."

Then he turned back toward Talia who still glared at him, unmoving as Jack groaned and held his face.

"A reprieve for your weak, little human, angel of death. For the moment. But I promise to return." He laughed. "And I always keep my promises."

In a sudden burst of flame and shadow, Abaddon disappeared from the room as the seraph's light dimmed.

Talia felt relief overwhelm her as she let her body go slack, wings folding against her back. "Archangel! Thank you!" she cried.

"Muriel alerted us the moment she felt Abaddon's presence near your suite."

Talia smiled and hugged Muriel, one of her best friends. Muriel's wings folded against her back, dark brown hair falling around her face, grey eyes still looking fearful.

"Thank you," said Talia. "Wasn't sure how we were going to stop Abaddon."

Muriel shook her head. "Neither were we, but then Azrael brought along the seraph. Cleared that problem right up."

"For the moment," Kesien added, looking alarmed.

"Talia?" Azrael motioned behind her. "It's Jack!"

She whirled around. He was on the floor, on his knees, hands clutching his face.

"Jack?" She fell down beside him, an arm sliding underneath his wings. "What's the matter? What's wrong?"

He groaned. "My eyes!"

She laid her hand against his head and rubbed the back of his neck. "Your eyes? Jack, I don't understand. What's happened to your eyes?"

"Oh, no!" Azrael moaned and moved toward her, dropping down on his knees beside Jack.

Talia shook her head. "Archangel, what's the matter with him?"

Azrael turned to her, his face contorted, pain in his voice. "The seraph. I've been so used to seeing Jack among you—and with wings—that I forgot he was human."

Then the words finally sank through her confusion. The seraph! The radiant light of a seraph was too much for human eyes. Her heart bounced into her throat.

Had Seraphina blinded him when she appeared in the room?

"Oh, Jack," she cried, sliding her arms around him, holding him close as she helped him to his feet.

His moans echoed through the room, the angels of death looking disturbed, glancing from Jack to the archangel.

"I summoned Berith," said Azrael who still looked unnerved as he laid his hand against Jack's shoulder. "Hold on, Jack. Forgive us. We'd forgotten you weren't one of us."

Jack writhed in pain against her and she just held him, terrified that Seraphina had permanently blinded him with her sudden arrival.

It seemed like forever until Berith appeared, wearing a pale grey, layered robe, dove grey wings flexed. She clutched an aqua gem in her right hand.

"Azrael, I'm here. What's happened to Jack?" she cried.

"The seraph's appearance was sudden. We forgot Jack was the only human in the room."

Berith gasped. "Oh, no...his eyes! Let's get him onto the bed where I can examine him better." She glanced at Muriel and Kesien. "Go find some ice. Hurry."

They nodded and blinked out of the room as Talia and Azrael carefully lifted Jack onto the bed. He curled into a ball, hands still clutching his eyes, his voice a hoarse, steady groan.

In a minute or two, Muriel and Kesien returned with a beige plastic ice bucket full of ice and a folded, white cloth napkin. They hurried to the other side of the bed. Kesien laid out the unfolded napkin and Muriel filled it with ice. She rolled it up and gently laid it across Jack's face as Talia slid his hands away from his eyes.

Berith laid the aqua gem on his forehead and pressed her palm against it, bathing him in pale gold light. The room shook as the stone began to glow with the purest white light she'd ever seen.

Talia took hold of Jack's shaking right hand and gripped it against her chest.

"It's going to be okay, Jack," she said in a soft, soothing soprano voice. "Just relax. You're going to be fine."

"Seraphina says that she infused Berith's healing stone with seraphim powers," said Azrael, a hand on Talia's arm. "To heal Jack's eyes. He was blinded by her presence, but her powers in the stone will heal his eyes. Restore his vision." Then the archangel sighed. "It's going to take a few days to restore though."

Talia leaned down and kissed his trembling lips. "Hear that, Jack," said Talia. She winced at the pain he felt, hating to see him injured like this. "Seraphina infused the stone with healing powers. Your vision will be fine in a few days."

"My eyes," he moaned.

He was shuddering and breathing so hard, his voice ragged from fighting pain.

In an instant, the room went dark as the seraph departed, bathing the room in darkness except for a crystal lamp on the ivory French provincial nightstand beside the bed.

"Talia," said the archangel in a deathly quiet voice. "Seraphina says that you and Jack can't possibly defeat Abaddon alone—even with your squad of death angels. God's Scribe is still trying to find a solution that will deal with Abaddon. Seraphina isn't certain that he'll find anything, but until there is a way to stop him, she is going to ward your suite. If this competition requires the two of you to go outside, tell Muriel immediately and she'll obtain seraphim wards to protect you out there. Until we find a way to stop Abaddon."

"Thank you, sir," said Talia, still gripping Jack's hand. "Can we try to tether him again? Without using a stone?"

"It would only be a temporary fix," said Berith. "As God's Destroyer, he'd eventually free himself with that key to the abyss. Thankfully, it won't unlock Lucifer's tether, but caging Abaddon isn't possible."

"I just hope Pravuil finds an answer before Abaddon returns," said Talia.

"As do the rest of us," said Azrael. "It is essential that we stop him. This isolated location on earth is a good place to draw him out, but we have to find a way to defeat him. If Abaddon succeeds here, then Lucifer will deploy him as his one-man army until he finds a way to untether himself from Hell."

Talia nodded. "I agree, sir, but without seraphim powers, none of us has the ability to stop him. And since he can't be killed or caged, we are running out of options fast."

Muriel held the ice pack gently across Jack's eyes as Berith kept her palm against the aqua gem stone pressed against Jack's forehead.

"Talia?" he cried out. "You there? Talia!"

She held his hand tighter. "I'm here, Jack," she said to him in soothing tones. "It's going to be okay." She stared at Berith. "Will it really only take a few days to heal his eyes?"

"I won't know until I get a look at the damage," said Berith in a calm, quiet voice. "But that's what the seraph says. Muriel, go ahead and remove the ice pack. I need to have a look at his eyes."

Nodding, Muriel slid away the ice pack and laid it in the ice bucket as Berith gently placed her hands on Jack's face. Scorch marks stretched across his swollen cheeks, under his puffy, red eyelids, and over his burned eyebrows.

"There's a lot of blistering around his eyes and across his face," Berith said, trying to sound calm and unaffected. For Jack.

Berith thought of Jack like a son and her worried, fearful expression spoke volumes. Terrifying Talia.

"It's bad, isn't it?" she whispered.

Berith turned her gaze toward Talia and gave her a deep, decisive nod. This was bad. Really bad.

Berith kept her hand against the healing stone pressed against Jack's forehead as she very gently touched his right eyelid, lifting it up with her thumb. The white part of Jack's right eye was red and swollen, making his pale green eyes look so wild as moisture streamed from the corners of his eyes and down his face.

"Blistered," she said. "Including his corneas."

She didn't know what that meant, but Berith's dark tone frightened her.

The healing light abruptly turned blue and Jack's body went limp. He was only wearing a pair of blue boxer briefs. His bare chest and stomach with lean, well-defined muscles and sculpted abdomen sculpted with those washboard abs were red and blistered. His beautiful body and face. She winced. And those irresistible, sexy, light green eyes of his—burned and blinded.

He was so beautiful. The burned and blistered skin made her ache all over. He was in terrible pain.

"All right, I've knocked him out for a bit," said Berith as she turned toward Talia. "There's extensive damage, Talia. It's not going to be an instant heal, not even with seraphim powers. But with my rare powers and the seraphim healing stone, we will heal him. The skin burns will take less time to heal than his eyes."

"What about my resurrect and omnificence powers?" Talia asked. "I remember Jack instantly healing Vassago's blindness after his eyes got burned away from looking upon the Maker."

Already, Berith was shaking her head. "Doesn't work that way on humans, Talia. Angels are beings of light, so those powers are much more effective on us. Beings of flesh can be instantly healed, but only by the Maker. Not even a seraph can heal these sorts of injuries instantly. It will take some time."

"The competition starts tomorrow!" Talia cried, a hand against her mouth. "What will we tell the cast and crew?"

Berith shook her head, wings shifting as she floated beside the bed. "You'll have to come up with something. He's not going to be able to see much for the next three days or so. And those burns on his skin will be painful."

She'd have to talk to Jack and come up with something.

"Maybe say Jack's vision issue was a food reaction or something?" Muriel replied with a shrug. "An allergy?"

"That's a thought, Muriel, thank you," said Talia, pacing as several possibilities rushed through her head.

She could guide Jack through whatever happened over the next few days or so. But what if Abaddon returned? Jack couldn't even see him coming. She winced.

An eight-foot demon and he wouldn't know Abaddon was there until it was too late.

"Squad, you'll need to stick even closer to him," she said. "He's going to need that protection until we handle Abaddon, especially until his eyes heal."

"It's our pleasure, Talia," said Kesien. "The kid did a lot for us. We consider it an honor to protect him."

Muriel smiled, patting her shoulder. "Kesien's right. Jack's done a lot for the guard. Protected us on several occasions. Now, we can finally return the favor."

"Just tell us where we need to place wards tomorrow and we'll take care of it," said Deemah, standing next to Kesien, her long, walnut hair flowing down her back.

"Muriel and I won't leave his side," said Anahera, her short red hair bright against the suite's white marble and white walls. "You have our word."

"Thank you, Anahera," said Talia, laying her hand on the sleeve of Anahera's grey robe.

Then she turned to Azrael who still looked concerned. "Archangel," said Talia. "Have they decided how to remove Jack's wings and halo yet? When that happens, will it affect the mirrored powers that he shares with me?"

Azrael's face darkened, those grey eyes turning steely as he glanced at his hands.

"Actually, Talia," he said as he stared at the floor. "The seraphim are still discussing that. It would appear that there are complications to removing them."

Talia's gaze narrowed as she fixed Azrael with her fierce gaze. "Complications? What does that mean?"

He sighed and finally met her gaze. "It would appear that we can't just remove them. That would banish him from the Heavens and turn him into a fallen angel."

She nodded. She already knew that. "We were told that already," she replied. "You said the seraphim were exploring other options."

"They are, but so far, there haven't been any plausible options. Pravuil is shaking his head over that problem and Abaddon. The problem with Jack's wings and halo is that they've changed his nature."

"Changed his nature? How?" she asked with a frown.

"One unintended consequence," said Azrael, sounding sheepish, "is that Jack has stopped aging."

"What?" Talia cried, frowning. "How is that possible? He's human. And he's back in his original timeline."

"Yes, that's all correct," Azrael replied. "But when we hid him among the guard by giving him wings, it changed him in ways we don't exactly understand. Like him not aging. It's like he's taken on some, but not all angelic characteristics. Pravuil is still investigating. We'll know more soon."

Jack would love that news. He'd just said to her that she would have to watch him get old, that he wouldn't look young forever. He seemed worried that she wouldn't love him anymore. Didn't he realize that she'd love him forever? Regardless?

Then Berith was beside her, the aqua story gem in her hand. She extended the large stone to Talia. "Talia, I've infused this stone that contains seraphim powers with my own rare healing light. You'll need to apply it to his eyes every night for three or four days until his eyes are healed. You can activate it with your angelic healing power."

Talia took the stone from her hands, realizing that she'd been standing here this whole time in front of the archangel dressed in only human undergarments. Abaddon's timing was the worst.

She moved over to the suitcases that sat just inside the door of the suite. A grey suitcase and a dark blue one. She laid down the grey one and unzipped it. On top was the short grey angel robe she'd laid on top. She pulled it on over her head and the silk fabric fell in layers around her body.

Once she had on a robe, she slid the stone in the front breast pocket of the robe and turned back to Berith.

"Will I need to apply the stone again tonight?" she asked.

Berith shook her head as she moved back to the bed and picked up the napkin-wrapped ice. She laid it gently across Jack's eyes again as he slept.

"Tomorrow," Berith answered. "Tonight, I made sure that he'll sleep for hours. Giving those eyes valuable time to heal."

Then Talia remembered that Jack had worn his Ray Bans on the drive to Santa Rosa. He'd tucked them into the pocket of his Henley. She moved over to the bed. Where their clothes lay piled against it. She bent down and collected them, grabbing Jack's shirt. It had his buttery scent and a hint of cedary cologne. She turned it around until she found the front pocket. The aviator Ray Bans were still tucked in the pocket. She removed them and set them on the nightstand. He'd need those tomorrow to hide the damage to his eyes. And protect them.

Jack would be so disappointed if this hurt their chances for that royal wedding. She'd dreamed of marrying him since she'd first laid gaze on him under the hot stage lights of Studio 22. Granted, they could still have their own wedding if they lost, but there was something about their journey coming full circle by winning this on-camera wedding.

And it would only increase the brilliance of his Hollywood stardom. She wanted to see him on top again. He'd earned it.

"Okay, thank you all for protecting us against Abaddon," said Talia. "I admit, I wasn't expecting him to show up this soon. I thought we'd have a few days before seeing our first demon."

Azrael nodded as he slid his arm around Berith's shoulders. "We did, too, Talia. The guard will stick close and place seraphim wards. And Seraphina is keeping careful watch, just in case she has to intervene again before Pravuil has a solution."

"Thank you, sir," said Talia. She turned to Berith. "And thank you for coming to heal Jack so quickly."

Berith smiled, patting her shoulder. "I'm happy to do it. For him and you, Talia."

"I'll be in touch soon, Talia," said the archangel, holding Berith close as she stood in front of him. "Hopefully with news on Jack's wings and Abaddon. Stay safe and guard her well, angels."

With a blink, Azrael and Berith disappeared from the room.

Muriel turned to the rest of the squad. "All right, guard, you heard the boss. Let's get these seraphim wards in place before Abaddon decides to return."

Pure white lights appeared around the room, wrapping the walls, windows, floor, and ceiling in a translucent white glow. The mark of a seraphim glowed within the light, protecting them from even Lucifer, not that he could break that tether anytime soon. But it made her relax a little, knowing that they'd be safe here.

Getting through the competition challenges was another story. Especially with Jack's injured eyes.

8

JACK AWOKE SEVERAL HOURS LATER. THE SET CALL TIME GOT CHANGED, so they didn't have to be down in the chateau's living room until ten A.M. for orientation and he was grateful. He was groggy and confused, the room so dark.

What time was it anyway? Why was everything so dark?

Then the horrible memory returned to him. The moment the seraph appeared in the room.

Like swords lancing his eyes, the light was so bright that it burned. His face and body felt sunburned.

Badly sunburned.

Panic washed over him as he stared into nothing but complete and utter blackness. Was he blinded? Like Vassago, the fallen angel after he'd looked on the face of God? The one that possessed Talia for Lucifer. The memory of that fallen angel's dark, empty eye sockets terrified him now.

Had his eyes been burned away, too? Empty and black like Vassago's? Before he'd healed them with the seraphim powers?

He laid his fingers against his eyelids. Hot, swollen, and aching.

If his eyes were just adjusting to the dark, he'd at least see outlines of furniture along the walls and windows of the suite. But all he saw was thick, fluid darkness. Not a single outline in the blackness.

"Talia?" His voice echoed through the large room and across the marble floors.

Silence.

"Talia!" he called.

No response.

"Anybody? Someone, answer me…please."

A hand pressed his bare left shoulder. "Talia?"

"It's Kesien, kid," said the soft but bright male angel voice, smooth and laid back.

"Kesien," he said, feeling the tension lift. "What time is it? Where's Talia?"

There was a pause. "Looks like it's about seven in the morning from that clock on the bed table. The sun's up and Talia is in the bathroom."

He laid his head back against the pillow, disturbed by the complete blackness surrounding him. How could he do this competition when he couldn't see a thing? And was it permanent? That thought terrified him.

"How am I going to explain this to the cast and crew?" he said with a groan.

Another pause. "Muriel suggested an allergy of some kind."

He shook his head and struggled to sit up, feeling restless and frustrated now. His face was sore and throbbed. He felt sunburn-like blisters around his eyes and similar pain across his chest, arms, and legs. How was he going to explain this? Maybe too much sun on the long drive without sunglasses? Too much sunscreen too late? Shellfish allergy? Sounded stupid. His head swam with other possibilities, but they all sounded like awful lies.

"Jack? How do you feel?"

Talia's lyric soprano voice filled the room, reassuring him. Her bare feet whispered across the marble floor. The bed shifted and he felt the presence of someone beside him.

"Talia?" he asked, awkwardly reaching out his right hand.

Long, damp hair, silky bare skin, faint scent of lavender.

"It's me, Jack," she said, her melodic voice calming him. "I asked how you feel? Can you see anything today?"

He just shrugged. "It's all utter blackness," he said, doing his best to slide that game face into place.

Even though he couldn't see anything.

Fingers gently tangled in his hair. Stroking.

"Give it time," she said, voice bright with reassurance. "Berith said it could be a few days before it's all healed. She gave me a healing stone infused with seraphim powers and her healing light. We're to use it once a day, Jack."

He struggled to cross his arms against his bare chest. Everything hurt. "How am I going to explain this to Herb? I don't want to get sent home after the first elimination round."

A hand cupped his chin. "Jack, we won't. We'll get through this—don't worry."

He sighed. "You deserve this wedding, Talia," he said, trying to keep his emotions out of the conversation, but he couldn't.

It pissed him off. After all the Hell and chaos they'd both endured at Lucifer's hands, Talia earned this happily ever after. And now Abaddon threatened it all with his sudden attack. And now, his sudden blindness.

"We'll get through it," she said against his ear.

Her hand slid to his cheek, caressing his face. Her touch and lyric voice eased his panic and frustration.

"We don't even know what the first challenge is going to be," he said, his voice in a quiet voice as his rested his hot, achy arms against the bed. "What if it's something crazy like an obstacle course or...well, doing anything that requires sight. And what the hell am I going to tell them happened to me last night? Oh, it's nothing. Just the most powerful angel in existence suddenly appeared, blinding me. But I'll be good in a few days—until the king of slayer demons tears me apart. No worries, Herb. It's all good."

Hands gripped his shoulders. "Jack," said Talia, sounding insistent now. "Don't worry. We'll come up with something."

"But orientation starts in three hours," he countered. "That's not much time to come up with a plausible story."

Something warm pressed against his lips. Talia's kiss. That was one thing he didn't need to see to identify.

"Does that help?" Talia asked him in a playful tone.

"It's a start," he said. "Do that again. For science."

Again, her mouth covered his in a warm, anxious kiss that burned through him. He kissed her back. Hard. Urgent. That connection in the face of this sudden darkness was comforting.

"Like this?" she asked, a smile in her tone.

Something thick and soft brushed across his chest. Reaching out, he felt the soft, silky tresses of her hair against his fingertips. He remembered how raven black and shiny her long hair was and how it tumbled in waves around her shoulders.

And then she was gone.

"Talia?" he called. "Talia!"

"I'm right beside the bed, Jack," she said. "Getting dressed."

"Now?" he cried.

The one thing he didn't need his eyesight for and she leaves him?

The mattress sank down and Talia's hands pressed against his thighs.

"Jack," she whispered against his ear. "The whole squad's still here."

And then the bed moved again, her hands sliding away from his legs.

"I knew that," he replied. "First Abaddon and now angels of death. Can't wait for the honeymoon. I'm sure Luci will be free by then to help out."

Kesien laughed nearby.

"Need help getting into the shower?" Talia asked from somewhere off to his left.

"That's a real big yes," he said, smiling as he felt for the edge of the bed.

The shower was someplace private. He and Talia could be alone there for a little while. Hands took hold of his arms, pulling him to his feet.

"Talia? That you?"

"Sorry, Jack—it's Kesien."

Was she trying to avoid him? If so, she was doing a fine job. He felt Kesien steering him through the darkness, the marble cold under his bare feet.

"We're in the bathroom now, Jack," said the tall, god-like angel of death.

Jack remembered Kesien's headful of coal black curls and large, light grey eyes. At six foot six or so, Kesien towered over him at six feet tall.

Something scraped across the marble floor and fabric rustled.

"Who's there?" he called, feeling uneasy.

"Still me, Jack," said Kesien. "I moved a bench beside the shower and put a couple of towels and your clothes on it."

Kesien led him forward until he felt the wooden bench against his knees. The angel of death took hold of his wrist, lifting it until Jack felt a cold metal lever against his right palm.

"Turning that lever will turn on the water and regulate the temperature. Talia said there were bottles of shampoo, conditioner, and shower gel already on the shelf behind you. At chest level."

He shook his head. "Can't see which is which," he said with a sigh.

"Talia put the shampoo on the left, conditioner in the center, and shower gel to the right."

Jack sighed. "Tell her she could have come in here and showed me where to find everything."

"I'll tell her," said Kesien. "Need anything else?"

"Just my eyesight, but thanks, dude. Appreciate it."

"You're welcome," said Kesien, armored boots clacking against the floor.

The bathroom door thumped closed and he felt self-conscious. Uneasy. Almost a sense of dread. Was someone—or something—in the room with him?

He held the shower lever in a death grip as he felt around for the shower door. It opened out and swung to his left. He felt the bench to the right.

He slid off his boxer briefs and dropped them beside the bench. Fumbling with the shower door, he managed to close it and turn on the water, regulating it to a temperature just warm enough not to aggravate his burned skin.

Sighing, he clawed at the shelf for the shower gel. Shower for one in the most romantic vineyard in northern California.

HE STRUGGLED to wash and rinse his hair and body. The burns still hurt, a sharp, throbbing ache that kept his back against the water. He turned off the water, dried off with the towel, and fumbled with his clothes to get dressed.

With one hand against the wall, he fumbled around the bathroom, wearing what felt like jeans and some pullover long-sleeved shirt Kesien put there. It felt like a T-shirt, but had no clue what he was wearing. He needed to find some socks and his Vans though.

His hair was still damp as he felt around for the bathroom door handle. But it felt like a window.

He held onto the wall, feeling a blank wall, and moved to the right. Still nothing.

Every movement in the dark—in this unfamiliar room—terrified him. How would he find his way out again?

His hands moved across what felt like a countertop. And then another window. Couldn't find the door to save his soul.

And he didn't feel alone in this bathroom.

"Kesien? You there?" he asked.

Silence. Thick. Heavy. Almost suffocating. God, he felt uneasy in here. Like he had an audience or something.

"Talia!" he shouted.

No response.

He waited. Listening. Not a sound around him except the last, steady drips of water from the shower head against the tile. Tick. Tick. Tick.

Like an old clock. A chill brushed across his skin. Or footsteps.

"Talia!" he shouted again.

Glass shattered, reverberating through the bathroom.

And dozens of hands grabbed hold of him. Wrapping around his chest. His arms. His legs.

"TALIA!"

He struggled, punching and kicking. Couldn't dislodge all the hands and fists gripping him like luggage handles.

They lifted him into the air.

He felt wind across his face. As several hands carried him. Outside. Into cooler darkness.

9

TALIA RUSHED OVER TO THE MURIEL WHO STOOD WATCH IN THE SUITE alongside Anahera. Kesien, Daidrean, and Deemah had been stationed outside the chateau, watching for demons. It was almost seven fifteen in the morning and no sign of Abaddon.

So far, the seraphim wards had held.

"Any problem with the wards?" Talia asked, dressed in a short jean skirt and ice blue sweater.

Muriel shook her head. "Everything's holding. How's Jack?"

"Frustrated and struggling," she said with a sigh. "I just hope his eyesight returns quickly. He said it was total darkness. He's really scared even if he won't admit it."

"Where is he?" Muriel asked, glancing toward the bed.

"Kesien got him to the shower while I got dressed."

Muriel frowned. "I don't hear the shower. Kesien just blinked out to return to his post on the roof with Deemah and Daidrean."

Jack probably needed help getting dressed. "I'll go check on him."

Her black flats slapped against the marble as she moved to the bathroom door. She knocked on the door.

"Jack? I'm coming in—in case you need help."

She opened the door.

The gold, padded bench stood in front of the closed shower door. One towel lay folded on the bench, the other was crumpled beside the shower door. Beside Jack's blue boxer briefs.

Sunlight warmed the empty room. Birds chattered and a cool breeze swirled through the space. Had he left the bathroom while her back was turned?

"Jack?"

Her voice echoed above the bird calls and the wind as something crunched under her flats. Broken glass. Scattered across the tiles.

Her heart leaped into her throat. The room was dark.

They hadn't warded the bathroom!

"Muriel! Kesien!" She shrieked out their names in angelic notes.

They blinked instantly into the room beside her.

"What's wrong?" Muriel cried, glancing around.

"It's Jack," she cried, her face contorting as she rushed toward the broken window. "The bathroom wasn't warded."

"Let's go!" Muriel shouted.

"On it," said Kesien, leaping out the broken window, wings beating the crisp blue sky.

Talia surged out the window behind him.

She circled the chateau in tight arcs, her breath coming in gasps, eyes filling with tears as she frantically flew low over the gardens, around the house. Checking the driveway, the terrace, and the pool.

Searching for Jack.

Did Abaddon already have him? Had that huge demon already killed him and taken Jack's soul? She'd never forgive herself if something happened to him.

Why hadn't she checked the bathroom for wards? Why?

Frantic, she circled around and drifted over the ordered rows of grapevines that rolled endlessly across the rich, green meadows surrounding Le Château des Angés.

The shockwave came out of nowhere. Rolling across her from behind, knocking her out of the air.

She somersaulted and caught an updraft, banking over the fields of grapevines as she turned toward a wooded area beside the vineyard. The shockwave made her grin and wipe away tears.

A murder marble. That was Jack telling her he was okay.

Flying high, she rode out the turbulence of another shockwave. From the woods ahead.

She called out to Muriel and her squad with angel notes and shot through the air toward the woods.

A third shockwave shook the air stream. She flew above it until she reached the tree line. And dived into the thick stand of trees.

Jack was on the ground, on hands and knees, surrounded by winged assassin demons. They hung at a distance as Jack flung murder marbles around him in a blind circle. His wings were flat against his back, halo in a wild, pale gold spin.

In a blink, Muriel, Anahera, and Kesien were at her shoulder. Another heartbeat later, Deemah was on her other side, long, walnut hair flowing around her face.

"Let's take out those demons," said Talia.

Kesien grinned. "Kid's doing really well—for a guy that can't see."

That was her Jack. Fighting hard.

"Time to eliminate Abaddon's vermin," said Muriel.

"On it," said Kesien, diving toward the ground.

Talia dropped out of the sky and landed in the circle of demons. Beside Jack.

"Jack, it's me! Talia!" she cried.

"Talia—Thank God!" he shouted, eyelids swollen shut, skin around his eyes still blistered and red. His burgundy Henley and faded Levi's were pristine, not a rip or tear from demon claws or teeth. "Did I take any of them down?"

"Sure did, Jack," she said with a teary smile. "You were awesome."

She summoned a sword of Holy fire and turned in a circle, cutting down two demons that approached from the terror of demons. A dozen or more. They had Jack surrounded, red eyes glowing, leathery red skin glinting in the sun.

Probably waiting for Abaddon to arrive.

Every time they tried to rush him, Jack tossed down murder marbles, knocking them backward. Destroying one or two.

But more came in their place.

The squad landed in a circle around her and Jack, shields drawn as Muriel threw down white seraphim wards.

Hissing and spitting, the demons backed off as the wards' searing white light burned their thick hides.

"It's working, Muriel," Talia cried, sliding her left arm around Jack's waist.

Holding him close. He was scratched up, his face bleeding and bruised, but Jack Casey was one tough human. He was still slinging murder marbles as the demons ambled away from him.

"That was too close," Muriel lamented as she turned her gaze to Jack. "Jack, I'm so sorry. Are you okay?"

He shrugged. "You tell me. Still can't see a damned thing. They threw me around and I think I took a punch or two. But I gave quite a few back."

Kesien laughed. "You did great, Jack. I'm really sorry about not warding the bathroom. That must have been a terrible shock to be attacked by demons like that."

"Terrible shock for them," he snapped. "They thought I was done. Totally different story when I started tossing down murder marbles though."

Talia pulled him close and hugged him. "Let's get you back inside and apply Berith's healing stone. Check for other injuries."

He just nodded.

With Jack in her arms, Talia lifted off into the air and shot toward the chateau. She circled around the roof and flew through the broken window. The rest of the squad flew in behind her. Anahera and Deemah paused at the broken window, using their angel powers to fix it. Kesien joined them, warding the bathroom in a bright wash of seraphim white light.

Talia and Muriel led Jack over to the bed and sat him down. He didn't even have on socks or shoes. He was barefoot.

"I'll get the healing stone," Talia said to Muriel. "Don't let him fall and hurt himself."

"Right," said Muriel, leaning over Jack.

"I'm not going to fall or hurt myself," said Jack in a low growl. "She thinks I'm helpless, but I'm not."

"I heard that," she called to Jack, hearing him snicker.

"Just in case, let me shout it then," he replied. "I'm. Not. Helpless!"

Talia rushed over to the armoire against the wall and found her grey angel's robes. She plucked the large aqua gem that Berith had given her from the robe pocket and hurried back to the bed.

"We were awfully lucky, Talia," said Muriel, a hand against Jack's head, her fingers combing down his damp blond hair that was sticking up. "What if that had been Abaddon and not just assassin demons?"

Her heart was still in her throat. She was terrified that she'd find Jack's lifeless body in Abaddon's hands after she flew out that window.

She'd gotten careless. She'd taken her gaze off him for just a few minutes. And it almost cost her the love of her life.

"I know," she said, her voice breaking as she leaned down and slid her arms around Jack. "I'm so sorry, Jack. I almost lost you just now."

Tears threaded down her cheeks as she laid her face against his blond hair and held him close again.

"We're okay, babe," he said in a warm, quiet voice, struggling to put his arms around her. "It's not your fault. Everything's going to be okay."

She held him so close that she felt his heart beating like a drum against her chest. His arms tightened around her.

"I didn't realize the bathroom wasn't warded, Jack," she said, her voice breaking again. "I'm so sorry."

"Babe, it's okay," he said in a soft, reassuring voice that was warm and smooth like hot caramel. "The demons got shut down, so don't worry. I'm fine."

With awkward movements, he found her face with his hands. He cupped her face, kissing her. His gentle, sensual kiss burned right through her heart. She kissed him urgently and pressed him against the bed, stroking his hair. She put the aqua gem against to his forehead, startling him.

"Need to apply Berith's healing gem," she said.

"Now?" he demanded, frowning.

"Gotta heal those smokin' hot green eyes of yours, Jack. And the blistered skin around them."

"I'll get some more ice," said Muriel as she hurried off.

Kesien came out of the bathroom. "Bathroom's warded from floor to ceiling like the rest of the suite. We'll scout all the locations for the competitions and make sure they're warded, too. Until we have a trap or a way to stop Abaddon, we can't risk dangling you and Jack as bait in front of him again."

"Agreed," said Talia as she held the aqua gem against Jack's forehead and kept her palm against it. "He means too much to me."

"Abaddon?" Jack replied with a snicker.

"You, smart guy," she said and kissed Jack's sexy smirk.

She summoned her gold healing light and soothing, warm light enveloped Jack.

"How many treatments will he need from Berith's gem?" Kesien asked.

Good question. She wished she knew.

"With the seraphim powers contained in the stone, Berith thought it would take three or four days to heal his body and regain his sight."

"Seraphim powers?" Jack cried. "In the stone?"

"That's right, Jack," said Talia, turning back to him. "Seraphina infused the stone with her seraph powers and Berith added her rare healing talents. She was confident your normal sight would return quickly."

He nodded, staring straight ahead through swollen eyelids. "Hope she's right. Wish we had a way to trap Abaddon with that stone—or at least send him back to Hell with it."

Talia caressed his arm. "Maybe Pravuil will come up with a solution like that? One that will send Abaddon back or give us a way to tether him like Lucifer? Without him being able to use that key to unlock whatever he needed to open."

"When all those hands dragged me through that window," Jack began with a sigh. "I was sure it was Abaddon. Didn't have a single defense to throw at him either. Figured I was a goner. Abaddon would have killed me. Or dragged me back to Hell for Lucifer to end and torture for eternity." He smiled. "Can't tell you how happy I was when I heard your voice, Talia. Thought I'd never hear it again."

"Oh, Jack," she cried, sliding an arm around him.

This attack scared him. He hadn't voiced it—until now. He had that actor's game face in place and kept it there so she couldn't see past it to his true feelings. He was certain that those demons were dragging him back to Hell again.

"Good thing you had the squad and all those seraphim wards," he replied. "Otherwise, I'd probably be Lucifer's bitch right now. Thank you. Appreciate the save."

She ran her fingers through his hair. "I'd have done anything to save you, Jack," she said against his ear, holding her healing light steady as it hummed through the stone against his forehead.

"I know you would," he said, smiling.

Not seeing those beautiful, expressive, light green eyes unsettled her. She just hoped the stone healed his eyes quickly. She loved the light in his eyes. It had always gotten her through even the darkest of times. Not having that reassurance right now disturbed her.

After she used the stone, she rose from the bed.

"Where'd you go?" Jack called out. "Talia?"

"Just putting the healing stone away," she said as she moved over to the armoire.

She dropped it into the pocket of her grey angel robes again.

"Where's that?" he asked.

"Back in my angel robe," she said and closed the armoire door.

Moving back to the bed, she picked up his gold aviator Ray Bans from the nearby nightstand. The stone had already healed the blistering around his eyes. It had taken down a lot of the swelling, too. His eyelids were still swollen though, showing only a glimpse of those light green irises that burned with an inner fire she'd only seen in other angels' eyes.

She unfolded the sunglasses and slid them onto Jack's face.

"What's that?" he asked.

"Your sunglasses. They'll hide the last bit of swelling across your face. Any change in your vision?"

He was quiet for a few moments, leaning forward, his head shifting as he surveyed the room. He shook his head.

"No," he said finally. "Nothing but darkness still."

Disappointed, she crossed her arms, feeling frustrated. She'd hoped that he could at least see a hint of light, but there was still no change to his eyesight.

"We'll give it a bit more time," she said, trying hard not to let her disappointment bleed into her voice.

He had to be feeling bad enough without her sounding discouraged. With the seraph powers and Berith's rare healing gifts in that stone, she had some high-powered tools at her disposal. They had to work.

"Speaking of time," said Jack, turning his head toward her. "Is it time for orientation yet? It's gotta be close."

She glanced at the clock on the bedside table. "It's nine-thirty, Jack. Why don't you just rest for now, let those healing powers take effect? We'll leave in about fifteen minutes to find the living room. I think Jennifer said it was just to the left of the stairs. On the first floor."

He sighed. "We still need to tell them something. They'll ask, Talia."

Everyone in that room would be keenly interested in what had suddenly happened to Jack's eyes. They had to come up with something plausible. The orientation started at ten o'clock. No pressure.

"We'll just say you had a food allergy," Talia replied.

"They'll ask which one," he replied. "And the vineyard staff will freak. Why don't we just say that I got sunscreen in my eyes and had a bad reaction to it. For a few days, my eyes will be swollen and healing."

She thought for a moment. That could work. Nobody would ask him a lot of questions about it, at least.

"Okay, let's say that," said Talia. "Let's just hope that the first challenge doesn't get us sent home."

"Hope not," he said. "If it does, we'll need to talk to Azrael about condo options in Heaven. To hide from Abaddon."

Hide from Abaddon?

For how long? That thought was terrifying. She wouldn't leave Jack alone here on earth while she returned to Heaven. Not even for a few minutes. It was too dangerous. Abaddon didn't have seraphim level powers like Lucifer, but he was still God's Destroyer. He was too formidable for an angel of death and a human—even one with rare angel powers like Jack. Especially when he no longer had seraphim powers.

Right now, with the wards, they were safe. And they had a competition to win. Come Hell or Abaddon, she was marrying this man.

10

JACK ARRIVED IN THE DOWNSTAIRS LIVING ROOM WITH HIS ARM IN Talia's. The room felt airy and cool, clack of shoes against marble reverberating, telling him it was a large room with tall ceilings. Laughter echoed through the space, so he knew he and Talia hadn't arrived first.

The first thing he smelled made him shudder.

That awful perfume that brought back all the bad memories of when they were together.

Head-ringing overdoses of jasmine and ginger, roses, and a sickeningly sweet musk tempered with sandalwood, patchouli, and what the hell notes of cloves, plums, and compost from last night's crème brûlée. And trace notes of cocaine's chemical tang that clung to the edges. Making him sweat. And wanting to run for the nearest exit.

Rachel Daniels. Wearing that hideous and expensive L'ange perfume.

Had everything around him been angels and demons—even back then?

Arms wrapped around him, holding him hostage in that cloud of over-the-top perfume. His nose burned. He wanted to gag.

"Rachel?" he replied.

He felt her kiss his lips. He recoiled.

"I wanted to thank you for everything, Jack," she said against his ear, a smile in her voice.

"What'd I do?" he asked.

"What'd you do?" she cried, sounding shocked. She lowered her voice to a whisper. "You know exactly what you did. You saved me."

He remembered the cage fight in Hell. She'd had blades for fingernails and he'd been unarmed. She'd punctured his lung, stabbed him multiple times. If it hadn't been for Berith, he'd have bled out right there in that cage. And then as Rachel was about to finish him off, he told her that he forgave her. He had no idea that his forgiveness would break Lucifer's contract for her soul. Releasing her from Hell.

"Guess I did," he said.

She was quiet for several moments. "I want to know why."

He wasn't even sure why. Because he was tired of all the cage fights. Of fighting demons. Of all the horrible things that this woman did to him. He just wanted it all to end.

He'd been a naïve kid from the Midwest, leaving college behind to try for his big break as an actor. Living in a big city for the first time. Alone. Ignorant. Trusting. He thought Lare Dumont was his best friend. He thought Rachel Daniels loved him. He had no idea that, to them, he was just another soul-gathering project for Lucifer. An insurance payout if he overdosed on flake.

"I was tired, Rachel," he said in a quiet voice. "Just wanted to end all the gaslighting and the lies and the staging. And because at one time, I loved you with all my heart."

More silence. Arms around him again, that horrible over-the-top perfume strafing his sinuses and seizing up his lungs.

"I didn't know what I had, Jack," she said in a whisper. "I regret it all. You were just a sweet, honest kid. Lare and I preyed on you like vampires. Did our best to turn you. Sacrifice you. We almost killed you—and yet, you still saved me. You're one in a million, Jack Casey. From my heart, I'm sorry."

And then the air cleared, that hideous perfume dissipating as the sharp rap of heels tapped against marble, the sound getting softer. Moving away from him.

"Talia?" he whispered, his body stiffening against the silence and the darkness.

In a few long, drawn out moments, he felt an arm slide around his waist.

"Talia?" he whispered again.

"It's me, Jack," said her melodic soprano voice. "Let's sit down."

He nodded, feeling the tension drain as he took hold of her arm and followed her through the room.

"Hello, Jack and Talia!" Gianni. He'd recognize that smooth, buttery voice anywhere.

"Hey, Gianni, good to see you. How are things with you and Izzy?" he asked.

Good to see you? Yeah, that was hilarious.

He had no idea when he'd get his eyesight back or if he was even looking at the daytime soap star. He didn't even know if Izzy was standing or sitting right next to the dude. Or even in the room.

"Jack?" Gianni said with a gasp. "What's happened to your eyes?"

Damn. Already busted. Didn't even get a chance to sit down before somebody noticed.

"Are you all right, Jack?" Izzy Castilla's mellow, precise alto voice. The voice of a TV news anchor.

"I'm fine," he said with a chuckle and held up his hand, game face firmly in place. "Had a bad reaction to some sunscreen that got in my eyes. They're all swollen and I can't see a damned thing until they clear up in a couple days. Until then, Talia will be my eyes."

"Sunscreen? Jack, that's terrible," said Gianni. "I hope it clears up fast. I want to kick your butt fair and square, not because you can't see."

He laughed. "No worries. I'll be fine. And you'll try to kick my butt."

Gianni laughed.

"Good to see you both," said Izzy, her voice just slightly off center from Gianni's.

"Take care, Izzy," he said, smiling as he felt Talia tug on his arm.

And they were moving again.

"Hey, Jack!" Mark Banks.

"Hey, Banks, good to see you. Glad you and Morgan are here."

"Same to you and Talia," said Banks, his voice loud and boisterous. "Take care of those trademark green eyes of yours."

"Thanks, dude," Jack replied, gripping Talia's arm tighter.

He followed her lead through the darkness until he felt her stop.

"We're in front of a sofa, Jack," she said in a quiet voice. "Just sit back. Cameras are filming. Devin Van Fossen will be here any moment to describe the competitions and get The Royal Wedding Hour off and running."

With awkward, jerky movements, Jack sat back against the sofa, not letting go of Talia's arm.

"Perfect," she whispered against his ear and let go of his arm. "You're doing great. Even despite Rachel Daniels kissing you."

He smirked. *A little jealousy in her tone?*

"You didn't like that, did you?" he replied.

"Not at all," she snapped. "Especially after watching that woman hurt you time and time again."

"Glad you weren't there in Hell for the cage fight," he said with a sigh.

"Me, too," Talia replied in a sharp voice. "Because I'd have smited her on the spot."

"That's my Talia," he said and smiled. "You realize that *she* kissed me, right? I couldn't see it coming."

The silence made him uneasy.

"Talia? You know that wasn't my choice, right?"

More silence.

"Aw, come on, Talia."

"Yes, Jack, I know it wasn't your choice," she said finally, but her voice sounded funny.

It made him nervous.

"Are you mad at me?" he asked. "I'm sorry. I couldn't see what was happening."

"No, I'm not mad at you, Jack," she replied. "Just a little worried. I don't trust her."

"Makes two of us," he said. "She's probably still trying to kill me for the insurance money, so stay close."

Silence again.

"You know I love you with my whole heart," he said in a quiet voice. "To my last breath."

He laid his hand against his heart and then held out his open hand to her. He waited a few moments and when she didn't react, he let his hand fall to his side.

He felt terrible. He had no idea Rachel would do that.

Had Talia walked away and left him alone on this sofa? Or was she simply pissed at him and was ignoring him now?

"Talia, talk to me," he whispered. "You're scaring me."

"What'd you say, Jack?" Talia said to him finally.

He sighed and bowed his head. "I said I love you with my whole heart and to my last breath."

"Oh, Jack—" she said and he felt arms slide around him, pulling him close. "I'm sorry. Jennifer needed some information from me, so I just gave it to her."

Again, he laid his open hand against his heart and then held it out to her.

"Forgive me, Jack," she said, her voice sounding sad and apologetic as she laid her hand against his and held it. "I love you with all my heart, too. And I gratefully accept your heart and all of you. Always."

He felt her warm lips against his in a soft, gentle kiss.

"But I won't accept your last breath," she said. "I want all of you instead. Forever."

He let the smile curve across his face. "Done. Marry me still?"

He felt her fingers entwine his hand. "Not even Lucifer could stop me." Her warm lips covered his again in a sensual kiss. He kissed her back, hard.

"Then let's get this party started," he said, gripping her hand.

"Looks like Herb just walked into the living room," said Talia, against his ear. "There are two camera crews with cameras and lights moving through the room. All four couples are in the room and Jennifer and Steve are here now, too. So, it shouldn't be long before we find out what we have to do for our first challenge."

Jack squeezed her hand. "Hope it's something I don't have to see to win," he said with a smirk.

"Good morning, princesses and prince charmings! Welcome to The Royal Wedding Hour."

Sharp footsteps ticked across marble.

Jack held in a groan at the melodramatic delivery and precise diction. Devin Van Fossen was in the house. Cameras were on and filming his and the other contestants every move.

He felt the presence of someone near him that passed quickly. Must be one of the cameras following in front of Devin as he walked through the spacious living room.

Then a shadow passed across his vision. It was dark on dark, but it was a definite change in the light. Was that a sign that the seraph's healing was working?

"Have you become too famous to associate with the cast now, Jack?"

Devin's voice.

He frowned. "Me?" he replied. "Devin, I've been kicked off more shows than Charlie Sheen. Why do you say that?"

"What's with the sunglasses?"

"Got sunscreen in my eyes and had a bad reaction to it," he explained to the dark shadow on his right. "I'm a little blinded right now, but not by my own success."

"Blinded?" Devin sounded shocked.

Jack nodded. "Gonna be a few days before I can see again, unfortunately."

"Jack, I'm sorry," said Devin, sounding concerned now.

"Cut!" Herb's voice rang out through the room.

Footfalls echoed through the room, more shadows falling over him.

"Jack, why didn't you report this?" Herb, standing over him now.

"Didn't want to cause any delays because I had a stupid reaction to sunscreen in my eyes," he replied.

The sound of Herb's voice got closer. "Jack, you're one of the biggest reasons we're in season four of this show. And I think I speak for the entire cast and crew when I say that we'll schedule around this as best we can."

"Appreciate that, Herb," said Jack, glancing at the shadows clustered on his right side. "Just didn't want to make any problems for the show or the other contestants."

"Anyone competing in this show mind if we slow down filming for a few days and give Jack's eyes some extra time to heal?"

"Take all the time you need, Jack." Gianni's voice carried through the room.

"I'm with Armand. Heal up, Jack."

He grinned. That was Mark Banks.

"Jack, I want to beat you fair and square, not because you can't see." Eric Saunders.

Jack couldn't hold back a laugh. "Thanks, dude. Thanks to all of you. Appreciate it."

"Just a minute," said the raspy, alto voice.

Rachel.

He winced. So much for that rare moment of niceness from her earlier.

He felt hands slide off his Ray Bans. His eyes ached and watered as another shadow fell against the other shadows.

"That looks awful, Jack," said Devin Van Fossen.

"Get some rest, Jack," said Rachel in a quiet voice. "I'm planning to kick your ass all over this competition, but only when you can see me doing it."

"All right," said Herb. "We'll go through and film the orientation. We'll schedule interviews and push back the completion of the first challenge a few days for Jack and Talia. Is everyone agreed?"

The room echoed with agreement, choking up Jack a little. He appreciated that.

"You dudes are the best," he said in a tight voice. "Thanks."

Someone laid a hand on his right shoulder and rubbed it, squeezing.

The shadows slid away from the darkness, footfalls growing softer. Was it Devin and Herb? Walking toward the front of the room? There weren't any more shadows beside him, so he assumed the others had returned to their seats, including Rachel.

"All right, roll the next take." That was Steve's voice, one of the set coordinators. Somewhere behind him. "Rolling in three, two, one."

"All right, princesses and prince charmings, I'm sure you're anxious to learn about your first challenge on The Royal Wedding Hour." Devin's voice carried through the room. "As part of your wedding planning duties, you must plan food for your wedding receptions. The wedding cake. Cocktails. Wine. The first challenge will have three parts. First, the cake sampling. Each couple will sample several cake flavors and rank them according to their beloved's preferences. Points will be awarded for each correct couple's answer."

Jack leaned against Talia. "Do you even like cake?"

"I'm an angel of death," she whispered in his ear. "Angels don't eat."

He sighed. Great. This was going to be tough. "I hope they have angel food and devil's food cake then. At least I can rank those."

Talia laughed.

"The second part of the challenge will be to create cocktails from ingredients on hand," said Devin, his voice sounding closer. "Each couple will put together two cocktails and present them to me and two other judges to be named later. The couple with the best overall score will receive the highest number of points."

Talia had never had a cocktail to his knowledge. This challenge would be tough, too.

"And the final part of the challenge is to participate in a wine tasting challenge. Each couple will taste three types of wine: red, white, and sparkling. These wines have been graciously provided by Celestial Vineyards. Each person will select their favorite and their partner's favorite from each type of wine. The couple with the most points from correct answers will win that part of the challenge. The scores of all three parts will be combined and the lowest scoring couple will leave on the first elimination round."

He didn't mind these challenges and he could almost do them without being able to see. But how would he match tastes with an angel of death—who didn't eat or drink? When she was human during the first season, she'd eaten food and drank alcohol, but her experiences were so few and so limited. He hated to think that they'd go home on the first round.

If they did, he would just have to plan a wedding for the two of them. Maybe get Gianni and Izzy to stand up with them? Besides, he still hadn't heard anything from the archangel about when Heaven was taking back their wings. Even if he still had them, Talia's abilities as an angel of death allowed her to hide his halo and wings from other humans. Either way, they'd be all right.

He'd miss being able to fly.

It had been a real rush and he admitted that he'd feel strange when they were gone. But they were never his to begin with, so he'd get used to not being able to fly.

Eventually.

"Cut and print," said Herb from across the room. "All right, everyone, Jennifer's passing out the interview schedules. Work with her to coordinate clothes with the stylists. There will be another group dinner tomorrow night and you'll all be on camera. Stylists will get with you to identify what you'll be wearing. We'll try to start the challenge on Wednesday after checking on the status of Jack's eyes. Tonight, there will be a meet and greet."

"All right, everyone," Steve announced, his voice booming through the room. "Clear the space. We need to setup for tonight's shoot."

Jack felt Talia take hold of his arm. "Let's get back to the suite and see if Muriel has any news from Azrael."

"Sounds good," he replied and rose to his feet, Talia helping him.

The shadows on shadows encouraged him as he walked beside Talia, shoes clicking against marble. The scent of Rachel's horrid perfume floated past him, heels sharp against the floor until he felt Talia stop.

"What's wrong?" he asked.

"Stairs," she said. "Eight up to the first landing."

He counted the steps to the landing and felt Talia turn him.

"Sixteen this time, Jack," she said. "Take your time."

He counted them to himself and then awkwardly stepped onto flat flooring again. The *tick, tick* of marble against his shoes echoed until he heard a door open. And slam shut behind him.

Then all Hell broke loose.

11

THE SUITE WAS DEVASTATED.

Talia got Jack inside and behind her. Broken windows were strewn everywhere. And demons.

A legion of them. Fighting her squad of death angels.

She pressed Jack against the warded wall behind her and spread her wings wide around him, sword of Holy fire raised.

"Muriel!" she shouted. "How'd they get inside?"

"Housekeeping!" Muriel shouted from across the room, shield-bashing three demons that rushed her.

Anahera stood at Muriel's shoulder, shield raised as she kicked a red-eyed demon in the teeth with her Eternean armor boots. The demon crumpled against the floor, two more leaping over it, at her face.

Deemah slammed her shield into one of the demons. Anahera took down the other one.

In the corner opposite the bed, Kesien swung his sword with one hand and shield-bashed demons with the other.

On the opposite side of the room, Daidrean pounded four demons with his shield, one after the other. Teeth gritted, wings spread wide, halo spinning with fury as he shouted and smashed his shield against a demon's head. Knocking it to the floor.

And still more demons poured through broken windows, the wards gone when the glass fell.

"Muriel, rewrap the seraphim wards while I hold them off!" Talia shouted.

Demons grabbed her arms, pulling her away from Jack.

"Jack!" she shouted.

Four and five demons grabbed Jack.

He dropped a couple of murder marbles at his feet. Splattering red demon spray all over the floor and walls.

He smirked. "Did I get 'em?"

"Look out!" Talia cried.

At the last moment, Jack dropped to the floor as demons leaped at him from all sides. He rolled two more murder marbles across the floor.

The demons joined the other horde, covering the floor and walls with more red demon goo.

"Calling in Azrael!" Muriel shouted between shield bashes.

"Formation around Jack," Talia called out. "Now!"

Her squad blinked across the room, forming a circle around Jack. Kesien grabbed hold of Jack and lifted him out of the floor, keeping Jack between him and Talia.

"Muriel, guard Jack!" Talia announced.

Muriel put her back to Jack, shield raised as she stood in front of him and Kesien. Talia blinked to the armoire and flung it open.

She cut down three demons with her sword of Holy fire and reached into her angel robe. She grabbed the healing stone, pivoted, and took down three more demons with her sword.

With another blink, she was beside Muriel again. She swung her sword in a wide arc, taking down two more demons and pressed the stone into Jack's hands.

"Jack, keep that stone against your eyes," she ordered. "It will keep you safe when the archangel arrives. And it will block light from the seraph if he comes with Seraphina at his shoulder."

She watched Jack slide off his Ray Bans and tuck them into his shirt pocket. He held the stone over his eyes.

Again, she swung her sword of Holy fire, taking down four more demons.

The air in front of the formation began to sparkle.

"Jack, avert your gaze," she said. "The archangel's about to appear and I don't think he's alone."

But he didn't respond.

She glanced back at him. The stone was glowing white, the gleam spilling onto him, enveloping him.

Why was the stone glowing like that? Flowing onto Jack.

"Jack, what's happening?" she cried. "Jack, the stone! What's it doing? Muriel, why is it glowing?"

Muriel bashed another demon with her shield and then glanced back at Talia, shrugging.

"No clue. Never saw it do that before."

Jack threw his head back, hand falling away from his face. He still clutched the stone in his right hand that had fallen to his side.

In a white-gold burst of light, the archangel appeared in the suite, the golden image of Seraphina behind him. All the angels of death looked away. Talia put her hand over Jack's eyes as Kesien turned him away. With their wings and bodies, she and Kesien blocked the huge burst of light that rolled through the room like a shockwave.

Azrael looked furious when he saw the suite teeming with a legion of demons and the broken windows.

"How'd they get in?" Azrael demanded, smiting a group of six demons with his outstretched hand.

Muriel sighed. "Housekeeping. Pretended to be delivering towels."

Azrael shook his head, smiting another group of demons with his other outstretched hand.

"So, in other words, you let them into the room?"

Kesien bowed his head and nodded. "Never dreamed they'd try something like that."

The archangel worked his way through all the demons until they retreated, leaving the suite in shambles and tons of broken glass all over the floors.

"Seraphina, would you please re-ward the room after I repair the broken windows and the damage?" Azrael asked.

He held up both hands, red-gold halo spinning faster as his soot-colored wings flexed.

One after another, pieces of the broken windows returned to their frames and reassembled into pristine panes of glass again. When all the windows had been fixed, the seraph swept the room with waves of white light that restored the furniture and reset all the wards from floor to ceiling.

Azrael brushed his hands together. "There, all cleaned up." He walked over to the squad.

Talia looked embarrassed as she laid her hands against Jack's arms and pulled him in front of her, turning him around.

"And next time," said Azrael, his voice sharp, "scan anyone entering to make sure they're not demons."

"Sorry, sir," said Muriel. "Thanks for getting here so fast."

"Appreciate the save, archangel," said Jack, head still bent toward the marble floor.

"You can lift your head now, Jack," said Talia, a hand on his shoulder.

He looked up, smiling, those light green eyes sizzling as he stared at her. Then she realized that his eyes had healed. He could see her again.

"Jack!" she cried, laying her hand against his cheek. "You can see again!"

He nodded, still holding the aqua gem. "Yeah, my eyes are back to normal."

Talia felt the tension drain out of her arms and legs, relief washing over her. His eyes were so unusual and beautiful. They made her weak in the knees whenever she looked into them—even now. The seraph must have healed his eyes after she arrived in the room.

"Thank Seraphina for me," she said, smiling at the archangel.

"Of course," said Azrael, turning toward the distant, brilliant white outline of an angel with three pairs of extended wings behind him. In a moment, they dimmed and then disappeared, the room darkening with her departure.

"She was happy to turn away the demons again," said Azrael. "She sends her regards."

Talia shook her head. "No, for healing Jack's eyes back to normal just now."

Azrael's brow furrowed and he stared at her for a moment or two, looking confused.

"Talia, the seraph didn't heal Jack's eyes. She just helped me smite the demons, repair the damage, and replace the wards."

Talia turned back to Jack. The faint white glow of seraphim energy still clung to the edges of his body.

"Jack?" she said in a wary voice, giving the archangel a worried glance. "How did your eyes suddenly get healed?"

"I used the stone," he said.

She let out the breath that she didn't realize she'd been holding until now. She felt relieved at that response.

"Like I told you to," she said. "Pressing it against your eyes?"

"No," he answered, turning toward her. "I just used omnificence to summon the seraphim power in the stone. And then I just imagined that my eyes were healed. And boom! They were healed."

The room went deadly quiet and Talia felt a cold chill dance across her skin. He'd used the omnificence power!

And summoned the seraphim power out of the stone?

She gasped. Jack gathered the seraphim powers out of the stone and back into his body. Oh, no—he had seraphim powers again!

"Jack! What did you do?" Talia cried, taking him by the shoulders.

"I just told you," he said with a shrug. "I summoned the seraphim power in the stone to heal my eyes." He grinned. "And it worked— who knew? So glad I can see again. That was brutal."

She shook him. "Jack! Don't you understand what you just did?"

He frowned. "I just healed my eyes fast."

"Not even close," Talia snapped. "You just put all the seraphim powers back into your body."

"No, I didn't," he said, looking surprised. "I just called them up to heal my eyes fast, that's all."

Talia shook her head. "No, you didn't. You pulled the powers out of the stone and into your body. Jack, those powers could kill you. Don't you understand that?"

He still seemed confused, not quite understanding that he'd used the omnificence power incorrectly. He hadn't enhanced the powers in the stone or made them react faster. He'd relocated the seraphim powers from the stone into his body.

"So, you're saying I have all those seraphim powers back because I took them out of the stone? Instead of just amplifying the healing process?"

She gave him a deep nod. "Your human body can't handle all those powers, Jack. Now, put them back."

He nodded, looking scared and pressed the stone back against his eyes. He gripped the stone with both hands, arms stiffening.

The moments ticked past, but nothing happened.

"Put them back into the stone, Jack," she repeated, her voice rising. "You have to put them back."

"I'm trying," he said through gritted teeth. "But they aren't leaving."

She put her hands on her hips, eyes narrowing. "Stop playing around and put them back," she snapped.

He smashed his eyes closed and clutched the stone with both hands.

"I'm trying!" he shouted. "Nothing's happening."

Talia gave Azrael a frustrated look and pushed past Muriel. She grabbed the stone out of Jack's hands and pressed it against his eyes.

"Okay, hold the stone with both hands," she said, unable to hide her concern which was manifesting as annoyance at poor Jack.

He complied, grasping the stone. "I'm holding it," he answered.

"I'll put it back using my omnificence power," she said.

Pravuil and Berith both told her she couldn't use her omnificence power on earth, but she was only using it on the healing stone. As long as she didn't use it to fight, there shouldn't be any devastation from using it.

She closed her eyes, summoning that strange river of information and images and power, focusing it all down through her hands like she learned from Jack. Into the stone—and on Jack.

Through the omnificence power, she saw the brilliant flame of white light that gleamed inside him like Holy fire. She did her best to grab the ribbons of Holy seraphim light that danced through his body, but she couldn't take hold of them. They resisted her grasp.

Next, she tried to direct the flame back into the shiny depths of the story gem, but the fire refused to budge. Or move toward her.

She even tried to grab hold of the flame itself, but her fingers passed right through it. Finally, she built up all the energy of omnificence within her and directed it at the white flame, but the omnificence power just flowed around it.

"Archangel," she cried, feeling frightened. "It's not budging. Not even with all my omnificence power focused on it."

"Let me commune with Seraphina a moment," he said and closed his eyes, head lifted toward the ceiling, hands pressed together as his wings folded against his back.

She glanced at Jack who looked embarrassed, his face flushed, eyes downcast. He hadn't meant to absorb the seraphim powers like that. It wasn't his fault. He wasn't an angel. He had only a rudimentary understanding of angel abilities and these rare powers. All of it had been thrown at him at once.

For a long time, the archangel conversed with the seraph in silence. Jack stepped away from the guard and walked over to the ivory sofa beside the French provincial white fireplace with its ornate swirls and ivy. He dropped down on the cushions, looking pale and contrite now.

She felt bad for getting short with him, but those seraphim powers could kill him. And it terrified her. She moved over to the couch and sat down beside him, holding his hands.

"I'm sorry for getting angry, Jack," she said and squeezed his hands. "Those powers are so dangerous in a human body. I just couldn't take it if something happened to you—especially because of those powers."

He smiled. "Guess it was a dumb thing to do," he said. "I just figured since I had the omnificence power, I might as well put in a rush order to heal my eyes. Didn't realize what I was doing. Sorry for causing trouble."

She ran her fingers through his hair. "You didn't know," she said. "Can't fault you for trying to heal your eyes."

At last, the archangel opened his eyes and looked around the room, blinking, like a flashbulb had gone off in his face. He turned toward Talia on the sofa and the look in those steely grey eyes was dire, frightening her all over again.

"The seraph has no idea how Jack managed to absorb those powers from the stone. It's never happened before. She must investigate the omnificence power applied to a story gem with God's Scribe. There may be a way to extract them from Jack and into another story gem, but until she knows for certain, she can't remove them."

Talia felt a cold chill rush down her spine. "But archangel! Those powers could kill him! Like they almost killed him in the haunted woods while battling Lucifer."

The archangel walked over to Jack and laid his hand against Jack's forehead. Jack gasped and sank back into the cushions.

"What was that?" Talia asked.

Azrael sighed. "The failsafe. To keep him safe. He'll experience a power drunk if he uses too much power."

Talia glanced up to see her squad of death angels grinning now, including Daidrean. Her gaze narrowed and she stared at them.

"What are all of you grinning about?" she asked, crossing her arms.

"We like power drunk Jack," said Kesien.

The rest of the squad nodded and tried to cover their chuckles.

Jack sat up and stared at them a moment and then Talia, finally shrugging. "Sorry for all the trouble," he said.

She laid her hand against his cheek. "You're definitely trouble, Jack Casey," she said with a smile. "But I just don't want to lose you. I guess that Abaddon's going to be in for a surprise the next time he tries to tangle with you."

Azrael moved over to the sofa, the expression on his face lighter this time. "Talia! That's a very good point. Abaddon might leave Jack alone if he realizes that Jack has seraphim powers."

Talia's smile widened into a grin. "Abaddon is powerful and he can't die, but he can't defeat a seraph either. Maybe if Jack shows off his powers, then Abaddon will realize it's a stalemate and return to Hell!"

At last, the embarrassment faded from Jack's face. "Think that'll work?"

"It's our best option right now," said Talia, squeezing his hand again.

The tension in the archangel's demeanor eased and he stood taller, straighter, wings unfurling like sails at his shoulders.

"With this mess cleaned up and the failsafe in place," he said, motioning at Jack, "I think we can all relax now. Until God's Scribe finds a way to put the seraphim powers back into the healing gem again."

"Thank you, archangel," said Talia, rising from the couch. She moved over to him. "Please thank Pravuil for us, too. We appreciate his input."

"Of course," said Azrael. Then he lowered his voice. "Keep a close watch on Jack. Even with the failsafe, those powers can get him into trouble."

She glanced back at him. "Trouble is his middle name, archangel, but we'll do our best to watch out for him. Thank you."

The archangel blinked. And disappeared from the room.

Talia whirled around to her squad, arms crossed, feeling annoyed. "Housekeeping? Really?"

Somebody began snickering. She looked up. It was Jack.

"You find that funny, Jack?"

He nodded, smirking at her. "That's something I would do. Just glad it wasn't me that let them into the room. I'd never hear the end of it."

Kesien began to snicker, Muriel along with him. In moments, all of them were laughing. Except Talia. She glared at them.

"Laugh all you want, but the outcome could have been fatal," she said, raising her voice. "What if Abaddon had been with them? What if we'd walked into this suite with Jack still blinded and walked into a trap that Abaddon had set for us?"

Kesien ran a hand through his black curls. "You're right, Talia. Again, it's more Jack's phrasing than what actually happened."

"Great," Jack said with a sigh. "Now, it's my fault again. Maybe I should use these seraphim powers to just smite myself?"

Talia's squad laughed again.

She turned back to Jack. "Oh, no you don't," she said and slid her arms around his neck. "That pleasure is all mine." She leaned over and kissed him.

At last, the smile returned to his face, those sexy green eyes brightening.

"All right, squad," she said to the other death angels in the suite. "Get to your posts. Jack and I need to talk about this first challenge coming up."

"Yeah, about that first challenge," he said, his mood darkening again. "How am I going to rate cake, cocktails, and wine that you've never tasted before? Because angels of death don't eat or drink."

She watched her fellow angels of death blink out of the room, returning to the rooftop. Only Muriel and Anahera remained in the suite, taking up positions on each side of the room.

That was a very good question. She had Jack's Book of Life and Death to view as an angel of death. That gave her insight into all his likes and dislikes, but she wasn't sure how they would handle that part of the challenge.

"Wish I had a good answer for that question, Jack."

"I think I'd rather deal with Abaddon than rate cake flavors," he replied, leaning back on the ivory sofa.

"Me, too," said Talia. "And wine."

"If we get sent home after this challenge, we'll just plan our own wedding," said Jack.

Talia nodded. "After we deal with Abaddon," she replied.

"Deal. Maybe he could be your maid of honor or walk you down the aisle?"

Talia laughed. "Wonder what size dress he'd need?"

Jack busted out laughing. "Those heels would be murder on his hooves."

She and Jack couldn't stop laughing even though it was all deadly serious. But she was amazed at how stressed out this wedding stuff had already made him. Fretting over cake and wine choices with an eight-foot demon trying to kill him.

They decided to walk through the gardens and talk about cakes and wine, making sure that the formal gardens had been warded first. Regardless, her squad was close, keeping watch. They had one more day until the first challenge. Hopefully, she and Jack could gather enough information to keep them from getting the lowest score.

But she worried about the rest of the challenges. She hoped they were more involved than cake and wine preferences.

JACK PACED OUTSIDE THE DINING ROOM AS HE AND TALIA WAITED FOR their turn at the food challenge. Eric and Rachel were in there now, being filmed. He and Talia were next on the schedule.

Wearing a pair of grey pants, grey loafers, and a thin, cream-colored V-neck sweater, Jack's footsteps ticked across the marble. He was nervous. Talia seemed unaffected. She looked so beautiful in her short black skirt and pale pink, long-sleeved top. She didn't seem concerned about the challenge at all, but he didn't want to go home during the first live elimination show.

Unlike other couples, they hadn't cooked and shared meals together. They had never learned what each other's favorite foods were—and what not to bring home for dinner. Of course, other couples didn't have to deal with their partner being an angel of death either.

How would he and Talia get past this one?

They'd talked about different cake flavors, but her eyes glazed over after vanilla and chocolate. It wasn't her fault. She had no reference points for these things. She'd enjoyed eating when she'd been human for a while, but eating was such an oddity for her. How could he guess her favorite flavors when even she didn't know what they were?

Together, they might be okay making cocktails, but tasting cake and wine? She barely knew vanilla from chocolate. Red wine from white wine. But liking a pinot noir versus a malbec? They all tasted red to her. And acidic.

Hell, sometimes, they all tasted red to him, too.

He felt a hand on his shoulder. He glanced up. Talia. Smiling at him.

"Jack, it's going to be fine," she said. "Don't worry."

"Can't help it," he said with a sigh and shoved his hands into his pants pockets. "This one's going to be tough."

He just wanted to give her the nicest wedding he could. Most of the money he'd made in the last three seasons of the show went to pay off the remaining debts he owed—beyond his former drug dealer. All the bills Rachel had left him. This season's paychecks would finally go to his bank account, so there wasn't a lot there yet. Especially since the government took nearly half the money that they won at the end of *The Prince Charming Hour*. He'd put what remained away for a down payment on a new place.

Not even knowing if Talia could stay on earth. With him—as his wife.

That nagged at him more than anything—even Abaddon hunting him. He didn't know what he'd do if Talia had to return to Heaven.

It would break him.

And Azrael still hadn't answered his questions about his wings or them staying together. But he couldn't think about that now. He had to focus on flavors of cake that Talia liked. And whether Talia liked chardonnay, merlot, or pinot grigio.

This first challenge seemed so trivial compared to everything that had happened since he joined this reality television show. Why was it stressing him out so much?

In about thirty minutes or so, Rachel and Eric exited through the dining room's closed black French doors, shoes clicking against the marble. Rachel stopped when she saw him, a grin on her face.

"Oh, Jack—" she said, laying a hand to his face and stroking his chin. "Got a surprise for you in there."

He frowned, laying a hand against his sweater. "A surprise for me?"

Now, he was really scared. Guess her gratitude toward him had expired. Like rancid milk.

She nodded and then giggled, her wavy auburn hair so bright against her ivory dress and matching ivory heels with those damned red soles again. She scuffed up every pair she'd ever owned and these looked brand new. He wondered if she could even afford them now that her contract with Lucifer had ended. Maybe her new financial planner boyfriend, Eric Saunders could? Lare Dumont was in Hell, so she had to find someone new. Rachel Daniels had never been alone in her entire life.

He hoped to hell that Rachel cared about Eric. That dude deserved a woman who loved him.

"Enjoy yourself now," she said, laughing as she and Eric ticked down the hallway, arm in arm.

Jack turned toward Talia and shrugged. "Wonder what that was about?"

With an eyeroll, Talia just shook her head. "Hard to tell. Wish you'd just let me smite her."

He nodded. "Tempting."

In a moment, Jennifer Collins stepped out of the dining room wearing a pair of turquoise glasses, her shiny dark hair pulled back into a knot at the nape of her neck. She had that clipboard in her left hand, phone on top of it. She wore a white blouse, dark blue pants, and black heels.

"Jack and Talia, we're ready for you." She squinted at Jack. "Jack, how are your eyes today?"

"Good," he said with a nod. "Eyes are back to normal now."

Thanks to those seraphim powers he'd regained after inadvertently pulling them from that healing gem. He had to be careful what he thought though. Like smiting Rachel Daniels. With all these powers tangled up inside him again, he could manifest a thought into some kick-ass angel power and accidentally smite someone.

"Glad to hear that." Jennifer opened one of the black French doors wide. "All right, both of you come onto the set. Devin will walk you through the challenge when cameras start rolling."

Jack cast a nervous glance at Talia. "Ready for this, babe?" he asked.

She nodded. Not looking as nervous as he felt, despite his game face. Still, he wondered what Rachel had been babbling about.

What surprise?

Jennifer led them inside the dining room with its crystal chandeliers, long rectangular table, and padded burgundy dining room chairs. He got a foot inside the door and halted in mid-stride, his mouth falling open.

"Jack! I'm so happy to see you!"

A stick-thin woman with a light brown bob dyed black cherry rushed at him, hugging him. She wore her trademark translucent red glasses, black skirt, and burgundy blouse. Her makeup was smoky and overdone. Like everything in her life.

He froze. His heart pounded, his annoyance rushing past surprised, shooting past shocked, and rampaging into the stratosphere.

Nina Westwood. Formerly Nina Westwood Casey—his mother.

Who had stopped talking to him the day after Rachel left him, insisting it was his fault. The same woman who refused to let him in the house for Thanksgiving dinner four years ago unless Rachel got out of the car first. A year later, she revoked his invitation to all family holidays. They hadn't spoken since he'd been fired from *SanFran Confidential*. Not even a Christmas card or a Happy Birthday text. Of course, until he got famous, he hadn't heard from her since he was ten years old.

She held him out at arm's length, grinning over those red glasses, pale blue eyes sparkling. Like he was her long-lost favorite son who'd finally come home to his adoring mother.

He wasn't her favorite son. And she only had one.

"What are you doing here?" he demanded, glaring, pulling away from her.

"The director hired me and my company to setup the wedding

challenges for the show, being Santa Rosa locals," she said without a moment's hesitation. "And your mother."

She had that matter-of-fact look, like it was the most obvious choice to make. Why, of course the show hired her! Why wouldn't they hire the mother of Jack Casey? Didn't matter that she hadn't spoken to him in years, refused his phone calls, and pretended like she didn't have a son when he got fired from SanFran Confidential. Now that the trades were talking about him again (in a good way), she acted like nothing had ever happened between them. Like they were tight.

They'd never been tight. And he wanted nothing to do with her.

She put her hands on her hips, looking annoyed. *She* was annoyed? He was livid.

"I just found out you were appearing on season four—on The Royal Wedding Hour. Planning to get married…when I haven't even met this girl yet. Why am I the last to know, Jack?"

He held up his hands. "All right, just stop! Right now."

"Stop what?" She gave him an angry glance over the top of those red glasses. "Don't have time to even call your mother once in a while, Jack? Not even when you're about to get married? And working almost in my backyard."

He began to pace around the dining table. "Call you? Call *you*? You refused my calls. You haven't spoken to me in over four years! Until you saw I was back in the good graces of the industry again. And now, you show up here like I'm your favorite kid? After *uninviting* me to all family functions and forgetting my phone number. Before that, I hadn't spoken to you since I was ten."

She crossed her arms. "I don't allow drugs in my house."

"I needed help," he said in a quiet voice.

Her stance didn't change. "I wasn't about to loan you money to buy drugs, Jack."

"Not one time in my life did I ever ask you—or anyone—for money," he said, slapping his hands against the table top. "Ever! I lost everything that year. My job. My place. The woman I thought I was going to marry. My self-respect. I was two days away from sleeping in my car, did you know that? But you didn't even bother to check on me. See if I was okay. Well, I wasn't. Just like that summer when Dad died. I was seventeen. You never even called me!"

She shook her head like he was exaggerating.

He wasn't exaggerating. And somewhere inside that granite exterior, she knew it, too. He'd never asked either of his folks for anything. He'd paid his own way through college—and quit after his first year. He rented his first place from the money he'd saved working three jobs in L.A. He never asked for a dime from his parents.

He motioned at the very silent film crew behind him. "If these fine people hadn't taken a chance on me, I probably wouldn't be here right now."

Then he gazed over at Talia. She probably wanted to crawl under a rock. He didn't want to talk about his family in private, much less on set in front of the entire cast and crew.

Talia's eyes were watery as she stared at him, fingers twisted together, a sad look on her face. He moved over to her and slid his arm around her waist, pulling her toward the table.

"And this woman is Talia Smith," he said, his gaze returning to his mother. "She's the biggest reason I'm still here. She saved me—and I love her more than my own life. To my last breath. And she's the woman I'm going to marry. So, mother, Talia Smith. Talia Smith, my mother. Now, you've met."

His mother looked unmoved and unimpressed.

He was used to it. She wasn't the kind of mother that had ever gushed over her kid's finger paintings or a coffee mug that said World's Greatest Mom. The one he'd bought her with his own money in third grade. He learned very early that his dad was the one that had gushed over the bird house he made in wood shop or the calculus test he'd aced.

His dad was the sentimental one. Kept all his Father's Day cards and things his kids made for him. Jack found all of them neatly stacked and labeled with his and his four sisters' names when he'd cleaned out the apartment after Dad died. He was seventeen at the time. Sat in the floor of Dad's room and cried his eyes out as he packed up everything. His oldest sister came over later and helped him move things to her place—he had nowhere else to go before he moved into his campus dorm room that fall. His mother never even checked on her youngest kid. To make sure he had a roof over his head. Or food to eat.

His mother was the driven one. Ambitious and determined. Tough love—and even that was rare. She went out and got what she wanted —even when it cost her relationships. And that included her husband and her kids. Family came second to her career. Always had.

Jack was the youngest with four sisters. His two youngest sisters (eight and ten years older than him) moved with his mother to California after the divorce. His two oldest sisters stayed in the Midwest near Dad. They didn't want to be the next casualties of his mother's latest business endeavor. He'd been ten years old at the time. Lived with his dad until he died of cancer a couple of months after Jack graduated high school. He lived with his sister, Meredith during breaks until he left college after a year and moved to L.A. to pursue his dream of acting.

His mother hadn't been a part of his life since he was ten.

"What about Rachel?" his mother asked. "I know you still love her, Jack."

He didn't know whether to laugh or punch a wall. Why not both?

"Did you not listen to a single thing I just said? Rachel dumped me the day after I got fired from SanFran Confidential. Remember? You told me it was my fault she left me and that unless we were back together, I shouldn't bother driving up to Santa Rosa for Thanksgiving or Christmas that year. Or ever."

She looked away from him, frowning. "I don't recall saying that."

"I remember the day well," he snapped. "That was the day Rachel kicked me out of my own place. Kept the furniture and the Porsche. I had to get an Uber to a motel that rented by the week."

Her anger kicked in and she glared at him. "Why didn't you call one of your sisters?"

"Because you insisted that they block my number because of my flake problem," he said, folding his arms against his chest as he began to pace again. "Tough love, remember, Mother? You told them I was out of my mind on drugs and that I'd be calling to ask them for money. And they believed you." He shook his head. "Reading the supermarket tabloids again."

She shrugged and adjusted those red glasses on her face. "There's always a core of truth in those rags."

"A quick phone call to your only son could have cleared that one right up," he replied. "But you were upset at me because you liked Rachel more than you liked me. My star had fallen, but hers was still on the rise and it preserved your bragging rights. But I took all that away when my life fell apart, didn't I?"

"When you got fired from that hit show, you were bad for business," she said and leaned against the table. "Clients canceled events. Switched to other event planners. You almost ruined me, Jack."

He had some nerve. Letting his life fall apart like that and ruining her business.

"Damn. What a selfish dick I was!" He thrust his hands in the air, voice rising. "Why didn't I just jump off a bridge instead of slowly combusting on flake? Then you'd have at least gotten sympathy business. That poor woman."

She shook her head. "Well, I'm glad you've cleaned up your act and I hope you're off all those drugs. Maybe now, Rachel will take you back?"

"See this woman?" Jack shouted, sliding his arm around Talia's waist again. "This is the woman I love. Get it through your head, Mother. This is the woman I'm going to marry."

His mother turned her back on him, moving toward some plastic tubs stacked against the white walls of the dining room.

"I'm sure Rachel misses you and wants you back, Jack. Give her a chance before you throw your life away again."

Jack let out an exasperated sigh. "I'm done," he snapped, letting go of Talia. "I need to get out of here."

He turned toward the door, seeing Jennifer standing beside Steve. Herb sat in his director's chair, mouth open, eyes wide, looking shell-shocked. Even Roy the camera man looked shocked. No one spoke a single word.

"Jennifer, can you please reschedule this challenge for later in the day? I apologize, but I can't do this right now."

She nodded as he stormed toward the door. Then she reached out and stopped him before he pushed open the door.

"Jack, wait!" Talia called.

"I'm so, so sorry, Jack," said Jennifer in a quiet voice, shaking her head. "I had no idea."

He did his best to force some sort of half-hearted smile on his face.

"Not your fault," he said in a clipped voice. "Sorry about all this."

He hurried out the doors and fled down the hallway toward the chateau's back doors that led into the garden. He couldn't breathe in here.

13

TALIA STARTED AFTER JACK, BUT HIS MOTHER GRABBED HER ARM, stopping her.

"Let him go," she said, her grip firm. "Jack's never handled the real world very well. Or the truth."

Talia pulled her arm free, glaring at this woman. "Never handled the real world very well?" Talia replied, her voice sharp. "How's this for the real world? Rachel Daniels got Jack addicted to cocaine. For months, she and her *real* boyfriend groomed him, pushed him into doing cocaine. And when he refused, they drugged his soft drinks until he blacked out and then forced the drugs into his system. Or didn't you know that she was living with Lare Dumont the whole time she was supposedly in a relationship with Jack?"

Jack's mother laughed. "Those are all tabloid fantasies, my dear."

Talia shook her head, eyes narrowing. She was going to smite this woman. And enjoy every moment of it.

"Rachel Daniels admitted it to him in a conversation heard by half this cast. Ask Armand Gianni or Izzy Castilla. Or the show's director. They all heard it—because the cameras captured it. Rachel was trying to get him to overdose, so she could collect insurance money on Jack. Get it through your head. She was trying to kill him."

At last, a motherly sort of look touched her features, eyebrows raising, mouth turning downward, a sad look in her eyes.

"What? Kill Jack? Why would Rachel do such a thing?" she asked, shaking her head.

She looked shaken. Had something finally gotten through that stone cold heart of hers? Talia felt terrible for Jack.

"Rachel needed money," said Talia as she stared down at the empty dining table and then at the large storage tubs against the wall.

The tubs were white with grey locking handles on both ends of the lid. They had a black and white logo of two crossed champagne flutes with the words Westwood Event Planning in a circle around them.

At this, Jack's mother wrinkled her nose, looking down it at Talia again, chuckling. "That's absurd. Rachel Daniels is a big television star. She doesn't need money."

Urge to smite rising. Talia gritted her teeth.

"You'll have to ask her," Talia replied, moving toward this horrible woman. "Jack's been through a terrible ordeal these past few years. Rachel broke his heart, lied to him about every review he'd ever gotten, told him he was washed up and a terrible actor. And he believed her. Then she got him fired from his television show and ruined his life with the drugs. And if you don't believe me, ask her."

Finally, the director got up from his chair behind the cameras and walked over to the dining table. He stood beside Talia, looking pale and concerned.

"Everything Talia's told you is the truth, Ms. Westwood," said Herb, looking a little shocked and quite sad, his blue dress shirt and Navy blue pants wrinkled. "She physically attacked Jack on the set of The Ever After Hour. After she gave him a list of everything she'd done to him over the years. It was quite lengthy, I assure you."

To Talia's amazement, Jack's mother still didn't look convinced. What was the matter with this woman? This was her son. Why wasn't she in Jack's corner, fighting for him? Like any mother when someone messed with their children. She acted like Jack deserved it somehow.

"She did some terrible things to your son, Ms. Westwood," said Talia. "Things he hasn't even begun to process yet."

Herb sighed and cast an uneasy look at Talia. "Talia's right. What Rachel did to Jack was brutal and savage. The only reason I allowed her to return to the show was because she wanted to apologize to Jack and thank him for helping her. Heaven knows why he's done anything for that woman after the abuse she put him through, but Jack usually puts himself last."

"Abuse?" Jack's mother frowned and glanced from the director to Talia. "What do you mean abuse?"

Talia wanted those words to sink in for a few moments. She needed to understand the hell that Jack went through. She sighed. Before he got dragged off to Hell by Lucifer—sacrificing himself to save her.

Herb turned around to the crew. "All right, turn off all sound and cameras to this room. And everyone, outside until I call you back."

Talia watched about a dozen subdued crew members file out of the room and close the doors.

Herb turned back toward Jack's mother when the doors closed with a thump. "Yes, Ms. Westwood. Abuse. And I don't use that word lightly. I still have the footage from the security camera. We put it in a safe place, so it didn't disappear."

"How do I know you Hollywood types didn't just put this together on a computer?" Jack's mother replied, still giving Herb a skeptical look.

Herb sighed again and flashed a commiserating look at Talia.

"What would I gain by doing that?"

Jack's mother laughed, tossing her head back with a horse-like laugh. "Ratings! A big, juicy story to sell to those paparazzi or whatever they're called."

"Jack Casey wasn't a spoiled, pampered Hollywood star that had everything handed to him," Talia replied, hands on her hips as she continued to glare at this woman and fight the urge to smite her. "He was victimized by his two costars. One he considered his best friend and the other was a woman he loved. Both of them betrayed him. Preyed on him—from the start."

Herb moved toward her, arms crossed as he walked around the

table. "Lady, for months and months, Rachel Daniels drugged your son's drinks, causing him to pass out frequently at her partner's beach estate."

"Why didn't he say something?" Ms. Westwood replied, looking irritated.

"Because he didn't know," Talia replied. "Before Rachel got him hooked on cocaine, she drugged his drinks and forced coke into his system. Later, he thought it was his fault that he'd done cocaine until he blacked out. But he hadn't. She was drugging his drinks the entire time."

Her irritation fled as the situation began to sink into her hard skull. That none of this had been Jack's fault.

"You're saying Rachel turned him onto the drugs? And not the other way around?"

"Yes!" Talia shouted. "Jack barely drank at that point."

Herb's voice was quiet but intense, his dark brown eyes filled with anger. "Whenever Jack regained consciousness, he found that he'd been moved. And undressed. A lot of times, it was in a bed at the estate. With Rachel—having her way with him. And with a ton of coke in his system. He was having terrible flashbacks at that same beach house during the filming of The Ever After Hour. Rachel told him all of this—we have it on film."

Her eyes got wide, her lips parting. She had on a heavy application of burgundy lipstick.

"Do you even care about Jack?" Talia demanded, hands on her hips. "Because, as his mother, I would expect you to be mad as hell that someone hurt your son like she did."

She went quiet. Talia hadn't heard her lie about anything yet, but it astounded her that a mother would take up for an ex-girlfriend over her own son. Her only son.

Talia took hold of the woman's arm and turned her around. "Don't you understand? Rachel was trying to get Jack to overdose on drugs—accidentally or intentionally—to kill him. So she could collect insurance money. Jack was just a game to her. A naïve kid that she and her partner preyed on. They did some awful things to him. As his mother, you should be furious! And wanting to protect him."

At last, some emotion touched this woman's triangular face. Her bobbed hair shifted toward her chin as she dropped down in a chair at the table, looking almost upset.

Finally!

She'd treated Jack like a child imagining things and overreacting when he'd been in the room. Talia didn't understand why either.

The woman sighed and propped her face in her hand. "It's not really Jack's fault. He's always been the spitting image of his father. Right down to those light green eyes."

Jack had the most beautiful eyes she'd ever seen.

"I don't understand," said Talia, shaking her head.

Jack's mother patted Talia's arm. "Jack's father was the most stunning man I'd ever met, but we were like gasoline and fire. When it was good, it was fantastic. When it was bad—it was hell on earth. And every time I looked at Jack, I saw Tom. And all the hurt he'd caused. Things Jack never knew. And I took it out on Jack."

With a sigh, Talia sat down at the table beside Jack's mother, studying her glassy blue eyes. "What do you mean?" she asked, trying to listen even though she wanted to smite this woman more than Rachel Daniels right now.

"I assumed he was just like his father and treated him that way." She thrust her hands against her face, looking unnerved. "Even when he was a little boy. But Jack worked hard for everything. What he said was true. He'd never asked family for money. Ever. And Tom had a drinking and drug problem the entire time I knew him. It nearly broke us."

There it was. She assumed Jack was just like his father and never even gave him a chance. He'd had three strikes against him his whole life with this woman.

"But Jack got half his genes from you, Ms. Westwood," said Talia.

It took everything she had to be civil to this woman.

"All I could see was Tom when I looked at Jack. His and Tom's baby pictures were absolutely identical. When Jack was four, we almost lost our house because of Tom's drug habit—something else Jack never knew. Tom was his hero and I didn't want to ruin that. When I heard about Jack's problem with cocaine, I knew he was becoming just like his father. And I wanted no part of it."

"He hasn't had any drugs for almost a year," said Talia. "By his choice. Rachel got him so addicted—and it almost killed him."

"He hasn't?" she cried.

Talia shook her head. "He's clean."

Jack's mother took off her glasses and swiped at her eyes. "And I blamed him for all of it. Told him it was his fault. Didn't even ask if he needed help. I just washed my hands of him, like he'd been an addict all his life."

Talia laid her hand on the woman's arm again. "He did need help. He was in bad shape. He overdosed one night and his heart stopped. He almost died, but Mark Banks and I brought him back."

The director's eyes bugged out and his mouth fell open. "What? When did that happen, Talia?"

Jack's mother gasped, her heavily made-up eyes wide, bottom lip quivering. "What? His heart stopped? When was that?"

"During the filming of The Cinderella Hour," said Talia. "And that was the last time he chose to do cocaine. He quit right after that. He's a good, selfless man, Ms. Westwood. He's honest and humble and he's always trying to do the right thing. Even if it hurts him in the process."

Herb laid his hand on the woman's shoulder. "And your son is the reason that this show is in its fourth season instead of lasting only a few months."

Jack's mother looked up at the director. "What do you mean?" she asked.

Herb smiled. "During the live finale of The Cinderella Hour, your son went off script and spoke from his heart when he offered it on camera to Talia Smith. Audiences loved it! They loved his and Talia's love story. And he's consistently done that through three seasons."

Her eyes lightened, turning misty. "My Jack did that?"

The director nodded. "He tells it like it is, Ms. Westwood—and he has no delusions about his success on the show. That's one of the things about him that makes him fantastic to direct. He's a talented actor, works hard at his craft, but he's the most honest guy I know. Cast and crew are all pretty crazy about your son. And this young woman right here loves him more than anything in this world."

Jack's mother smiled at her. "You really love Jack?" she asked. "Not just because he's a Hollywood star?"

Talia chuckled. "When I met your son, I didn't even know who he was. I don't own a television. But those light green eyes melted me to my core the very first time I met him. He loved the fact that I didn't know who he was that night."

"His eyes—that I understand," said Jack's mother. "Jack's even better looking than his father. And he's been breaking hearts since he was about seven. Little girls falling in love with him and he just wanted to swim. Even when he landed that role on SanFran Confidential, he had no idea how stunningly beautiful he was."

"He still doesn't," said Talia with a laugh.

Jack's mother nodded. "Rachel Daniels said he blew her mind the day he showed up on set, wearing tight, faded jeans and an old grey Purdue T-shirt to read for the part of Davy Pierson. She said the casting director lost her mind when she saw him."

Talia would never forget how hot and sexy Jack Casey had been under the sound stage lights that afternoon at the studio. That windblown blond hair, light green eyes sizzling under the bright lights, that sexy smirk quirking his lips. He looked like he'd just rolled out of bed. Made her heart race. All she wanted to do that day was run her fingers through his short, thick blond hair and stare into the depths of those light green eyes. At twenty-six, he was utterly stunning. She'd never seen any human or that beautiful until she met Jack Casey.

And even now, after everything he'd been through, he was still stunning. Those smoldering green eyes. His hot, lean body. She sighed. And that devastating smirk that burned right through her heart. Along with his kiss. She couldn't believe it when she learned that his was the soul she was supposed to save. She couldn't get him out of her thoughts. He made her lightheaded and all the blood rush to her cheeks. All she'd wanted to do was touch him, hear him laugh, feel his arms around her.

By the end of the show, she'd managed to enchant him, but he had forever burned his way into her heart. She couldn't forget him even if she tried. He meant everything to her and she'd do anything and everything to stay with him.

"Trust me, Ms. Westwood," said Herb, smiling at last. "As you can see from Talia's face, Jack Casey is still setting women's hearts on fire. He's the major draw for this show and even though he hasn't asked us for any sort of special treatment—or even any riders in his contract— we like to keep our stars happy. That's why we hired you to setup the wedding challenges for the show. We thought that since you were Jack's mother, it would please him. Obviously, we made a mistake."

Jack's mother's face turned as pale as the dining room's white walls and marble floors.

"Please don't fire me from the show," she said, her gaze flicking to Herb. "Jack's my son and regardless of what's happened between us in the past, I want to be a part of his wedding. He and I haven't been close over the years, but I'm the only parent he has left. At least give me a chance. My company is one of the best event planners in the region. And maybe it's time for Jack and I to mend our relationship?"

Talia still wanted to smite this woman. Whether or not she stayed on with the show should be Jack's decision. Not hers.

Herb leaned against the table, arms crossed. "That decision belongs to Jack Casey, not me. If he agrees to it, then I'm okay with you continuing on the show."

"I agree," said Talia. "This is Jack's decision to make."

Ms. Westwood rose from the chair and fluffed up her bobbed hair. "Fine. I'll let Jack make that decision."

"We'll give him some time to unwind a bit," said Herb, stepping away from the table. "And then I'll see what he has to say about you continuing with the show, Ms. Westwood."

"Thank you," she said in a quiet voice and moved over to the tubs against the wall of the dining room.

She pulled her phone out of one of the tubs and began to go

through a list of items on the screen as Herb led Talia by the arm toward the black French doors. He pushed open the doors and they stepped into the hallway. Jennifer Collins stood ten feet from the door, hugging her clipboard, her face looking pale, her eyes filled with fear and anxiety.

Herb motioned her over.

"Yes sir?" she asked, wide-eyed as her gaze flicked from Talia to the director.

"Reschedule the other three couples doing the first challenge. Get the filming schedules changed and reposted for the week, starting with Jack and Talia."

"Right away, sir," she said, pulling a pen from behind her ear and writing things on the clipboard. "Are we keeping her on?"

Her eyes looked empathetic and almost apologetic as she looked at Talia.

"We're going to leave that decision to Jack Casey," said Herb. "I feel bad. I should have checked with him first. This had to be a very painful surprise."

Talia nodded. "It was," she replied. "He didn't even want to sign onto the show when I told him it was filming on location outside Santa Rosa. Because he knew his mother lived here. It took some convincing to get him to sign onto the show this time."

Herb exchanged an anguished look with Jennifer.

"Dammit, this is all my fault," he said, hands on his hips as he stared at the floor. "I thought it'd be a nice surprise. A pleasant one— not a painful one."

Jennifer nodded, brows pressing into an angry expression. "The way she talked to him. I wanted to walk over there and slap her."

"Thank you, Jennifer," said Talia, crossing her arms. "I wanted to ring her neck. Especially when Jack told her that he'd needed help and she acted like he was just being self-centered."

"Yes!" Jennifer cried. "And when he told her he'd been two days from having to live in his car…she just didn't seem to care. That broke my heart. I had no idea he'd been through all of that."

"He's been through a lot," said Talia. "He hides things like that, doesn't want people to know. And then he just quietly accepts the blame, like it was his fault when he had no control over things—like Rachel Daniels getting him hooked on cocaine."

Jennifer shifted her clipboard to her other hand, studying Talia for a moment. "That broke my heart when I heard it on The Ever After Hour. The things she did to him...and knowing that he let himself get fired from his hit television show to protect the rest of the cast."

"All this time," said Talia, studying Jennifer's concerned gaze, "he's blamed himself for things that weren't his fault."

"So sad and so unfair," said Jennifer. "And he didn't even try to clear his name. He just took the punishment for all of it—while they just went on with the show. But I heard that ever since Jack was fired, the show has all but tanked."

Herb was nodding. "Especially since Lare Dumont just up and disappeared from Los Angeles. No one knows where he is—including Rachel Daniels. And no one's talking about it either. Probably hiding to avoid being prosecuted for that film we have of Rachel confessing everything. Serves the bastard right."

That horrible man was in Hell where he belonged. Sent there when his contract with Lucifer expired. And Rachel Daniels knew exactly where he was, too. A shame that Rachel hadn't stayed there with him. All of this was her fault. Even now, she just couldn't help herself from being cruel to Jack at every turn.

It made Talia so angry. She wanted to face this bitch in a cage fight herself—and smite her with every angel of death power she possessed. Rare or otherwise.

"If you'll excuse me," said Talia, moving away from them. "I need to go make sure Jack's okay."

She needed to go find him. Make sure he was safe back in the suite —where her squad could guard and protect him from Abaddon.

14

JACK FLED TO THE GARDENS, HIS BRAIN SPINNING, HIS HEART FEELING like someone had just put a bullet through it.

Struggling for air, he rushed down a footpath that led between two symmetrical flower beds along both sides of the chateau's formal gardens. The air was cool and crisp, carrying the sweet scent of gardenias and roses as he ran past box hedges that made square borders around each section of the grounds.

White seraphim wards gleamed around the manicured hedges as he ran past their walls of light that only demons and angels—and apparently him—could see.

Toward the vineyards.

He hated admitting how much his mother's hard exterior had always hurt him. The unconcerned attitude, the lack of empathy, the *suck it up because others have it worse* remarks. Or the fact that no matter what it was, it was his fault in her eyes. Nothing he'd ever done had been good enough for his mother. When he got the part on *SanFran Confidential*, she wanted to know why he hadn't tried for the lead role. Even though it was Laren Dumont's show and that part wasn't available, she thought Jack should have done more. When he got his first salary raise, she told him he screwed up. That he should have negotiated for more.

Jack didn't stop running until he reached the middle of the vineyards, surrounded by ordered rows of meticulously staked grapevine stalks. The vines had green leaves, gangly shoots, and long runners tangling around the beginnings of tiny grape clusters bursting out across the rows of grapevines.

This fourth season of the show could have been the best one yet. But now, his mother was in charge of all the challenges (like that wasn't a conflict of interest?) and hell-bent on getting him and Rachel back together. He wanted nothing to do with Rachel Daniels—or his mother.

And the woman he loved was an angel of death who didn't eat or drink. Yet he was supposed to choose her favorite wine and cake preferences. And if all that wasn't bad enough, Abaddon, Lucifer's newly appointed ambassador from Hell, was still trying to kill him.

He ran down the rows of grapevines thriving in the warm spring sunlight, headed away from the chateau. He needed to get away from this place. Away from all of this bad history. Clear his head.

He tripped over a stake along the vineyard rows and rolled headfirst down a hill. Landing at the bottom of a tree-lined valley. That looked like an orchard.

Little pink flowers covered the branches of small saplings, laid out in even, methodical rows. The trees reminded him of the dwarf peach trees his dad grew at the house back in the Midwest. Before the divorce. Small little peaches with white flesh, juiciest and sweetest peaches he'd ever eaten. Beyond the rows of small, pink-flowered trees stood taller trees with large white blossoms. They looked like apple trees.

He got to his feet, brushing off his grey pants, and walked through the long rows of fruit trees, soft scent of apple and peach blossoms reminding him of when he was a kid. Before his dad's cancer. Before the divorce. When Dad worked as a carpenter by day and built furniture at night in the garage. The scent of fresh-cut wood and blossoming fruit trees stayed with him after all these years.

The valley here was quiet, peaceful. Just him, some big fuzzy bees, and chittering birds. The wind was a soft, cool whisper through the leaves, blowing through his hair. He walked away from the rows of fruit trees, toward the wild tangles of brush around the orchard's edge. In the shade of a large sycamore tree, he leaned against its white trunk, branches popping out green with new leaves. And tried to process this conversation with his mother.

The peace and serenity of this orchard soothed his soul. He drank it in, the cool breeze soft against his face.

"I knew if I waited, I'd get you alone, little human. I am very patient."

Jack smashed his eyes closed, not turning around.

Damn. Should have known something demonic would show up to ruin the moment.

"Dude, seriously," Jack said, squaring his shoulders against the sycamore tree's trunk. "Why do you let someone like Lucifer order you around like one of his sniveling little demon servants?"

"What makes you think I let Lucifer order me around?" the baritone voice demanded, the harsh timbre carrying through the treetops.

Groaning, Jack turned around.

Abaddon towered over him at about eight feet tall. Ashen white and leathery skin, glowing red eyes. Made the Incredible Hulk look like a child.

"Because Lucifer's the one that wants me dead—not you," said Jack, holding out his hands. "From what the angels told me, you have much better things to do than to play hitman for Lucifer. Besides, you'd never heard of me until Lucifer. Am I right?"

"Correct, little human," said Abaddon, thundering closer.

His steps shook the ground as he moved toward Jack, but the angel-turned-demon stopped about twenty feet away. A distance Abaddon could cover in two steps if he needed to react quickly.

"Then why come after me?" Jack asked. "Why would you bother?"

"Because until God unleashes me on humanity, I have nothing better to do except guard the key to the Gates of Hell."

Jack crossed his arms against his chest. "So, you're bored," he said, pacing behind the sycamore tree. "I get it. But it's such an easy job. What will you do ten minutes from now? Listen to my screams in Hell for the next century or so?"

"Has a nice ring to it, Jack Casey," Abaddon replied, his deep voice rumbling through the valley.

"Really? You're that bored? Damn, dude—take up surfing or sailing or something. Takeover a public library and read all its books, watch all its movies or something. But this bounty hunter shit is really anti-climactic. Especially when you have to return to Hell empty-handed."

A curious smile carved across Abaddon's ashen, leathery face. His long chin jutted out, red eyes filled with amusement.

"Am I now?" he replied, taking a step toward Jack. "And why would you assume I'll be returning to Hell empty-handed?"

Jack threw down a huge burst of Holy fire that lit the ground and rolled toward Abaddon in a massive ten-foot wave.

"Because of that," he said. "Surf's up, dude. Hang loose."

Abaddon let out a shout as Jack flexed his wings, letting them unfurl from his shoulders. He rose into the air, floating above Abaddon as the massive demon cursed at him.

"What was that?" Abaddon demanded with a groan, holding his left arm.

"A little taste of seraphim powers to get your attention," he replied.

"How do you have seraphim powers?" the demon sputtered. "Or wings? Lucifer said you were human."

"Mix up in Heaven's distribution chain," Jack said, still hovering. "They're working on the problem. Until then, you'd best run along back to Hell and tell Luci you're taking up a new hobby. Like cage fighting or scrapbooking. Or hell—why not both?"

Abaddon bared his pointy teeth. "You're going to be very sorry you did that, human."

Jack gathered another large ball of Holy fire in both hands, tossing it back and forth like a basketball.

"What?" he cried, raising his eyebrows. "Sorry about this?"

He flung the ball of Holy fire at the ground and it rolled across the grass in another ten-foot wave that smashed into Abaddon, knocking him to the ground.

The eight-foot demon cursed at him again and struggled to his feet as Jack gathered another basketball-sized ball of writhing Holy fire between his hands.

Abaddon shook his fist at Jack. "This changes my plan of attack, human. Nothing more."

Jack laughed. "I'd say my seraphim powers combined with some rare powers like…omnificence…should make you pause a little, Aby."

Abaddon froze, a look of surprise burning deep into his long, demonic face. "You have omnificence?"

Jack just nodded at him and held out his right hand, palm down, focusing down the omnificence power to the valley floor. Omnificence was all-present, so he'd just appear in two places at once for ol' Aby.

He summoned the flood of power roiling underneath his hand, power that threatened to overflow his control and swamp him with energies and information and data. Gritting his teeth, he held it tight between his fingers, summoning his presence on the ground beneath the tree.

Sweat poured down Jack's face as he held onto the omnificence power, his hands beginning to shake.

Abaddon's mouth fell open and he backed away, holding up his hands. He glared at Jack from a safe distance.

The ball of Holy fire fell out of Jack's hands and smashed against the ground, burning the grass to cinders as another ten-foot wave of Holy fire washed over Abaddon. The ground shook, a fissure cracking open the valley floor as Jack let the omnificence power fade.

Talia warned him that omnificence would cause devastation. He'd forgotten that.

"I will return soon, little human," Abaddon called to him from a distance. "That, I promise you. Soon."

Only when Abaddon departed did Jack let go of all the powers. He couldn't keep his wings moving though and he dropped from the sky.

He'd only been about ten feet off the ground, but he hit the valley floor hard, the grass blackened and smoking around him. At least, he hadn't aimed his Holy fire bursts toward the fruit trees. But he'd torn a swath of devastation across the rolling grasslands in the valley below the chateau.

It was a little noticeable. Like all of Anaheim going up in flames.

He laid his sweaty face against an unburned patch of green grass and called up a small rain cloud to put out the flames. Then he collapsed, spent as the beginnings of a power drunk started to wash over him like a gas station bottle of scotch. Damn.

But he'd had no choice.

He had to defend himself against Abaddon or he'd be dead right now, his soul in Lucifer's torturing hands for eternity. Not his idea of a good time. He'd been there. It was definitely not a fun place.

He tried to get to his feet. Couldn't. He was too weak.

The seraphim powers and then omnificence had sapped all his strength. Muscles burned from exertion. His head throbbed, his stomach turning. After not having those powers for a little while, he'd forgotten how taxing they were to his body.

He'd overused them—all of them.

A flock of birds took flight, fluttering overhead across the crisp blue sky. Thick fluffy clouds softened the horizon as he stared up at them, fighting off a wave of nausea. He had to stay conscious until his legs could hold him again—or at least his wings. If he passed out, Abaddon might return and finish him off.

But the rush of seraphim power was going straight to his head, making his thoughts—and the world around him—fuzzy and out of focus.

Another flock of birds took flight, winging over the treetops and underneath the clouds. They were larger than the first group. Like Canadian Geese. Huge grey bodies. He squinted. No, those were wings. Big grey wings.

Angels of death.

He was in trouble. He'd ducked under their wards and their supervision. They were coming to yell at him. His head already hurt enough for three tongue-lashings. And that was before Talia found out.

The whole squad landed around him, Talia leading the way.

Shit. She looked furious.

"Jack Casey!" she shouted. "What did you do?"

"Nuthin'," he said, slurring. "Went. Fora—walk." He hiccupped.

They were all snickering except Talia.

"A walk?" Talia cried, hands on her hips. "You practically destroyed this area! Deemah, Daidrean, fix this mess. Muriel, close that fissure."

"It wasss a—brisk walk," Jack replied, struggling to focus both eyes on Talia, but she just kept getting blurry.

Kesien and Muriel broke into a fit of laughter. Even Deemah had to turn away as she began to laugh.

"I love power drunk Jack," Muriel said to Kesien.

"So do I," Kesien replied.

Talia dropped down on the ground beside him and slid her arms underneath his shoulders, helping him sit up.

"Jack," she said in a loud, insistent tone. "What did you do?"

"Sssschooooooled Aby," he said, holding his head high. He hiccupped again.

Talia just shook her head as Kesien dropped down beside her. "What does that even mean?" she said in a quiet voice to the curly, black-haired angel of death.

"I think it means he fought Abaddon, Talia," said Kesien, grinning. "And from the looks of this area, Jack must have thrown down lots of Holy fire. Lots of it."

"And omnifischenceisheneshes…power. Hic!"

Jack tried to stay sitting up, but the world began to tilt. He tried to focus on Talia. Couldn't.

Talia gasped. "Jack, you didn't! No wonder there's all this damage. We were told not to use omnificence on earth."

"Easy—foryoutosay," he said, slurring, his head bobbing.

Muriel and Anahera laughed harder.

"You're lucky nothing worse than that fissure opening up happened."

Then he noticed the fissure. He crawled over to it and looked inside.

"Hey! I can see Luci's place from here! Hic!"

The squad broke up laughing again. Even Talia was smiling now.

"Ev'body wave—at Luschi now!" he shouted, waving his hand wildly above the fissure as Muriel stood over it. "'Cause his leash doesn't reach—this far."

He fell backward into the grass, the sky tilting again.

"Let's get him back to the suite," Talia said to Kesien. "Everyone else, put this area back the way it was. Before Jack takes another brisk walk through it."

The squad laughed harder.

"Blame Aby," said Jack.

He wanted to tell them about what happened and how he'd thrown three waves of Holy fire at Abaddon and then terrified the big hulking demon with the mere mention of the word omnificence. But he couldn't even say that word right now, much less try to form coherent sentences as the power drunk hit him full force. Like he'd drank an entire fifth of whisky. And a bunch of beer chasers—five or ten at least.

Kesien grabbed hold of Jack and hoisted him over his shoulder like a sack of potatoes and with Talia beside him, they flew over the treetops toward the chateau of angels. It was the last thing he remembered before the world went dark.

15

THE DARKNESS DISSIPATED AND JACK FOUND HIMSELF BEING DROPPED onto the bed in his and Talia's suite back at the chateau.

"I think he'll probably sleep this off for a while," said Kesien.

"Notshleepy," Jack replied, trying to sit up, but Kesien and Talia held him down. "Jushtalildizzy."

"I think that's Jackspeak for he's not sleepy," said Talia. "He's just dizzy."

Kesien nodded, still smiling. "I'd guess that, too. Well, whatever happened out there, Talia, it ended with Abaddon retreating for now. I'd say that's a good thing. We could have gone out there and found Jack dead and his soul on its way to Hell."

"Damn, Keshien," said Jack. "Way t'shugarcoat thingsh."

Kesien laughed. "Sorry, Jack. We were afraid Abaddon had killed you when we couldn't find you."

Talia put her hands on her hips. "Yes, we were, Jack," she said, those luminous grey eyes glaring at him again, fire in her voice. "Now, I need to know what happened out there. I need you to tell me."

"Can't...hic!"

He was just too power drunk to speak coherently. It was all clear in his head, but his mouth couldn't properly translate it right now.

"Kesien, can you try and heal away some of this power drunk?" Talia asked. "We really need to find out what happened down there. I know you've had a lot of experience with healing humans in this kind of condition."

Jack squinted, seeing Muriel and Anahera walk up behind Talia. Back from cleaning up his mess below the chateau. They were both frowning.

"Aw, already?" Muriel cried. "We were just going to pull up some chairs and enjoy the Power Drunk Jack Casey Show." She grinned at Talia. "That never gets old."

"Happy to entertain," said Jack with a hiccup.

Kesien floated beside the bed, dove grey wings fluttering softly as the white marble floors and crown molding spun around him. Jack felt warm gold light engulf his body as Kesien held out his hands.

"This won't take the power drunkenness completely away," said Kesien, his voice warm and resonating, "but it may lessen it enough that he can tell us what happened out there."

"Good," said Talia as she sat down on the bed and leaned over Jack. "We need to know what happened with Abaddon."

Her raven black hair hung over the left shoulder of her pale pink top, short black skirt showing off her long, winter pale legs. She was so beautiful, a soft blush in her cheeks, those big grey eyes so intense, full lips pursed. He could only guess what had happened between her and his mother after he'd walked out of the dining room. He hadn't seen any smoking wreckage at the chateau from the valley below it though. He was afraid that his mother won that round.

Jack laid back against the headboard, the room still spinning, and let Kesien's healing light do its work for ten minutes. Finally, the gold light dissipated along with the bed spins. Things were looking up.

"That's as good as it's going to get until some time has passed," said Kesien, sliding back from the bed.

He landed beside Muriel, watching Talia with a bright expression. Kesien looked happy and content in most situations. Dude had incredible patience.

Talia laid her hand against the side of Jack's face. "How do you feel, Jack?" she asked.

"Still feel a little drunk," he said with a smirk as he laid his hand against hers.

"Well, you're not slurring," she said, stroking his face with her fingers. "So, maybe you can tell me what happened out there?"

"Needed to cool off, so I went out to the gardens," he said with a sigh, staring into her eyes. "But that wasn't far enough away from her."

Had his mother's responses colored how Talia saw him now? His heart sank. Did she see him as the loser that his mother had portrayed him as?

"Your mother?" Talia asked, her eyes turning sad.

He nodded, his gaze falling to the lavender comforter on the bed. "Let's just say she's never been my biggest fan."

Talia ran her fingers through his hair in long, soothing strokes. He closed his eyes, losing himself in her touch.

"I don't know who I'd rather smite," said Talia. "Rachel Daniels or your mother."

"Why not both?" he asked.

"Don't tempt me," she said and leaned down to him. "Your mother was so cruel to you. The whole crew is upset over how she treated you."

"They are?" His eyes widened, staring at her.

He figured everyone would side with his mother. The moment the word cocaine came up, everyone changed their opinions pretty rapidly. Everything became his own damned fault the moment people found out drugs were involved. Didn't matter that Rachel had shot him up with it after he'd passed out from whatever she put in his drinks.

Even if he had gotten himself hooked on the flake though, it shouldn't have mattered. Addicts were people, too and sometimes, they needed help. Like he had.

But his mother saw his flake problem as his own personal failing. A failing of his character. And maybe it was? Regardless, it was up to him to fix it himself. No matter the problem, she'd always expected him to fix it all himself. By the time he was seven years old, he knew better than to go to her with a problem.

"Herb and I set her straight on the fact that Rachel Daniels did some horrible things to you. Herb explained that they had Rachel admitting it on film. The director really stood up for you, Jack."

"He did?" Jack couldn't help but smile.

She nodded. "And your mother admitted something that you need to hear."

He stiffened. He didn't want to hear anything that woman said.

"I don't want to hear it," he said with a growl and turned away from Talia.

Talia laid two fingers against his chin and gently turned his face back toward her.

"Jack, listen," she insisted. "Your father had a drug and alcohol problem when you were little. Your mother says they almost lost their house because of it. You were very young and she didn't want to ruin your hero worship of your dad."

His dad had a drug problem? His brow furrowed and anger rose hot in his veins.

"What's she talking about? Dad never had a drug problem! I never once saw him do drugs. Not once! And I lived with him for years! Just him and me—from the time I was ten until he..." He choked up. He swallowed a breath and then finished his sentence. "Until he died—of-of cancer. When I was seventeen."

"Jack," said Talia, her voice empathetic. "She said it was when you were really young. She wanted to preserve your dad's memory for you, but when you had the cocaine problem, she thought you were becoming just like your dad. And she wanted no part of that. She said you look just like your father and every time she looked into your eyes, she saw your dad there. And that was her fault."

His heart smashed against his rib cage. "She said all that? And she's never once told me any of this stuff. She didn't even check on me, Talia. Not when Dad died. And not when I got fired either. Just let me waste away after Rachel dumped me."

Talia nodded. "I know. It doesn't excuse her bad behavior toward you, Jack, but it does explain it. Herb told her that he was letting her go from the show, but she begged him not to—said she wanted to be a part of your wedding if you won. And she wanted to try and mend yours and her relationship."

That was a good one.

She probably wanted to mend their relationship because he was getting good reviews again. And he was back in demand in Hollywood. That was good for her event planning business. It was the only reason she wanted to be involved with his wedding, too. How would it look if she wasn't part of it? Clients wouldn't even believe he was her son if she wasn't planning his wedding.

"Because it helps her business," Jack snapped. "Can we talk about something else now?"

Talia kissed him. "Of course," she said, sitting up again. "Let's talk about Abaddon."

"What's there to tell?" he replied.

She frowned. "Plenty. Like how'd you get him to leave for starters?"

"Introduced him to my seraphim powers." In a big way. Abaddon never saw that part of the story coming.

"What'd you do?" Talia asked.

"I threw down some bursts of Holy fire," said Jack. "Each one surprised him. Knocked him off his feet."

"I can't imagine that would have stopped him for long," said Talia, her gaze scrutinizing his face.

Abaddon seemed very surprised that he'd had seraphim powers, but the omnificence power turned the tide of the fight. The huge demon looked openly frightened when he brought it up. And when he used it, Abaddon looked visibly shaken by it.

"It didn't," said Jack, shaking his head. "But he kind of lost his mind when I told him I had the omnificence power. It really seemed to scare him. But I had to use it to prove it to him."

Talia turned her gaze toward her squad and they stared at each other for several long moments. Finally, she turned her gaze back to him, still looking pensive.

"That's surprising," said Talia. "Has Abaddon lost some of his power?"

"Or maybe he will only possess those powers when he's sent to earth as God's intercessory," said Kesien, glancing at Talia and then Muriel. "Regardless, he thought Jack was just an average human that Lucifer couldn't reach because of that tether."

Muriel's face brightened, her mouth falling open, eyes wide. "Maybe you're right, Kesien?" Excitement quivered in Muriel's voice. "Maybe Abaddon saw this as a quick and easy accomplishment?"

Abaddon said he was tired of waiting. "The dude said he was getting bored waiting around for the apocalypse to happen, so he could do his job," Jack offered. "He sounded like hunting me down was something that got him away from Hell and into his hunting grounds. Like he was aching to hunt down some humans. I told him he should get a hobby. Like surfing. Or cage fighting. Or scrapbooking."

Muriel snorted, Kesien snickering alongside her.

"You actually said that to Abaddon, Jack?" Muriel asked, grinning at him.

He nodded. "Yep. Told him he better get a hobby because he was showing up to Hell empty-handed. That's when the fight started and I hit him with three ten-foot waves of Holy fire."

Kesien gasped. "Ten-foot waves of Holy fire? No wonder everything was burned. Surprised it wasn't still burning when we got there."

"I called up some rain clouds to put out the fires," said Jack, rubbing his forehead.

"And that's how he got power drunk," said Muriel, shaking her head. "Jack, you used a lot of seraphim powers doing all of that."

"Most of that was before I even used omnificence," said Jack.

He'd made Abaddon think he could be in two places at once. Attacking the eight-foot lummox from above and below. He nearly passed out doing it, but Abaddon didn't know that.

Talia gripped his biceps. "Jack, how did you use omnificence?"

Frowning, he shook his head. Why'd that even matter now? "I

made him think I could be in two places at once by...well, by...um, being two places at once. I sent myself to the bottom of the tree I was hovering beside. He thought he'd have to fight two of me—both with seraphim powers."

The hush in the room made him glance around at the other angels of death. They looked shocked.

"That's...incredible," said Kesien as he glanced from Talia to Muriel. "For a human to command seraphim powers like—"

"A seraph," said Talia, turning back toward Jack. "Jack, do you have any idea how dangerous that was?"

He sighed and sat up on the bed. "Well, considering that I was about to be destroyed by an eight-foot demon, I didn't have much choice."

Talia's face flushed. "Well, you shouldn't have been out there alone. And you shouldn't have gone past the wards." She shook him. "You of all people should have known better, Jack! You should have known better!"

He started to defend himself, but she just pulled him into her arms and held him. She was shaking.

"That was so, so very dangerous!" Her breath caught and he heard her voice hitch, a sob in her throat.

Surprised, he slid his arms around her, holding her tight. "Talia... everything's fine now. I'm fine."

She pulled back from him, anger burning in that grey gaze again. "But what if it hadn't been, Jack Casey! What if it hadn't been? Abaddon could have killed you! And you could have killed you with those seraphim powers!" She glared at him. "I'm so mad at you right now!"

He couldn't help it. He busted out laughing. He'd never seen his angel of death girlfriend so rattled before and he didn't understand why.

"Why are you laughing?" she demanded, still holding onto his arms.

"Because, I'm not sure if you're going to smite Abaddon first or me." He smiled at her. "I've never seen you like this before."

"That's because you were in Hell when she was like this before, Jack," said Muriel.

"I love you," she said in a tight, strained voice. "I won't lose you— even if you're doing your best to get yourself killed, Jack Casey."

She was shaking now, those intense grey eyes growing misty. Tears? What had gotten into her? Had he scared her that badly?

"I'm sorry, Talia," he said finally, letting his smile fall away. He gripped her forearms. "I didn't mean to upset you like this. I just did what I had to do to get away from Abaddon. Thought you'd be proud of me."

She shook her head. "Not if it gets you killed." Her eyes brimmed with tears. "Jack, don't you understand? If you die, you'll go to a part of Heaven that I can't access. Forever. For eternity. And I'll never see you again." At last, those tears ran down her face, turning to crystals. "I couldn't take not ever seeing you again. Of being away from you."

He pulled her against his chest and held her tight. "I love you more than my own life, Talia," he said in a soft voice against her ear.

"And that's what I'm terrified of, Jack," she said, her voice breaking. "Don't sacrifice yourself for me. Ever again. I don't want to exist without you. Apart from you. Understand?"

Sighing, he stroked her hair. He understood more than she'd ever know. The thought of being apart from her made him shake all over. Woke him up at three A.M., worrying him about what would happen once they handled Abaddon. Even now, he had no idea if they could stay together or if Heaven would call Talia back there.

Without him.

"Understand?" he said in a raspy whisper. "I'm terrified at what happens once we take care of Abaddon. Will they call you back to Heaven and leave me here—where you found me?" He swallowed a breath, his voice small and strained. "I'll die without you, Talia."

She pressed her face against his, her lips finding his mouth in a hot, frantic kiss and he returned it, desperate to stay with her. Here, Heaven—he didn't care. As long as they were together, he'd handle the location change.

It took a few minutes, but her shaking subsided. Finally, he let her sit up. He gripped her hand, smirking at her.

"See, I've got this plan," he said.

She smiled, wiping away tears and crystals from her face. "What plan?" she asked.

He tapped his index finger against his right temple. "I'm going to hold the seraphim powers hostage until my demands are met."

She chuckled, reaching out to caress his face. "What demands?" she asked, sniffling.

"You—in exchange for the seraphim powers." His smirk curved into a smile. "I can be reasonable."

She laughed and threw her arms around him, holding him close again. "I like being your hostage."

"Still want to marry me?" he asked.

"More than ever," she said in a quiet voice and kissed him again. "And I want to walk into that first challenge and set fire to it tomorrow."

He laughed as she let him sink back against the headboard.

"I'd settle for third place," he said with a chuckle. "As long as we don't get sent home, I'm good."

She leaned over and kissed his lips and then rose from the bed. "We're not going anywhere just yet, Jack Casey. And after using all that seraphim power, you need to rest." She tapped him on the nose. "And realize just how taxing those powers are on your human body. Especially these rare powers we share. You expended so much power today, Jack. Now, rest."

At last, Kesien stepped over to the bed. "She's right, Jack. You may not be feeling it right at this moment because of the power drunk numbing your system. You used a full range of seraphim powers and then omnificence. I'm glad the seraph put that failsafe back in place. Power like this could kill a human."

He was feeling sleepy, but he remembered those devastating hangover effects that arrived the next morning. Damn. He hoped he wouldn't have to deal with that again tomorrow. It had been just long enough that he'd forgotten.

"I'm gonna be hungover like a kid after his first kegger, aren't I?" he asked, wincing.

Kesien nodded, a look of commiseration on his face. "Sorry, Jack. I can help a little with that, but it took Berith's special healing gift to ease that after-effect last time."

"You could just smite me," he said with a sigh.

"Wish I could help, Jack, but I think Talia would have something to say about that."

Talia gave him a very deep nod.

"See?"

Jack sighed and looked toward the bathroom. "Guess I'd better go swallow a whole bottle of ibuprofen before I fall asleep."

Muriel stepped out of the bathroom with a big glass of water and a bottle of ibuprofen.

"Here, Jack," she said, holding them out to him. "Hope this helps."

He smiled at her. "Muriel to my rescue. Thanks."

She blushed, a grin spreading across her face. "You sure you're going to marry him, Talia?"

"Without a doubt," said Talia, crossing her arms. "Sorry. He's all mine."

"Awww...fine," said Muriel with a groan.

Jack took three ibuprofen and drank the glass of water and set them on the nightstand. He laid down on the bed, waiting for the sledgehammer to bludgeon his cranium and everything inside it. It would be a long day tomorrow. If he could even lift up his head.

16

TALIA WOKE UP EARLY THE NEXT MORNING, JACK STILL ASLEEP AND moaning. He was running a fever after he'd used all those seraphim powers at once—and then omnificence on top of it.

He just didn't realize how much damage those Holy powers caused his human body. Those powers were meant for seraphim to use in battle against demonic forces. Those abilities were too powerful and caused damage, even to angels that possessed rare powers—like her and Berith.

For a human being? Those powers were devastating.

He'd forgotten the toll they'd taken on his body the last time. How could he forget? He fought Lucifer who had full seraph powers. He used those seraphim powers without the failsafe to protect him and his body took dozens of Lucifer's seraphim-level blows. Without that protection, those powers devastated his body, causing fatal damage. Thanks to Seraphina and Berith, he survived.

She'd gotten more ibuprofen down him and he'd gone back to sleep, but he was hurting. She had no idea if he'd be in any kind of shape for this afternoon's challenge. Kesien planned to use more healing light on him later. She hoped that would be enough to get him through the challenge.

They were the last couple scheduled today. She doubted if Herb would let them reschedule again though. Especially with that first live elimination broadcast on Friday. And then she and Jack had interviews after today's challenge. Separately and together.

No, they had to get through today's filming schedule. And this challenge.

After dressing in a short jean skirt, black flats, and a light blue, long-sleeved top, Talia went down to the small dining room to the left of the entryway's tall gallery. Sunlight warmed the white and black marble tiles as she headed down a short hallway toward the small breakfast room (as the chateau staff called it). The smell of butter and bacon warmed the air.

The room had soft green and fuchsia striped wallpaper interspersed with cherry blossoms and a small crystal chandelier that hung over a round table with an aged white base and a dark walnut top. A gold and white sideboard with an ornate gold mirror over it stood against one wall. The other wall had a tall china cabinet in that same French gold and white style. The cabinet glistened with fine, gold-edged china trimmed in black and surrounded by delicate crystal glassware. The black French doors had beveled glass and overlooked a small courtyard filled with box hedges and yellow and white flowers.

Armand and Izzy sat together at the table, Mark Banks and Morgan on their right, Rachel and Eric on their left. A platter of scrambled eggs, round sausage patties, and crispy strips of bacon set on the table, a small plate stacked high with browned toast set beside it. A pitcher of orange juice was also on the table, passed around as some of the cast filled small, clear juice glasses with the bright orange liquid. The sound of conversation and silverware clicking against plates echoed through the room.

"Talia!" Izzy called, motioning her over. "Good morning."

"Join us, please," said Armand.

"Good to see you, Talia," said Mark as she walked around to the chair that Izzy slid beside hers.

"Good morning, everyone," said Talia, forcing a smile on her face as she sat down beside Izzy.

No one asked where Jack was yet. They would. The whole sordid conversation between Jack and his mother had no doubt made the rounds through all the contestants. Armand looked concerned as he glanced toward the door and then back at her. Looking for Jack, she knew.

"Jack running late this morning?" Armand asked in a nonchalant voice, worry in his big brown eyes as he glanced at Talia and then at Izzy.

Izzy wore black yoga pants and an orange, long-sleeved top. Armand wore jeans and a blue rugby shirt. Mark wore a long-sleeved yellow T-shirt and jeans. Morgan had on jeans and a half-zip blue sweater. Eric wore a red polo shirt and khakis, Rachel in a light pink, figure-hugging dress and matching heels.

"He's sleeping," she said and filled her glass with orange juice. "He wasn't feeling well this morning."

She didn't need to eat, but she needed to understand all of this food that humans ate. Especially with that cake and wine challenge still ahead of her and Jack.

Rachel looked surprised. But she was an actress. Probably still playing her role as Jack's tormentor to the hilt.

"Hope it isn't anything serious," said Armand, picking up a corner of buttered toast and taking a bite.

"I hope so, too," said Talia, glancing at him as she took a sip of the orange juice.

"That orange juice is fresh squeezed," said Izzy, smiling as she leaned toward her. "It's amazing."

Talia squinted at her glass. It was sweet and acidic—refreshing. She liked the taste of it. Did that mean that just because it was the color orange and it was juice, it wasn't always fresh squeezed?

"It's delicious," she replied and took another drink.

Armand finished off his piece of toast and stared at her for several moments.

"All right, I'm sorry, Talia, but I have to be nosy," he said, his gaze still full of worry. "We all heard what happened."

Mark leaned around Armand, nodding, his light brown hair sliding into his face.

"Yeah, so, how's Jack?" Mark asked.

Armand nodded, glancing at Mark and then back at her. "I can't imagine how badly he must have felt."

Rachel set her knife down hard against her plate, a fork in her hand. "Badly? What are you talking about?"

Talia glared across the table at her. "Like you don't know."

"Don't know what?" she said. "Jack hasn't spoken to his mother in years. Wasn't she thrilled to see him?"

Talia shoved the glass of juice out of her way and snapped up from the chair. She moved around the table, glaring at Rachel.

"She devastated him," Talia snapped, hands on her hips. "Like you knew she would."

Rachel's eyes got big and she stared at Talia, shaking her head. Talia reached for her angel powers. If this woman was lying, she'd feel the heat burn from her words.

"No! She didn't..." Rachel rose to her feet. "Talia, that was supposed be some closure for Jack. My way of thanking him. I wanted to do something nice for him."

"By releasing that harpy on him?" Talia shook her head. "That was so kind of you, Rachel. Letting her smash him to bits like that. He didn't even want to do the show when he found out it was being filmed on location in Sonoma County. I had to talk him into it."

She hadn't felt any heat coming from Rachel's words. As much as she hated to admit it, there hadn't been any malice behind this woman's actions.

"What happened?" Rachel asked.

"What do you think happened?" Talia shouted. "That woman treated Jack like garbage! She blamed him for everything that happened in his life. She didn't seem to care that he'd needed help and that he'd been two days away from living in his car before this show's first season started."

Gasps filtered around the table, the others looking shocked and concerned now. Concerned for Jack, Talia realized.

"And then she had the nerve to blame him for almost ruining her business after he got fired from his show. When the tabloids reported it and his cocaine addiction."

Rachel's brows pressed into an angry line. "The nerve! Jack had nothing to do with that. I can't believe she wasn't on the phone to him the moment she read that in the tabloids or the trades." She sighed, her face screwing up into a look that was a mixture of guilt and concern. "None of that was even Jack's fault. It was mine—and Lare's."

Talia could barely hold in her shock. Rachel was admitting it to the entire cast?

"What does that mean, Rachel?" Armand asked. "That you're finally owning up to what you did to that poor guy?"

He looked pissed. His face was a mirror image of her own. She wanted to smite this woman. Hard. Back to Hell for what she'd done to Jack. For what she'd let people believe about him. And he just took the punishment and the derision, letting anyone and everyone believe whatever they wanted to believe.

Rachel hung her head, nodding, staring down at her plate, fingers struggling to hold the fork she'd been gripping.

"I am," she said and looked at Armand and then Talia. "What I did to poor Jack Casey was horrible. He was just a sweet, innocent kid. A drop-dead, smoking hot twenty-year-old who just wanted to act. I fell so hard for him, but then Lare and I preyed on him, breaking him down over the months. Jack didn't even drink back then. A beer if he was driving. A couple if he wasn't. I tried to get him to do cocaine so many times. Finally, I had to drug his drinks and shoot it into his system."

"My God," Armand cried, snapping up from his chair. He glared at her, shaking his head. "Why would you do something so horrible? Why, Rachel?"

"For sport," she said with a sigh. "Lare and I had been doing it for years. Wanting to see who we could turn. It was all just a game. The cast of SanFran Confidential was a pretty rough crowd. That poor kid had no idea what he was getting himself into. And besides, Lare was so jealous of him. Jack loved me and I wanted him so badly, but I knew it could never happen."

Armand was staring at Talia in confusion, his gaze wondering if she was buying any of this story. Talia felt no malice or heat from any of Rachel's words. She was telling them the truth. And Jack hadn't told her much about what happened in Hell between them—in that cage fight. Talia just shrugged and shook her head.

Rachel's eyes filled with tears as she glanced at Talia and then her attention returned to Armand. "See, Lare made me into a star. I owed him—couldn't leave him. But I wanted Jack Casey so badly. The press loved us—one of Hollywood's power couples they said. The paparazzi followed us relentlessly. Then Lare wanted him fired. He was stealing Lare's spotlight. The whole time, Lare pretended to be Jack's best friend and I pretended to be his lover. Even though I was still living with Lare at the beach estate when Jack thought I was with him."

Armand looked disgusted. Mark Banks looked horrified.

"You played him," said Armand, his voice rising. "The entire time he was on that show. When you were in a relationship with him. Everything was a lie. As despicable as you getting him hooked on cocaine was, the rest of it is just as deplorable."

Talia put her hands on her hips. "Don't forget that she gaslighted him the entire time. For years. Read him fake reviews, told him he was the worst actor in Hollywood. Until he believed it."

At last, she understood why she'd been sent to save Jack's soul in the first place. Because everything that happened to Jack had been caused by Lucifer and he didn't even know it. Heaven wanted to fix the horrible injustices that Lucifer had perpetrated against him. Azrael chose his soul as part of that first wager because of Lucifer's meddling.

Armand's face had gone pale, but the rage in his big brown eyes smoldered. Mark looked angry, too, his hazel eyes burning.

"Is that true?" Armand asked. "Did you really throw gasoline on a chemical fire already burning?"

Talia couldn't imagine hearing all this for the first time. Or that Rachel had been brave enough to admit to all of it. But Lare Dumont was no longer here on earth. He was in Hell where he belonged. Rachel belonged there, too. Jack hadn't intentionally gotten her released from her contract with Lucifer. He didn't even know about those contracts—she sighed—until he found out she was an angel of death. And Lucifer showed up at his apartment to drag her off to Hell.

Collapsing into her chair, Rachel threw down the fork and pressed her face into her hands.

"I did so many terrible things to Jack. I made most of the industry hate him. I made him think he was the worst actor in Hollywood. I turned him into a drug addict. I took away his hit show—and almost killed him."

"And so much more than that," Talia replied, unaffected by Rachel's tears.

She still wanted to smite this bitch. Hard. All the way back to Hell.

Armand was nodding now. "So true, Talia," he said, glaring at Rachel. "And so much more."

"Jack hasn't been part of his own family for years," said Rachel, taking her hands away from her face, smoky eyeliner and mascara smudged. "I just wanted to try and reconnect him with his mother if I could. Get him back in contact with his sisters. He has four older sisters."

Even though Talia still wanted to smite this bitch, she made a good point. She'd never heard Jack mention anything about family except his dad who passed away when Jack was seventeen. He'd mentioned that he had sisters, but with everything in Jack's life, there was a vast distance. Reconnecting him with his sisters made sense. She wasn't so sure about his mother though.

The legs of Armand's chair screeched across the marble as he shoved it away from the table, fury in his eyes.

"How can we believe any of this sudden goodwill toward Jack, Rachel?" he demanded, hands on his hips. "Why help him now?" He moved over to Talia and laid his hands on her shoulders. "He has family right here. Talia Smith is the love of Jack's life." Armand gestured at Mark and then Izzy. "And he has us. We care about Jack and we don't want to see you get any more opportunities to trash that man. He's been through enough."

Talia patted Armand's shoulder. He was such a good friend to Jack and to her. Armand and Mark had gotten really close to Jack by the end of *The Cinderella Hour*. It made her eyes sting when she thought about how protective of Jack they'd become.

"You're right, Armand," said Rachel, rising from her chair. "Jack Casey's been through enough. That's why I asked to come on the show. I wanted to see Jack finally get rewarded. Eric and I are happy together, so if we win, we'll get married. But I was hoping to set things right for Jack. He deserves some happiness at last."

Armand crossed his arms against his chest. "I couldn't agree more. We'll just see how things go, but just know that we're watching for any foul play or malice leveled at Jack. And we will stop it. Just so you know."

Mark gave her a sharp, deep nod. "What Armand said. We're looking out for Jack and we'll keep looking out for him until this season's over. And then as his buddies afterward."

"Fair enough," said Rachel. "I'm glad Talia's not the only one looking out for him."

With a timid slide of her chair, Izzy slid back from the table. "I need to get to my interview with Devin now."

"I'll be following you today," said Morgan who scraped her chair legs across the marble tiles. She kissed Mark. "See everyone later. Bye, Talia." Morgan reached out and squeezed Talia's shoulder as she walked behind her.

"See you later, Talia," said Izzy. She kissed Armand and hurried out of the small dining room.

The rest of the cast finished eating and left under the awkward silence, including Talia. She needed to check on Jack.

She hurried up the grand staircase to the second floor, her footsteps clacking across the tiles as she walked past the tall, white columns toward the black French-styled doors leading to the Halo Suite. Full of angels of death. And Jack, who still had his wings and halo. Hidden by her angel of death powers.

When she closed the suite door behind her, she found Jack sitting on the bed, head in his hands. Kesien floated beside him, enveloping him in gold light.

Moving to the bed, she sat down beside him and rubbed the back of his neck.

"How do you feel today, Jack?" she asked in a soft voice.

He looked up from his hands, one eye closed. His short blond hair was disheveled in that sexy, just woke up look, but the one eye open worried her.

"Like I need to walk out in front of a bus to end this headache," he said with a moan.

Muriel flew past Talia, a big glass of chilled water in her hand. She handed it to Jack along with three ibuprofens.

"Thanks, Muriel," he said and tossed down the ibuprofen, chasing it with the big glass of water.

"My pleasure, Jack," she said, giving Talia a concerned look. "He's got a bad power hangover."

"I can see that," said Talia, still rubbing his neck. "Gotta get you on your feet though. We've got to be in the dining room by two o'clock. For our first challenge."

He made a sour face and laid a hand against his stomach. "I'm gonna yak if I have to eat cake and drink wine."

Kesien and Muriel chuckled.

"I'll add my healing light to yours, Kesien. See if together, we can heal some of this."

"Ready when you are, Muriel," said Kesien with a nod.

Together, they stood on Jack's right side and summoned gold healing light, engulfing Jack in a double dose. They kept it flowing for several minutes until the color in Jack's face improved.

"Any better, Jack?" Kesien asked.

He nodded. "Better than it was. Thanks, dudes."

She hoped he'd feel better when it was time for their first event this afternoon. She wanted to beat Rachel Daniels—in more ways than just at this first challenge.

17

JACK SHOVED HIS HANDS IN THE POCKETS OF HIS GREY PANTS, THE shirttails of his white and grey striped button-down shirt hanging loose as he leaned against the wall beside the closed dining room door. Already, his heart pounded in his throat. His mother was in there, setting up the three phases of this first challenge and he had no idea what to expect.

From her or the challenge.

His head still hurt, but the ibuprofen had pushed the steady pounding at his temples back into the distance. And thanks to Kesien and Muriel, his nausea had fled. The thought of eating cake with all that sweet icing made his stomach shudder. He was more of a salt eater than a sweets person and preferred pretzels to chocolate.

Talia looked hot as hell in a short, ice blue skirt, tan flats, and a lacy white top, her raven black hair tumbling in waves down her back. Her grey eyes were luminous in the sunlight streaming into the hallway from all the windows. She smiled and gazed outside.

She just took his breath away.

Finally, Jennifer opened the door and motioned them into the dining room. His stomach twisted into a knot at the thought of facing his mother again. He'd already been nervous about this challenge without her adding more stress. He had no idea what she'd say to him today. Maybe the demons did?

"Welcome back, Jack and Talia," said Jennifer.

Jennifer wore a pair of black leggings and a long-sleeved lavender T-shirt with *The Royal Wedding Hour* logo on it. She had on a pair of purple glasses that made her brown eyes look bigger, her hair in a tight ponytail at her nape. She smelled like vanilla and coffee, that clipboard in her left hand pressed against her thigh and a grin on her face.

"Hey, Jennifer," he said and entered the dining room, Talia behind him, a hand on his left arm, gripping it protectively.

Talia greeted her as she passed.

"Ready for your first challenge?" Jennifer asked.

The room's furniture had been cleared. A large cloth divider in rich purple satin trimmed in sparkling gold piping stood in the center. A raised, wooden throne-like chair stood beside a heavy rectangular wood table on each side of the purple satin divider. The carved, oak thrones looked like dusty old museum pieces (something Steve had excavated from the studio's warehouse in Burbank).

One place setting of that black and gold china set on each table. Three big, goblet-like red wine glasses, three angular white wine glasses, and two tall, tapered champagne flutes sparkled on the right. To the left of the forks, a small computer tablet set beside a royal purple cloth napkin. Talia would hate to see that tablet.

He felt bad. This whole challenge would be difficult for her.

At the other end of the table was a large, shiny silver tray with a silver dome covering it. Arranged around the tray were six bottles of wine, wrapped in midnight blue paper with gold stars and crescent moons to obscure the labels. And two bottles of champagne, also wrapped in that star and moon paper.

His mother wasn't in the room and that made him breathe a sigh of relief.

Last thing he needed right now was another argument with his mother who insisted that she was always right. He didn't need another headache on top of the massive one he already had.

Two camera crews were in the room, managing lights and four cameras: two on each side of the divider. Herb's director chair stood at the end of the long room, giving him an unobstructed view of both sides of the divider. Steve stood beside Roy the lead cameraman who had a stationary camera between the divider. This camera captured both sides of the divider simultaneously and the entire room.

Another camera moved through the room on Rhonda's shoulder. And two smaller cameras were fixed on each side of the divider, focused on the table. Phil managed the divider camera with a couple other crew that Jack hadn't met before.

Jennifer took Talia by the shoulders and steered her around the divider to the table on stage left. She motioned toward the tall, wooden throne.

"All right, Talia," said Jennifer, pointing to the tablet and the place setting. "Jack will go first. He'll be seated on the other side of the partition and when Devin Van Fossen arrives, he'll take Jack through the first two parts of the challenge. You will wait outside until he's done. Then he'll wait outside while you select your answers on the tablet. Once you've completed your answers, Jack will rejoin you for the third part of the challenge. Any questions?"

She shook her head.

"Jack?" Jennifer asked, motioning stage right toward the other table. "Any questions?"

"Nope, let's do this," he replied, wanting it to be over.

"All right, Talia, you'll need to wait out in the hall, so you can't hear any of Jack's responses."

Talia nodded as Jack moved toward her. He put his arms around her and kissed her.

"Good luck, babe," he said.

"You, too, Jack," she said, smiling at him. She reached up and ran her fingers through his blond hair. "Choose well. I love you."

He grinned and pulled her back into his arms for a longer kiss. "I love you, too," he said and laid his hand against his heart, holding out his open hand to her.

She kissed him on the lips as she closed her hand into a fist and pressed it to her heart. With a wistful glance, she turned away toward the black French-styled panel doors and opened one, stepping into the hallway.

When he turned back toward the set, Jennifer was smiling at him.

"Ready, Jack?"

He nodded and followed her over to the tall, wooden throne on stage right of the divider. Gently, he sat down, his body still aching from using all those seraphim powers. He glanced past Herb and the cameras toward the closed doors.

Waiting for Devin to return from Mark and Morgan's couple interview they'd just filmed, according to today's filming schedule.

He wondered what would have happened if he'd stuck to that very first script. Would he have matched with Claire—even though he'd lost his heart to Talia? Where would he be right now if he hadn't fought back? If he'd just followed what was written in black and white and accepted that Claire was his match?

There wouldn't have been a fourth season of this show. Would he have overdosed on flake shortly after that? Would Lenny Overton, his drug dealer's enforcer, have killed him when he couldn't pay his debt? Would Talia and Archangel Azrael have still intervened somehow?

He'd never know the answer to that question, but he was so glad he'd found the courage put his heart on the line that night, offering it to Talia.

The thought of her not being in his life made him shake all over. If she got to stay with him here on earth, his time would be over so fast. And he'd still be separated from her for eternity.

Somehow, when all of this was over—and Abaddon dealt with—he'd go off script again. Throw himself on the mercy of Heaven and the seraphim. Beg them to let him and Talia stay together. Somehow. On even footing together. Forever.

It was the least they could do after he'd trapped Lucifer in the Garden—which cost him his life. After Talia brought him back, he battled Lucifer again, stopping him from taking over the Heavens.

All he wanted was to stay with Talia.

In a few moments, one of the black doors opened and Devin Van

Fossen walked into the dining room, brown Ferragamo's ticking across the marble floor toward the set. His over-highlighted hair was bright in the wash of set lights shining throughout the long dining room, every hair pomaded into submission. His highlights almost drowned out the glow from his over-whitened teeth. Dude didn't need all that stuff. He was good at his job and didn't need to out-glam Hollywood to prove it. Devin wore a brown tweed jacket, light blue dress shirt, and brown pants. He was clean-shaven and smelled like some stinky aftershave with fake ocean scent. No ocean stunk like that unless a bunch of shark carcasses had washed ashore.

"Good afternoon, Jack," said Devin, extending his hand. A gold class ring gleamed on his hand, from some east coast college, its big red jewel sparkling. "Was wondering if something had happened to you and Talia."

He shook Devin's hand, but the ring's red glow reminded him of demon eyes and made him uncomfortable.

"Nah, we're fine. Just needed to reschedule some things. How are you, Devin?"

"Good. Glad you and Talia are here. It will make this season so much more exciting. And the ratings so much higher." He chuckled, flashing those over-bright white teeth.

"Hope so," said Jack. "Hope we still have some fans out there, routing for us."

Devin gave him an astounded look. "Jack, if you could see all the studio's fan mail for you and Talia, you wouldn't say that." He glanced around and lowered his voice. "There have been a ton of letters asking if the network would give you and Talia your own reality television show."

Jack laughed. "The Jack and Talia Hour? Seriously?"

The show's host nodded emphatically at him. "That's what they're all asking for, Jack. A long running show that follows you and Talia around in your new life together."

With death angels and demons and seraphim and Lucifer? Yeah, that would be a pretty entertaining show, he had to admit. He'd watch that. From a long distance.

"It's got a strange ring to it," said Jack with a shrug.

"Doesn't it though?" said Devin with a knowing look.

"But I want much more than an hour or a season with Talia," Jack replied, settling back in the uncomfortable wooden throne. "I want a lifetime."

Devin grinned at him. "And America wants to see that happen, Jack. They want to see all the juicy details of your lives together. They want the fairytale, too, Jack. They want to see the happily ever after."

"That makes two of us," Jack replied, running a hand through his hair.

He had a feeling that Abaddon—and Lucifer—didn't much care for fairytales. Or happy ever afters. Just horror stories. He wondered about angels of death. He couldn't picture Talia at home with a dog and two cats, baking pies and chasing kids around the yard. Kids... Talia wasn't human. She couldn't have kids. If they did have kids, how would he explain to them that their mother was an angel of death?

He snickered. And they'd get to meet Aunt Muriel, Uncle Kesien, and Grandpa Azrael. He made a note to call Azrael *Grandpa* the next time he saw the archangel.

Devin looked over at Herb who was busy talking to Steve and Jennifer as the script supervisor stood beside him. Along with camera and lighting crews. It was several minutes before Herb looked up at him and Devin.

"All right, gentlemen," said Herb, "let's get this challenge in the can for Jack and Talia. Devin, introduce the challenge to the cameras and Jack."

"Got it, Herb," said Devin, pulling some cards out of his jacket pocket as he watched for Steve's cue.

"Rolling in three," said Steve, a hand in the air.

Like most of the crew, Steve wore a short-sleeved grey T-shirt with *The Royal Wedding Hour* logo in purple on the front. He had on Doc Martens and faded jeans, his hair tied back in a dark brown ponytail, no glasses today, beard short and trimmed.

"Three, two, one—rolling," Steve announced in a quiet voice.

"And now, my royal subjects," said Devin in his melodramatic delivery as he turned toward Roy, the lead camera crew member's lens, "we welcome Jack Casey, former star of SanFran Confidential and the film, You and Me. Jack and his lady fair, Talia Smith, will be completing the show's first challenge as royal taste testers."

Devin walked toward the table, shoes ticking against the marble as he turned to Jack, still seated in the wooden throne at the end of the polished square table. The dark walnut finish stood out in the white room.

"Jack, ready to have your cake and eat it, too?" Devin asked him with that stupid euphemism.

He leaned against the right arm of the throne as Devin stood beside him. Game face on. He was having a grand time. Devin's banter was riveting and the wittiest thing he'd ever heard. He couldn't wait to try and guess what kind of cake and wine an angel of death preferred.

He offered Devin his most devastating and charming smile.

"Bring on the cake, Devin. I just hope Talia will forgive me if I get these wrong. I think she'll be as surprised by her favorite cake flavors as I will be."

Especially since she hadn't even tasted them all before. She was an angel of death. She crossed over dead humans. Unless a few of them died in bakeries, at weddings, or during birthday parties, she probably hadn't eaten much cake.

"Well, Jack," said Devin, his gaze drifting from the main camera and back to Jack. "America's hoping the two of you nail this challenge." Devin pointed at the other end of the table. "As you can see, there's a large covered tray, concealing six slices of cake. Each slice is numbered. You will sample all six slices and then rate them according to how you think Talia will rate them. Using the tablet computer beside you on the table."

Jack glanced at the tablet on the left side of the table. It had the first question on display and a *tap to continue* message on the screen.

"And the second part of the question is which flavors you prefer. You will enter those answers on the tablet as well. Any questions?"

Jack shook his head. "Got it."

"In the second part of the challenge, you will sample three white wines, three red wines, and two champagnes."

"You trying to get me drunk, Devin?" he asked with a smirk.

"If it'll get me a laugh, I will," Devin replied back to him.

Jack chuckled.

"You will select one wine in each category as the choice you'd serve at your wedding," said Devin. "You'll select your preferences and the choices you think Talia will make—on the tablet."

Jack nodded. "So, I choose one white wine, one red wine, and one champagne that I'd serve? And then the ones I think Talia will choose?"

Devin turned to the main camera and smiled. "He's quick, isn't he, my royal subjects?" Devin turned back to Jack. "That's exactly right, Jack. After the wine, you'll switch places with Talia and she'll go through the challenge. Once she's made her choices, you two will compete in the cocktail challenge."

"That's the third part, right?"

"Quite correct, Jack," Devin replied and studied him for a moment or two. "Together, you and Talia will each craft a cocktail from the items on hand at our royal bar. Each drink will be evaluated by myself and two of the crew and given a score. You won't know your scores until the first live elimination round."

So, he and Talia won't have a clue how they scored until Friday's show. Terrific. He just hoped they at least came in third place. That's all he cared about. Staying on the show. Maybe the rest of the challenges would be something Talia had experience with—like smiting demons? Or telling humans they were dead and it was their time to go? Winning this royal wedding competition was going to be harder than dealing with Abaddon. He sighed. Especially with his mother working for the show.

"All right," said Devin, glancing around the room. "Let's have Jack sample our cake flavors."

A grey-haired man in black pants, black shoes, a white tuxedo shirt, and black bowtie entered the room. He picked up the tray, a pair of white gloves on his hands, and set it in the center of the table.

With a little white glove waving, the attendant removed the silver dome lid.

Revealing six small dessert plates, each one numbered one through six in gold leaf. The man picked up the first plate and set it on the gold and black charger plate in front of him.

A small wedge of white cake with white icing.

"You may begin, Jack," said Devin.

Jack picked up the dessert fork at the top of the plate and cut a small bite of cake with it. He slid it into his mouth.

Vanilla with buttercream icing. Moist and fresh. Tasted homemade, not out of a box. Really good—for vanilla.

He set down the fork and nodded at the attendant beside him. The man took the plate and fork away, setting them on the big silver tray. With a pause, the attendant set the plate numbered two in front of him. A rich, chocolate cake with chocolate icing.

Grabbing another fork, Jack cut off a small bite of chocolate cake. The icing was a chocolate ganache—really good. One of his favorites. Not cloyingly sweet like a lot of sugary icing tasted. His favorite so far.

The third plate was a yellow cake with some sort of golden glaze. It wasn't too sweet and the lemon flavor was good. He wasn't crazy about lemons though, so this one was a clear third choice for him.

He sampled plates four and five, tasting a classic red velvet cake with buttercream icing and a spice cake with cream cheese icing. He was surprised that he loved the cinnamon, nutmeg, and nuts in the spice cake, the cream cheese icing delicious. That one went to second place in his book.

The last one was a pink layer cake with white icing. He had no idea what it was. Strawberry? Cherry?

He took a bite of the cake. And tasted champagne with a little vanilla. It was moist and had a unique flavor. He put it third in his list.

"All right, Jack," said Devin, glancing into the camera. "If you're ready to rank your choices, go ahead and select them on the tablet. Set the tablet down to indicate that you're ready for the next part of the challenge."

Nodding, Jack set down his last fork and picked up the small touchscreen tablet as the attendant cleared the last slice of cake and his fork from the table. While the attendant replaced his forks, he tapped the screen and saw his name. Empty numbered boxes on the left. List of cake flavors on the right. He dragged the flavors into the numbered boxes in order of his favorites: chocolate, spice cake, champagne, red velvet, vanilla, and lemon. And tapped enter.

The next question was to rate the cakes for Talia. She'd be intrigued by the champagne cake first, followed by red velvet. After that, he had no clue—except that vanilla would be her least favorite. He ordered the other flavors as: chocolate, spice cake, lemon, and vanilla. He thought through the answers again, but he knew that Talia had never tasted most of these flavors before. She did like unusual things, so he went with those first and the more expected flavors last.

It was the best he could do. Sighing, he set the tablet on the table.

Devin motioned to the attendant who covered the silver tray with the dome lid. Next, the attendant gathered three blue-wrapped bottles of wine and placed them in front of Jack. On the front of each bottle was a gilded letter and number: R1, R2, and R3.

The attendant picked up the first bottle and poured a sip of red wine in the first glass. Jack took the glass and sniffed the wine. It had a whiff of pepper, blackberries, and flowers. He sipped it. It was dry, tasting a bit like cedar with a hint of brown sugar and cloves. Not bad.

The attendant added a sip or two to the second glass. It had a rich garnet color. He sipped it. It had a touch of cherries and raspberries, a hint of tobacco leaves, and a little bit of an earthy taste. Not too acidic. He liked it better than the first one.

The third glass of red had an almost black cherry flavor with a hint of plums and vanilla. It was smooth and had an oaky flavor. It tasted like a warm fire on a cold, snowy night. He preferred it to the other two reds.

"Whenever you're ready," said Devin, motioning toward the tablet, "please select the wine you'd choose and the one you think Talia will choose."

He chose the third red for him and Talia.

Next, the attendant poured the first angular glass of white wine.

He sipped the first glass. It tasted like ripe apples and pears—even peaches. Like someone had bottled the summer sun and poured it into a glass.

The next glass had a crisp, lemony taste and smelled almost like the ocean for a moment—with a hint of smoke. Like how the Pacific Ocean smelled and felt in December. With a bonfire on the beach at sunset.

The third glass of white wine had the soft taste of green apples and flowers, a hint of herbs and spices. It reminded him of spring, the smell of apple blossoms, fresh-cut wood, and fresh-mown grass.

He chose the second glass of white as his choice and he chose the first glass for Talia. The first white wine reminded him a little of Eolowen's meadows and the scent of flowers that hung on the sunny breezes.

When he set down the tablet, two flutes of champagne sparkled in front of him, bubbles churning through the golden liquid. He sipped the first one. It had an almost apricot flavor and citrus with a hint of toasted nuts.

The second glass tasted like a hint of peaches, a touch of caramel, and yeasty baked bread.

He chose the second champagne for him and Talia. He set down the tablet.

"All right, thank you, Jack," said Devin. "Please exchange places with Talia in the hallway. We'll bring her in and get her choices now."

With a nod, Jack rose from the wooden throne and walked toward the closed doors. To wait and see what Talia chose before they mixed Frankenstein cocktails together. As he opened the door, he wondered if Talia had even tasted a mixed drink before. This would be interesting.

Tending bar with an angel of death.

TALIA WAS NERVOUS ABOUT THIS FIRST CHALLENGE AS THE DOOR OPENED and Jack exited the chateau's main dining room. Normally, he showed no vulnerabilities during these challenges, that actor's façade in place, but this time, he looked worried. A rare expression on his gorgeous face.

He kissed her as they passed and wished her good luck.

And she quickly understood his concern when she walked across the marble floor and sat down on the other side of the purple silk partition. Seated on the other wooden throne, she stared at the elaborate place setting with all its confusing forks, knives, and spoons. And array of wine glasses.

So many wine glasses!

She remembered having to learn all the etiquette that humans tied to these objects and how some ridiculed anyone that used the wrong fork at the wrong time. Or, Heaven forbid, the wrong spoon!

It made her eyes roll at all the pretense, all the fancy gold-trimmed black and white china. And everything just so. She wanted to rearrange it all and see if anyone noticed. That made her smile. It would have made Jack laugh, if he'd been in the room.

After Devin explained the challenge to her on camera, a thin, grey-haired attendant in black pants, white shirt, white gloves, and white bowtie served her the first plate of cake.

Seeing all the cake slices, the bottles of wine, and all the wine glasses did she understand why Jack seemed so out of sorts. And she felt a little overwhelmed, staring at six pieces of cake on that silver platter in front of her. She knew almost nothing about human foods and flavors.

And the computer thing set on the left side of the table. Jack warned her about that. The tablet, as he called it, reminding her that it reacted to the touch of her fingers. He'd shown her a smaller one before. One he used to read books. And his phone (still in Hell) with a screen that he poked and prodded all the time with his fingers. She laughed, remembering Jack say that he hoped it blew up down there—Jackspeak for endlessly ringing—and drove Lucifer crazy.

She hoped she didn't mess this tablet computer thing up.

The first bite of cake was the white cake that she and Jack talked about yesterday. Vanilla he called it. It tasted okay, but it was bland and bored her. And the icing was too sweet. She tried not to wrinkle her nose as she set down her fork, waiting for the next slice of cake.

When the attendant removed the first plate and set down the next piece of cake, it looked more interesting. Chocolate cake and chocolate icing. But there was a sameness to it, even though she liked the icing better. It wasn't so lip-curlingly sweet.

The third slice of cake was yellow without a heavy layer of frosting. When she took a bite, it had a strong citrus flavor. Lemons! It was light and refreshing and a little sweet with a sparkly clear glaze. A lot more interesting than the other two slices, although she liked the chocolate icing.

Red cake surprised her. It was called Red Velvet on the tablet and that made her grin. It did look like red velvet fabric! The white icing made the red look so bright. She didn't know that cakes could be so brightly colored. When she took a bite, it surprised her again. It tasted like chocolate with vanilla icing. She'd expected a fruity flavor. She loved being surprised by this one.

The fifth piece of cake was dense and dark with a thick layer of icing that made her leery. She didn't want another mouthful of sickeningly sweet icing. She touched the icing with her finger and brought it to her mouth. But it wasn't so sweet. It had a rich flavor that was a little sweet. Her favorite icing so far. And the dense cake tasted like cinnamon and nutmeg. Almost like gingerbread. And the icing was perfect!

But the final piece of cake was pink! Like bubblegum. With white icing again.

She grinned, surprised by the champagne taste. She loved champagne, especially the bubbles. Like fireworks underwater! She loved the color and the taste of this one. It was her favorite. Just seeing it made her smile.

"All right, Talia," said Devin, standing a few feet from her in his tailored tweed jacket and brown trousers. "Are you ready to rank your cake flavors?"

His hair looked pressed into place, every hair perfect as he nodded at her and pointed at the tablet.

"Yes, Devin," she said, smiling for the camera. "I'm ready."

"Please record your preferences on the tablet and then what you think Jack chose as his favorites."

Nodding, Talia picked up the tablet. The instructions were at the top of the white screen that read, *drag the flavors on the right into the boxes on the left. In the order from best to least favorite. Press enter when finished.*

It took her several attempts to drag the cake names into the fields, but she got the hang of it quickly. She put them in order: pink champagne, red velvet, spice cake, lemon, chocolate, and vanilla. She tapped enter on the screen and the second question appeared. *Please drag Jack's preferences into the boxes in order from best to least favorite.*

She knew Jack liked chocolate more than vanilla and he didn't like the fruit flavors unless they were sweet versus sour. She put the lemon cake last even though it wasn't sour. Chocolate was his favorite though, so she put that one first. He didn't much care for vanilla either, so she put that one next to the last. She put the red velvet cake second, the champagne cake third, and then the spice cake.

Taking a deep breath, she tapped enter on the screen.

Next came the wine as the attendant brought over three bottles of wine wrapped in dark blue paper with shiny gold moons and stars. He poured a sip of red wine in the first really large wine goblet. It had a deep burgundy color. She sniffed it. It smelled like old wood and some sort of spices. The taste had a hint of fruit and a touch of flowers. It was okay.

The second wine was a deep garnet color. It smelled like cigars, almost like the woods. She tasted some fruit and an unpleasant spice. Pepper? It burned her tongue, but she swallowed it. It was awful. She tried not to make a face as she set it down. She didn't care for this one. At all.

The third glass of red wine had a ruby-garnet color and smelled a little like cherries. It had a charred wood aroma, like smelling a campfire. Like when they had bonfires on the beach at the Malibu estate. The nights had been chilly, but snuggled up to Jack made her warm and cozy. This one reminded her of those nights. This wine reminded her of Jack and it made her smile.

Turning to the tablet, she dragged the R3 wine label into the preference for her and for Jack.

Next came the white wines. The attendant poured a sip of white wine in her first glass. It was cold and tasted like apples and fragrant flowers. Like the gardenias that grew along Eolowen's pergolas in the Heavens. She liked the taste.

The second wine tasted more like icy lemons and a bit like smoldering wood. It was refreshing, like something to drink on a hot day, but she preferred the first wine.

The third glass of wine had an almost green taste to it. Like how new plants smelled before they bloomed. She didn't care for its almost unfinished taste.

She picked the first wine for both her and Jack.

Grinning, she watched the attendant pour a sip of champagne in the first crystal champagne flute. The bubbles danced through the golden liquid. She loved watching the bubbles flow through the chilled champagne. Closing her eyes, she drank the sip, tasting a little hint of lemons and an almost roasted nut flavor. Like the ones Jack liked in his coffee. What was it? Hazelnuts?

It reminded her of those first meet and greets on *The Cinderella Hour*. Watching Jack from a distance. Aching to speak to him. Hear his voice. Listen to his stories.

Back then, she was supposed to save him and she knew nothing about him. When she got to know him, kiss his lips, feel the beat of his heart against hers, she had to save him. She couldn't bear the world without him in it and she ached to be with him.

The second glass bubbled and foamed a moment as she brought it to her lips. Smelling that scent of bread fresh from the oven and juicy, sweet fruit. It reminded her of nights on the beach in Jack's arms. Waking up to his sultry green eyes and that tousled, sleepy-eyed sexiness when he first woke up and said good morning. She remembered the first time he made love to her as misty waves rolled onto the moonlit beach below their suite. That memory burned through her body and would stay with her forever.

She liked this champagne best. She chose it for both her and Jack on the tablet and set the computer on the table.

"Thank you, Talia," said Devin, motioning her toward the hallway. "Please wait outside with Jack while we convert our royal dining room into the royal bar."

With a smile, Talia rose from the wooden throne, her flats tapping across the marble floor. She opened the door and exited into the hallway.

Jack leaned against the white wall beside a large gold-framed portrait of angels in storm clouds. Not bad. Almost like the artist had seen angels flying before. But Jack was a much finer image and she wanted to kiss him.

"How'd you do?" Jack asked, stepping away from the wall.

She leaned up and kissed him hard on the lips, bringing a smile to his face.

"Not sure. It was hard to choose."

"Sure was," he said with a shake of his head.

She ran her fingers across the curve of his cheek. "But I'm glad the next part is us together."

He slid his arms around her. "Me too," he said. "Now, kiss me again and take my mind off our scores."

"Gladly," she said with a laugh, kissing his warm lips again.

"Please tell me your favorite cake was champagne," he whispered in an anxious voice, his green eyes sparking.

She grinned at him, nodding. "That was my favorite flavor."

He fist-pumped the air. "Yes! I got one right. Least favorite still vanilla?"

When she nodded, he matched her grin.

"Got two right. I'm happy."

He kissed her in a long, sensual kiss that made her whole body pulse with heat.

She ran her fingers through his blond hair. "Can't wait to see how you'll kiss me if you got three right."

He pressed his forehead against hers, taking hold of her hand as his hot caramel voice burned through her in a half-whisper. "Me, neither. See, there's this really cool suite upstairs with a four-poster bed and—"

The dining room door opened and Jennifer stepped out. Jack sighed.

"Jack, Talia—we're ready for you," she said, clipboard cradled under her left arm, phone gripped in her left hand. When Jennifer saw them in an embrace, she smiled. "Sorry to interrupt."

"Me, too," he whispered in Talia's ear, letting her go.

She leaned up and kissed him again as he took her hand and pulled her through the open dining room door.

The partition and two tables were gone, a round, dark wood dining table brought into the space. A rolling metal cart set beside the table with at least two dozen bottles of alcohol. On the table were several kinds of fruit juices, teas, coffees, and honey. She saw a small pitcher of cream, bottles of colored syrups, soft drinks, herbs—even candies like chocolate and caramel. And two huge bowls of fruit. Measuring cups and spoons set beside an ice bucket, two electric kettles, and two blenders. And a dozen crystal glasses in various sizes set beside the blenders and kettles.

Talia's eyes widened. She was overwhelmed. She had no idea what most of this stuff was and she didn't have time to learn about all of it. Was this part of the challenge timed?

"Talia, Jack, please come over to the table," said Devin, standing beside the cart as two of the cameras focused on him.

Talia tried her best to look at the table and not the cameras as she gripped Jack's hand tighter. He was smiling. That concerned look had already faded, replaced by his game face, as he called it. He made sure that no one knew what he was thinking when he was on camera. Only what he wanted the camera to see. He was calm and collected, looking excited by the challenge. She had no idea how he really felt about it and she wouldn't until they were back in the suite.

As soon as they reached the table, Jennifer and Steve walked up behind them and slipped white aprons over hers and Jack's heads, tying them at their waists.

"As my royal assistants have so graciously provided you with aprons, we're ready for the last part of the challenge," said Devin, glancing into the camera to the right. "Talia and Jack, here is your royal bar. The two of you must craft two cocktails together. The first cocktail is the embodiment of the first time you met and fell for each other. The second cocktail will represent the two of you as a married couple. Your cocktails will be scored based on presentation, originality, and taste by myself, the director, and two crew members. You have one hour. Any questions?"

It was timed! Her heart began to race.

Jack nodded and pointed at the table and the cart. "I'm assuming we can only use what's in front of us, correct?"

Devin nodded. "That's correct, Jack. You may use only what's on the cart and the table. Any other questions?"

Jack turned his gaze to her. "Any questions, babe?" he asked and let go of her hand.

She shook her head. She had no idea how to make cocktails. She just hoped that Jack did—and that he had some ideas.

"Please begin your challenge," said Devin.

Devin turned away from the table, gazing into the camera as he stepped back toward the wall.

"All right, my royal subjects. We will check in with Talia and Jack a little later as they discuss their ideas and create two drinks befitting Cinderella and her Prince Charming."

All smiles, Jack turned toward her, sliding his arms around her and pulling her close. "So, two drinks together. That sounds serious. We sound serious."

She brushed his blond bangs out of his eyes. "Almost like we want to get married or something." She held her hand up with his ring on it.

"Now until forever," he said, kissing her, a soft brush of his lips against hers.

"The first drink is supposed to be like the first time we met," she said.

His smile widened into a grin as he glanced at the table and then back at her. "I don't see any fireworks on the table," he said, shaking his head. "No flames either to set my heart on fire. Not even a good ol' fashioned California heatwave to scorch my soul. Because that's what you did to me the very first time I saw you standing on that Studio 22 sound stage, Talia." He kissed her again.

Even now, his kisses burned through her human soul, through her wing tips, and down to her toes. She returned his kiss until he was pulling in a ragged a breath.

"Damn," he said in a raspy whisper. "Still setting me alight after four seasons. Even when I'm 80, you'll still be lighting up my world, Talia—hope you know that."

She didn't think she could love him more than she did in this moment, like she was the only person in the room as he told millions of viewers how much he loved her. And that he intended to stay with her a lifetime and beyond.

"And you, Jack Casey," she said, leaning toward him, "will be turning mine upside down and teaching me how to fly for an eternity and beyond. Just like you did the first time your gaze met mine. And I melted right there on the spot."

Laughing, he pulled her into another sizzling kiss that made her weak in the knees.

"Think we can capture all of that in a cocktail?" she asked with a chuckle.

"Not sure," he said with a smirk and turned her toward the table. "Think I need to sample that one more time," he said and kissed her again. "For science."

She laid her hand against his cheek and leaned up, sipping his lips. "For science."

He gripped her hand again as he scanned the table and the cart beside it.

"It needs to be a hot drink," he said to her. "Because everything about being with you is heat and fire, Talia."

She smiled at him. She'd never felt so much heat before—except whenever Lucifer popped up somewhere.

"You were all hot summer nights, Jack Casey. Nights by the pool. Days in the wafting summer heat and the palace's fragrant, blooming flowers."

He brought her hand to his lips and kissed her fingers. "Melting with you by the pool." He sighed, a wistful smiling playing across his lips. "I lived for those stolen midnight moments."

Even now, his light green eyes sizzled. Only for her. And she loved him for that.

"We even have a song," she said to him. "I Melt with You."

He nodded. "We do. More heat."

He was right.

"Then we have to make a hot drink," she said with a nod and turned toward the table. "How do we start?"

"Let's each pick a couple of items that remind us of the first time we met," he offered.

"I like it," she said. "You start."

He moved over to the liquor cart and looked at all the bottles until a grin touched his face. He snatched a bottle from the cart and set it down in front of her, still grinning.

"What is it?" she asked, staring at the bottle.

"Fireball whisky," he said. "Because you're smokin' hot and have the most devastating arsonist's wit I've ever encountered. Burned me to the ground the first time I tried to flirt with you."

He started laughing when she shrugged at him. "I feel like I should apologize."

"Never! God, I laughed for days over the first thing you ever said to me."

"What'd I say?" she asked. She couldn't remember.

"That very first dinner," he began, staring into her eyes. "I sat across from you. And you picked up your sweating water glass, so I asked, *hot?* Because I meant that you were scorching hot." He laughed again. "You didn't miss a beat. You looked right across that table at me and said, *is that an observation or a compliment?*"

She couldn't help but smile at him. He was so attractive and that devastating smile of his burned right through her heart.

"And you threw it right back at me," she replied, reaching up and stroking his face. "Remember? You were so smooth. Didn't even hesitate. You asked me if that was a question or a come on."

He shook his head. "You still burned me right to the ground on that one, too. That's when you said, *welcome to the game, Mr. Casey.* I wanted to kiss you right then and there."

"I wish you had," she said. "You were the hottest thing I'd ever seen. The heat just radiated from you."

He gave her a quick kiss and patted the bottle of whisky. "Then our first ingredient has to be Fireball. Your turn."

She glanced around the table. And the first item that got her attention was the caramel. Every time she heard Jack speak, his voice was like hot caramel. Even now. She grabbed the plastic package of wrapped caramel cubes and set it beside the whisky bottle.

"Caramel," she said.

"Interesting," he replied, eyebrows lifting as he studied her a moment. "Why did you pick that?"

She slid her arms around his neck and planted a soft kiss on his lips. "Because when I heard you speak for the first time, your voice was like hot caramel," she said and let him go. "Even now, that's what I feel like when I hear your voice."

He smirked at her. "Really?"

She nodded. "Your turn."

Jack turned toward the bottles of juice that set on the table and grabbed a plastic, half gallon jug of cloudy amber liquid and set it down on the table in front of her.

"Then the best thing I can think of to go with Fireball and caramel is apple cider," he said. "Your turn."

She glanced over and saw the small pitcher of fresh squeezed orange juice. It was delicious this morning. She picked it up and set it beside the jug of apple cider.

"And a little fresh squeezed orange juice. It reminds me of California."

That sexy smirk rose on his lips as he nodded. "I like it." He grabbed a small glass jar with some brown tubes that he set beside the cider. "And some cinnamon sticks. Anything else?"

She shook her head. "Not from me. Anything you want to add?"

"Yep," he said and he reached toward those spices again. "Some cloves for the cider."

She had no idea what a clove was, but she trusted Jack's judgment.

"Okay," she said, studying him. "What do we do first?"

"Grab one of those electric kettles," he said.

The tall, stainless steel kettles matched the stainless-steel blenders. They were already plugged in, so she moved one as close as the cord allowed and opened the lid.

"Okay, we're limited by the kettle's size," he said, squinting at the front of the kettle. "Says 2 liters, so most of this jug of apple cider to start. Gotta leave room for the other stuff."

"I'll unwrap caramels," she said and grabbed a one-cup dry measuring cup. "How much?"

He shrugged. "Fill that cup with caramels to start and we'll add them until it's right."

As she unwrapped caramels and filled the cup, Jack grabbed a glass measuring cup and poured almost a cup of fresh squeezed orange juice into it. He poured about three-quarters of the apple cider into the kettle and added the orange juice. Then he tossed in three cinnamon sticks and a few of those strange looking brown things he called cloves. They smelled really strong and she was glad he hadn't thrown a bunch into the mix.

"Caramels," she said and slid the cup over to him as he turned on the kettle.

He shook a bunch of the caramels into the kettle and then opened the whisky bottle. He poured almost a cup of the whisky into the kettle and tossed in a few more caramels. Smiling, he closed the lid.

"Okay, we'll just let that heat all the way through and melt the caramels," he said and turned back to her. "And now, for our second drink. What we'll be like as a married couple."

She chuckled. "Can we just light this drink on fire and call it married?"

Jack broke into a fit of laughter as he stirred the melted caramel in the kettle. "Are you insinuating that I'm going to be trouble once we're married?"

Nodding, she slid her arms around his waist and pulled him close. "Going to be? You're already trouble, mister. Lots of it! And that's what I love about you."

"That I'm trouble?" he said with a snicker and kissed her lips.

"No," she replied with a smile. "I didn't think I could love you more than I did when you proposed to me during the finale of The Prince Charming Hour. But when you—"

She halted a moment. She had to phrase some of this carefully. No one knew about the sacrifices that Jack had made for her. Or how he hadn't quit trying to rescue her from Lucifer.

"When I what?" he asked with a smirk.

"When you've made so many sacrifices to be with me," she said. "Putting your career on hold. Saying you'll go anywhere to stay with me. Hell or Heaven. I fell in love with you all over again. And you know what?"

"What?" he asked in a quiet voice, his eyes glassy.

He knew exactly what she meant—him sacrificing himself to keep her safe. He spent months in Hell being tortured by Lucifer and his demons to protect her. And then he locked himself into the Garden with Lucifer...to keep her safe. She had to watch him take his last breath which nearly broke her, but through their bond and some rare angel talents, she brought him back again. And he almost destroyed himself again with an overload of seraphim powers while fighting Lucifer. To save Heaven—and her.

"I will never stop falling in love with you, Jack Casey," she said, holding his hands. "Ever."

He took her in his arms and kissed her in a sizzling, frantic kiss that almost made her dizzy.

"When I'm with you, Talia, I'm home. Doesn't matter where we are. You're a warm hearth on a cold night. A December bonfire on a chilly Pacific Ocean beach. Fourth of July fireworks on the Vegas strip. And I'll never feel cold and alone again as long as I'm with you."

She felt her eyes turn misty as she pulled him close, wrapping him tightly in her arms.

"I love you, Jack Casey," she said, kissing him.

He let her go. "I love you, too, Talia." He glanced back at the table and the booze cart. "Okay, let's do the same thing as the first drink. Pick an item and say why you chose it. Go!"

He turned to the table and rifled through the candies, the fruit juices, and then stopped, grabbing a box of tea. She frowned. Tea?

Her eyes were drawn to the small ripe peaches. He was eternal summer to her. Golden sunlight, green grass, crisp turquoise skies, fluffy white clouds, and warm breezes. And the sweet, refreshing smell of these ripe peaches reminded her of him.

She set the two white-fleshed peaches on the table in front of him as he set down the box of tea bags. She read the label. Earl Grey Tea.

"Why the tea?" she asked.

"Because when I think of Earl Grey tea, I imagine sitting under a soft wool blanket beside a roaring fire, sipping hot tea with honey. With you. Growing old together. Snuggling under that soft wool blanket, basking in the warm firelight and our own glow, drinking hot tea and sipping your lips."

Thinking of him as old made her sad. Once he crossed over, he'd go to the part of Heaven where she couldn't follow him. That would destroy her. She didn't ever want to lose him. He meant everything to her. She gripped his hands.

"And why the peaches?" he asked, pointing to the fruit beside the box of tea.

She grinned, her eyes still misty. "Because you're all summer, Jack. Bright blue skies, warm sunshine, blooming gardenias, and green grass. Like a grand white marble hall. Being with you is like an eternal summer."

His pale green eyes lit with recognition and she knew he was picturing Eolowen. But he was also remembering their time at Cinderella's palace, where they filmed the first season of this show as he kissed her again.

"Okay," he said, "Let's check on our first drink."

He reached for the spoon and stirred the concoction in the kettle again. "Caramel's all melted now. It's on low, so we'll let it simmer a bit. Next ingredient. Go!"

Her gaze immediately went to the bear-shaped plastic bottle of honey. She grabbed it and set it beside the peaches. He was so sweet and romantic. And she loved him for daring to show that vulnerable part of himself to her. And the world.

Jack scanned the bottles of liquor and grabbed one. He set down a bottle of wine. She glanced at it. It read Celestial Vineyards, Angelsong Pinot Grigio.

"Why did you choose that wine?" she asked.

"Because you're my angel and I know that a Sonoma white wine is a bottled California summer. And that it'll remind you of marble white halls and pergolas. To quote someone we both know, Parrish blue skies and fluffy Constable clouds."

She couldn't help but grin. He understood that she got homesick for Heaven sometimes, especially Eolowen. And those clouds and skies, as only Archangel Azrael could describe them.

Jack squinted at the honey. "You chose honey. Why?"

"Because beneath that game face of yours is the sweetest and most romantic man I've ever met. And I think he'll grow sweeter and more romantic as time goes by."

He laughed and bowed his head, his cheeks a little flushed. Finally, he lifted his head, looking through that thick fringe of eyelashes with those scorching light green eyes.

"I guess we're making a sort of wine and tea cooler then," he said. "Okay, why don't you cut up those peaches while I grab a couple of those tea bags and fill this other kettle with water. Gotta make some tea first."

"I'll peel and slice the peaches," said Talia.

He poured water from a pitcher into the kettle and turned it on high as she grabbed a small wooden cutting board beside the bowls of fruit. She picked up a small paring knife and began peeling the skin from the peaches. Then she cut them into slices.

In a few minutes, the kettle water was boiling, so Jack turned off the kettle, tossed the two tea bags into the water, and closed the lid. He opened the other kettle with their first drink and stirred it with a spoon again. Then turned the kettle's dial to warm.

Next, he grabbed a tall, empty pitcher and set it in front of him.

"Twenty-three minutes left," Devin announced from across the room.

Jack's head snapped up. He glanced over at her and smiled as he grabbed a can of peach nectar and opened it.

"Let's add the peach nectar, too," he said.

She nodded her agreement as she set the cutting board aside and wiped her hands on the white apron she wore.

Jack poured a cup of peach nectar into the pitcher. Next, he opened the bottle of wine with an opener and pulled out the cork with a pop. He poured the entire bottle into the pitcher and stirred the two liquids together. Then he picked up the bottle of honey and squeezed about a quarter cup of honey into the liquid, stirring it with a spoon.

"Babe, toss in those peach slices, will you, please?" he asked.

She loved cooking with him in that beach house kitchen for *The Ever After Hour*. He'd been so excited and patient—so sexy. Like right now. Would he be like this once they were married? She knew he would. One thing about Jack Casey, he'd never been anyone but himself on this reality television show. That's why he'd been such a big ratings' draw, according to Herb, the director.

Taking another spoon, Talia held the cutting board up to the pitcher and pushed the peach slices into the wine and peach nectar. He tasted the mixture in a small glass and then handed it to her.

"More honey?" he asked.

She sipped the wine and peaches. It definitely needed some more honey. "Whatever you added before, add that much again."

"On it," he said and grabbed the honey.

He squeezed in more, stirring. He filled the glass again with another sip or two and tasted it. "Better?" he asked, handing it to her.

She took another sip. "Much better."

He opened the kettle with tea and left the lid up for it to continue cooling. With a smirk, he poured a couple sips of the warm liquid from their first drink concoction into another glass.

"Here goes nothing," he said and tipped it to his lips.

He grabbed the bottle of Fireball whisky and poured another couple of shots in it, stirred it, and poured another sip or two into the glass. And smiled.

"That's definitely you and me, babe," he said and handed her the glass.

She drank the warm liquid. It tasted like that hot June day when she saw Jack Casey for the first time. When she'd first looked into his eyes. She sighed. And felt the burn of attraction—from her flushed cheeks to her toes. A little heat from the cinnamon whisky and the warm, caramely apple cider with its hint of oranges. Like the first time she'd heard his warm, smooth voice—talking only to her. It was perfect! It reminded her so much of that day at the studio.

"It's perfect, Jack!" she cried, setting down the glass, and threw her arms around his neck, hugging him. "It's us."

He slid his arms around her, holding her tight a moment or two and then he let her go.

"What do we call it?" she asked.

"A Sizzling Glass Slipper," he said with a wry smile.

"Done! Okay, what's next?" she asked, stepping back.

His eyes widened a little. "Now, we wait for that tea to cool a bit before pouring it into the wine and peaches. Check to see if we need more honey after the tea's added. Then we toss in the ice and we're done."

"Fifteen minutes left," said Devin to them from across the room.

They waited about five minutes or so. Jack picked up the kettle with the tea and poured a cup of tea into the pitcher. He stirred it all together and had her taste it.

"A little more tea," she said and he filled a measuring cup and poured it into the mixture.

She tasted it again. "I like it," she said.

He tasted the mixture, nodding and then added a little more honey. When she tasted it again, she smiled and gave him a thumb's up.

"We need a name for this one," he said.

"Six minutes, Talia and Jack," Devin called out.

"How about a Now Until Forever?" she offered.

"Perfect name for our let's get married wine cooler," he said. "You pour the Now Until Forever's into four of those crystal glasses. Leave room for ice. I'll grab four more glasses and fill them with our *Sizzling Glass Slipper* drinks."

She laughed and slid glasses over to him. "Here, lover," she said.

He picked up the kettle with the warm caramel cider and whisky drink and began filling four half-height glasses. She grabbed four tall glasses and filled them two-thirds of the way with the wine and tea cooler. He unwrapped four caramels and plopped one into each glass as she took a measuring cup and scooped ice into all four glasses. Then she saw a package of honey straws in a glass beside the juices. She plopped one into each glass.

"That's perfect, Talia!" Jack cried, pointing at the honey straws.

"Two minutes," said Devin.

Together, they lined up the four glasses at the opposite end of the table from all the mixes and fruits.

"Time!"

Jack slid his arms around Talia and hugged her. "We didn't do too badly," he said as two attendants entered the room.

One was the grey-haired man that had supervised her cake and wine challenge. The other one was a woman with bobbed almost burgundy hair and light blue eyes. She was dressed in black pants, a white tuxedo shirt, and a black bowtie. She wore white gloves as she picked up four of the glasses and set them on a silver tray like the grey-haired man.

Talia felt Jack stiffen, but his expression didn't change. Then she realized that the other attendant was Jack's mother. She carried the drinks over to Devin who motioned for her to set them down on the sideboard. The male attendant set down glasses on the sideboard to Devin's right.

"Our judges, made up of myself, the director, and two crew members will now judge your two drinks, Jack and Talia," Devin announced, turning toward one of the cameras. He turned back toward them again. "You will both find out how you did on the entire challenge Friday night." He turned toward the main camera this time. "During The Royal Wedding Hour's first elimination round, live on Le Château des Angés' candlelit terrace. Best of luck to both of you."

"And...cut! Print that." Herb rose from his chair and moved toward the drinks setting on the sideboard beside Devin. "Talia and Jack! That. Was. Fabulous! Your fans are going to love this episode. Good luck with the drinks."

Devin nodded as Jennifer and Steve moved toward the drink trays from the back of the dining room.

"Great job, you two," said Devin. "See you both in interviews tomorrow."

"Thanks," said Jack, peeling off his apron.

He glared at his mother as she stood beside the sideboard. He threw the apron down on the table and stormed out of the room.

"Jack, wait!" Talia called.

The door to the dining room slammed shut, the sound of his footsteps echoing in the hallway outside the room.

Talia hurried to remove her apron. She set it on the table, but Jack's mother touched her arm.

"Talia, that was a beautiful scene with you and Jack," she said, smiling. "I thoroughly enjoyed watching the two of you together. I see what enchants him about you. You're good for him."

She smiled at the woman, her urge to smite fading, but she kept her guard up just in case.

"I just wish I could get him to speak calmly with me," said Jack's mother. "Give me another chance. I'd like to apologize, explain to him about his father—and why I did what I did. He deserves to know those things and so do his sisters."

Talia reached out and touched the woman's shoulder, white tuxedo shirt pressed and wrinkle free.

"I hope you get that chance, Ms. Westwood," she replied. "He deserves to know the truth—and he deserves to know that you love him."

Her eyes widened. "Of course, I love him! He's my son."

"He thinks you only loved his Hollywood fame. You need to make sure he knows that you love him for who he is, not how much he earns—or how famous he is or was."

She nodded. "You're right, Talia. I'll try to talk to him later."

"I wish you luck," said Talia as she hurried out the doors.

That woman needed all the luck in the world. Jack never wanted to speak to her again. And she wasn't sure how Jack's mother was going to prove to him that she loved him regardless of how famous he was when she'd stopped speaking to him after he lost that fame. That woman had a big job ahead to convince him otherwise.

And Talia wasn't sure she'd accomplish it.

19

Furious, Jack slammed through the dining room's double doors and pounded down the hallway. After the horrible fight he and his mother had in that very room, the studio makes her a damned attendant on the show! Without even telling him she was going to step onto the set while he was on camera.

He stomped up the stairs, his footsteps echoing through the entryway's gallery to the third floor, carrying in layers as he reached the second floor. He thumped open the suite's door and slammed it behind him, wanting to bust up something. But not in this place. Anything in this chateau would earn him a reputation and cost him a fortune. And he couldn't afford either one.

"What's up, Jack?" Muriel asked as he grumbled to himself and slammed open one of the armoires.

He kicked off his dress shoes. "My mother's now an attendant on the show." He grabbed a pair of jeans and a grey Henley out of the armoire and slammed the door closed.

"What?" Muriel shouted, moving over to him. "I thought you made it clear that you didn't want her on the show."

"So did I," he snapped, gritting his teeth as he slid his feet into his blue Vans slip-ons. "Of course, I get to learn this fact when she just nonchalantly steps onto the set toward the end of the challenge. No advanced warning. Not even a whisper. They just let me discover the fact when she showed up with a tray, delivering our drinks to Devin for judging."

He stormed into the bathroom and snaked off his grey dress pants, dropping them back onto the hanger he'd left in the bathroom. He hung the hanger on the doorknob, kicked off his Vans, and slid on his jeans over his blue boxer briefs. He unbuttoned the dress shirt he'd been wearing and draped it over the vanity's chair, pulling on the grey Henley. He stepped into his Vans again and rushed out of the bathroom.

He hurried past Muriel, but she stopped him, a hand on his arm.

"Where you headed?" she asked, eyeing him with concern.

"Out to the gardens, so I can curse and shout and hope that Abaddon hears me. I'd love a fight right now."

She shook her head and grabbed him by the shoulders. "No way, Jack. Remember what happened the last time?" she asked.

"Yeah, I kicked his ass. Hard." He stared at her a moment. "And I really, really want him to show up again, so I can burn something down. And feel good about doing it instead of setting the valley below the vineyards on fire. Abaddon has an ass-kicking coming to him if he's still around the vineyard. So, yes, Muriel—I'm definitely up to no good and I am definitely looking for all the trouble I can handle. And then some."

"Kesien!" Muriel called. "Need some help here."

"I heard all of it," said Kesien, stepping away from the window to stand beside Jack. "Jack, you can't go out there and just shout out for Abaddon to return and challenge you. For all you know, he's been back to talk to Lucifer and they've already schemed up something horrible and nasty to do to you. Besides kill you and enslave your soul for eternity."

Jack sighed and leaned against the wall. He hadn't forgotten the months he'd spent in Hell. Being tortured. Pursued by demons and people like Lare Dumont and Tyler Hughes. He remembered the cage fights with those horrible demons and then with Rachel who'd wanted him dead every bit as much as those demons had. And he remembered all the mind games that Lucifer had inflicted on him.

Giving him food. And cold water. Placing that succubus near him. And all the earth-like buildings that made him almost forget where he was. Then putting Berith in a position to be kind to him in the midst of all the hate and torture. And that horrible, unending ache of being away from Talia, knowing he'd never see her again.

How he'd burned for her every single day as he felt the pain of Lucifer's lash or the sudden attacks by his demons. That he hadn't seen coming. And Hell's constant, blistering heat. It had all been a terrible nightmare. That he didn't want to repeat again. Ever.

"You're right," he said with a sigh and bowed his head, toeing the marble tiles with his Vans. "Last thing I want to do is end up in Hell again. I wouldn't escape from there a second time."

Muriel walked over and rubbed his shoulder. "If you ended up in Hell again, Talia would absolutely wreck that place until she got you out." She laughed. "That I can guarantee you, Jack. And then she'd wreck you for getting yourself back down there again."

She was right. Talia would destroy everything in her path to get to him. And that included him once she got him out again. He smirked at the thought of seeing her with eyes glowing gold as she brought down the wrath of the Heavens on Hell and Lucifer—and him.

"Good point," he said, glancing up at Muriel. "I'd be more afraid of her than Lucifer."

Kesien nodded. "A wise choice, Jack."

"I can't imagine how hard it is to deal with your mother like this, Jack," said Muriel, patting him on the shoulder. "But we're ready and willing to smite her for you. Just ask."

He laughed. "I'm afraid that I'm going to accidentally smite her with these seraphim powers."

Kesien broke into a loud laugh. "Hadn't even considered that, but you're right. It's possible, so be careful."

"That's why I walked out just now," he said, rubbing his neck. "If I'd stayed, I might have done something I regretted."

"How'd you and Talia do on the first competition?" Muriel asked.

"I just hope it was enough for us to stay around to the next challenge," he said. "I really want to give Talia the Cinderella fairytale wedding she deserves."

She'd earned it, putting up with him all these months.

"Let's hope the seraph puts a good word in for you two with the Maker," said Muriel.

He sighed. "Enough that we can stay together. I'd hate to win that fairytale wedding and then…"

His throat tightened, his voice cutting out. He couldn't even say it. Just the thought of losing her made him shake all over.

Muriel patted his shoulder and then moved away from him, back to her post at the window. "It's okay, Jack. We're all hoping that High House inserts itself into this one. And makes it right. You and Talia have been through enough. You've earned the right to stay together."

He nodded, bowing his head again. His heart hurt at even the thought of Talia returning to Heaven. Without him. Forever. He couldn't even say it. It was just too painful.

"Hang in there, Jack," said Kesien, patting his right shoulder.

Kesien fluttered across the room, back in front of the windows to keep watch.

The door to the suite banged open and then slammed shut, Talia storming into the room.

"Muriel! Kesien!" she shouted, rushing to Muriel. "Have you seen Jack? I—"

Muriel's mouth pressed into a crooked line as she pointed behind Talia.

Talia whirled around, looking relieved when she saw him leaning against the wall, hands stuffed into his jeans' front pockets.

"Jack!"

"What's up, babe?" he asked, his gaze flicking from Muriel to Talia.

Talia visibly relaxed, taking a deep breath as she stepped toward him and threw her arms around his neck.

"I was so afraid you'd gone out alone and become Abaddon's target," she said in a worried voice.

"Wanted to start another fight with the big dude, but Muriel and Kesien talked me out of it."

Talia's eyes got wide and she exchanged a glance with Muriel who just shook her head. She let him go, crossing her arms and glaring at him.

"Jack Casey, you just get that thought out of your head right now. Do you hear me?"

He just shrugged. He wasn't making any promises.

"Jack! I mean it!"

He stared into her intense grey eyes that flickered with gold light, the glow of her halo brightening. Her wings flexed at her shoulders as she let them unfurl after being flat against her back all day. Like his. Hidden from the rest of humanity. He felt his every time he shifted his weight under the scrutiny of the set lights and the numerous lighting and sound checks.

"I'm going to have to fight him again sometime, Talia," he replied. "And you know it. Will be easier than dealing with my mother, believe me."

"She wants to make amends, Jack."

"Amends?" He snickered. "Yeah, I could tell that from the first time I talked to her. It had been years since we last spoke and she still insisted everything was all my fault."

Talia had no idea how difficult his mother had been to please even as a kid. And how cold and callus she'd been when Dad died. He'd just graduated from high school, wasn't even eighteen yet. She didn't even come back from California for the funeral. Or check to make sure he had food or a place to stay. Even though he was six weeks away from turning eighteen, it was still his problem. His two oldest sisters made sure he was okay. Until eventually, his mother convinced them he was poison.

"Did you hear me, Jack?" Talia asked in a quiet voice. "She wants you to know the truth."

He scowled, his lip curling. "The truth about what?" He poked his chest with his thumb. "Her truth or the whole truth? Believe me, Talia, there's a huge difference between those two things."

She caressed his cheek. "She told me that she liked our scene together. She said that she sees why you're enchanted by me. And that I'm good for you."

What? She wasn't still pushing Rachel Daniels?

"First thing we've ever agreed on," he said, the edge in his voice disappearing.

"See?" Talia cried, kissing his lips. "There's some middle ground here. She just wants the opportunity to apologize to you."

"Apologize? She's never—"

She laid her hand over his mouth. "She said it in front of the entire crew, Jack. She meant it. I'm an angel, remember? I can sense lies in humans. She wasn't lying."

Talia slid her hand away from his mouth, kissing it gently again.

"Can you sense when someone's told themselves so many lies that they believe them?"

She gave him a deep, emphatic nod. "Yes, Jack. And she wanted to apologize to you. To sit down and tell you things she should have told you a long time ago."

He shook his head. He wasn't letting that woman back into his life to carve a new path of destruction through it. Like Rachel. He wanted no part of either of them.

"Not happening," he said, crossing his arms as he leaned back against the wall again. "Every time I've given her another chance, it's become a sneak attack on my life. She's the one that cut me out of her life. I called her on her birthdays, Christmas, and Mother's Day when that's all I could afford. Later, I sent her gifts or showed up with them. I drove up to Santa Rosa for all the family holidays—until she uninvited me. It was always me making the effort, Talia. I got tired. Because it was never enough."

She ran her hands up and down his arms. "Promise me that you'll listen? If she talks softly?"

"Talia, I'm tired of listening to her berate me and tell me I don't measure up," he said. "I think I preferred her when she was ignoring me."

"Promise to listen if she's not trying to hurt you," said Talia. "That's all I'm asking, Jack."

He sighed and ran a hand through his hair. "I'll think about it."

"Why don't we go for a swim?" she asked, taking his hand.

A swim? How would he swim with wings? Talia had hidden his with her angel powers, but just because others couldn't see them didn't mean they weren't still there.

"How will I swim with wings?"

She let out a breath. "That's true. You'd have to learn to swim with them—like I did. Angels of death have to train for all kinds of human situations." She chuckled. "Including water landings. But you might look a little strange to the other couples—even though they can't see the wings."

"A little?" He laughed. "More like they'd wonder if I'd been inhaling a few eight balls again."

"We could just sit by the pool," she said, kissing his fingers.

He thought back to those times during the first season of the show, when she'd sneak outside and meet him at midnight beside the pool. In that red string bikini that made his blood boil.

"Still have that red bikini?" he asked, hopeful.

She gave him a sad look. "Sorry."

Muriel stepped between them, holding up a skimpy red bikini. "This one?"

He just nodded. *Yep, that was the one.*

"Muriel, where'd you get that?" Talia asked, wide-eyed.

"It was still in the suitcase when I helped you pack up for the beach house. When the guard grabbed everything from Jack's Explorer for this trip, it was still in the luggage."

Jack grinned at Talia as he slid the red bikini out of Muriel's hands and handed it to Talia.

"I'd love to sit by the pool if you wear this bikini," he said, sliding an arm around her waist and pulling her close.

"Do I get to admire you in a skimpy swimsuit, too?" she asked, returning his grin.

He chuckled. "All I've got is a standard, boring swimsuit, babe," he said. "In blue this time."

"How about this one?" Kesien asked, handing a suit to Talia who began to giggle.

Talia never giggled. That made him nervous.

Kesien broke up laughing as Talia held up one of those thong swimsuits that looked like a marble bag. In red.

"Forget it!" he shouted, waving her off. "I'm not wearing a marble bag thong!"

She tried to keep a straight face. "Why is it okay for me to wear a skimpy bikini and not okay for you to wear the male version of it?"

"Because you can burn eyes out of their sockets with that red bikini, Talia," he said. "If I put on that marble bag, I'd be all over the tabloids by nightfall. And not in a good way. Jack Casey had a break from reality today when he donned a bodybuilder's swimsuit and claimed he was on a callback for a new comedy film."

"Nobody would laugh at you if you wore this," she said to him, dangling the red swimsuit in front of him.

"That's not a swimsuit, Talia," he said with a groan and snatched it out of her hand. "It's a slingshot and I'm not wearing it."

She stepped back from him. "Fine," she said. "I'll go find my black one-piece swimsuit."

"Works for me," he said. "You'd burn my eyes out of their sockets if you wore a paper sack. You know that, don't you? This way, I don't have to share you in that red bikini with anybody else."

She turned around and kissed him hard on the lips. "You say the sweetest things, Jack." She held up the marble bag again. "Maybe you'll model this for me later?" She pointed toward the four-poster bed and nodded her head toward the three angels of death in the room. "In here? When they're on patrol?"

"I'll think about it," he said and crossed his arms.

"Will my wearing my red bikini change your mind?" she asked, dangling the tiny bikini in front of him.

"Changed," he said.

She laughed, motioning for him.

He glanced over his shoulder at Muriel and Kesien. "Squad, take a few trips around the block, will ya?"

"A few trips?" Kesien asked, raising an eyebrow.

He nodded and tossed the red slingshot over his left shoulder. "Like fifty," he said and moved toward Talia, grinning. "And then start over."

"Come on, Kesien," said Muriel with a sigh. "Let's patrol the rooftops."

They lifted into the air and blinked through the wards, up to the roof as Jack took Talia in his arms.

"Alone at last," she said, hands sliding under his grey Henley.

"I thought they'd never leave," he said and slow-walked her over to the four-poster bed.

20

TALIA HURRIED JACK INTO HIS SHINY BLACK DRESS SUIT, THE SUN already low on the horizon. It would fall behind the tree line by seven o'clock. Already, the three arched windows along their west-facing suite glowed with the golden hour. Jack's favorite time of the day.

But it was Friday.

In a little over an hour, the first live elimination show would begin. They needed to be on the patio in five minutes.

Yesterday, she and Jack spent most of the day doing interviews for the show, passing each other in the hallways as they did a bunch of individual interviews. Finally, they did couple's interviews together, hand in hand, talking about the three parts of their challenge.

When they did their after-challenge couple's interview, Jack was coy about how they'd performed, that game face firmly in place. And afterward, when she'd tried to ask him how he thought they'd done, he avoided answering.

Whenever Jack avoided a question, that meant trouble. He didn't think they'd done well. She felt it. Saw it in his demeanor.

The closer they got to the first elimination, the more nervous Jack became, pacing the suite, looking visibly distracted, deep in thought. She knew how much he wanted to give her this fairytale wedding, but as long as she was with him—and got to stay with him—she had her fairytale ending.

Didn't he know that?

But he really wanted to do this for her. Said she'd earned this storybook wedding. It would be fun and it would make her feel like Cinderella at the ball again. Like a princess. But all she really wanted was Jack. As long as he loved her, she had everything she'd ever wanted. Including a human soul that allowed her to experience humanity and all it offered like he experienced it, allowing her to share it with him.

He stood there in front of the arched windows lit with golden sunlight, wearing that slim-fitting, shiny black suit that hugged his beautiful, leanly muscled body in all the right places. And he just took her breath away. He wore a white silk T-shirt under his jacket and no socks with his black loafers. He looked stunning, that blond hair so light against his pale green eyes. Hypnotic. Scorching her down to her wing tips whenever he fixed her with his encompassing gaze.

She glanced at Jack's ring still on her left ring finger, the silver band that belonged to his dad. She hadn't taken it off since he'd given it to her during the finale of *The Prince Charming Hour*. Tonight, they would find out if they scored well-enough to stay for another round of challenges.

To plan another phase of their wedding.

But she hadn't seen Jack brood like this since he had to erase her memories to break Lucifer's control over her. Was it still about his mother's presence on the show? Or Abaddon? Or something else that he hadn't shared with her? He'd been distant since they'd arrived—about some of these intensely personal things bouncing around inside his head.

He was visibly worried about something that he'd chosen not to share with her yet. She had no choice but to keep a close eye on him. And wait it out.

She pulled on a short, strapless red dress and black heels, admiring Jack again as he paced in front of the window, hands in his pants pockets. She brushed her long, raven-haired locks into waves that hung past her shoulders.

"I'm ready," she said and stepped toward the window where Jack's shoes ticked against the marble tiles.

He stopped and turned, whistling sharply, a smile touching his lips. "Babe, you're a knockout in that dress!"

"Thanks," she said, smiling.

He moved over to her, taking her in his arms. His deep, anxious kiss left her breathless.

"You make my blood boil in that dress," he said in a husky whisper against her ear, his hot caramel voice sending shivers through her.

"And you make me want to throw you on that bed and slowly undress you, Jack Casey," she said, gripping his jacket lapels and pulling him close again.

He exaggerated a cough. "Call in sick?"

She shook her head, leaning up and kissing his warm lips. "Sorry, lover. We have to show up."

"We'll talk about your wish list later then," he said with a smirk and brushed a lock of black hair out of her eyes. "Ready to see if we'll be back next week?"

"I'm ready," she said with a nod and reached out, taking hold of his hand.

He motioned toward the door with a nod. "Let's head for the terrace. There's some candles and moonlight I'd like to share with you."

She loved it when he got romantic. "Lead the way," she said in a soft voice. "And I'll follow you anywhere."

He turned around, a funny look in his eyes. He looked...vulnerable.

"Even if it's in Hell?" he asked in a quiet voice. "If Abaddon gets hold of me and drags me back there?"

There was her answer—the reason he'd been brooding.

She felt the fear and rage well inside her. "If Abaddon drags you back to Hell, I will storm those gates so fast his horns will spin into orbit. And then I'll take Hell—and Lucifer—apart, demon by demon, until I find you, Jack Casey. I'll never let anything separate us again. Not Hell and not Heaven."

That hot, sexy smirk lifted the corners of his mouth. "I love you with all my heart, Talia," he said in a shaky voice, leaning down slowly and planting a scorching hot kiss against her lips. "To my last breath."

She shook her head and grabbed his face in her hands. "Never again, Jack Casey. I love you from my first breath to eternity. From the first time my heart beat. From now until forever."

"Now until forever," he whispered. "That has a nice ring to it." His mouth covered hers again.

Nodding, she smashed her lips hard against his hot mouth, wanting to drag him back to that four-poster bed and make love to him. But they had a live show to do. She reached up and brushed blond bangs out of his smoldering eyes.

"We have to go, lover," she said, tugging on his hand.

He sighed, nodding, and let her pull him out the suite door, their shoes clacking against the marble. They trotted down the steps, across the landing, and down the last flight into the candlelit entryway. The golden hour's light filled the lofty space as the sun fled from the sky, flicker of set lights and candles so warm against the huge cobalt urns brimming with roses, lilies, and lavender.

The lilies' bold fragrance, softened by roses, filled the foyer, a hint of clean-smelling lavender as they turned right and hurried past gold framed, masterful paintings of angels. Some contemporary and some great masters like Titian and Raphael.

They followed the hallway past the dining room with its burgundy chairs as the corridor made a right turn. Toward the back of the house. Through a blue and yellow sitting room with blue velvet couches and antiqued ivory-painted furniture in a French provincial style.

Ahead, flameless candles flickered through black French doors with frosted glass panes. The dull murmur of voices hung in the chateau's calm silence as they drew closer to the double doors.

Jack hurried ahead and opened the door for her, bowing as she stepped outside onto the concrete patio with its rounded edge framed by columns. Cobalt urns filled with more roses and lavender dotted the patio that overlooked the symmetrical, box-hedged formal garden squares on either side. The setting sun illuminated the distant vineyards, casting long, hard-edged shadows across the velvety green grass surrounding the chateau. The air was cool and smelled like fresh-mown grass and those fragrant lilies in the urns.

"Talia and Jack," Steve called, carrying several white sheets of paper in his right hand, wireless mic pack attached to the back waistband of his jeans. "Find your purple mark on the patio and I'll take you through sound and light checks."

Steve wore gold wire-framed glasses, his hair in a brown ponytail. He wore a jean shirt over a grey *Royal Wedding Hour* T-shirt, jeans, and white leather tennis shoes.

"Thanks, Steve," said Jack as he reached out for her hand.

Talia smiled and gripped his hand, following Jack across the patio where Devin stood between two cobalt urns, wireless mic already in place. Devin wore a traditional black tailcoat, a royal purple bowtie, and a white tuxedo shirt. His hair was pomaded into place like it had been epoxied and he mumbled to himself as he stared at a stack of white index cards in his hands.

Jack pointed at the purple square made from masking tape—their blocking mark for this scene.

Behind them, Armand and Izzy stepped onto the patio. Izzy's warm coppery hair was in a loose bun and she wore a burnt orange long dress that hugged her body. Armand wore a Navy blue suit and white shirt, no tie. Armand patted Jack on the shoulder as he moved past him, finding the yellow triangle that was his and Izzy's mark.

"Jack," said Armand, smiling at him. "How are you tonight?"

"Good, Gianni," he said with a nod. "Nice suit. Brioni?"

"Yes, very good eye," said Armand, holding open the lapels.

"I still have a few left in my closet back in my apartment," he said with a shrug. "Maybe now I can auction them off for a few bucks?"

She watched Armand's eyes widen. "Auction them off?" he asked, looking surprised. "Why?"

Jack smiled and pulled Talia close. "Gonna need every last cent to fund a new place for the two of us after we're married."

Armand seemed to relax a little. "I'm sure your salary for this show will cover a better mansion than what you had before."

"Mansion? Are you kidding me?" Jack chuckled. "Dude, those days are way over. I'm looking at a thirty-year mortgage no matter what we get."

This time, Armand laughed. "That's funny, Jack."

Jack's eyebrows pressed into a frown. "What's funny?"

"You," he said with a chuckle. "A mortgage."

"Don't think I can get one?" he asked, looking scared.

Armand's smile widened into a grin. "Oh, Jack—you really have no idea how big of a comeback you've made, do you?"

He shook his head. "Comeback? I know Talia and I have some fans from this show, but—"

Armand pointed at Jack with his thumb and nudged Izzy. "Izzy, someone hasn't been reading Variety lately."

Izzy gave him a strange look. "What are you talking about, hon?" she asked, glancing from him to Jack and back again.

"Jack thinks he and Talia have *some fans* from the show," he repeated, grinning at her.

"Some fans?" Izzy's mouth fell open. "Jack, are you kidding me?"

He just shrugged. "I'm really confused."

Izzy was smiling now. "Jack! The Royal Wedding Hour premiered last night. It was the number one show in the country. Over fifty million viewers are expected to watch tonight's live show. And you're one of the biggest reasons that they're watching, Jack. You and Talia."

"Tell him the rest," said Armand, patting Jack on the shoulder again.

"Evan Bellows put an ad in Variety, Jack," Izzy continued. "An open letter addressed to you. He's begging you to contact him. He wants you back starring on SanFran Confidential, Jack. He says money's no object—just call him."

Jack's mouth fell open. "What?"

"And you want to take out a mortgage," Armand said, elbowing

Jack's side. "You are back on top again, my friend. You can write your own ticket this time."

A funny look touched Jack's face. A wistful, faraway look in his eyes, that smile fading away.

"How long you think that'll last this time, Gianni? A year? Two years? When this season is done, they'll all forget they know me again."

Armand shook his head. "Jack, they want you and Talia to do your own reality television show. That's the fans asking. Herb said he was in talks with the network and other interested parties. I'm sure you've gotten a bazillion calls already on your cell phone about it."

No wonder he didn't know anything about these offers and things. With his phone lost in Hell. She needed to remind him again to replace that phone right away and not just talk about it.

"Armand," said Talia to the tall, handsome daytime soap star. "Jack's cell phone got broken during The Ever After Hour and he hasn't had time to get it replaced yet."

"See, Jack!" Armand replied, holding out his arms. "Maybe you need to make time to replace that phone and call your agent?"

Jack glanced over at her, nodding. "Yeah. Maybe."

"Maybe?" Armand shook his head, arms still out. "Jack, you're killing me here! Apparently, all of Hollywood's been trying to get hold of you for a month or two. Get a new phone and then take your old life back when it's being offered to you. You went through hell to get it back. You earned it."

Armand didn't know just how accurate that statement was. Jack had been through hell in so many different ways. He'd earned that old life back, but the look in his eyes was confusion. Like he wasn't sure he wanted that life back again. It surprised her. No, it scared her.

"I'll see if Jennifer would mind picking up a new phone for me," he said. "Same number and all."

"Jack," said Izzy with a chuckle, "I know Jennifer wouldn't mind taking care of that for you. That way, she knows she can contact you."

"I guess that explains why you didn't return any of my calls," Armand said with a laugh and slid his arm around Izzy's shoulders.

"We tried to invite you and Talia over for supper a few times, but you never answered. Thought you were just ghosting us."

Jack shook his head, a sad look in his eyes. "No, I really wasn't," he said, his voice tight. He looked hurt. "You dudes are very good friends and I'd like nothing better than to get together for a cookout or something. Seriously. I wasn't ignoring your calls."

"Relax, Jack," said Izzy, laying her hand against his forearm. "He's just kidding you, trying to guilt you into accepting a dinner invitation when the show ends."

"Hell yes I accept!" Jack replied and then pulled Talia against his shoulder. "We accept." He gave Talia a funny look. "You accept, too? Don't you, babe?"

All three of them burst into laughter.

"It's Armand and Izzy," she said, kissing Jack on the cheek. "Of course, I accept, but I appreciate you asking me first."

Behind them, Mark Banks and Morgan walked past, headed to the edge of the patio where a blue half circle was taped to the concrete patio on Armand and Izzy's right.

"Hey, Banks," said Jack with a nod. "Hi, Morgan."

"Hi, Jack and Talia," Mark called to them, wearing a tan suit, white shirt, and black dress shoes.

Morgan grinned and waved. She wore a short white dress with small lime green flowers on it, the skirt a flouncy A-line.

But Talia stiffened as Rachel sauntered onto the patio wearing a sleeveless, shell pink dress cut above the knee. It was so tight that it looked painted on her. She wore pale aqua high heels—with the red soles that Jack always grumbled about. Talia didn't know what the red soles meant, but he got grumpy every time he saw them. Beside her, Eric wore a charcoal grey suit, light grey shirt, and dark grey dress shoes. They found their red circle to the right of her and Jack.

Eric Saunders held Rachel close and whispered against her ear, making her giggle. They seemed really into each other. Maybe after Lare Dumont's influence was gone, Rachel had mellowed out a little?

Talia still didn't trust her and she couldn't forget all the terrible things this woman did to Jack, but if Jack forgave her, she would be civil. And she wouldn't smite her—unless she tried to hurt Jack again.

This time, Rachel wouldn't get the chance. She'd make certain.

She glanced at Jack who watched the other couples, looking…sad. His expression sent a chill of dread through her. Had he changed his mind about her after seeing all the human couples together?

"You okay?" she asked, her lips against his ear.

He smiled and slid his arms around her, holding her close. "Just wishing that you and me could be together like that once this show is over."

"Like this?" she asked and put her arms around his neck, kissing his lips.

He laid his hands against her elbows, his hot touch sending sparks across her skin.

"That and more," he said in a quiet voice. "I just want to stay with you, babe. That's all. That's all I want." A smirk touched his lips. "Well, that and someplace that isn't my shithole studio apartment with the squeaky Murphy bed."

She nipped his bottom lip. "I kind of like that squeaky Murphy bed."

He sipped her lips. "Only when you're in it," he whispered as his lips slid down to her neck, sending shivers across her wing tips and turning her skin to gooseflesh.

More and more candles lit the patio and then Steve was standing beside them, clearing his throat. Lighting technicians set up lights along the patio to enhance the candlelit atmosphere. Steve carried two wireless mic packs and ear mics in his hands.

"Ready to mic up for sound checks?" Steve asked, holding out the mics.

Sighing, Jack let her go and took the battery-powered mic pack. He clipped it under his suit jacket, at the waist of his suit pants. Steve clipped hers to the back of her dress and handed her the ear clip. Jack slipped his clip over his ear and adjusted it as she put her mic on, too.

"Okay, Jack," said Steve, glancing down at some sort of meter in his hand. "Sound check in three, two, one—go."

"Sound check. This is Jack Casey. Checking sound. Check. Check."

"That's perfect, Jack," said Steve, giving him a thumbs up. "Okay, Talia, sound check in five, four, three, two, one…go."

"Testing, testing," said Talia. "This is Talia. Testing, testing."

Steve reached over to her battery pack and made an adjustment.

"One more time, Talia," said Steve.

"This is Talia Smith. Testing, testing, testing." She glanced up at Jack.

"How does Casey sound?" Jack asked.

"Casey?" she asked.

He smirked at her, leaning down toward her earpiece. "This is Jack Casey, testing sound for soon-to-be Mrs. Talia Smith Casey. Testing, testing."

She felt a chill brush across her skin as she turned and smiled at him. "Casey sounds just perfect to me," she said and reached up to his face, caressing his cheek. "Just perfect."

Steve grinned at them. "Like your sound, Talia. Good luck you, two."

Behind them, cameras swiveled and rotated, doing tests against the lighting. It was almost seven o'clock.

The crew moved around the patio, setting up mics and checking lighting for the rest of the cast. Jack seemed right at home in that atmosphere even though to her, it felt frenetic and chaotic.

She glanced at the black mansard roof that crowned the three-story limestone chateau of angels, as the winemaker called it. Le Château des Anges. She smiled. Where Kesien, Deemah, Daidrean, Anahera, and Muriel perched, dove grey wings unfurled and catching the last rays of golden sunlight. Their pale-yellow halos spun so bright against the darkening sky. The squad stood ready to defend them against anything demonic.

Like Abaddon.

All around the patio, over it, and across the concrete, surfaces glowed with a pure white sheen. Seraphim wards were in place. Protecting her and Jack against Abaddon. Had Jack's seraphim powers set Abaddon off guard, enough to rethink coming after him here on earth? She just hoped that Jack didn't think something he shouldn't and set off those seraphim powers by mistake.

Then she'd be forced to call Azrael down to fix it.

High House still didn't know how to remove the seraphim powers that Jack had absorbed from the healing stone using omnificence. Like his wings and halo apparently. Not even the seraphim had omnificence.

Jack was constantly doing things that Heaven hadn't anticipated. They didn't know how to deal with his wings and halo situation any more than they did these seraphim powers. Or him.

No, Jack was an enigma that had confused High House from the start and they were still struggling to compensate.

Then there was the issue of an angel of death possessing a human soul. And her and Jack staying together after they handled Abaddon. So many questions and still no answers.

She and Jack needed those answers.

At fifteen minutes before seven, the set was ready to broadcast the live elimination show. She kept her arms around Jack's waist, watching the vineyards darken as the sun disappeared in a wash of indigo and citrine.

"All right, everybody! Stay sharp and watch Devin and Steve for your cues," Herb called out across the set. "Lighting techs have done an amazing job making the patio look candlelit, so in the dim lighting, remember your blocking and stay on your marks."

Everyone turned toward the director, listening and waiting for any last moment instructions.

"Devin will work through the list of couples," said Herb, pointing toward Devin Van Fossen who stood between two cobalt urns, the heady scent of lilies, roses, and crisp lavender intense on the breeze. "He will announce the first couple in jeopardy in the first fifteen minutes. First couple called will move to the orange X marking a spot to Devin's right. Last couple in jeopardy will stand on the green star to Devin's left."

Steve moved beside Herb who stood beside his director's chair behind the cameras on the left side of the patio. Herb wore black trousers and a light blue V-neck sweater.

"If you're safe, stay on your marks," said Steve. "Is that clear? Couples that are safe, don't move from your marks. Period. And for Heaven's sake, do not even think about wandering off this patio or I will personally slay you!"

Cast and crew laughed.

"Or Abaddon will," Jack whispered in Talia's ear.

She gave him her best, *don't go there, Jack Casey* look and he just smirked at her.

"They think I'm kidding," said Steve, nudging Herb who stood on Steve's right at the edge of the patio.

Herb pointed at Steve. "He's not kidding. Trust me. And you thought I was mean. Anything else, Steve? Jennifer?" He looked over at Jennifer who stood to Herb's right.

She shook her head, that clipboard in her left hand. She wore a camel-colored pant suit with a gold top, tortoiseshell glasses perched on her nose, dark brown hair against her shoulders.

"Best of luck, couples," she called out to them. "I wish you could all stay. After the broadcast, we'll have a meet and greet with wine and appetizers in the living room."

"Okay, good luck to all of you," said Herb, sitting down in his chair. "Get ready to roll."

Steve glanced at the clock. "And it's four minutes and twenty-eight seconds until we're live. Good luck and stay on your marks."

Jack sighed as he glanced around the darkening patio. "Guess we'll know soon enough how we did," he said in a quiet voice.

She reached up and cupped his smooth-shaven chin a moment. "We did well on our challenges, Jack. It'll be fine."

"Hope you're right," he said and held her close, his chin resting against her shoulder as he wrapped his arms around her waist from behind. "It's not like we've had much time together to learn about each other's likes and dislikes. Not even talking food and drink here. We've been too busy smiting demons and fighting Lucifer to even focus on the little things."

He had a point. They hadn't spent much time together as a couple. Even when Azrael hid Jack among the guard, they hadn't spent time doing all those get-to-know-each other things that most couples did when they dated and moved in together. She and Jack hadn't done any of those things yet.

"Saving the world—and the Heavens—came first," she whispered against his ear.

"Couldn't agree more," he said.

"One minute thirty-eight seconds, people," Steve announced. "Places. Stay on your marks. Devin, camera two for introductions then camera one for canned footage and stay there until break."

Devin nodded at Steve as he gripped those index cards in his right fist. He glanced over his right shoulder at camera two and then to his left at camera one. He turned his body to face camera two and studied his first index card again.

"Devin looks nervous tonight," said Talia.

She'd never noticed him that nervous before. Probably because he was the only one that knew the final scores right now. And it was the season's first live show.

"He's not the only way," said Jack.

"Thirty seconds," Steve called out, head phones on his head covering one ear.

Jack pulled in a long, deep breath and held it. Then let it out slowly.

"Ten seconds," Steve called out. "Stay on your marks…and five, four, three, two, one…rolling."

Devin stared into camera two. "Good evening, my royal subjects, and welcome to The Royal Wedding Hour's first live elimination show on this beautiful patio. Located in the heart of Sonoma County in wine country. Tonight, we must say goodbye to one couple." Devin turned toward camera one. "But first, let's see the outcomes of our couple's cocktail hours. First up is Mark Banks and Morgan Boyer, making two cocktails fit for a princess and a prince charming."

"Cutting over to pre-recorded footage, Banks and Boyer…now," Steve said in a soft voice.

The large monitor behind Steve rolled with footage of Morgan and Mark making their two drinks. When the clip finished, Devin spoke into camera one.

"And let's see what Morgan and Mark had to say about their first challenge."

"Cut over to canned footage complete," said Steve. "Banks and Boyer interview rolling now. First commercial break in four minutes thirty-one seconds."

The footage of Mark and Morgan's first couple's interview rushed by on the monitor and then the broadcast cut back to Devin.

"Thirty-two seconds to break, Devin," Steve said as Devin stared into camera one.

"Next up," said Devin, gazing into camera two. "A little romance and cocktails from a daytime soap star and a regional news anchor. Winners of The Ever After Hour, Armand Gianni and Isabella Castilla. Stay tuned, America. We will also announce the first couple moving on to the next challenge shortly and you don't want to miss that."

"And we're clear," said Steve. "Five minutes and three seconds until cut back. Stay beside those marks. I will slay you if you step off this patio."

Talia glanced up at the rooftop. Three angels circled the chateau. Two angels stood stoic above the patio, wings extended as sunset faded into twilight. Kesien and Muriel. Jack's gaze moved to the sky and then to the rooftop.

"I see the squad's keeping watch," he whispered.

She nodded. "I wanted to make sure this broadcast wasn't interrupted."

"By demons?" he asked.

"Among other things," she replied, glancing at him.

Jack's game face slipped a little, surprising her. He jerked his gaze past Gianni and Banks. Toward the darkening edge of the patio as the sun's last fiery trails dimmed.

"What is it?" she asked, studying his demeanor.

"I thought I heard something," he said, staring off into the twilight.

He didn't move. He just stared.

"Heard what, Jack?" she asked.

His face turned pale, the color washing away. And she felt suddenly frightened and uneasy.

"Jack," she snapped. "Talk to me. What did you hear?"

"Holy shit," he muttered, shaking his head. "It can't be…can it?"

"Can't be what?" she demanded in a sharp whisper. "Jack, what are you talking about?"

"I thought I…" His voice trailed off.

She glanced up at the roof. Both Muriel and Kesien had disappeared. Only two angels circled above the chateau now. Where were the other three?

She glanced around the patio, checking the white seraphim wards. All intact. Above them. Around them. Beside them.

"Thought what, Jack?" she asked in a sharp whisper.

"Heard something," he said in a low, raspy voice. "Something…familiar."

A chill danced across her skin. She glanced around, behind, in front. But only the growing twilight and the set's candlelight glow clung to the patio.

"One minute fifty-four seconds," Steve called out.

Talia turned to Jack. "Jack?" she whispered. "What did you hear?"

A chuffing sound echoed across the vineyard. And a low growl. Near the patio. And the sounds chilled her blood.

"Hellhounds," he said in a low voice, fear shining in his pale green eyes.

His gaze shot around the patio.

Hellhounds? Here?

Only Lucifer controlled hellhounds. Unless it was Cerberus or his brother, Orthrus. She shuddered at the realization.

Abaddon had the key to the Gates of Hell. Had he brought them? To hunt Jack?

Her heart began to race as she glanced around the patio and back up at the roof.

All five angels of death—her entire squad—were gone now.

Had they been duped and led away from the chateau? Leaving her as Jack's only protection? And the seraphim powers that he'd inadvertently plucked from the healing gem.

A low, feral rumble vibrated across the patio followed by a mountain lion's raspy caterwaul. It made her skin turn to gooseflesh.

She glanced over at Armand and Izzy. At Mark Banks and Morgan. Eric and Rachel. They were all engaged in quiet conversation together, whispering and smiling at each other.

Oblivious.

Only Jack heard that horrifying caterwaul.

He looked pallid, terrified. His eyes were wide, gaze frantic as it moved around the patio. "Where is it?" he demanded, shivering, his whisper sharp.

"Doesn't matter," Talia replied. "We're warded. We have rare angel powers. And you have seraphim powers. They can't get through those wards. If they do, we smite them. Fast."

"Hope you're right," he said with a nervous sigh, his gaze drifting from right to left.

"Twenty-nine seconds." Steve announced. "Find your marks and stay there."

A shadow shifted somewhere off to her left. Past the set lights. She swallowed a breath.

Past the set lights?

Her gaze shot skyward. The darkening sky looked clear. No angel wings or demons shot past overhead.

She followed the white glowing wards with her gaze, tracing them around the patio's edge and along the chateau's limestone walls.

No gaps or holes.

Again, the nails against chalkboard sound of a feral yowl bayed across the patio and reverberated against the limestone chateau.

"Talia..." said Jack in a low, frightened voice.

"Trying to locate it," she answered, her breaths quickening.

Again, a shadow passed in front of the set lights.

She snapped her gaze right, toward the shadow. Nothing but clear, dark sky.

"Ten seconds," said Steve. "Stick to those marks. Devin, camera one and then camera two for every canned footage introduction."

Devin nodded, turning to camera one as he shuffled the top index card to the bottom of the stack in his hand.

"Back in five, four, three, two, one—rolling."

"Welcome back, my royal subjects," Devin said into camera one, his over-the-top delivery echoing across the patio.

Jack's game face slid back into to place, but his gaze kept tracking around the patio. Searching for hellhounds.

She sensed them. Smelled the hint of smoke and brimstone in the air.

Jack sniffed the air and tried to hold his attention on Devin, the show's host. His grip tightened on her hand, fingers trembling.

She squeezed his hand, letting him know he was safe and she was right beside him.

"And it's time to watch America's favorite primetime doctor and her financial planner prince flirt and craft cocktails in royal fashion. Let's watch."

"Cutting away to canned footage," Steve replied in a quiet voice. "Daniels and Saunders rolling."

The monitor behind the cameras showed the segment of Rachel and Eric laughing and creating two cocktails together.

"Cutting back in three, two, one—" Steve pointed at Devin who turned to camera two.

"And now, a special treat, America," said Devin into camera two. "Let's watch as fan favorites, Jack Casey and Talia Smith flirt and romance their way through creating two cocktails fit for a king and queen."

"Running canned footage," Steve announced. "Casey and Smith is rolling."

Jack bit his lip, watching the darkening edges of the patio. Talia laid her hand against his chest, feeling the frantic beat of his heart. Maybe Abaddon brought the hellhounds to intimidate Jack?

Unfortunately, it was working.

Talia glanced over at Steve. To her surprise, Nina Westwood, Jack's mother, stood beside Herb. She was dressed in a purple tunic, black flats, and black leggings, hair in a crisp bob the color of black cherries.

Oh, no! That's all Jack needed right now.

He was already worried about the results and now, there were hellhounds outside the wards. Now, his mother was behind stage at a live broadcast.

No pressure. Poor Jack.

He'd blow his top if he looked over and saw his mother standing there. She had to keep him distracted. From his mother and hellhounds? How would she possibly do that?

"I'll mix drinks with you any day, lover," she whispered in Jack's ear and nibbled his earlobe.

"Same, babe," he said and smiled. "Although, I'd like to go back to your other activities first."

"Other activities?" She frowned. "Like what?"

That sexy smirk lifted the corners of his hot mouth. "That throwing me on the bed and slowly undressing me thing was at the top of my list."

She put her hands on her hips, chuckling. "I'll just bet it was."

"It was at the top of your list before it was at the top of mine," he countered, giving her a shrug.

She laughed. He had a point. "Okay, you got me. It was at the top of my list. For later."

"Just want you to know that I'm clearing my entire calendar for you and your list," he said with a wink. "The entire calendar."

"You have no calendar," she said to him and kissed his lips. "Remember? You lost your phone in Hell."

"How do you think I cleared it?" he asked, raising his eyebrows.

"This is Jack Casey. Yeah, *that* Jack Casey."

Looking confused, Jack glanced around, squinting into the deepening twilight.

"That's your voice," said Talia, glancing around.

None of the other cast or crew reacted to it, but it was clearly Jack's voice filtering out from the growing darkness that surrounded the patio.

"If I owe you money, leave me a message with the details, so I can delete it."

Jack's mouth gaped. "Talia! That's my voicemail greeting on my cell phone."

His phone? Had Abaddon returned from Hell with it? And now, he was taunting Jack with his phone. She swallowed a breath.

"If you're my mother, the number you have reached is no longer in service. If you're my agent, please leave a message and tell me you've got a job for me. Otherwise, you're welcome to try your luck by leaving a message."

"Recognize that, Jack Casey?"

Abaddon's deep, gravelly voice permeated the twilight calm. And then time paused.

Jack glanced around as everything halted.

"This isn't how I hoped the elimination round would go tonight," said Jack, looking pale and annoyed now.

Abaddon stood at the edge of the wards' gleam, a pack of hellhounds surrounding his thick, eight-foot muscular frame. He clutched Jack's phone in one hand.

"With your physical elimination?" Abaddon asked with a chuckle. "I thought it would make a nice presentation back in Hell."

Abaddon tossed the phone at Jack and he caught it in his right hand.

The clear protective case had melted, but the phone still seemed to work. Jack clutched it.

"Lucifer sent your phone and his regrets that he couldn't be here personally," said Abaddon, nodding at Jack as the huge demon stepped closer to the patio. "Thanks to you and that halo tethering trick you pulled on him."

"Just returning the favor," said Jack.

Abaddon motioned at five thin, leathery-skinned hellhounds surrounding him. Their thick hides looked mottled charcoal and burgundy as they whined and pawed at the grass, digging along the edges of the wards. They had long snouts, wiry bodies, and lots of claws and teeth. Lucifer used them to attach a soul tether to Jack—through a hellhound's bite. Cerberus. And his brother, Orthrus.

Jack looked unnerved by their presence and fear burned in his pale green eyes again.

"Lucifer sent the hellhounds to welcome you back home, Jack," Abaddon said with a deep, rumbling laugh. "Lucifer said he misses you and promises to torture you at a much more relaxed pace this time. For him. He's promised the angel to me though."

Jack bristled, pushing Talia behind him. "You're not touching a single feather of her wings, Abaddon. Back off. Now!"

Abaddon just laughed. "Prepare to die, Jack Casey."

21

JACK GLARED AT THE FIERCE, TOWERING DEMON AS ABADDON ADVANCED toward the patio. And crashed hard into the seraphim wards surrounding them.

"They're seraphim wards, dude," said Jack as Talia struggled against his hold. "You're not going to be able to break them."

"Jack, stop trying to protect me!" Talia shouted.

"No way I'm letting him get close to you," he said.

She meant everything to him. He wasn't about to let Lucifer's stooge and his Hellpoodles near her. Not on his watch.

"Jack!" she cried. "I'm an angel of death, remember? You're the frail human. I should be protecting you."

He sighed. That stung. But she was right.

She pulled away from him, standing her ground.

He was feeling a little lost now. Abaddon wanted to destroy Talia because she'd tricked him, but this demon wanted to overnight his soul to Lucifer. Still, Abaddon was hunting Talia as frantically as he was hunting him.

"I wasn't trying to dominate you," he said in a sad tone. "I was just trying to keep my body between him and you, to protect you. You mean everything to me, Talia."

Talia stepped in front of him, wings spread wide, gold halo a dull whine in the sudden quiet. The wind turned cool with night's approach.

"And you mean everything to me, Jack Casey."

His cell phone began to ring. It played a ringtone he hadn't heard before. He glowered at it. *Sympathy for the Devil* by the Stones. He answered it.

Lucifer.

"Luci!" he shouted into the phone and tapped the speaker icon. "Got you on speaker, you maniac! How are the wife and kids? Still stealing cable and Wi-Fi from Heaven? Still in therapy for those daddy issues? How you been? How's that tether holding up?"

"Jack. Shut up."

He almost felt the intense wash of acid from Lucifer's voice surge through the phone, but he couldn't help himself. He just had to poke the bear again.

"Sorry you couldn't be here to watch Talia and I kick your mascot's ass. But hey, I can stream it for you like a pay per view. Still using God as your password down there?"

"You know, Jack," said Lucifer in a sharp tone, sounding so icy and British. "I'm going to enjoy disemboweling you and feeding it to my hounds every morning when Abaddon returns you to Hell. I think I'll give you the Prometheus treatment."

Jack laughed. "You mean I'd grow them back every night? Kind of like your balls? Aww...still waiting for them grow back though, aren't you? After we neutered you in Heaven. How long's it gonna take them to grow back this time, Luci?"

"Oh, Jack, I do miss your smart mouth," said Lucifer in a smooth, bright voice. "Almost as much as I miss shutting it. With your phone, for example."

Jack frowned. "Not following you, Luci."

Lucifer chuckled. "Oh, but you will, Jack. See, that phone was your property, so it passes through the ward without a problem."

"Jack, drop the phone!"

Talia's words rang in his ears and he let go of the phone.

"Plenty of room in there to conceal a soul tether and tunnel my demons past the wards. And Abaddon. Can't wait for your arrival, Jack. We'll have so much fun in the cages again. With you begging me to kill you. Can't wait!"

Shadows seeped up through the concrete patio as demons and hellhounds rose through the wards.

Dammit! They'd gotten past the wards!

He backed away, toward the French doors of the chateau as the demons advanced.

"Lucifer, your gifts really suck, you know that," Jack replied. "A gift card would have been much more thoughtful. I'm afraid you're off my Christmas card list this year."

"And you're on my wish list. Just in time for Hell's annual easter egg hunt. This year, I'll be hiding pieces of Jack Casey instead of eggs. It will be glorious!"

"Hope nobody hides anything past Hell's Gates, Luci," Jack shouted at the phone. "'Cause your leash doesn't reach that far."

"Shut up, Jack!" Lucifer fired back at him through the phone. "Abaddon, take them. Now."

Jack summoned murder marbles in both hands, tossing them across the concrete.

Hellhounds yelped as the spheres exploded, spraying demon goo in a fine red mist across the patio.

He turned, sword of Holy fire raised, and ran two assassin demons through with it.

Talia swung a flaming sword of Holy fire in a wide arc around her, forcing the massing demons and hellhounds back as she pushed Jack behind her again.

But he was already gathering a wave of Holy fire in both hands. He threw down the writhing white, basketball-sized sphere against the patio. A ten-foot wave of Holy fire swept across the expanse.

Engulfing the demons. Burning them down.

A hellhound jumped him. Knocking him to the concrete.

He held its snapping jaws away from his face as Talia ran it through with her sword.

Abaddon leaped at them, grabbing Jack by the throat. He flung Jack into the air.

Jack spread his wings and shot upward, away from the huge demon's reach. He did a somersault in the air and banked around Abaddon, grabbing Talia's hands and lifting her into the air.

She caught an updraft and rose. Out of Abaddon's reach.

They floated ten feet above Abaddon, six assassin demons, and four hellhounds that leaped and snapped at them.

"Does he still have wings?" Jack asked Talia.

"He did when he was sent to oversee Hell," she said. "But he looked like an archangel then. Not like this. When he turned to Lucifer's cause, it probably shriveled up his wings and caused his halo to go dormant."

"So, we just stay up here until they leave?" he asked with a shrug.

"If we do anything else, we'll destroy things below," Talia replied, flipping waves of that shiny, raven black hair off her shoulders, the beat of her wings steady as night descended. "Jack, did any of those hellhounds bite you?"

He shook his head. "No, but Lucifer said the tether was in the phone."

She grabbed hold of him and pulled him against her, fingers searching his hair and around his right ear.

"What are you doing?" he asked.

"Searching for a mark," she cried. "Any connection to that phone could have implanted a tether on you."

The thought of another soul tether made his stomach twist into knots and his heart race. Had Lucifer managed to tether him again? Just the suggestion of it terrified him.

"See anything?" he asked as he pulled in an anxious breath.

"Nothing yet," she said in a hushed voice.

Her fingers raked through his hair and scraped across his ear. Frantic, she slid her hand across his jaw and down his neck.

"I'm not finding anything, Jack," she said, her voice sounding frustrated. "And where's my squad?"

"Here!"

Muriel swooped past her, Kesien at her shoulder. Daidrean and Anahera slammed into Abaddon, fighting with shields and swords as Deemah bashed her shield against the huge demon's head.

"Where were you?" Talia demanded.

"Battling about a hundred or so demons and a herd of hellhounds," Muriel shouted, gritting her teeth as she stabbed Abaddon in the neck with her sword. "A diversionary force, but they're all down now."

"We'll repel them, Talia, don't worry," Kesien shouted.

Jack held out his hands to Talia. "Calvary's here, babe," he said with a brief smile.

He hadn't flown at all since he'd returned to earth. The sudden shift—and using a seraphim power—made him feel lightheaded. He reached up to his forehead and rubbed it, the muscles already tightening into a headache.

But Talia wasn't smiling. Her mouth was open.

His forehead felt sticky. He glanced at his hands. The right one had an open wound in his palm. Leaking blood.

He touched his forehead with his left hand and it came away bloody.

The tether! It had attached itself to his soul through his right hand. When he'd caught the phone and answered it with his right hand.

"Jack! Your hand."

"No…" He gasped, sickness rising through him.

Talia's eyes were full of tears as she shook her head. "No, Jack—no!"

Was it over? Had Lucifer gotten the last laugh?

"You have the resurrect power, remember," said Jack, feeling unsteady. "That's what we used to break the tether last time."

She nodded, hundreds of thoughts rushing across her eyes.

"Yes, the resurrect power. You're right, Jack. I'll send up a call to Azrael. He and the guard will help like they did before. But this time, you have seraphim powers. Lucifer won't get you back. I won't allow it, Jack."

Below, Azrael and Berith appeared on the patio. Together, with the squad's assistance, they destroyed Jack's phone and expelled the demons and Abaddon from the wards. Only when the ward gleamed bright white again and Abaddon pounded on it from the other side of the patio did Jack and Talia land.

"Jack! Talia!" Berith took hold of Jack's shoulders as he slumped.

Talia held him up as Berith took hold of his right hand, examining the bleeding wound in his palm.

"You're right, Talia," she said, her frightened gaze fixing Jack now. "He's been hit with another soul tether. I need to bandage his hand and slow the tether's plunge through his flesh. It will eventually reach his soul, but this will slow it down." She reached out and plucked a feather from Jack's silver-grey wings.

"Ow!" he cried. "That hurt."

"Sorry, Jack," said Berith as she laid the silvery grey feather from his wing on a swath of sparkling white fabric in her left hand.

When the feather touched the fabric, it exploded into a burst of gold light and the cloth absorbed its energy. The bandage had a faint gold sheen to it as she wrapped it around Jack's hand, between thumb and index finger, over and over until it was tight. The fabric was sticky and clung to his skin, holding fast.

"There," she said and ruffled Jack's hair. "That should slow down Lucifer's soul tether until you can use the resurrect power to break it, Talia."

"I won't have to go through the ritual of awakening it again, will I?" she asked Berith.

Berith shook her head. "No, but you will need to refer back to the parts of the power. You'll draw those same elements from the Creation itself and place them like you did on Jack in the Garden." She reached out and laid her hand on Talia's shoulder. "And no last breath required. A breath from Jack is all you'll need."

"There's good news," Jack said with a smirk.

"If you like, I'll return and walk you through using the power, Talia." She reached over and hugged Jack. "The tether can't be broken until it touches his soul, so we have some time."

"How will we know when it reaches my soul?" Jack asked, feeling uncomfortable about waiting.

The longer they waited, the deeper the tether embedded itself.

"The bleeding will worsen. Lucifer kept bleeding your wound last time, Jack," said Berith, motioning toward his left shoulder. "Your blood fed the tether. It's what fueled it. We need to keep a close eye on this one. It won't take more than a couple of days, even by slowing down its progression, to reach your soul. As soon as it begins to bleed profusely, Talia will need to sever it with the resurrect power."

Azrael looked all kinds of pissed as he surveyed his squad and how the demons got past the wards.

"I'll consult with Seraphina after I erase the damage done here," said the archangel. "Berith, help Talia and Jack prepare to enact the resurrect power to break this tether. There's got to be a way to get Abaddon to stand down. We've just got to find it."

"No information from Pravuil?" Talia asked.

Azrael shook his head. "Nothing yet," he said with a sigh. "He's still combing the archives, looking at information about when Abaddon was chosen for his role as God's Destroyer and as the key holder to Hell's Gates."

Berith laid her hands on Azrael's shoulders as he flexed his wings. "Go ahead and finish the cleanup. I'll head back to work out the details for the resurrect power and return in a couple of days."

"I'll be along soon, Berith," he said, squeezing her hand.

"Don't worry, Jack, Talia," said Berith as she lifted off from the patio, charcoal grey wings spread wide. "I'll be back in a day or so to break the tether. It'll be fine."

"Thanks, Berith," said Jack as she disappeared into the clouds.

Azrael tossed waves of gold light across the patio, repairing concrete and returning the landscape to its pristine condition before Abaddon showed up. When he finished, he stretched out his soot-grey wings in a wide arc behind him.

"I'll hold the time pause until you and Jack are back into position. And then I'll let it expire. We'll talk tomorrow, Talia, Jack. Once Berith is ready to walk you through another tether break."

"Thanks, sir," Talia called as he blinked off the patio and disappeared into the deepening darkness.

Jack moved with uncertain steps over to the purple square taped to the patio floor. He let his wings fall against his back and go flat. Talia folded her wings back in place and in a burst of gold light, she hid their halos and wings again. She slid her arms around his waist and he pulled her close, feeling violated. Lucifer's attack came out of nowhere.

Talia leaned up and kissed him hard on the lips.

"That's just to reassure you that you're not going anywhere without me, Jack Casey. Got it?"

He pulled on his game face. For her. He'd feign confidence and an unconcerned demeanor for her. He wouldn't let her see the fear and uncertainty permeating his body. The thought of returning to Hell terrified him almost as much as the thought of being separated from her forever. Almost.

He returned her kiss as the first movements twitched across the patio.

"One minute and eight seconds, people," Steve called out, startling Jack.

He turned to see the crew animated again, Steve gripping his headset with one hand as he glanced across the patio.

"And we're back," Jack whispered against Talia's ear.

"Are you scared?" Talia asked him, fixing him with those wide, luminous grey eyes as she laid a hand against his face.

He nodded. "Only of losing you," he whispered.

Talia reached down with her other hand and gently gripped his right hand. She smiled at him.

"You'll never lose me, Jack Casey because I won't let you. We have the power to break this thing, remember? You're not going anywhere without me."

Her reassurance was infectious and it cut through his anxiety. He smiled.

"Glad to hear that," he said and kissed her, a long, slow-burning kiss that set his heart afire.

"Twenty-eight seconds. Hit your marks, everyone. Devin, you're all camera one for the results."

"Got it, Steve," said Devin, turning his body toward camera one as he put the top card in his stack on the bottom.

Jack's heart pounded like a jackhammer. He pulled in a deep breath, held it, and let it out slowly. Already, his right hand ached. Blood seeped from the wound in his palm. It wouldn't stop bleeding until Talia severed Lucifer's soul tether. He hated the idea of this thing slithering through his body and harpooning his soul with a homing device that would yoink him back to Hell.

"Eight seconds. Nobody move from their marks."

His hands began to shake again. Jack pressed his arms against his sides, but Talia took both hands in hers and gripped them tightly.

Steve pointed at them, hand against his headset again. "Five, four, three, two, one—and we're back."

Jack pulled his game face back on and smiled at Devin, looking focused and excited. Even though he was screaming inside, wanting to run for the nearest exit.

He couldn't go back to Hell. He couldn't!

"All right, my royal subjects," said Devin, his melodramatic delivery filling the silence as he gazed into camera one's lens. "I'm afraid we've come to that moment where we have to send home one royal couple. So, now, we discover the results of this week's wedding reception challenge."

Devin turned toward Banks and Morgan. He walked toward them, the candlelight casting his shadow in a long, flickering line across the patio.

"Our first couple, Mark Banks and Morgan Boyer."

Morgan gripped Banks' hands tightly, a nervous smile on her face as she glanced from Banks to Devin.

Devin tapped the card in his hand against his fingers. "I have here the scores of your first challenge."

Abruptly, he turned toward camera one.

"And America, your first princess and prince charming scores have been compared with the three other couples on this patio. This week, Mark Banks and Morgan Boyer..."

He whirled back around toward them. "Unfortunately, you and

Morgan are in jeopardy of leaving tonight. Please stand here beside me."

Banks looked defeated and Morgan looked sad as they moved toward the red mark on Devin's right.

Next, Devin turned to Gianni and Izzy who looked uneasy as he approached, an index card still in his hand.

"Our second couple, Armand Gianni and Isabella Castilla, won last season's Ever After Hour challenge, beating out fan favorites, Jack Casey and Talia Smith."

Devin walked around them, flicking to the next index card in his stack.

"Tonight, after reviewing their scores."

He whirled around, pointing the card at them. "Tonight, our second princess and prince charming couple is…safe. You move on to next week's show."

Gianni grinned and threw his arms around Izzy who let out the breath she'd been holding as he spun her around and kissed her.

Jack gave them a big grin and a thumbs up. He felt bad that Banks and Morgan were in the bottom two, but he was happy for Gianni and Izzy. He was afraid that he and Talia would be joining Banks on that other mark.

He stiffened as Devin approached him and Talia, that white index card in motion as he circled them.

"America, our third royal couple and fan favorites, Jack Casey and Talia Smith."

He moved around them and then turned abruptly toward the camera again.

"Runners up in The Ever After Hour challenge. Here for a rematch against Armand Gianni and Isabella Castilla. Will last season's winners beat them out again?"

One more time, Devin circled them.

Jack held his breath, gripping Talia's hands so tight they were probably going numb.

Devin turned toward them, holding out that index card.

"Scores were tallied and compared against our other three couples.

And tonight, the results of Jack and Talia's first challenge are right here. On this card."

He pulled it back from them as he whirled around and stared in camera one's direction.

"Tonight, Talia and Jack," he said, turning toward them. "You are…safe."

Jack felt the anxiety rush out, his body going slack like a worn radiator belt. Talia threw her arms around him and he kissed her hard on the lips, turning her around and around. He couldn't hold back his grin. Despite Lucifer hitting him with that tether and Abaddon getting past the wards, he and Talia knew each other's likes and dislikes! Well enough to not go home tonight. He was thrilled.

"And incidentally," said Devin, standing beside them with a grin on his face. "Jack and Talia's two drinks received the highest score of all the couples. Not only were their drinks delicious, but they were the perfect embodiment of Jack and Talia's journey as a couple. Well done, you two!"

"You hear that, Talia?" he cried, spinning her around again. "Our drinks didn't kill anyone!"

Everyone laughed, including Talia.

Devin moved toward Rachel and Eric. Rachel cast a dark glance at Jack as Devin circled them like a vulture. He turned toward the camera.

"Unfortunately, that means that Rachel and Eric are also in jeopardy of going home tonight. Rachel and Eric, please come stand beside me."

Rachel glared at him as she gripped Eric's hand and held her head high, moving toward the green star taped on Devin's left as Devin returned to his original mark.

"And now, America, after the commercial break, we will send one royal couple home. Stay tuned."

"And we're clear!" Steve announced. "Four minutes and twenty-seven seconds. Everybody, hold positions."

Rachel crossed her arms, her dark stare still encompassing him.

Like it was his fault somehow. He hadn't done anything to harm her chances in this challenge.

He stared back at her.

"Cameras on," Herb said in a low voice.

"Gloating, Jack?" she asked.

He shook his head. "Why would I do that? We were all competing against ourselves during this round."

"Still, you're enjoying my failure, aren't you?"

"Again, why would I do that?" he asked. "I wish no one had to go home. This season's about marrying your fairytale princess. Or prince charming. I'd like to see all of us get that storybook ending. On camera or off it."

He pulled Talia into his arms and kissed her.

"I hope all of you have found that ever after," he said, motioning around the patio. "And seeing a big royal wedding with four prince charmings marrying their princesses would be the coolest show ending ever. If Eric's your prince charming, Rachel, I'd love to watch you marry him in royal style."

She sighed and held Eric's hand tighter, her eyes brimming with tears.

"God, you really are a bright light, aren't you, Jack?" she said as tears slipped down her cheeks. "After everything I did to you and you can still stand there and wish me well. Even now. I'm so sorry Lare and I hurt you, Jack, but I'm so grateful that we didn't break you."

"Busted up, but fixable," he said and gazed at Talia. "In the presence of angels."

Talia tilted his head toward her and returned his kiss.

"Thirty-one seconds," said Steve.

Rachel smiled at Talia. "So, I've heard."

"Devin, camera one until we're clear. Stick to those marks, people."

Devin nodded as silence descended across the terrace.

"Twenty seconds."

"Regrets, Rachel?" Gianni asked.

Rachel kept her gaze on Jack. "Hundreds," she replied. "But that's how we learn, isn't it?"

Jack nodded at her. It was a start at any rate.

"Eight seconds."

Rachel smiled at him. "No matter what happens next, Jack, I will be watching you get married, if you and Talia win this thing."

"Thanks, Rach," he said in a soft voice.

"Cut and print that," said Herb in a quiet voice.

"Live in three...two...one..."

"Welcome back, my royal subjects," said Devin, motioning to his right and his left. "As you can see, two of this show's most popular couples are standing beside me tonight. And one of them is going home. The moment has arrived."

He gestured to his right at Banks and Morgan and then he turned to his left, motioning at Rachel and Eric.

"And the couple leaving us tonight is..."

Devin held out that index card and stared at it for several, long seconds.

"Mark Banks and Morgan Boyer," said Devin in his over-dramatic delivery as he held out a hand to them.

Banks looked dejected as Morgan's bottom lip quivered. He slid his arms around her and held her tight as Rachel threw her arms around Eric, grinning in relief. He turned her around and kissed her.

"Good night, America, and stay tuned next week as our three remaining couples challenge each other to set the stage for their weddings. Find out what obstacles are in their paths next week on... The Royal Wedding Hour. Until next week, my royal subjects."

"And—we're clear!" Steve announced and slumped back in his chair.

"Great show, everyone," Herb called out.

Steve and crew flooded the patio, picking up the wireless mic sets from Jack and Talia and the rest of the cast.

"We survived the first round, babe," said Jack, sliding his arms around Talia and holding her tight.

He was still feeling lightheaded and a little weak.

"Don't forget tonight's meet and greet in the living area," Jennifer announced. "There will be plenty of wine and appetizers for everyone."

Abruptly, Talia turned him away from the cameras. He frowned.

"What's the matter?" he asked.

"Someone you don't want to see," she whispered.

And his hackles rose. His mother.

He turned his head, anger rushing through his veins as she stepped out from behind the cameras and onto the patio. Moving in his direction. First, Abaddon, then getting soul tethered by Lucifer, and now his mother was on set.

He glared in his mother's direction. Would this bad day ever end?

"Let's get out of here," he said and moved toward the French doors.

22

TALIA HAD TO SPRINT TO KEEP UP WITH JACK AS HE RUSHED THROUGH the French doors and inside the chateau. His mother called his name, but he didn't slow down, hurrying inside. He'd been through enough today and dealing with his mother now, after getting his soul tethered by Lucifer was just too much—even for Jack.

He rushed past the living area, a big open concept space with more of those tall white capitals spread across the black and white marble tiles. Pale blue couches were grouped into three conversation areas against white walls and around yellow area rugs. The center set of couches stood between two turn-of-the-last-century white fireplaces. End tables in a French provincial style stood on either side of the couches with soft, velvety fabric that had a cloud-like feel.

The white walls were covered in ornate gold framed classical masterpieces. Lavender scented the room lit with three sprawling crystal chandeliers that reflected the gold frames across the shiny marble-tiled floors.

Talia smiled. More angel prints.

The room looked like a museum, like it shouldn't be touched or the couches used—just admired from a distance. It made her feel uncomfortable to be in these areas. Like she was going to break something. In the center of the room stood two rectangular tables draped with white tablecloths. One table had drinks and the other had trays of hot appetizers.

The cast had already gathered and the crew was filtering into the room as the hurried tick of Jack's shoes headed toward the stairs. She rushed after him, following him into the foyer. Wanting to blink ahead of him, but there were too many people around.

"Jack, wait!" she called.

He didn't slow down. His anxious footsteps pounded across the marble above her and slammed the suite door behind him.

He wasn't all right.

She ran up the stairs and hurried into the suite. The sound of running water echoed as she stepped inside.

Muriel stood there and just pointed toward the bathroom.

Nodding, Talia blinked through the suite and into the bathroom doorway.

He was at the sink, no shoes, water running as he scrubbed his face with a washcloth. Berith had washed away the blood across his forehead, but he gripped that washcloth in his left hand and scrubbed it across his forehead.

"Jack?" she said in a patient voice. "What are you doing?"

"Getting the blood off," he said, his voice sounding shaky.

She walked over to the counter and turned off the hot water as it began to fog up the mirror. She slid the wet cloth out of his left hand.

"There's nothing on it," she said, draping it across the sink. "Berith got all the blood off before Azrael resumed time. Jack, what's the matter?"

She grabbed an ivory hand towel from the rack and pressed it against his left hand with both of hers, gently drying his fingers. They were shaking.

"Nothing," he said and turned away from the mirror. "Just wanted to make sure the blood wasn't showing."

She ran her fingers through his hair. "Jack, talk to me. Is this about Lucifer or your mother?"

"Is there a difference?" he snapped, avoiding her gaze.

"Yes, there is, Jack," she said, stroking his face. "Lucifer just wants to hurt you."

His eyes narrowed, anger burning like green flames. "That's her goal, too, babe. I'm not giving her another chance to shred me again. And I don't trust her motivations. Now that apparently even my old show wants me back, she only wants to make peace with me for her business."

Talia shook her head. "Jack, no—she wants you to know why things turned out the way they did. Why she reacted to the drugs like she did."

He pulled his hand free from the towel, shaking his head. "She had that chance and she just doubled down on her being right and me being the villain. Again. I'm done, Talia. I'm just done."

"This isn't about your mother, is it?" she asked as he backed away from her, his breath quickening.

"I'm just a little freaked out right now," he said, biting his lip. "This tether...what if we can't break it this time? What if I..." His eyes turned glassy, his voice tight and thin. "Talia...what if he pulls me back to Hell again? I can't go back there. I can't."

His panic broke her heart. She slid her arms around him and held him, his heart pounding like pistons.

"You won't, Jack," she said in a comforting voice, rubbing his back. "We won't let that happen. We have the power to break the tether, remember?"

His wings shifted as he sucked in a pained breath, his body still trembling.

"Before he drags me back there again?" he asked, voice unsteady.

"Of course," she said against his ear. "You won't be dragged back to Hell. Berith and I will sever it the moment it's possible. I'm not about to lose you. I'm going to marry you."

She held him until his shaking subsided. "Ready to go to the party?"

He sighed. It was deep and heavy and it made her sad to hear that weight on his soul again.

"But my mother will be there," he said and pulled away.

"Jack, I'll be right there beside you," she said, kneading his shoulder. "Let her start the conversation, but if she starts to be hurtful, cut her off and have her removed from the set."

"It's already been a difficult day." He held up his right hand. "This thing's already starting to bleed."

She tried not to show her surprise at the blood already seeping through the bandage. She'd used her angel powers though to reinforce the bandage and keep the blood hidden from human eyes.

She was a little surprised that Jack could see it. Berith used a feather from his wing to hide the bleeding from him, too. To keep him calm. Maybe Jack saw past the energy it because of her mirrored powers—and the seraphim powers he carried?

Fear still shined in his eyes. He had a right to be scared after what he went through in Hell.

And if Lucifer got hold of him again, Jack wouldn't survive. She had to do everything Heavenly possible to keep him from being pulled back to Hell.

Or she'd lose him forever.

She gently took his right hand in both her hands and cradled it against her cheek.

"I know, lover," she said in a soft voice and kissed his fingers. "This was a terrible shock and I remember how weak the last tether made you. That's why we have to act fast. And we will."

She pulled him against her and kissed his lips.

"But for tonight, we can't fix it. What we can do though is celebrate the fact that we got through this first challenge." She kissed him again. "And our two drinks got the highest scores."

Focusing back on the challenges distracted him and she was thankful for that.

"That's right," he said, those green eyes brightening. "Our drinks did pretty well, didn't they?"

She nodded. "They did. So, why don't we go celebrate with Armand and Izzy and commiserate with Mark and Morgan."

The corners of his mouth lifted. "And ignore Rachel and my mother?"

"Whatever pleases you, my prince charming," she said with a chuckle and bowed.

He began slow-walking her backward out of the bathroom, his hands gripping hers.

"What pleases me, Cinderella..." he said with a smirk.

She felt the bed against the back of her calves.

"Is that wish list of yours," he continued, cupping her face in his hands and gently kissing her lips. "Where you throw me down on the bed and slowly undress me. Much more fun than drinks with my mother and Rachel, wouldn't you say?"

"Sure about that?" Talia asked and nodded behind him.

He turned around.

Kesien leaned against the wall behind him, Muriel beside him. Along with Anahera, Daidrean, and Deemah.

"We're uh..." Kesien stammered. "supposed to uh—stick to both of you...I—like glue."

Muriel tried not to laugh as she crossed her arms and leaned against the wall beside Kesien.

"But don't let us stop you," she said as Anahera giggled and covered her mouth. "Carry on, you two. I enjoy watching the occasional wild, depraved death angel monkey sex like the next angel."

"Apparently, not in this suite," Jack said with a growl and shook his head. "I'll get my shoes," he said. "Damned guardian angels, blocking my shots even from half court."

Kesien covered his mouth, hiding his laughter, but Anahera couldn't hold hers back.

Jack turned toward the armoire that stood against the other wall. "All these damned angels and not one wingman in the squad. Not one!"

He mumbled to himself, but angels had hypersensitive hearing. Of course, Jack had forgotten that.

Talia glanced over at Kesien. He still had his mouth covered, laughing harder, wings shuddering. Muriel was trying so hard not to laugh, but she couldn't help herself either.

Jack slid his feet into his black loafers and turned around. Talia put her arms around him, nibbling his earlobe.

"I'll make it up to you later, lover," she whispered. "After I send them on long-range patrol."

At last, his smile returned. "To New Zealand? By mule train?"

She laughed and took his arm in hers and they headed out the Halo Suite's black door, into the hallway. Headed to the cocktail party.

23

JACK WALKED WITH THE SLOWEST STRIDES HE COULD GET AWAY WITH down the stairs and through the dim-lit entryway. His and Talia's footfalls echoed through the gallery as they turned right and headed around the hallway to the back of the sprawling chateau. Toward the huge open-concept living room with all the blue couches and the Edwardian fireplaces. Three large, pale blue couches with off-white, aged end tables, a glass coffee table, and a butter yellow area rug adorned each conversation area. The line of six tall, white capitals cut through the space, making the room feel like an airy Greek temple.

This living room took up more than a third of the space in the back of the chateau. White crown molding adorned the ceiling above each of the three crystal chandeliers and framed the ceiling. Wide white baseboards trimmed the walls. The two fireplaces, along the outside wall, dated back to around 1914 when this mansion was built. It had eight of those big cobalt blue urns throughout the room, each one stuffed full with stargazer lilies, pastel pink roses, and fresh lavender that scented the air.

In the center of the room between the two fireplaces, two tables with white tablecloths had been setup by the show. One had wine and mixed drinks and the other had several silver trays of hot appetizers with a stack of small, clear plates and light blue cocktail napkins. A hint of bacon and tomato sauce hung above the scent of stargazer lilies.

The cast had gathered around Banks and Morgan and he immediately felt badly for them, having to leave so soon. He bet Morgan was heartbroken over not getting that fairytale wedding with Banks. But if he knew Banks, the dude was already planning one for her. He glanced down at the bandage on his right hand, already stained with blood.

The tether wound had already begun bleeding. Even from Hell, Lucifer would try and keep his wounded hand stirred up, his blood feeding the tether.

Talia had to sever this thing quickly. Lucifer would act on it the moment the tether anchored itself to his soul. Would the seraphim wards prevent Lucifer from dragging him out of the chateau? The regular angel wards hadn't stopped the tether at the beach house, but that had been Lucifer's place. He could have poked all kinds of holes in the death angel wards before that afternoon in the escape room.

Gianni glanced up and motioned him over.

He gave him a thumb's up and took hold of Talia's hand, hurrying over to the drinks table.

"What'll you have, babe?" he asked.

God, she was so hot in that red dress that hugged all her curves and showed off her long legs. But with a suite full of guardian angels, he was grounded until they took care of Abaddon.

"Don't you already know?" she asked with a smile and caressed his cheek.

"Good evening," he said to the short, stocky, dark-haired attendant in black pants and white tuxedo shirt. He glanced at the wines. They were the same six wines from the challenge. "My better half will have a pinot grigio."

He turned to Talia. "And what will I be having, my better half?" he asked with a smirk.

She leaned toward him, kissing his lips in a scorching kiss that burned right through him.

"The gentleman will have a merlot," she said to the attendant.

"Very good," he replied.

That was his favorite. His dad's influence.

With a nod, the attendant filled a wine glass with pinot grigio for Talia and one with merlot for him. The attendant handed the white wine to Talia and the red wine to him.

"Hey, you're Jack Casey," said the attendant with an excited grin. "You used to be on SanFran Confidential, didn't you?"

He nodded. "A few years ago. Thanks for remembering."

"Detective Davy Pierson." The dude was still grinning at him. "You were my favorite character on that show. Always giving the other cops hell for not doing the right thing. You were the best thing about that show."

"Appreciate that," said Jack, unable to hold back a smile. "It was a good run. I had a lot of fun playing Davy."

"Think you could take a selfie with me?" the dude asked, sliding out his phone.

"Sure," he said and stepped around the table.

He stood close, a few inches taller than the attendant, and smiled into the dude's camera as he held it out and took three or four shots.

"Would you also sign an autograph for me?" The dude slid a pale blue cocktail napkin and a black Sharpie across the table to him.

"You want my autograph?" he said, surprised.

The dude nodded. "Could you write it to James?" He grinned, pressing a hand to his chest. "That's me."

"Sure thing, James," he said and uncapped the black Sharpie.

He wrote, *To James, thanks for watching! Jack Casey, Detective Davy Pierson.* He recapped the Sharpie and slid it and the napkin back across the table to the attendant.

"Thanks, bro! You're the best. Seriously—thanks! Can't wait to insta and snap all this!"

"Thanks for the wine, James," he said and slid his arm in Talia's, turning toward the cast a few feet away.

"Don't you want some appetizers?" Talia asked.

He glanced at her. "Why don't you grab some for both of us?"

"But I only know what kind of cake you like," said Talia with a shrug. "Not what kind of appetizers."

Laughing, he nodded toward the appetizers. "Let's go pick some out then."

He handed her a clear plastic plate and grabbed one for himself, watching her eyes fill with wonder at all the choices. Stuffed mushrooms, mini egg rolls, little stuffed pastry triangles, meatballs, and shrimp skewers.

"I can't decide," she said, glancing from one to another.

"Then get one of each," he said. "That's why I plan to do."

She grinned. "Really?"

He nodded, urging her to try them all. She picked up silver tongs and took one of each appetizer. He took a spoonful of cocktail sauce and put it on the edge of her plate and then a spoonful of sweet and sour sauce.

"What's that?" she asked.

"Red stuff's for the shrimp. Pink stuff's for the egg roll."

He took one of each appetizer and then took an extra mini egg roll and an extra shrimp. He put a spoonful of cocktail sauce and sweet and sour sauce on his own plate. Grabbing four napkins, he handed her a couple and they moved toward the cast again.

Until his mother stepped in front of him.

"Jack?"

She had a glass of white wine in her hand, hair in a sleek bob. She'd worn that black cherry color for a decade or more. Even before she left Indiana. Hiding more and more grey every year. He couldn't remember her hair in any other color—or style.

"Mother." He stared at her, fighting the growing urge to duck out of the room.

"Could I talk to you for a moment?"

"For a moment," he snapped with a sigh. "Then I have to go talk to Banks and Morgan."

She motioned him over to a light blue couch behind her. The last thing he wanted to do was to sit down with this woman and talk about anything.

"Jack, I can go talk to Izzy and Morgan if you like," said Talia in a quiet voice.

"Oh, no you don't," he said in a sharp whisper. "Don't you dare leave me now."

She smiled. Guess she liked the idea that he needed her.

"I'll stay right with you then," she answered and followed beside him.

He took a big drink of merlot and sat down on a couch diagonal to the one where his mother sat down. She wore a long-sleeved purple tunic, black heels, and black leggings. She took a sip of her wine and then fixed him with her gaze.

"Jack, I owe you an apology," she said in that matter-of-fact way of hers, pushing aside any trace of warmth or emotion.

She never showed emotion or that motherly warmth that he'd needed and wanted as a kid. She'd always been like stainless steel. A quick sweep of her hand could erase any fingerprints that might have imprinted on her heart. Hot in summer, cold in winter. With no sympathy for anyone that didn't share her stainless-steel exterior. Especially her only son who'd been made of glass.

"I'm listening," he said in a quiet voice, stiffening.

Her jaw relaxed a little, those blue eyes flicking from his face to her wine glass, never staying too long on either one.

"I realize now that you went through a really difficult time in your life. And I wasn't very supportive. I should have tried to help you. And I apologize for that. It was more about your father than it had ever been about you. I wanted to explain that to you."

He frowned. "Dad? But he's been gone so long. And you've been divorced forever."

She nodded, took a sip of her wine, and then cradled the glass in both hands, staring into it. Not looking him in the eye.

"Jack, you've seen Tom's baby pictures. You look just like him. Act just like him. Even more drop-dead gorgeous than he was with lighter green eyes and blonder hair, and he was the most attractive man I'd ever met."

"That's a little creepy, mother," he said, shaking his head.

"Just listen, please," she snapped, staring into her glass again. "I loved your father deeply. Despite the drugs and alcohol problems."

"You said that before," he replied. "I never saw any of it."

"Because I covered it up," she said and took another drink of wine. "He'd disappear for days at a time, Jack, on drug and alcohol binges. I told you he was away on a job. Or at a conference."

He thought back to his childhood, remembering that Dad had been away a lot. She'd always said he was away on business and he'd never thought much about it. He winced. Until Dad got home and they'd fight like cats and dogs in their bedroom.

She'd been covering for him. A lot.

"Why'd you cover it up?" he asked, staring at her.

She looked up from her glass. "Because Tom was your hero, Jack. And I didn't want to take that away from you. You looked up to him. When he was home and clean, he worshipped you. He wanted a son so badly and I wanted to make him happy. I don't regret my four daughters at all, but I hadn't planned to have five kids."

For a moment, he was stunned, staring at her in surprise. She'd never gone out of her way for any of her children, but she'd had five just to give his dad a son? He'd had no idea.

"But you sure as hell regretted having me," he replied, finishing her statement. "You've always made that perfectly clear."

Her eyes turned glassy. "Not after I held you in my arms, Jack. But you were the sun, moon, and stars to that man. I hope you know that."

He nodded, feeling a little choked up. He took care of his old man through the cancer treatments and in hospice those last few months. He'd never doubted that his dad loved him. His mother, yes, but not his dad.

"And I took my decision out on you a lot, Jack," said his mother as she took another sip of wine. "I blamed you for Tom's drug and alcohol addictions. I blamed you for being born when I didn't want any more children. I blamed you for staying married to him and taking care of five children—and him. I'd go find him at the bars or his dealer's house and drag him home. I called in sick for him when he was in withdrawal or was passed out drunk. And I got a job to help pay the huge amount of debt he'd racked up."

He sat back on the couch, his brain just beginning to chew on what she'd said. He had no idea that his dad had substance abuse problems. Or that she'd loved him enough to cover it up.

"Finally, when you turned ten, I couldn't take anymore," she said, her voice turning shaky. "I had to get out. So, I filed for divorce. I got custody of your sister, Tara who was still seventeen. Tom got custody of you."

He already knew that. "You left your ten-year-old in that kind of environment?"

"Your sister, Meredith made sure you weren't neglected, Jack. That's why she and Whitney stayed in Indiana. To make sure you were okay."

That made his chest tighten. Meredith and Whitney stayed because of him? He had no idea.

"My point, Jack, is that I blamed you for Tom's behavior and I expected you to be just like him when you grew up. When I heard about the coke habit, I blamed you for it because you were your father's son." She sighed, her voice becoming tight and thin. "I didn't know that Rachel had forced the drugs on you. And I'm sorry for that. I should have stepped in and helped my son instead of just cutting you out of my life." Her eyes filled with tears. "I just couldn't deal with more drug and alcohol abuse, Jack. I'd been through decades of it with Tom."

He took a long sip of his merlot and set his plate on the end table, trying to process all of this information. So, his dad was a drug addict and an alcoholic. Great. That would have been nice to know up front.

"I get it," he snapped. "You saw him in me and wrote me off, too. No need to explain further."

"Jack," she said and reached out, taking hold of his hand. "I didn't mean it like that. I should have been your mother instead of a disgruntled ex-wife. And I wasn't. I blamed you for what happened and I didn't do anything to help my son. A son that I love every bit as much as I love my four daughters. Love I've never shown you, Jack. And I'm so sorry for that."

He pulled his hand away from her grasp and stood up, glaring. "Why the sudden urge for affection now? When I'm twenty-six. You never even hugged me as a kid. You didn't even come to Dad's funeral, back when I'd have killed to get you to show me the slightest bit of affection. I didn't see you for a decade, Mother. A decade! You offloaded me when you divorced Dad and you never looked back again. Not even a card or a call on my birthdays or on Christmas. Not until I got that part on SanFran Confidential. That was the first time you'd spoken to me since the divorce. And we lived in the same damned state by then!"

She scrambled up from the couch. "Jack, that's what I'm trying to explain to you. Your father's drug abuse made me treat you like you were a carbon copy of him. That's what I'm trying to apologize to you for—for running from Tom's drug and alcohol problems instead of being your mother."

He shook his head, stepping back from her, but she grabbed hold of him and put her arms around him, holding him close.

"Jack, I'm so sorry," she said, her voice breaking. "I should have been your mother and I failed you. I want to fix that going forward. I want you to know that you're my son and I'm proud of you no matter what. And I love you."

"Even if I don't marry Rachel?" he asked.

His mother let him go, staring at him. "Marry Rachel? What are you talking about?"

"Is this all conditional?" he snapped, taking a step back. "You trying to get me back with Rachel?"

"I'll admit that I'd love to see the two of you back together again—because you loved her," said his mother.

"Past tense," he said. "Besides the fact that she tried to kill me."

His mother gripped his upper arm. "I want you to marry whoever makes you happy. I don't know Talia, but if she's the one you love, then yes, I want you to marry her."

He frowned. That didn't sound like the mother he remembered.

"I made a lot of mistakes as a mother and most of them, I made with you, Jack. Because I was afraid Tom's addictions would become yours and ruin your life. And I couldn't be there to have my heart stomped again. It hurt too much."

Putting the wine glass to his lips, he drank a big mouthful of merlot and tried not to slam the whole thing.

"I don't know what to say," he said finally.

She let go of his arm, her hand sliding up to his face.

He froze. He wasn't used to affection from her and it just felt awkward to him.

"I know I can't fix the past, Jack," she said in a soft voice. "Just let me try again. That's all I'm asking. I want to see you get married."

He took a step back from her and slammed the rest of his wine.

"Like be on the show's wedding—if we win?" He gave her his darkest smile. "Should have seen that angle from a mile out. Be on the show, let your company plan the wedding. It'd be a shame if all that publicity went to somebody else, wouldn't it?"

"Jack, no," she said, reaching out to him. "That's not what I'm saying. Win or lose, I want to see you get married. Not as an event planner. As your mother."

He laughed. "Yeah, how would that look to have my mother and her company barred from the event? Gotta keep up appearances, don't we? My life's bad for business."

She shook her head. "Jack, please—this isn't about my business. It's about my son getting married. That's it. No cameras. No event planning. No publicity. I just want to be there when you get married."

Talia was beside him, an arm sliding around his waist. He was about to bolt out of this room and she knew it. She handed him another glass of merlot. He set the empty one on an end table.

"You've heard what your mother has to say, so for now, just think about it," she said to him in a soft voice that blunted the sharp edge of his anger and his flight response.

Finally, he nodded. "I'll think about it, mother," he said and backed away from her.

Talia picked up the two plates of appetizers and nudged him

toward the center of the room. Where Banks and Morgan stood, talking to cast and crew.

"Come on, let's go talk to Mark and Morgan," said Talia against his ear.

He took a long sip of merlot and let her lead him away from his mother.

Gianni eyed them as they approached, his gaze shining with concern.

"Everything okay, Jack?" he asked, glancing over at Jack's mother and then at him.

Whole room probably heard his mother's loud voice, letting everyone know about his shit childhood and losing his dad at seventeen. And when they all heard that his dad had been a drug addict and an alcoholic, they'd add two and twelve together to get four. And more rumors would haunt his career. Just what he needed.

"Just fine," said Jack, grinning as he patted Gianni's shoulder, shoving away his anger and resentment to make room for his game face again. "How's Banks doing? Pretty disappointed, I'm sure."

Gianni relaxed a little, that Cary Grant grin lighting his face, but the daytime soap star kept glancing over at his mother and then back at him.

"He and Morgan both are pretty down about it," said Gianni who glanced at Rachel and Eric on the other side of the group. "They thought Rachel and Eric would leave first."

Jack shook his head and took a sip of merlot. "Unfortunately, it was never a competition between other couples. It was with ourselves. How well we know our partners."

"True," said Gianni as he smiled at Talia. "And it looks like you and Talia are off to a strong start."

"So are you and Izzy," he replied and nodded at Izzy who chattered away with Talia and Morgan in their own little huddle. "Things going as well as they appear?"

A bright smile curved across Gianni's face, lighting it up. "Even better," he said and nudged him. "I couldn't be happier, Jack. Izzy is definitely the one. And I can't imagine my life without her."

That made Jack grin. "Dude, I can't tell you how happy that makes me. I'd love to see the two of you get married."

"You will," Gianni replied. "I'd really love to have you as my best man, Jack."

"Me? Really?" He laid a hand against his chest, getting a little choked up. "You want me as your best man?"

Gianni patted him on the back. "We've been through a lot together on this show, Jack and I consider you one of my closest friends. Even if you don't return my calls."

He sighed, feeling badly about losing his phone. "Seriously, dude— I really did lose my phone. I don't ghost people—except Rachel and my mother. And that was just returning the favor."

Gianni laughed. "Just giving you a hard time, Jack. But really, would you stand up as my best man at my wedding? Whether it's here or later."

"Of course, I will, dude. I'd be honored. But only if you'll stand up for mine."

Gianni's big brown eyes got even bigger. "Your best man?"

Jack nodded. "Hell yes, you're my best man. I'd like to ask Banks to stand in my party, too, but you've been my best man through four seasons, Gianni."

"Even the first one, Jack?" he asked with a laugh. "We were both vying for Talia as I recall."

For part of that time, he'd thought that Talia was using him to get to Gianni, but it was just a story Morgan Boyer made up because she was jealous of Talia. But Gianni stood up for him again and again— even saved his life when Lucifer tried to drown him in the ocean. And Banks stopped him from sending Talia home that first season, using his only veto—which would have been the biggest mistake of Jack's life. And saved his life after he'd overdosed on flake.

"Even the first one," Jack replied. "You knew how crazy about her I was and you stepped aside—even when I'd behaved like the world's biggest dumbass."

"True," he said, nodding. "But she never gave up on you, Jack." He glanced over at her and Izzy. "And she never will. Don't forget that."

Jack shook his head. "I won't. I love her to my last breath, Gianni. For me, there will never be anyone but Talia."

"Can't wait to see you two tie the knot," said Gianni. "But you know, I rather liked what you said to Rachel during the break. How nice it would be to see all of these couples get married in a royal wedding."

"That would be my kind of fairytale ending," said Jack. "Where all four Cinderellas married their Prince Charmings. Hey, if the glass slipper fits..."

"What was that about a glass slipper fitting, Jack?" Banks asked, moving toward him and Gianni.

"Jack was just saying how fitting it would be if all four of us got to marry our princesses in that royal wedding," Gianni replied, motioning at Jack.

Jack nodded.

"Cool idea, Jack," said Banks, his gaze turning dark. "But it's over for Morgan and me now. Up to you or Gianni to win this thing."

"Listen, Banks," said Jack, leaning closer as he lowered his voice. "Regardless of whether we get married on this show or off it, I'd like for you to stand up with me as one of my groomsmen. You're a really good friend."

Banks just stared at him a moment. "Wow, Jack—seriously?"

"You stopped me from making the biggest mistake of my life," he said with a smile. "You also saved it when you did CPR on me. When my heart stopped from doing those eight balls of coke."

Banks smiled and extended his hand. Jack shook it. "Jack, I'd love to stand up with you at your wedding. Just tell me when and I'll be there."

"Thanks, dude," he said. "I appreciate it. I'll let you know when as soon as Talia and I finalize the date."

"So, maybe you'll answer your phone the next time I call?" Banks said with a grin. "Left you four messages over the past few months."

Gianni burst out laughing. "I just gave him hell about that, Mark," said Gianni.

Jack sighed, hanging his head. "I lost my phone, dude—I swear I did. During the finale of The Ever After Hour and I haven't had a chance to replace it yet."

"It's really true," said Gianni. "He's had everybody in Hollywood blowing up his phone, Mark and no one's gotten hold of him. Including his agent."

Mark made a face. "Is that what that open letter from Evan Bellows in Variety was about? Him begging Jack to call him."

"Exactly," Gianni said with a laugh. "Everyone thinks Jack's been blowing them off, not knowing that Jack lost his phone."

"Dude, I swear it on my mother's grave," Jack replied. "I really did lose my phone."

Gianni frowned. "But your mother's not dead."

He sighed. "A dude can hope, can't he?"

They both laughed.

"So, that's how you get call backs from Hollywood directors?" Banks replied, elbowing him. "By losing your phone."

"Dude thinks I'm ghosting him," said Jack with a shrug. "And I'm not."

Banks grinned and shook his head. "That guy really wants you back on SanFran Confidential, Jack. Bad. I heard that Lare Dumont just combusted and stopped showing up. He wasn't returning calls either. Bellows is probably losing his shit and he's trying to save the show."

Jack just smiled. Lare Dumont got what he deserved—unlike Rachel Daniels—and he was in Hell after his contract with Lucifer came due. He didn't think Lare's cell phone plan extended to Hell.

"You going back?" Gianni asked him point-blank.

"Nah," said Jack, taking a drink of his wine. "Don't want to end up doing flake again. Or getting back in with that crowd. Bad environment for me."

"But Jack, Bellows said money is no object," said Banks.

Jack shrugged. "What happens if I go back and the show still tanks? Gets cancelled? I get screwed again. Besides, don't think I could trust the rest of my costars after what happened to me there. Even without Lare and Rachel."

Banks poked his shoulder with his fist. "Good call, Jack. But damn, that's a lot of money to ignore."

"It's just promised, Banks," he said. "What good is it if the network pulls the plug on it."

"You're right."

"What does Talia think?" Gianni asked.

"I…haven't exactly discussed it with her yet."

Gianni stared at him in surprise. "You've already made up your mind without talking to Talia about it? She won't like that, Jack."

"I'll talk to her before I officially decline it," he said. "I haven't actually heard any of these offers yet, just heard about them. We'll talk as soon as I get a new phone and go through my voicemails."

Suddenly, Gianni frowned and pointed at his right hand. "What happened to your hand?" He squinted. "Wow, that's fresh blood, Jack! Talking to your mother make you slit your wrist?"

He glanced down at the bandage. His palm had already bled through the sparkling white bandage that Berith had applied to his hand. But now, everyone else could see it, too. Looked like the tether had overridden whatever power she'd used on the bandage.

"Damn, Jack!" said Banks. "That looks bad."

"Don't tempt me, Gianni," he said and turned his palm downward. "Cut it on some broken glass. Dropped a couple wine glasses in the suite. It may need stitches. It just keeps seeping."

Gianni shook his head. "Jack, let the set doctor look at it. She may send you into Santa Rosa to get that checked though."

"I will if it doesn't stop bleeding," he said. "But it was just before the live show, so it hasn't had time to heal yet."

Jack stayed until the meet and greet was over, wishing Banks and Morgan the best before he returned to the suite alone. Talia stayed and chatted with Izzy and Morgan. He couldn't wait to get out of there, wanting to rest up before Sunday orientation for the second challenge. In the dining room at 8 A.M. for breakfast and instructions. This wound had already taken a lot out of him, so he wanted to be well-rested for the next challenge.

24

WHEN TALIA WOKE UP ON SUNDAY MORNING, JACK WAS ALREADY IN THE shower. He'd been asleep when she returned Friday night which surprised her. But he'd had a difficult day Friday with his mother and Lucifer tricking him into a new soul tether. He was already worried about ending up back in Hell, but now, he was being bled by the new tether wound.

And it was weakening him.

All day Saturday, she tried to get him to relax and rest, but even walking around the gardens had taxed his energy. He came back tired and went to bed early last night, too, leaving her alone to hang out with Gianni and Izzy on the patio.

She'd hoped Berith would give the okay today to use the resurrect power on Jack. When that soul tether reached Jack's soul, Lucifer would retrieve him. They were running out of time.

Lucifer's tether frightened her more than anything right now. She couldn't lose Jack. She wouldn't.

She pushed the lavender comforter off her shoulders. Angels didn't sleep, but with her human soul, she found herself falling asleep beside him for hours at a time. Not as long as humans slept, but long enough that she hadn't heard him get up and climb into the shower.

Beside her, his blood stained the sheets where his hand had rested all night. She shuddered, her stomach dropping. The circle of blood was at least eight inches in diameter.

So much blood for such a small wound. It made her worry even more.

She rose from the bed, wearing Jack's long-sleeved blue *The Cinderella Hour* T-shirt. She slid her bare feet into some white slippers and put on a white terrycloth robe with a sun, moon, and stars embroidered across the front pocket. Provided by the vineyard.

Still, the shower ran. He liked to take long, hot showers when he was tired or didn't feel well.

She padded out into the suite's living area where her squad kept vigil at the three windows and near the black French doors.

"Muriel, how long has Jack been in the shower?" she asked.

She knew her best friend was watching Jack like a hawk for her. She always had.

"More than fifteen minutes now," said Muriel. "You might want to go check on him. He was a little unsteady this morning when he got up."

"A little unsteady?" Talia cried.

Her heart began to race. She turned around and blinked to the bathroom door. Locked.

Using her angel powers, she stepped through the door. Into the steamy bathroom.

"Jack? Are you all right?" she called into the bathroom's thick fog. "Jack?"

"Yeah, Talia," he answered.

She moved through the mist toward the shower door, all fogged up as she opened it.

He sat in the corner of the shower, water washing over him as he hugged the wall. The bandage was gone from his right hand. A thin stream of bright red blood trickled across his hand and down his thigh, running into the drain.

"Jack!"

She threw off her robe and kicked off the slippers, stepping into the hot shower. She dropped down beside him and slid her arms around him.

"Jack? Talk to me!"

"I'll be out in a minute, babe," he answered, his voice sounding weak and disoriented.

"You weren't supposed to remove that bandage, Jack," she said with a sigh and glanced around for it.

When she glanced out the shower door, she saw it lying on the white marble countertop.

She blinked out of the shower and over to the countertop, retrieving the bandage. And a lavender bath towel. She hurried across the warm marble tiles and back to the shower. Turning off the water, she bent down to him, dried his hands, and slid the power-infused bandage back over the tether wound in his right palm.

Gripping the bandage around his hand, she called up her angel powers, fitting it tight against his hand again. It was already soaked with blood.

He needed Berith to apply a new one. Right away.

Gently, she dried him with the towel and grabbed the robe she'd dropped in the floor. She got his arms into the sleeves and wrapped the terrycloth robe around his beautiful body, tying the robe closed.

She half-carried him to the door and unlocked it. She blew on the door, her angel powers opening it as she carried him out of the bathroom and over to the bed.

"Jack!" Muriel cried, rushing over to the bed. "What's the matter with him?"

Kesien and Anahera were behind her, looking worried.

"I'm fine, Talia," he said in a thin voice. "Just a couple more minutes in the shower and I'll be out."

"Of course, lover," she said and held him against her on the bed. "Just a couple more minutes."

Jack's hair was still dripping wet, so she dried it off with the towel. And her brightening halo. He was shivering.

"Muriel, get Berith down here right now. He needs a new bandage and more healing." She glanced over at Kesien. "Kesien, freeze time until we get this healed."

The tall, curly black-haired angel nodded and turned toward the windows. He held out his hand until a pale blue light rolled through the room. Pausing time on earth.

Already, Jack's bloodied hand had soaked through the bandage and dripped down his arm onto the robe.

"Here, Talia," Muriel said, carrying a small lavender hand towel.

She wrapped it around Jack's hand and held it there, holding it up his head.

"Did you summon Berith?" Talia asked, cradling Jack against her as he laid his head against her neck, eyes closed.

Muriel nodded. "Yep, when I went to grab another towel. She should be showing up soon."

"This tether isn't acting like the first one, Muriel," she said, glancing at her. "It's like it has accelerated the process or something."

"Yeah, he wasn't quite right last night when he came back to the suite either."

Talia's eyes widened. "Not right how?"

"A little dizzy," said Muriel, nodding at Jack. "And a little unsteady as he got undressed. Kesien and I helped him hang up his suit and crawl into bed. He seemed okay when he got into the shower this morning though, but we only saw him for a second or two as he hurried into the bathroom."

Talia pointed at the circle of blood on Jack's side of the bed. "See how much this thing has already bled."

"Wow, Talia," said Muriel, moving closer to the bed. "This is bad. You said Lucifer put the tether inside Jack's lost phone?"

She nodded. "Abaddon tossed it through the ward. Because it was Jack's property, it passed through the ward without a problem. Infecting Jack. It all happened so fast."

"Gotta admit, that was a Lucifer-level sneak attack," said Muriel. "Never dreamed he could do something like that."

Talia shook her head. "Neither did I," she said and glanced around the suite. "Where's Berith?"

"Hope she gets here fast," said Muriel and laid her hand gently against Jack's damp hair. "He's not doing very well. He's really out of it."

She nodded. She'd never seen him like this before.

It seemed like an hour before Berith appeared in the suite, an aqua story gem in her hand. She looked worried, haggard, grey eyes sharp and piercing as she rushed over to the bed.

"Sorry, had to get another stone from Pravuil," she said and lifted one of Jack's eyelids. "How is he?"

Jack didn't even react to her presence or her touch.

Talia shook her head. "Not good. The tether wound is bleeding profusely, Berith."

Her eyes widened as she sat down on the lavender comforter. "How profusely?"

Talia pointed to the sheets. "That's how he woke up. When I found him in the shower, blood ran down his body and stained the water circling the drain red."

"That's a lot," she said.

"He took the bandage off to shower," Talia replied. "I got it back on him fifteen or twenty minutes later, but it wasn't stopping the bleeding."

Berith shook her head. "It shouldn't be bleeding like this, Talia. Not continuously."

"It's been accelerated somehow, hasn't it?" Talia looked deeply into Berith's light grey eyes.

She nodded grimly and took hold of Jack's right hand. When she removed the towel, it was soaked in bright red blood already. Underneath the towel, the entire bandage was damp and reddish brown.

"We've got to slow this down," said Berith and pressed the aqua gem against Jack's bloodied palm.

She held it there and closed her eyes until a deep yellow light surged down her right arm and into Jack's hand. The light enveloped his arm and crept across his chest to his heart.

"Glad he's right-handed," said Berith.

"Why?" Talia asked with a frown.

"He caught the phone with his right hand. So, the tether has to cross his chest to reach his heart. Takes longer that way. If he'd caught it with his left hand, the process would have been almost instant."

Talia shuddered. "Instant?"

Berith nodded. "Let's see how far the tether's already traveled since insertion last night. And my power countering it."

The yellow light disappeared as the aqua stone began to glow. The aqua light traveled down his fingers and wrist to his elbow. The tether had traveled almost to his shoulder.

"There's still time, Talia," said Berith, nodding at Jack's shoulder. "It's accelerated, but it still has to travel across his chest to his heart." She grinned. "And I'm about to throw more obstacles in front of it."

Again, she closed her eyes. A burst of yellow light washed down Jack's arm and into his chest from Berith's hands.

Talia watched the dripping blood become a slow drip until finally, it began to congeal. And stop bleeding. Only when the glow subsided did Berith open her eyes.

"There," she said with a smile and lifted the stone from Jack's palm. "That should make that tether move at a crawl until we can cast the resurrect power on him. Just need to rebandage his hand with a fresh bandage."

"Why not just do that now?" Talia asked.

"Because we have to gather the parts of Creation again to cast it," said Berith. "Lucifer knows that. And he's counting on that taking longer than the tether's activation because most of those elements can only be found in Heaven, Talia."

She felt her heart smash against her chest. "I can't leave him right now and return to Heaven."

Berith patted her shoulder. "You won't have to, Talia. Because of my rare healing powers, I learned that can awaken the resurrect power, too. I will reenact the process using the splinters that Jack brought back from the Garden."

"You can?"

"Yes," said Berith, nodding. "When I have awakened spheres from all those splinters, I'll bring them here, so you use the power on him. I'll bring a small piece of Aeonium and some of Eolowen's soil from beneath the willow tree, so I can extract a green orb from the last grain of sand. And the first drop of water, so I can awaken the power. You will need an orb of Jack's breath to break the tether—but not his last."

Talia couldn't help but smile. "Thank you, Berith."

"My pleasure to help both of you, Talia," she said. "And you can help me awaken the resurrect power. Don't worry. Lucifer won't get a second chance at Jack."

"But what about Abaddon?" Talia asked, nodding toward the windows. "He's out there, waiting for Jack's tether to reach his soul, so that big monster can drag him off to Lucifer. Why hasn't Pravuil found anything yet?"

Berith bowed her head. "He's still researching it. He hasn't given up. High House is still trying to figure out what to do about Jack's wings and halo, too." She glanced over her shoulder and turned back to Talia. "Apparently, there isn't a precedent for it. And they haven't found a way around rendering him a fallen angel if they remove his wings and halo."

"They wouldn't do that, would they?" Talia asked, terrified they'd proceed with that decision if there weren't any other options.

"No, they won't make him a fallen angel, Talia. Don't worry. They don't want to punish him for his sacrifices, but they're struggling to make things right. It's hard, especially now that Jack has stopped aging."

"What? Stopped aging? Then that means—"

Berith nodded. "That he's not completely human anymore—exactly. You didn't hear that from me though."

If Jack had stopped aging, maybe they had more time to resolve this issue of staying together? And she wouldn't have to watch him grow old and die. But what did that mean for his soul? He'd earned his eternity—to hopefully see his dad again and anyone else he lost throughout his life. No matter what happened, he was being forced to give something up. It wasn't fair.

"I know that look, Talia," said Berith, giving her a warning glance. "Nothing is set in stone yet or even been decided, so don't fret over anything. Heaven wants to reward Jack, not take things away from him."

Finally, Talia nodded. She knew that Archangel Azrael and Seraphina were both fighting for Jack. She just had to hope for the best outcome. That she and Jack could stay together. It was the only thing she wanted. And he wanted. If that didn't work, she'd fight for it. To her last wing feather.

"Thank you for telling me this, Berith," said Talia, reaching out to grip Berith's hand. "It means a lot to me—and him."

Berith smiled. "Jack's like a son to me, Talia."

"I just met Jack's mother this week, Berith," she said with a sigh. "And I can guarantee you that he sees you like the mother he always wanted. She's starting to come around a bit though, so there's hope."

"I'm glad," said Berith. She kissed Jack's cheek and rose from the bed. "Okay, I'll return tomorrow night with everything we'll need to use the resurrect power, Talia."

"Tomorrow night?"

Berith nodded. "Azrael and I have to go see the Scribe and appear at High House tomorrow. For Jack. The barriers I placed in the tether's way will dramatically slow it down. Tomorrow night, call when you're back in the suite. Azrael and I will arrive with the shards, the Aeonium, and the soil. And more of the guard just in case Abaddon and Lucifer sense me awakening resurrect and you using it."

"We'll be ready," said Talia. "Will he be okay until then?"

Berith cast a worried glance at Jack. "He's going to be a little lightheaded from the blood loss. The barrier I put between Jack's soul and the tether won't halt the blood loss, just slow it down. He'll start to lose blood again by tomorrow night. So, try not to let him do anything too strenuous until then, okay?"

She gasped. She had no idea what the second challenge was for the show. They were supposed to find out at the eight A.M. orientation.

She glanced at the clock on the nightstand, to see where it had stopped when Kesien froze time.

7:42 A.M. They still had time to dress and get to the orientation. She'd just have to get the guard to help her heal Jack as much as possible. To get him through the events.

"I'll do my best," she said. "But you know Jack."

Berith rolled her eyes. "Yes, I do," she said. "And you have your work cut out for you."

Berith reached out and pressed the stone against his forehead, letting gold light spill over him and onto his chest. She kept the stone in place until Jack came into some sort of awareness.

"What's wrong?" he mumbled. "I'm up. Just need to get in the shower."

Talia ran her hands through his damp hair.

"You're fine, lover. Berith's here, doing a bit of healing on that hand of yours."

He opened his eyes to slits and glanced past Talia to Berith.

"Hi, Berith," he said, sounding almost a little drunk. "How long you been here?"

"Just a little while, Jack," she said and cupped his chin. "You hang in there, okay? We'll have this ridiculous tether broken by tomorrow. Now, I'm going to rebandage your hand."

Berith wrapped a fresh, sparkling white bandage around and around his hand, between index finger and thumb, in several layers, and used her angel powers to seal the ends against the bandage's fabric.

He looked up at Talia. "By the way, you made my blood boil in that dress last night. Just saying."

Talia laughed and held him tighter.

"I love you, Jack Casey," she said and kissed the side of his face.

"I love you, too," he said in a quiet voice. "We need to get going. Don't want to be late for the next challenge's introduction."

Berith finished healing him and pulled the stone away from his forehead.

"That should make him feel better," said Berith, sliding the stone into the pocket of her grey robes. "But as that wound starts to bleed again, he'll struggle with it. See you Monday."

"Bye and thanks, Berith," Talia called as she blinked out of the suite.

Jack reached up to his hair with his left hand. "Why is my hair damp?" he asked.

"You passed out in the shower, so I carried you out here and called Berith."

"I already took a shower? Thought I dreamed it."

She shook her head as he glanced down and saw the white terrycloth robe she'd tied around him. His leanly muscled body looked sexy in it, especially with his damp hair and those light green eyes burning like embers.

"Thanks, babe," he said. "This tether's bleeding as much as the last one. Kind of took me off guard. And a hot shower just feels so good."

She cradled his face in her hands and kissed him. "Well, you're doing better now. Let's get dressed and ready for orientation."

He nodded and struggled out of her arms. Onto his feet. A little shaky, he tottered over to the armoire on the right side of the room and took out a pair of teal boxer briefs and faded Levi's. He seemed to have an endless supply of those jeans, but she never got tired of seeing him in a pair that hugged his lean frame in all the right places. He put on boxer briefs under his robe and pulled on jeans, a pale mint green V-neck sweater, and tan socks. He slid his feet into tan loafers.

As he combed his damp hair, she pulled out a jean skirt and a button-down chambray shirt over a pale pink tank top. She slid on black flats as he stepped out of the bathroom. She couldn't breathe for a moment.

He was stunning with that short, light blond hair, bangs soft and feathered against his forehead, that smirk turning up the heat in those piercing, pale green eyes. He just took her breath away.

She walked over to him and laid her hands against his smooth-shaven face, kissing him hard on those smirking lips. Wanting to fall into his arms and feel his hot hands against her body.

He kissed her back in deep, kissing sips that were like hot coals against her mouth. She ran one hand across his neck, into his blond hair, fingers tangling in the soft, damp strands as his fiery mouth covered hers. But he struggled a bit with his right hand as it slid around her waist, pulling her against him.

"Wish we had a private room," he whispered against her ear, his lips brushing across her earlobe, sending chills down her back.

"But we do—"

"Angel free?" he asked, letting her go.

She sighed, frowning. "No. But they could go on patrol."

His mood lightened. "Until you call them back?"

"Mostly," she said.

"Mostly?" He shook his head. "Guess I'll have to wait until our honeymoon."

She'd heard the word before, but didn't know what it meant.

"What's a honeymoon?" she asked.

He gave her that bad boy smirk again, taking her in his arms. "It's what comes after the wedding ceremony and the reception. The bride tosses her bouquet and then she and her new husband leave the reception for a holiday together." He brushed his lips across her ear again. "They lock themselves in a hotel room somewhere and have wild monkey sex for days."

She stared at him. "You're making that up!"

He looked a little surprised by her reaction. "It was just a joke, Tal. A lot of couples have already slept together before that, but that first night of the honeymoon is the first time a couple makes love as husband and wife."

Talia felt bad for her knee jerk reaction. It was the locking themselves into a room that she didn't like.

"No, no—locking themselves in a room. They both have the key, right?"

At this, he laughed. "Of course," he said and smiled. "They go on holiday and check into a suite like this and then spend several days in the room. Having wild monkey sex."

Now, she understood. She gently reached out and caressed his face. "Is that where I get to finally throw you down on the bed and slowly undress you? Just you and me?"

"Or quickly...I'm flexible," he said, that smirk turning up the corners of his sexy mouth again as he reached out and caressed her face with his left hand.

"You're the hottest thing I've ever seen, Jack Casey," she said and leaned up to his mouth, kissing him again. "But we'd better get downstairs and find out about our next challenge."

He glanced around the room, seeing Muriel, Anahera, and Kesien checking the wards at the windows and along the floors.

"Since I can't make love to you," he said with a heavy sigh, "let's get going."

"How's your hand feel now?" she asked, stroking the fingers of his right hand.

"Better," he said. "And I don't feel like I'm going to pass out again."

"For now," said Talia. "Berith said that by tomorrow, you'll be feeling weak and lightheaded again. She showed me how far the tether had traveled."

His eyes got wide. "You could see how far it had gotten?"

She nodded. "It was almost to your shoulder. Berith slowed down its progression again."

He let out a breath that he'd been holding. "There's some good news."

"Ready?" she asked.

She needed to ask Kesien to unfreeze time.

Jack nodded.

She turned to Kesien and gave him a nod. With the wave of his hand, he unfroze time.

He glanced at the clock as it turned 7:42 A.M. "Guess we'd better head down now."

Talia slid against his side and gripped his left hand. "I'm ready," she said.

She waved at Muriel who nodded and kept checking the wards as they headed out of the suite and down the stairs. As they reached the landing, she could already smell the heavy, spicy scent of those lilies in the first-floor urns. Their scent drowned out the delicate smell of roses and the clean scent of lavender.

They moved through the entryway and turned right into the hallway. Bound for the dining room and the introduction of the show's second challenge.

25

JACK AND TALIA PULLED OUT TWO BURGUNDY CHAIRS AT THE LONG, rectangular table and sat down in the dining room. Attendants in black pants and white tuxedo shirts set two white carafes of coffee on the table.

The coffee smelled hot and rich. A small metal pitcher of cream and a white ceramic container with sugar packets set on the table. A heavy white mug with the purple *Royal Wedding Hour* logo had been placed at every chair.

He turned his mug up and waited for the carafe to slide his direction. Talia sat down on his left. Gianni was already seated to his right. Across the table from Gianni sat Eric and Rachel. He frowned. Rachel watched him intently.

"Good morning, Jack and Talia," said Gianni, leaning toward him with the carafe.

"Hi, Armand and Izzy," said Talia with a nod.

"Hey, Izzy, Gianni," Jack replied and took the warm carafe. "How you doing?"

He poured steamy coffee into his mug and leaned toward Talia.

"Coffee, babe?"

She shook her head.

He set the carafe back in the center of the table and picked up his mug. Smelled good and strong. He poured a little cream in it and swirled it around the cup. After a moment or two, he drank a sip. Tasted good with the cream.

When he glanced up, Rachel was still watching him. He ignored it, only glancing up when Herb, Jennifer, and Steve walked into the room. They sat down across the table. Near the door.

Jack slid the carafe over to Talia. "Pass that to Jennifer, please."

Nodding, she handed it to Jennifer, who sat down on Herb's right, Steve on Herb's left.

"Good morning, cast," said Herb, leaning back in his chair.

Everyone around the table said hello and good morning.

Herb was casual today, in dark jeans and a grey dress shirt, sleeves rolled up. Jennifer had on a red, long-sleeved top and black leggings, her dark brown hair in a loose bun. She laid her clipboard in her lap. Steve had on faded jeans and a jean shirt over a deep purple T-shirt with *The Royal Wedding Hour* logo on it. His brown hair was loose around his shoulders, his beard short and trimmed.

"Good morning, Herb, Jennifer—Steve," said Jack, settling back in his chair, mug of coffee cradled in both hands.

His right hand hurt this morning, but the warm coffee made it feel better. His brain was still fuzzy about what had happened since this morning. He remembered waking up and getting into the shower. And still felt cold. The last thing he remembered was hitting his hand against the shower door, causing it to bleed a lot. As the steam rose, he got lightheaded. Then he found himself in a robe on the bed in Talia's arms. With Berith healing him.

He was still missing some moments in between. It felt much later than eight o'clock.

"Breakfast will be served right after our orientation," said Jennifer, "so, stay put after we finish. It won't take long."

Herb nodded. "Jennifer's right. This won't take long. Because the second challenge is very straightforward. First challenge was about food. Second challenge is about venue and flowers."

Eric raised an eyebrow. "Flowers?" Rachel looked at him and shrugged.

"That's right, Eric," said Jennifer as she addressed the whole group. "Flowers. The second challenge will be a scavenger hunt of sorts."

"Of sorts?" Rachel asked.

"More or less," Jennifer said, smiling. "See, there are three hidden places located here at Le Château des Angés: a fountain, a ballroom, and a parlor. First couple to find and claim a spot gets married in that location on the grounds. If they win."

Hidden places on the estate? That sounded intriguing.

He loved the idea of a secret staircase in this crazy, museum-like mansion. Or places from 1914 that people had forgotten. Places preserved from that time period. He gazed at Talia who smiled and held his left hand. He squeezed her hand.

"And the next part of the challenge is for our brides to select four flowers from a list. Then as a couple, our brides and grooms will locate where each of the four flowers in the bride's bouquet are growing on the grounds."

"How will you record that information?" Izzy asked.

Jennifer held up a physical paper map and a small tablet computer about the size of a paperback book.

"Each couple will carry one of these small tablets. It has a map on it, but you'll get the paper map today. You'll use the tablet to scan a QR code for each flower you locate. Since this is an historic estate that was once open to the public, there are placards in the gardens that identify each flower by name with a QR code. That's what you'll scan. The couple with the fastest time for locating all four flowers and one of the hidden venues wins the challenge. Any questions?"

Rachel spoke up. "How will we know where to search for the venues?"

Jennifer grinned. "Very good question, Rachel." She held up the tablet again. "On your tablets, you'll find a document with the history of the property and an original map of the chateau. You'll find the tablet outside your doors first thing Monday morning. I'm handing out the list of flowers and paper maps today for you to study. I won't let you out of this room without turning in your flower list though. And just so you know, none of this information is available on the web."

"Times will only be known by me," said Steve, leaning forward with his coffee cup. "I'm monitoring the network drive and the database as it gets updated with your scans. You'll scan a QR code inside the hidden space as well. All of the codes are entered into a database with a device number and time stamp for each couple. And I'll also be checking in your devices—to make sure everything matches."

Jennifer nodded and glanced around the table. "And just to clarify, the couple with the slowest time will leave us on Friday at the live show."

"How long will we have to do this?" Jack asked.

"From Monday morning until sunset on Wednesday, Jack," she replied. "Interviews will be on Thursday. Of course, the longer you take, the higher your risk of getting the slowest time—and the lowest score. Couples can decide which venue you want to search for by Monday. But you must pick four flowers today. From the list. Before leaving this room."

"Got it," he said. "That's clear enough for me."

Jennifer gazed around the table. "Any more questions?"

Talia shook her head. No one else spoke.

"All right then," said Jennifer, rising from her chair, clipboard in hand. "Let's have breakfast."

Getting up from the table, Jennifer hurried over and opened the door to the dining room. Three attendants in white pants and white kitchen jackets carried in two trays.

Jack smelled tomatoes and peppers.

The three attendants, a woman and two men, set down trays and a stack of small white dishes. Breakfast burritos!

"Two trays of sausage, cheese, and egg breakfast burritos," Jennifer announced. "One tray is rice and veggies for the vegetarians. With cheese and eggs on the side for any vegans in the room—like me. Dig in!"

Everyone got up from the table and formed a line around it as the attendants set down napkins and a fork at every person's chair. When Jack got to the trays, he saw that the burritos were made from small tortillas, so he took two with sausage.

"Hungry, babe?" he called across the table.

She nodded. "One of whatever you're having."

He grabbed another plate and put a third burrito on it, carrying both plates over to his chair. He slid the plate over to Talia.

"What is it?" she asked, poking it with her fork.

He chuckled. "It's a breakfast burrito."

She wrinkled her nose, staring at him with those intense light grey eyes. He loved her reactions to human food. Most of the time, it just confused her.

"What's that?" she asked.

"It's sausage, egg, and cheese. With onions, peppers, and tomatoes in a flour tortilla. With salsa."

She shook her head. "All of that together? Humans are weird," she said and cut into it with a fork.

He just laughed, wondering if she'd hate it or like the taste. He loved burritos for any meal.

Talia made her *it's not bad* face and kept eating as he picked up his first breakfast burrito in his left hand and took a bite. Talia's eyes widened when she saw him holding the burrito in his hand.

"All that silverware I had to learn about and you use your hands?" she said in surprise.

"Try it," he said with a smirk. "It's rolled into its own container. No silverware needed for this meal."

With an awkward sweep of her hand, Talia picked up the burrito, balanced it between her fingers, and took a bite. She smiled.

"It's much better this way," she said. "I hate trying to remember when to use all those forks and spoons."

"Me, too, babe," he said and took another bite of his burrito.

As everyone ate, Jennifer dropped off a purple pen and a list of flowers to Talia, Izzy, and Rachel. Talia gazed at it in between bites of her burrito. Jack leaned over and glanced at the list, printed in color.

About twenty flowers listed in two columns, front and back. With pictures of each flower in a column beside the names.

He watched Talia's face light up as she went through the list.

"So, the flowers I choose will be in the bride's bouquet if we win?" she asked, the light just dancing off her beautiful oval face.

He couldn't help but smile. She was intrigued by this bouquet. He had to make note of what she chose, because if they didn't win, he'd get her the biggest bride's bouquet of those flowers she'd ever seen.

"That's right," he said and brushed a lock of shiny black hair off her shoulders that had fallen forward. "You choose the four flowers you like best and we'll go find them on Monday."

"My bouquet?" she said, a hand against her chest.

"Your bouquet," he repeated. "With your favorite flowers."

"What are the flowers in the urns around the estate?" she asked. "I love those flowers together. I recognize the roses, the palest pink I've ever seen. And there's some sort of lily, right?"

He took the pen off the table and made a mark beside roses. "Okay, roses—the palest pink. That's one." He scanned the list until he found stargazer lilies. "Stargazer lilies, that's two."

"Those are the lilies that have that wonderful scent?" she asked.

He nodded. "They're pretty incredible."

"I love their name, too," she said.

He did, too. Reminded him of Talia every time he saw them. Because of her unquenchable sense of wonder at everything, including watching the stars and seeing flowers in bloom.

"They remind me of you," he said.

She turned her wide eyes to him. "Me? Why?"

He smiled. "Everything about them is unusual and they remind me of all those times we watched the stars by the pool at the palace. Remember? Midnight at the pool?"

"Of course," she said. "I loved spending those moments with you, Jack. And I love that these flowers remind you of me."

He put a mark beside the lilies. "Okay, that's two." Again, he scanned the list and pointed to the lavender. "Those urns have a ton of lavender in them, too."

"Good! Mark lavender."

He added a dash beside the lavender. "Okay, that's three, babe. You just need a fourth flower."

She went through the list and turned it over. Then she turned it back again. Finally, she pointed at a big purple cluster of flowers.

"What are those?"

"Hydrangeas," he said.

"Do you like those?" she asked, looking hopeful.

It was obvious that she loved them. He nodded. "I think hydrangeas will look spectacular with the palest pink roses, stargazer lilies, and the lavender. You have amazing taste, babe."

She looked up at him and laid her hand against his cheek. "I can't believe that all these flowers could be in my bouquet, Jack. I've never had a bouquet before."

That made him feel sad. He'd never even had a chance to get her flowers. Couldn't do that during the show—against the rules. He'd been on a quest to get her address after the first two shows. And by the time the third show began, he found out she was an angel of death and they were running for their lives from Lucifer and his demons.

He sighed. Kind of like right now.

As soon as this challenge was over, he was getting her flowers. This exact bouquet. To see if she liked them all together.

"I'm going to have to fix that," he said, reaching out and stroking her long, black hair.

"How? You can't pick the flowers at the chateau."

"We have florists, babe," he said in a quiet voice. "And places where they grow flowers on farms just like our food."

"A place where they farm flowers?" she asked, wide-eyed, that look of wonder on her face. "Why?"

It was that same look that he'd fallen in love with way back on *The Cinderella Hour*.

"So, when the love of my life wants a bridal bouquet with these four flowers," he said and laid his hand against her face. "I can buy them and have them put into a bouquet for her wedding."

"You can do that?" she cried. "Without seraphim powers?"

He nodded, grinning at her. God, she was the most enchanting person he'd ever met.

"I can," he said. "Like every other dude in love on this planet. Or woman."

"Do I know this love of your life?" she asked, teasing him.

"You might," he fired back and leaned closer. "Her name's Talia Smith. She loves to fly and she's not from around here. Ring any bells?"

At last, she smiled at him. "Wedding bells."

"That's her!" He said with a laugh and kissed her.

She kissed him back, playfully nipping his bottom lip. What he wouldn't give for an empty suite.

"Are you okay with these flowers, Jack?" she asked.

"Babe, this bouquet is all about your preferences, but I love all four that you chose, if that helps. After staying in this chateau, I'll always think of you when I see any one of those flowers, especially those stargazer lilies."

Her smile stretched into a grin as she threw her arms around him. "That's what I wanted to hear."

He handed her the purple pen. "You mark all four of those flowers and we'll hunt for them first thing on Monday."

Still grinning, she took the pen and circled all four of the flowers. Excited, she jumped up from her chair and handed the sheet of paper and pen to Jennifer. Then she picked up the physical map of the property that Jennifer laid beside her plate. She looked it over and then turned to him as he picked up his second burrito and took a bite.

"Jack, what do you think about the secret locations?" she asked.

He shrugged and finished chewing his bite of breakfast burrito. "I think that's way cool to have three secret spots at this estate. Whichever one you like the best, we'll search for it. It's where you're going to marry me, so I want to find the one you like best."

"What's a parlor?" she asked in a quiet voice.

He set down his burrito and picked up a napkin. "Back in the 1800s, it was this formal room with the best furniture, the best artwork, and the nicest curtains. The best room in the house. It's where people showed off while they entertained guests they wanted to impress—or where single women got chaperoned when they wanted to date single dudes."

Talia bristled. "Chaperoned? As if."

He nodded. "That was eons ago though. Most women don't have to put up with shit like that anymore." He sighed. "Just actors with angels of death in their suites."

She laughed, but she looked angry still. "Why weren't the men chaperoned?"

"If they were both single, they both got chaperoned," Jack replied.

"Why?" she asked, frowning.

He shrugged. "Because the Victorians were uptight and terrified of sex or something. No clue." He lowered his voice to a half-whisper. "But I'll bet they hooked up—a lot."

She shook her head, pressing her mouth into a line. "Well, I don't like it."

"Hook ups?"

"No, treating women like property."

"Me neither, babe, but this old parlor may still be a beautiful room," he countered. "With furniture and stylings around 1914 when this place was built. It might be a space untouched for over a hundred years. Could be rad."

"So could this ballroom," she said and crossed her arms.

"Agreed," he said. "I just want you to be happy with whatever location we choose—and find. If you like the ballroom best, then we'll look for that space."

"What about the fountain or pool or whatever?" she asked, studying him.

Trying to gauge his reaction.

"I like the idea of it being outside," he said and set the napkin beside his plate.

"Me too," said Talia, letting her arms fall against her sides. "Reminds me of Eolowen."

"I thought it might," he said in a quiet voice. "I'll be fine with whatever you choose, Talia. I want this wedding to be about your choices."

"Thank you," she said and took his left hand in hers again. "But it's your wedding, too, Jack. I want you to be happy with everything, too. Do you have a preference?"

"I kind of like the idea of an outside wedding," he said and squeezed her hand. "It reminds me of Eolowen, too."

"I'd prefer outside to inside," she whispered.

"Are you sure?" he asked.

She nodded emphatically.

He knew that she missed Eolowen a lot after she'd been on earth for a while. And he understood. That was her home. And it was the Heavens. He had to admit, he'd gotten comfortable there. But she was a creature of air not earth. Angels loved those air currents and wide-open spaces. Not stuffy old buildings surrounded by walls and windows.

But as long as she was with him, he was home, so it didn't matter to him as long she was beside him.

"I'm sure," she said, a smile lighting her face. "Let's look for the fountain."

"Works for me," he said and kissed her again. "As long as you're happy with that location. That's all I care about."

"I love you, Jack Casey," she said and put her arms around his neck.

He laughed. "I love you, too, Tal. For as long as the universe will let me."

"That better be forever," she whispered in his ear.

He grinned. "I'm counting on it," he said.

"I have one more announcement," said Jennifer as she turned away from Herb.

Talia let him go as the conversations around the table fell silent. In a couple of moments, everyone looked at Jennifer.

"Forgot to mention one tiny detail that Herb reminded me about," she said, smiling, those red glasses perched on her nose. "You're all grounded to your suites except for dinner."

"What?" Rachel shouted. "What do you mean by that?"

"She means," Herb replied. "That after you've turned in your flowers and you leave this room, you'll be escorted to your suites. All the chateau's outer doors will be locked, monitored, and manned. Can't have any couples scouting out flowers or hidden locations until the start of the challenge on Monday morning."

"Makes sense to me," said Jack. "It's only fair."

He took another bite of his burrito.

"Jack's right," said Izzy. "This way, no one gains an unfair advantage."

Gianni nodded. "Agreed."

"I'm good with it," said Eric as he picked up the last bite of his breakfast burrito.

"Okay," said Herb. "Just remember, we've got cameras on all the doors. All doors and windows have sensors on them, so alarms will go off if you try to use them."

"No worries, Herb," said Jack, leaning back in his chair. "We'll all be good."

Herb grinned. "The tech will make sure you're all good. If you're found outside, you and your significant other will be sent home. Is that clear?"

"Like a summer day, Herb," said Jack.

"All right then," said Herb, rising from his chair. "Then we begin filming first thing Monday morning. At 8 A.M. sharp, tablets will be left at your suite doors, so do yourselves a favor and prepare for this challenge."

Herb left the dining room, Steve behind him.

"Rachel, have you and Eric picked your flowers yet?" Jennifer asked.

Nodding, Rachel rose from the burgundy dining room chair and handed her list to Jennifer.

"Thank you," said Jennifer, rising from her chair. She clutched her clipboard to her chest. "I now have all three couple's choices. Good luck with the challenge and enjoy your day together."

"Thanks, Jennifer," said Jack and waved.

He finished his last burrito, wiped his hands with the napkin, and waited for Talia to finish. When she was done, they took the map upstairs to start investigating the grounds for possible locations. Like where the original builders might have hidden a fountain or pool around the chateau. It would be a long week—especially with this tether wound and the possibility of Abaddon showing up again. He just hoped the surrounding grounds of the mansion had been thoroughly warded like the chateau.

26

ALL AFTERNOON, TALIA REVIEWED THE MAP OF THE CHATEAU AND ITS grounds with Jack and they marked places on the map where they remembered seeing flower beds, including the patio and the pool. They pinpointed three possible locations where a fountain pool could be hidden on the estate and hoped to find it at one of possible spots.

Talia worried that all three couples would search for this outdoor spot, but she was an angel of death. She had angel powers that helped her locate hidden places.

She sighed and leaned against the wall beside the old fireplace, letting her wings settle against her back, gold halo slowing its spin.

She didn't want to cheat though, so she'd let Jack handle the searching. And she'd make sure he didn't call up seraphim powers to locate the hidden fountain pool either. She wanted to win this challenge fairly. Not by cheating.

Even though she knew the others were using their phones and those tiny computers right now, using this internet thing that Jack always talked about.

"You look worried, Talia," said Muriel, standing in front of the suite doors.

Jack was at the window, studying the rear gardens to gather clues.

"The others have those intelligent communicators to use and Jack doesn't have one right now," she said with a sigh.

Muriel smiled. "You mean the cell phones?"

Talia nodded. "They've probably looked at all kinds of maps of the chateau and surrounding area by now, using that search motor thing to look up history."

"Search motor?" Muriel replied, cocking her head, grey eyes squinting.

Talia motioned at the door. "That goo thing that searches information almost like my omnificence power."

"Oh, a search engine," said Kesien with a smile.

"Not today they're not," Muriel replied.

Talia frowned. "What do you mean not today?"

"Kesien and I blocked all internet traffic coming into the house," Muriel said with a smirk, flexing her wings. "Not going to get fixed until tomorrow."

Talia threw her arms around Muriel, hugging her. "Thank you, Muriel!" She turned around and hugged Kesien, too. "Thank you, Kesien for ensuring that we're all on level ground."

Kesien nodded. "I knew that you and Jack were doing your best not to use your powers on this challenge. Muriel and I just wanted to make sure no one else got an unfair advantage either."

"Like Rachel," both Kesien and Muriel said in unison.

That made Talia laugh. Rachel was probably furious right now, storming around her suite in that cloying perfume and red soled shoes that Jack hated because she couldn't use her phone to find that information ahead of time.

"Hey, Talia," Jack called, pointing out the window. "I think I see the roses from here. I know where I want to look first. Can't see that far, but it looks like the blooms are pink."

"That's great, Jack," said Talia as she stepped away from the fireplace.

She sat down on one of the couches and spread out the paper map on the coffee table again. He rushed over with a blue ballpoint pen in his hand.

"Here, let me mark it on the map as a good place to search," he said and made a big blue X on the map. "If those are roses, maybe we can find the lilies by scent?"

She liked that he wasn't even thinking about the seraphim powers. He was just using all the human senses at his disposal.

"Shouldn't be too difficult to find them by scent," she said as he glanced at her, those light green eyes burning with excitement.

They lit up his whole face. Her gaze moved to his right hand and she examined the bandage. Still looked pristine and white. That was good. It meant that Berith's healing was still working and that her barrier had slowed the progression of Lucifer's tether. The longer they kept it away from Jack's heart, the more time they had to summon the resurrect power and sever the soul tether.

Before Lucifer or Abaddon tried to drag Jack off to Hell.

Too bad that Berith and Azrael had to meet with the seraphim at High House first. It was about Jack's wings and halo. That made her nervous.

Regardless, she wouldn't let Lucifer take Jack again. No matter what it cost her. She wouldn't let Lucifer have him. The thought of that terrified her.

She knew it had shaken Jack to his core and he was doing his best to hide it.

He glanced up from the map. "And the hydrangea blooms should have grown big by now. We should be able to spot them from a distance. Lavender's really delicate though, so we'll have to be close to it in order to spot it."

He'd been focused on that map—and the window—all afternoon. She smiled. The sun had already sunk low on the horizon, twilight approaching. She wanted him to relax for a while, let his body and mind rest after losing so much blood from that wound. It hadn't been enough to bleed out or anything, but it was enough to make him pass out in the shower. And he'd been at that map for hours without a break or distraction.

Sliding her arms around his neck, she pulled his attention away from the map.

"There's plenty of time for that map, Jack Casey," she said and kissed him.

"What'd you have in mind?" he asked in a quiet voice that was all hot caramel and intense, those green eyes sparkling with mischief.

The corners of his mouth turned up in a playful smile.

"A little us time," she said and gave him a soft, lingering kiss.

He glanced over at Muriel and Kesien. "Not happening," he said with a sigh and turned back to the map.

"Patrol," she said against his ear. "Long range patrol."

He laughed. "Nice thought, but we both know they'd patrol in shifts."

"I just want you to take it easy before tomorrow, Jack," she said with a frown. "You've been at that map for hours. I don't want you to get lightheaded and pass out again."

He held up his right hand, showing her the pristine bandages. "Nah, I'm good. Whatever Berith did, it's holding nicely."

"I do need the squad to ward all around the chateau grounds. Otherwise, we may run into Abaddon while hunting for those flowers and that hidden fountain pool. That has to happen before tomorrow morning."

Jack nodded. "I'd hate to find the fountain and then battle Abaddon until I was drunk off my ass."

"Muriel," Talia replied, turning toward the dark-haired angel of death, her grey eyes soft. She smiled. Who still had a crush on Jack. "The squad needs to put seraphim wards in place around every square inch outside the chateau before morning."

"Already begun," said Muriel with a motion toward the surrounding areas beyond the windows. "Daidrean, Deemah, and Anahera are already warding everywhere around the chateau and across the entire grounds to the vineyards. In a few minutes, Kesien will join them. Azrael insisted that one of us remain in your presence at all times."

Talia saw the annoyed look on Jack's face.

"Sorry, Jack," said Muriel, patting him on the shoulder. "With this active soul tether threatening you, Azrael forbid us to leave the two of you alone."

"Lucifer better stay the hell away from my honeymoon," Jack said with a grumble, "that's all I've got to say. Or I will smite him so hard he'll have little demons orbiting him."

Muriel and Kesien both laughed.

"Jack isn't taking this guard change very well," said Talia to them.

Jack whirled around. "No, Jack is definitely not taking this guard change very well. He just wants a little privacy with the love of his life in the bedroom."

"That's my cue to go handle those wards," said Kesien.

"Sorry," Jack said with a sigh and rubbed his forehead. "Feeling a little edgy and a little weak from Lucifer's attack."

"I understand, Jack," said Kesien. "But we'll keep you and Talia safe."

The tall, black-haired angel spread his wings and blinked through the window.

"It's okay, Jack," said Muriel and patted his right shoulder again. "Not your fault. You lost a lot of blood already. That's got to make you feel a little weak and cranky."

Talia took hold of his left hand and gripped it in hers. "Why don't we turn in early after dinner, Jack? So you can get plenty of sleep before the challenge starts on Monday? Berith said we'll be ready to apply the resurrect power to the tether tomorrow night. She also said her barrier would erode by then, so that wound will probably start bleeding again soon."

"I'm okay," he said, deflecting their concerns, that game face of his firmly in place.

He was acting again. She felt it. He'd just lied to her, forgetting she had an in-born ability to detect lies. He was feeling much worse than he let on and was trying to hide it from her. He'd forgotten to use those angel powers he carried to block intrusions. Probably being back on earth again with all its distractions made him forget about those powers he'd honed up in the Heavens. But here, his life hadn't depended on using them.

"Forgot that you're dealing with angels instead of humans, Jack?" she asked, hands on her hips.

He squinted at her. "What do you mean?"

"Muriel and I could have sensed that lie you just told from the vineyards."

"Busted," said Muriel in a quiet voice.

"You're feeling really badly and you're trying to deflect and hide it with that actor's game face of yours." Talia shook her head. "Doesn't work on angels, Jack."

"Dammit," he muttered. "Forgot that I needed that block in place."

"So, you've made lying to me a habit?" she asked.

His mouth fell open, surprise sparking in those pale green eyes. "Talia, I'm not a liar," he said, frowning. "But I just know how you worry. It's not like you couldn't sense when I'm using it anyway—since I'm mirroring the ability from you."

He had a point there. Good confession. She'd make sure she looked for it in the future, when she was worried about his health. Issues that he always tried to hide from her.

"You telling me that you're fine, Jack, doesn't make me worry any less," she said, crossing her arms.

He stared down at his grey socks. "Still didn't want you to worry."

She moved toward him and held his hands. "I will worry about you for the rest of my existence, Jack Casey," she said with a smile. "So, get used to it. You mean everything to me."

He looked up, a smile lifting the corners of his mouth. "When you put it that way…" He kissed her in an anxious kiss.

"Let's get supper and turn in early," she said and squeezed his hands.

Finally, he nodded. "I'll get my shoes," he said and moved a little unsteadily toward the armoires.

She'd have to keep a close eye on him tomorrow—with the help of her squad. Keeping Jack safe from Lucifer was her top priority and even if it cost them the win here, she didn't care.

She was marrying this man and Lucifer wasn't taking him away from her ever again.

27

AT 8 A.M., JACK CLIMBED UNSTEADILY OUT OF BED IN BLUE BOXER briefs and hurried to the suite door. Talia was already up. When he opened the door, he found a small white box in front of it. And Jennifer Collins standing there in jeans and a yellow striped button-down shirt.

"Uh...hi, Jennifer," he said.

"Oh, my," she cried, those brown eyes widening. "It's really good to see you." She blushed and thrust a hand over her mouth. "I mean—good morning, Jack."

He laughed and picked up the box. "Thanks for dropping this off," he said.

"Made my day," she said in a quiet voice. "To see you!" she added quickly. "I mean, to get you started on today's scavenger hunt."

A little starstruck over him? After four seasons? It wasn't like she hadn't seen him in swim trunks before.

"Take care, Jennifer," he said and closed the door.

When he turned around, Talia and Muriel were standing there.

"You just broke her mind, Jack," said Muriel with a chuckle.

He just shrugged. "Didn't know she'd be standing there when I opened the door in my boxers."

Jack set the box on the coffee table between the two lavender couches and flipped open the top. A small mini tablet with a camera was inside along with a folded paper floor plan of the house and a paper map of the property, folded in half.

"You handle that table thing," said Talia as she picked up the papers from the box. "I'll look at the maps."

Table thing? He chuckled. "It's a tablet computer," he said and pressed the *On* button.

The small, eight-inch tablet had a color touchscreen and front and rear cameras. The splash screen displayed the purple *Royal Wedding Hour* logo. He touched it and a browser opened with a webpage that read, *welcome Talia and Jack. Please touch the word FLOWERS or VENUE to scan your first code.*

Looked simple enough.

There was also a link for maps and clues. He touched his index finger to the map button.

It took him to an interactive map of the grounds and chateau floor plan, allowing him to pinch and stretch the map, zooming in or out. He'd wait to touch the *clues* button until Talia had seen it.

He carried the tablet over to the bed and laid it down, looking at the map as he pulled on a pair of Levi's. He slid his room key in his front right pocket and his wallet into his back right pocket. Then he pulled on a dark green Henley. And struggled to deal with his wings. Even with them flat against his back, they were uncomfortable in human clothing and most of the time, they didn't fit under his shirts and hoodies. Until Talia used her angel powers on his wings.

He called up the power and just like that, they slipped through the fabric like it wasn't even there. She said he had the ability too, through her mirrored powers. He hadn't needed to even try summoning that power yet though. And he expected Azrael to show up any day now and retrieve these wings and the halo that spun around his head like a night light.

He put on a pair of dark blue socks and slid his feet into his blue Vans slip-ons. Then he pulled on his Navy blue hoodie, leaving it unzipped. He grabbed the tablet off the bed and carried it into the suite's sitting room.

"Ready to head outside yet, babe?" he asked.

Talia turned away from the window, Muriel beside her. Talia wore a short jean skirt, a tight-fitting, ice blue T-shirt that hugged her body, and his grey hoodie. That looked a hell of a lot better on her than it did him.

He whistled and she smiled.

"Almost," she said and moved toward him, cupping his stubbled face in her hands. "Not shaving today?"

He shook his head, rubbing his left hand across his jaw and chin. "Does it look bad?"

She shook her head and let her fingers brush through his blond hair. "You look sexy, like you just woke up."

He chuckled. "Because I did."

"You sure made Jennifer's day with this look," she said and kissed him. "And you've already made mine, too. How do you feel?"

He didn't feel like trying to block how he really felt this morning from her and he didn't want to pretend everything was fine. She knew better.

"A little tired and a little weak," he said with a shrug. "But you already knew that, didn't you?"

She nodded. "Angel powers," she said with a frown. "By tonight though, that wound will be healing after we sever Lucifer's soul tether." She kissed him. "Just don't overwork yourself today, Jack."

"No promises," he said with a grin and held out the tablet. "I want to win this thing."

She gripped his forearms, staring deep into his sultry, pale green eyes.

"So do I, but not at your expense," she said in a quiet voice.

He'd be fine. He was still young enough to take whatever Abaddon —or his cast mates—could dish out. He'd lost some blood, but Berith had halted that process. He didn't know for how much longer, but he hoped it would get him through this second challenge.

"It won't be, babe," he said and nodded at the map in her hands.

"You ready to check some of those locations?" He held up the tablet and pointed to the *clues* button. "See this? They've got clues for us to follow."

She smiled and her whole face brightened, but she looked fearful, too, like he might fall over from exhaustion after one lap around the chateau. Being a little lightheaded was nothing like the bite Cerberus had inflicted when that hellhound implanted that first soul tether in his left shoulder. One that Lucifer had intentionally bled at every opportunity. He wasn't feeling one hundred percent, but he wasn't feeling ten percent either.

"That's wonderful," she said and slid the room key into the pocket of her jean skirt. "I'm ready when you are, Jack."

He patted the front pocket of his jeans, feeling his room key there. He still felt strange without his phone in his front pocket though. The screen on his old one—rigged by Lucifer—had been broken before the angels of death destroyed it, so he'd needed a new one anyway. He sighed. One without a soul tether.

He nodded. "Let's do this."

Talia turned to Muriel. He didn't hear them exchange any conversation, but angels made those piercing high notes—notes too high for human ears to hear. He assumed that she'd told Muriel to stick close to them. Just in case Lucifer had any more tricks up Abaddon's sleeves.

They hurried out of the suite and down the stairs, shoes tapping against the marble. A rusty-haired attendant dressed in black pants, white gloves, and a white tuxedo shirt opened the door for them and they hurried outside to the front of the chateau. Talia gazed at the paper map as he stared at the tablet.

JACK LED Talia around to the back of the chateau and right to the correct flower bed garden with huge, pale pink roses. The one he had seen from their suite window.

The April sky was a vivid blue, wisps of clouds that allowed the sun to glisten across the sprawling limestone French chateau. Its formal, blooming gardens had short walls edged with crisp, green box hedges with perfectly sculpted lines. The air smelled pungent with fresh-mown grass, distant buzz of a lawn mower hanging above the buzz of a plane passing overhead. A hint of sweet gardenias touched the air.

He looked around the ordered garden plots and past the squares of crisp green box hedges. This plot was one of four, ten-foot squares with stone paths intersecting at right angles in the center. He located a small sign with the QR code and some words on it and pointed.

"See, babe," he said and held out the tablet. "This grey and white sign says that they're English roses. This one's called Rising Spirits."

"I love it!" Talia cried. "Scan it."

Nodding, he touched the *flowers* button on the browser page. An input box opened on the screen and the camera light turned green. He pressed the onscreen button to take a picture of the QR code.

The browser page flashed and a message read *QR code has been successfully scanned.*

"Got it! Now, let's look for lavender, hydrangeas, and stargazer lilies."

She leaned up and kissed him. "How did you know so much about flowers?"

"Four sisters and an event planner for a mother," he said and rolled his eyes.

Their backyard had been like a florist's shop. His sisters and mother grew every flower he could think of, creating bouquets for brides and events when his mother started her business out of the house. He had to read the little tags on everything when he had to help weed and water those damned things.

"Thank God for soccer, track, and baseball," he replied. "Got me away from home and out of dealing with all those flowers in the summer. Always pissed off my mother when Dad enrolled me in sports. She lost her slave gardener."

Talia slid her arms around his neck. "Well, I like that you know all about these kinds of things."

"Do you?" he said, kissing her lips. "I'll have to tell you all about those flowers." He sighed. "If we're ever alone."

She took hold of his arm. "Let's check the rest of the beds for the other flowers."

"Split up or together?"

"Together," she said, her eyes looking almost sad.

He pulled her closer and slid his arm around her waist. "Together's much better."

Together, they looked at all the flowers in the bed with the roses. The blooms were all pink.

"Wait a minute," he said and turned around, a hand over his eyes as he looked around at the other flower beds.

One bed had yellow flowers. The bed across from it had purple flowers. And the bed diagonal to the yellow flowers had all red flowers.

"Babe, look! They're arranged by color!"

"You're right," Talia cried.

They ran down the concrete pathway over to the purple bed and glanced around it.

Jack grinned. Hydrangeas! Right in front.

"There's your hydrangeas, Talia."

He pulled her by the hand and pointed at the leafy bush in the center with several green blooms already beginning to blush purple. He moved over to the little grey sign and touched the tablet screen, waking it up. He touched the *flowers* button on the screen again and the camera light winked green. Pressing the button, he scanned the QR code and it returned a message that read, *scan successful*.

"Okay, let's see if there's any lavender in here?"

Together, they looked through all the flowers, but no lavender grew in the bed. Then he remembered the other formal garden around the side of the chateau.

"Come on!" he cried, tugging on Talia's arm.

He pulled her around the back of the house, across the patio, and to the other side. Where four more ordered beds of flowers soaked up the sun. Gianni and Izzy stood between the flower beds with their tablet. And at the farthest plot was Eric and Rachel. It was a regular party.

"Looks like we've got company," said Jack, leading Talia along the path.

He waved at Gianni and Izzy who stood along the path beside the adjacent flower bed. Flowers in these beds were planted along a diagonal line like a wave in each of the squares. He looked at the flowers where Gianni and Izzy stood. All white. Below it, a bed of deep pink flowers soaked up the sun. The bed beside it had more bluish-purple flowers. The bed they stood beside was filled with red flowers.

They headed toward the bed where Eric and Rachel stood.

"Morning, cast mates," he said with a wave as Talia gripped his arm tighter and pulled him close.

He chuckled. She was so protective. He worried that she might still smite Rachel if given half the chance.

Even twenty feet away, he caught wind of that God awful perfume Rachel wore. Crazy expensive kitchen sink of over-the-top scents. Way too much jasmine, heart-stopping amounts of musk, I can't breathe anymore clouds of sandalwood and patchouli mixed with drown me in gardenias and orchids.

"Eric," he said with a quick nod and glanced at Rachel. "Rachel."

"Good morning, Jack," Rachel said with a smile.

Didn't even acknowledge Talia. Nice. He shook his head. Good way to get smited.

She had on a short, peach-colored skirt that wrapped tight around her hips and a lacy white blouse. He frowned. And a brand-new pair of white heels with those red soles.

"You remember, Talia, right? My fiancée."

"Hi, Talia," she replied. Like it almost hurt to say her name.

Why was she suddenly acting like a spoiled starlet? Especially around him. She was lucky he even spoke to her after everything she'd done to him.

He tried to ignore the cloying perfume that would probably start wilting all these flowers. Glancing at the diagonal planting of flowers, he searched until he saw lavender at the top of the bed. He smiled. Opposite Eric and Rachel. Relieved, he motioned Talia forward and gripped her hand, pulling her around the flower bed, past Eric and Rachel.

Rachel followed him with her gaze, but she didn't say anything as they passed by, Eric scanning something with the tablet in his hand.

Jack nudged Talia over to the top corner of the bed. He bent down and tapped the *flowers* button on the tablet screen. When the camera turned on, he hit the button, taking a picture of the sign that read, *French Lavender*. The *scan successful* message appeared on the screen.

Once he was downwind of Rachel's overwhelming perfume, he smelled a familiar scent. He grinned.

Even before he turned around, he recognized that spicy scent of stargazer lilies.

"Smell that, babe?" he whispered in Talia's ear.

She grinned. "I can now," she said.

He motioned her to follow as he turned around and rushed toward the bed of deep pink and fuchsia flowers across from where Eric and Rachel stood, examining signs.

At the closest edge, stargazer lilies grew tall with deep, waxy green leaves. Three deep pink and purple, spotted blooms had opened, casting that unusual scent into the air.

Talia gasped. "Oh, Jack...they're beautiful!"

He leaned down and inhaled their intoxicating scent. Made him a little lightheaded in a good way. He wished he could give her a bouquet of these flowers to enjoy.

"Is that the fourth one already, Jack?" she asked against his ear.

He nodded, giving her his best smile.

After locating the little grey sign beneath the leaves, he knelt beside it and touched the *flowers* button on the tablet screen. As soon as the camera turned on, he snapped a picture of the code. It took a moment or two before the *scan successful* message appeared in the browser.

"Okay, let's go back to the patio," he said in a quiet voice and took her hand again.

Grinning, she ran past him. "Race you!"

"You're on!"

He burst into a sprint down the concrete path, back around the house. Talia was fast, but he'd been a sprinter in high school and college. And he was still fast. He blew past her. Until she blinked ahead of him.

Two could play that game.

He held out his hand and pointed at the patio. And blinked. He greeted her as she blinked onto the patio.

"Jack Casey!" she cried, hands on her hips. "You out-cheated me."

He laughed and tapped his temple with his index finger. "Seraphim powers, babe."

She threw her arms around his neck and kissed him.

"Okay," he said, "Let's look at these clues we've got."

She nodded and leaned toward the tablet, watching the screen as he tapped the word, *clues.*

Three buttons appeared on the screen: *parlor, ballroom,* and *fountain.*

"We staying with the one we chose last night?" he asked, glancing from the tablet to her expressive grey eyes, so full of light.

She nodded.

"Here we go then," he said and tapped the *fountain* button.

Three purple buttons appeared on the screen, each one labeled *one, two,* and *three.*

"First clue." He read the two sentences out loud. "It says, I was the first fountain, but I was much too small for such a big estate."

"So, the fountain is much smaller than the huge fountain pool in the front of the chateau," Talia replied. "So, that means we're looking for a much smaller space somewhere around the house."

"Second clue," he said and pressed the second button. "It says, I was a little coy about my location though and most people walked past me without even knowing I was there. Hmmm. Coy…" He smiled. "It's gotta be a play on words, babe. Like a koi pond or something."

Her expression brightened, that glow of wonder in her eyes. "That's good, lover. What's the third clue?"

He pressed the third button. "Things grew and grew until the world forgot about me burbling away. Until a drunk Olympic sprinter stumbled upon me."

Beside the third clue was another button that read, *scan QR code*.

"A drunk Olympic sprinter? That's your department, Jack," Talia said with an infectious laugh.

"Hey!" he shouted, breaking into a laugh. "I'm an addict not a drunk. And don't make me tickle you."

"I've smited humans for less, Jack Casey," she said, giving him that look.

He laughed harder.

Finally, she put her arms around his neck and kissed him again. "Okay, so we know it's a much smaller fountain than the one in front. It may have a koi pond. And a drunk Olympic sprinter found it. Whatever that means."

"If it's a fountain, then it's gonna make some noise, right?" said Jack as he led her around the patio toward the other formal gardens. "If it's still working."

She nodded. "The clue mentions it making noise."

That was true. Burbling away, it said.

He moved past the patio, into the backyard and beside the swimming pool. A tall, sculpted line of cypress trees stood on each side of the swimming pool. And one row at the back side of the pool. The upper part of the backyard was framed with concrete and had two long, narrow fountain pools on either side with green space between them. Each fountain had two sprays of water.

He stared past the fountains. The swimming pool was built on the lower tier of the yard and framed with cypress trees on all sides. He noticed a ring of spruce trees off to the left side of the endless backyard, barely visible above the cypress trees.

Then he smelled it.

A faint, spicy, almost savory scent hung in the air above the pungent scent of spruce trees. His gaze traveled across the backyard as he searched the plants and shrubs. Squared, precise lines of box hedges edged the acreage behind the house. And a similar line of box hedges grew in front of the ring of evergreens.

But the eucalyptus and oregano-like scent still carried on the wind.

It wasn't overpowering. It was faint, but just enough that he recognized it. Those hedges in front of the evergreens weren't more box hedges. They were bay laurels!

His mother grew bay laurel back in the Midwest, a scent he'd never forgotten. The scent of the fresh-cut bay laurel leaves filled the whole house whenever she brought them inside.

That's why that third clue mentioned an Olympic sprinter. They gave out laurel wreaths to the winners in ancient Greece during the Olympics. The fountain had to be behind that bay laurel hedge!

"Come on!" he shouted, breaking into a run across the backyard.

Talia blinked, catching up with him as he passed the modern fountain pools on both sides and ran past the swimming pool. When he reached the bay laurel hedge, he leaped over it like it a hurdler and slipped between two tall evergreens.

"Jack, wait!" Talia shouted.

He froze. Listening. And heard the gurgling of water.

"This way, Talia!" he shouted over his shoulder.

He wound his way through the sharp, tangling bows of evergreens, the air tanged with the scent of pine nettles and bay laurel. And found his way into a secret, oblong clearing surrounded by spruce trees.

In the center of the clearing stood an old three-tiered limestone fountain that bubbled water into a round, algae-laden stone pool. Filled with red and white koi fish.

A small, white wrought iron bench stood beside the fountain. It was so quiet and peaceful here with sunlight peeking through the evergreens, crisp blue sky bright, and the soothing sound of flowing water from this little fountain. Plenty of room in this secret garden for a wedding ceremony.

A little grey sign stood beside the fountain. With a QR code.

He moved toward it and touched the tablet, waking it up. He tapped the *clues* button and then touched the third *clue* button. Beside the clue was a button for scanning the code. He tapped it and an input box appeared on the screen, green camera light flashing.

He snapped the picture and got an *input successful* message. Then the browser loaded another page.

Congratulations, you've completed the second challenge.

When Talia rushed out of the evergreens, she looked almost afraid as she grabbed him and held him close.

"Talia?" he said and slid his arms around her. "What's the matter?"

"I'm what's the matter, Jack Casey," said the deep, throaty voice from the tall stand of spruce trees.

Shit. He held Talia tight.

Abaddon.

TALIA SPREAD HER WINGS WIDE IN FRONT OF JACK, HALO SPINNING faster, turning pale gold as she faced Abaddon. The ashen-skinned angel-turned-demon lumbered out of the evergreens, standing eight feet tall. He leered at her, red eyes glowing in the shade, his thundering steps shaking the ground as he approached.

This hidden garden hadn't been warded. Of course, it hadn't. Her squad didn't know it was there!

"Think you're enough angel to stop me, little angel of death?" He laughed. "I'll deal with you after I've harvested this annoying little human's soul."

"You really want to try me again, Aby?" Jack replied.

Abaddon waved his meaty hand in the air until the sun dimmed, creating shadows all through the space.

The shadowy length of Jack's soul tether appeared. It was thick and ropey, mostly darkness with only a hint of bright red blood threading its way through the tether.

Abaddon tried to grab hold of the soul tether, but it was still just a shadow and it passed through his thick demon hands. A frown pressed his eyebrows into a flat, angry line that framed those glowing red eyes.

"What's this?" he demanded, sounding almost surprised. "The tether hasn't completely connected to his soul yet. It should have attached itself yesterday." His angry gaze moved toward Talia. "What did you do to it?"

Talia laughed. "Put a damper on yours and Lucifer's plans. Deal with it. You're not taking Jack Casey."

A loud rumble shook the trees and the ground as he laughed at her, pointing with a clawed index finger.

"And you intend to stop me, little angel of death? Alone?"

His amusement made her angry. She glared at him.

"No, but we intend to stop you," Jack called out from behind her.

Abaddon's eyes narrowed.

He waved at Abaddon. "Remember me? Dude with seraphim powers? And omnificence?"

"Until that tether activates, you're just an annoyance with those powers, little human." He laughed again. "I taught Job the word patience, so I'll wait. It's close." He pointed at Jack. "I'll see you tomorrow, little human. Once that tether activates, I can easily subdue you. Doesn't matter what powers you have."

The flutter of wings caught her attention.

Her squad landed between her and Abaddon, blocking him. Azrael was at the head of the squad, Berith behind him.

"Feel free to try an archangel, Abaddon," said Azrael, his silver-black hair glinting in the sunlight that trickled into the hidden garden, illuminating his clear gold Eternean armor.

"Tomorrow, Azrael." Abaddon laughed and faded into the shadows.

After Abaddon's heavy presence had dissipated, Azrael whirled around and laid his hand against Talia's shoulder.

"Talia, are you and Jack all right?"

Jack stepped out from behind her wings, anger pinching his gently sculpted features, those pale green eyes lit with flames.

"I couldn't unleash even a murder marble," he said, glowering toward the evergreens.

"Why not, Jack?" Azrael asked, his worried gaze encompassing Jack now.

Jack motioned at the fountain and this beautiful hidden oasis with its soft, murmuring fountain and colorful red and white koi fish. Soothing and relaxing—so peaceful.

"I couldn't wreck this amazing secret garden," he said with a sigh. "This is where Talia and I are gonna get married. Not gonna wreck it for that little bitch, Abaddon." He clenched his bandaged hand into a fist. "I swear, I'm gonna strangle that red-eyed, leathery bastard with every last inch of my soul tether. Slowly and painfully. Smug little bitch."

The squad held their shields up to hide the laughter. Even Berith covered her mouth and turned away. Azrael tried to speak, to reprimand Jack for being reckless, but he gave up. He was laughing, too.

"Jack," Azrael said, serious again. "If that tether activates, all those rare and seraphim powers will be useless to you. I know you understand that better than anyone."

"Unfortunately," he said with a growl.

Berith moved beside Azrael and motioned at Jack. She patted the small gold satchel that hung at her side, against her dove grey robes.

"I have the items for the resurrect power," she said with a smile.

But her charcoal grey eyes grew wide, her lips pursing. She pointed at Jack. "Jack, your hand."

Talia's gaze snapped to his right hand. It bled through the bandages.

"Just in time then," said Berith. "Jack, let's get you back to your suite and break this thing before Abaddon returns tomorrow. He's correct though. Without intervention, Jack's soul tether will activate by tomorrow."

"Little bitch is in for a big surprise when he shows up tomorrow," Jack said with a raspy growl. "Smash his leathery ass with Holy fire he's never felt before."

Talia glanced at the guard. They were trying not to grin at Jack. And failing.

Jack turned back to her, gripping her hand. "Well, what do you think, babe?" he asked, motioning toward the fountain. "Think you'd like to get married in this spot?"

She nodded and put her arms around him, holding him close. "It's stunning," she said, kissing him. "Like you."

He gave her one of his crooked smiles. "In a taser kind of way or a drop-dead gorgeous, Talia Smith kind of way?"

"In a stop-demons-in-their-tracks, Jack Casey murder marble kind of way," she said with a wry smile.

He nodded. "I'll go with that," he said and returned her kiss.

"Let's go take care of that tether now, Jack," she said and let go of him.

He stepped away from her, moving toward the evergreens. Talia gasped. His tether wound left a little trail of red blood as he walked.

"Jack!" she cried. "Your hand."

He stopped and turned around, seeing the little droplets of blood behind him and then glanced at his right hand. The bandage was bright red and dripping. Sighing, he bowed his head.

"Damn it, Lucifer."

"Muriel, freeze time," Azrael ordered. "So Kesien can carry Jack back to the suite."

Jack shook his head. "No need for that," he replied. "I'm fine."

"Really need to block those lies, Jack," said Berith. "We, angels always know otherwise."

"Does everybody know when I tell a lie?" Jack said, sounding annoyed.

"Yes." Every angel in the garden replied in unison.

"Fine, get me an Uber, Kesien," he said with a groan. "I'm not feeling so good right now."

His face was starting to turn pale, but that sexy spark in his pale green eyes remained as Kesien picked him up. Muriel was already summoning her angel powers to freeze time. She couldn't let anyone see Jack get carried back to the chateau by angels.

AFTER KESIEN GOT him back to the suite, he carried Jack over to the bed, laying him down as Talia arrived behind the tall death angel. Followed by Azrael and Berith. One by one, the rest of her squad returned to the suite, Muriel arriving last.

"Okay, I restarted time, so no one saw us fly Jack back to the suite."

"Not even a free drink on that first-class flight," Jack said with scowl.

Talia moved over to him and removed his Vans, setting them beside one of the armoires against the wall. She helped him out of his hoodie and put it away as Berith floated beside the bed, wings in a gentle motion at her shoulders.

Berith wrapped Jack's hand in another thick bandage over the other one that dripped rich, dark blood. Then she took yellow shards and red shards from the small gold satchel and laid them on the bed. Beside the shards, she set down a small dented square of blue Aeonium metal and a small silver box about four inches square that she removed from her satchel. She opened the box, revealing a handful of soil.

"The soil came from the roots of the willow tree behind Eolowen," Berith replied as she gazed at Talia. "We can take the first drop of water from the Creation from this piece of Aeonium and then gather a breath from Jack."

Talia flexed her wings, shifting around the bed toward Berith. And the shards.

She had bad memories of those shards. It broke her heart every time she thought about that moment in the Garden. Her eyes welled with tears, remembering Jack's broken body cradled in her arms and watching—no feeling—him take his last breath. Feeling his heart beat for the last time. And that horrible stillness. That memory still ached through her.

She turned away, covering her mouth as tears slid down her face.

"Talia, are you all right?" Berith asked, a hand on her shoulder.

Taking deep breaths, she fought down her anguish at those terrible memories of losing Jack for what she thought was forever.

Berith was in front of her now, grey eyes glassy.

"Those memories in the Garden are still so painful, aren't they?"

Talia nodded, unable to halt the tears slipping down her face.

Berith put her arms around Talia and hugged her. "I can't imagine how horrible those moments were for you. Just know that Jack won't be taking a last breath any time soon. We're about to remove this tether and I'll be awakening my resurrect power. You'll just need to summon yours once all the spheres have been created and placed."

"Thank you," she said in a tight, pained voice.

Arms slid around her shoulders. She looked up. Jack was beside her now.

"I'm so sorry to put you through all this again," he said in his smooth, hot caramel voice and pulled her against his chest.

Holding her tight.

She couldn't hold it all in this time. She held onto him, body and wings trembling as she cried against his chest.

"It's okay, babe," he said in a soothing voice, stroking her hair. "It's all going to be all right this time."

She looked up at him and he gently cupped her face in his hands. "I still remember feeling your heart stop, Jack. And you taking your last breath. It hurts so much every time I remember it."

He kissed her softly and just held her, stroking her hair and whispering that everything was going to be all right. She didn't want to let go of him.

Right now, at this moment, he was safe in her arms and as an angel of death, she could still protect him. From Abaddon. From Lucifer. From any humans that wanted to harm him.

But she couldn't protect her heart if the Heavens took him away from her.

"I can't lose you, Jack," she said in a broken voice. "I just can't."

"You're not going to lose me, Tal," he said against her ear. "First, we break this tether and next, we find a way to send Abaddon back to Hell. And then we get married. Easy, right?"

The enthusiasm in his voice won her over. She loved him more than her own existence.

Finally, she nodded at him. "I hope it's that easy," she said finally.

"We'll just make it that easy then," he replied and kissed her again. "Let's start with this tether, okay?" He lifted her chin. "Okay, babe?"

She nodded again as he brushed away the crystalline tears from her face with his thumbs.

"I love you, Talia," he said and let her go. "Now until forever."

She watched him weave a little around the bed, holding onto it as he slid back onto the mattress. He was weak and shaky, pretending he was fine. That was her Jack. Always the actor and the protector.

Kesien took hold of him, towering over Jack's six-foot height at least six foot six, and helped Jack back onto the bed.

"Ready?" Berith asked.

She nodded. With a deep breath, she turned back toward the bed.

"Ready," she said. "How do we start?"

Berith pointed to the red shards. "First, I'll create orbs out of these shards as I awaken the resurrect power."

Berith closed her eyes, reaching into that river of light and air and energy that flowed through every celestial body until little whorls of white light floated above her fingertips when she reached for the red shard.

"That's the lifeblood of Heaven and earth," said Talia. "First blood spilled from the Creation. In the Garden—the Maker's first experiment."

When Berith touched the red shards, they spun together, twisting into a tight, ruby red orb that gleamed with an inner white core.

"Now, remnants of the first sparks of fire," said Talia, motioning toward the yellow shards.

Berith slid her fingers to the yellow shards.

"The yellow shards are from the first light in Creation. Daylight. Firelight. Starlight."

Berith's fingers glimmered with gold light as the shards began to spin, glowing inside a bright yellow orb.

Talia let her hands rest against the bed as she glanced over at Jack. He watched her, smiling, those intense, pale green eyes so vibrant. Burning through her—into her human soul.

"Good work, Berith," she said.

Berith was on Talia's left side now, wings only a whisper through the room as all the angels crowded around the bed.

"I'm starting to feel a little uneasy with this many angels of death crowded around my bed," Jack replied. "You sure this isn't last rites or something? If I see a priest, I'm totally bolting."

His humor made Talia smile.

"We're sure, Jack," Muriel said and poked him in the shoulder. "I've seen your Book. You're not crossing over any time soon."

He relaxed, his posture not so stiff now. "Good to know," he said.

"Okay, next, the first drop of water from the Creation," said Talia, pointing the blue square of Aeonium metal. "Draw that first drop from the Aeonium, Berith."

Berith laid her hand against the bluish metal. And closed her eyes.

Again, that river of light and air stirred around them. A cool breeze brushed across Talia's face as the currents of air swirled around Berith's fingertips again. Berith pressed her fingertips against the clear blue metal that gleamed with an inner gold flame.

Berith gasped. "It feels so cold!"

"Pluck the orb from the metal," said Talia.

Nodding, Berith stretched out her fingers, dipping their tips into the metal until she balanced a frosty blue orb between them. She let it roll into her palm and shifted it onto the bed beside the yellow and red orbs.

"Now, the soil," said Talia.

Berith opened the little silver box and held it out to Talia. "Ready," she said with a nod.

"You're seeking the last grain of sand from the Creation," said Talia. She pointed at the tiny box of soil. "Find and free it. And it will become an orb."

Wind currents shifted through the room and blew across Berith's right hand. A soft moan of wind rushed around the eaves of the chateau's rooftop as Berith dipped the tips of three fingers into the soil.

The cool, loamy scent wafted through the room as Berith gently sifted through the rich black soil, searching for a grain of sand. The last grain from the Creation—still present in the Heavens and on earth.

It seemed like forever until Berith gasped and glanced at her.

"I feel something sharp and stony," she said. "It's pressing against the tips of my fingers."

"Call to the power awakening in you," said Talia, "and summon the grain of sand. When you free it, it will turn into a green orb."

Berith kept turning the soil over with her fingers until a small green orb pushed to the surface like a seedling reaching toward sunlight.

"I did it!" Berith cried and plucked the green orb out of the soil.

"Fantastic job, Berith," Talia cried as Berith laid the orb beside the other three. "You and I are the only two angels in all the Heavens that possess the resurrect power."

Berith's eyes widened. "Only two of us?" she asked.

"Just you and me—and Jack," said Talia with a smile. "Your rare healing gift is even more valuable to Heaven now, Berith."

"Thank you, Talia," said Berith. "Now you need to capture a breath from Jack."

"How do I do that?"

"Your tears will work," said Berith. "But you can also just reach out and touch his breath. That will also capture one."

Talia called to the air currents of power flowing through her body. Cool air rushed over her hand, swirling around the ends of her fingers as she reached toward Jack's face. She held her fingers in front of his mouth, under his nose, waiting until a frosty white sphere formed. It fell against the lavender comforter.

"That one didn't hurt a bit," Jack replied with a smirk.

"It didn't hurt me either," she added and picked up the white orb.

"We'll need to place them across his body now," said Berith.

Talia laid the orbs together on the lavender comforter. "Okay, I remember that the white orb goes in the well of Jack's throat."

She plucked the marble-sized white orb off the comforter and laid it in the indentation at the base of his throat.

Berith moved around the bed to Jack's right hand and began unfastening the bandages, laying them open. His right hand was bloody from fingertips to wrist. And more blood bubbled up from the wound.

"Lie still, Jack," said Berith.

"Place the red orb on the wound, Berith," said Talia, motioning at Jack's hand. "In his palm."

Talia floated over the bed, her wings moving a little faster, the sound rhythmic in the silence as Berith placed the red orb in the center of Jack's palm.

"The first spark of light goes on the forehead," said Talia.

Berith retrieved the yellow orb and laid it on his forehead, against Jack's hairline, so it didn't roll away. But the orb adhered to his skin the moment it connected and it stayed where Berith had placed it.

"The last grain of sand, the body of the world, goes on his stomach."

Berith reached over and slid Jack's dark green Henley up, revealing his pale, flat stomach with its well-defined muscles.

Talia took the green orb and pressed it against his belly button.

"That tickles," Jack said with a chuckle, making Talia smile.

"And the last orb, the blue one," Talia said as she gazed into Jack's sexy green eyes. "Goes on his heart."

Talia slid her hand and the blue orb past the unbuttoned collar of his Henley and across his smooth chest. To his heart.

She pressed her palm there, feeling its steady beats as the orb stuck to his skin. With a caress, she slid her hand back and brushed her fingers across his stubbled jaw. He smiled at her.

"Now, what?" Berith asked.

"Call up the power and direct it into all five orbs," said Talia as she laid her hand on Jack's shoulder. "Until they each shatter and release their energy."

"Jack," said Berith, "this is going to be a little uncomfortable for you. Just stay still and get through each stage as best you can. You'll be fine."

Jack sighed. "I'll pretend I'm being audited by the IRS. That should prepare me for any pain and make me really patient."

Talia laughed along with Muriel.

"Okay, Talia," said Berith, taking a deep breath. "I'm going to summon the power into the orbs now."

Berith lifted both hands in the air, palms up, pinkies touching.

In moments, pale gold light engulfed the orbs. Bright light flashed and then dimmed.

Taking a deep breath, Berith closed her eyes and reached into the currents rushing across their angelic forms. Talia felt the ebb and flow, the rise and fall of the wellspring of powers within Berith. She felt the bright white light resting in the currents like a seashell.

"What do I do now?" Berith asked.

"Take hold of the white light and focus it on the orbs," said Talia.

For a moment, Berith struggled. She held her breath, struggling, and then lifted the bright white light from the currents and focused it on all five orbs.

With a sigh, Berith opened her eyes. She blew on her hands and released the breath of energy, scattering white light across Jack's body.

One by one, all five orbs shattered. The blue orb on Jack's heart shattered first and the first drop of water in Creation enveloped his body in ice. The green orb disintegrated next, swirling into a cone of primordial dust that coated the layer of ice in rich, loamy soil, burying Jack.

"Can he breathe?" Berith asked.

Talia nodded. "Don't move, Jack."

"Trying not to," he said in a muffled voice beneath the ice and soil.

The yellow orb shattered next, exploding in a shower of sparks. Scattering the soil. Melting the ice.

The red orb dissolved into sticky, bright red blood that covered Jack in the thick fluid. It floated on top for several long moments and then sank into his body through clothes and skin.

And finally, the frosty white orb at Jack's throat burst, releasing coils of pure white smoke into the air. The smoke ringed his head and face and then sank into his skin, drifting into his nose and mouth.

Floating above him, wings fluttering, Talia leaned down and kissed his lips.

Sparks flew when he kissed her back. Hard.

"The blood on his palm is drying up," said Berith, pointing at Jack's right hand.

The blood that had dripped from his palm and ran down his fingers, coating the bandages, turned to dust and blew away.

It was done. The soul tether had been broken. He was free of Lucifer's impending control again.

"It worked, Jack!" she cried, laying her hands against his face.

"That's what I wanted to hear," he said and reached up, pulling her out of the air and on top of him.

Into his arms. He kissed her again.

"You're safe from Lucifer again, lover," she said and kissed him again, her arms sliding around his neck.

"What a relief," he cried with a sharp exhale. "Can't tell you how much I've worried about that tether."

She ran her fingers through his blond hair. "I know. I could tell it was really upsetting you. I know how much it was upsetting me."

Jack slid into a sitting position and pulled her close, glancing over at Azrael who stood stoically behind Berith. Talia knew that the archangel was making sure nothing broke through the wards while they summoned the resurrect power.

"I'm glad that issue has been fixed," said the archangel, almost sounding tired. Like there was another part to that statement he'd left unspoken. His steely grey eyes were piercing and he looked annoyed.

"As opposed to other issues that haven't been fixed?" Talia asked. "Like dealing with Abaddon."

He nodded. "Amongst other things, yes."

"Things are still complicated," said Berith, glancing at Azrael. "Pravuil, God's Scribe, still hasn't found a way to recall Abaddon or deal with him yet." Her gaze flicked to Jack and back to Azrael. "And the seraphim are still discussing the other issues."

That meant there was no definitive decision on what happened to Jack after Abaddon had been dealt with—if there was a way to deal with an angel that had been turned and hadn't fallen. Abaddon still had shriveled wings and a faint glow of what used to be a halo above his head that only angels could see.

Well, angels and Jack. Jack was an anomaly in Heaven and no one knew quite how to handle the situation. Like her—an angel of death with a human soul.

Berith turned around and leaned over Jack, laying the back of her hand to his forehead.

"He's starting to get feverish, Talia," she said, glancing at her. "Keep him in bed tomorrow."

"Hey, he's still in the room," Jack snapped. "How about talking to him, too. And if one of you angels starts spelling stuff in those damned angel notes, I will wreck this place."

Kesien and Muriel started laughing.

Berith reached over and brushed the hair out of his eyes with calming energy. "And he needs to stay in bed for a day because the resurrect power takes a lot out of humans. As he might recall."

"He might not," Jack said with a growl, shaking his head. "Because Lucifer beat the hell out of him and killed him, so he wasn't exactly feeling like himself that day." He sighed. "Okay, enough of this third person bullshit!" He held out his hands. "I get it. I'm gonna feel lousy for a day or so. Talia and I finished our challenge today. So, I should be fine in time for interviews."

Berith gazed at Talia again. "When are these interviews?"

"Thursday."

She nodded. "You'll be fine by Thursday, Jack."

Berith looked over at her and spoke in angel notes that Jack couldn't hear. "Keep him in bed until Wednesday. No matter how many times he says he's fine."

"Got it," said Talia.

Jack frowned. "Got what?"

"I get that you need to rest," she said and pulled him into a quick kiss. "You've lost blood and had resurrect angel energy scouring away every last trace of that soul tether. It's going to tax your human body a bit, Jack."

His eyelids began to droop.

"Nah, I'm good," he said, his voice getting softer.

He began to blink his eyes, struggling to keep them open, Talia realized.

"You sure?" Talia asked, smiling at him.

"Golden," he said. "Ready to—explore the grounds…a bit. And turn in—tablet."

Jack slumped against Talia's shoulder, eyes closed, breaths deep and even.

He was asleep.

"That was fast," said Berith. "I expected him to fight the exhaustion for a few more minutes."

"With the blood loss, he was just too tired," said Talia as she flexed her wings and rose from the bed.

She slid her arms underneath Jack and lifted him up. "Someone turn down the covers, please."

Berith and Muriel quickly pulled the comforter and sheet down. Talia laid Jack on the bed and Berith pulled up the covers. She pressed the back of her hand to his forehead again.

"He's spiking a fever," she replied. "He'll be fine by Wednesday once all of this passes through his system."

Talia smiled. "Thank you, everyone," she said. "Thank you for protecting him against Lucifer. I don't think I could have stood it if Lucifer had dragged him back to Hell."

"Heaven wasn't about to let that happen again, Talia," said Azrael, lifting his chin high. "We owe Jack a huge debt. Something we're still discussing with High House."

"I understand, sir," said Talia.

"We'll be in contact soon," said Azrael. "Pravuil has some little detail that he's pursuing. We're hoping it bears fruit. Until then, keep the seraphim wards in place and keep Jack out of trouble."

With that, he and Berith blinked out, leaving Talia and her squad to stand guard over Jack while he recovered from the soul tether's removal. It might be a long day or two until their Thursday interviews.

She picked up the tablet computer that Jack used to scan all their codes from the bed. She needed to find Steve and turn it in before anything happened to it.

JACK HAD SEVERAL WILD DREAMS ABOUT LUCIFER AND EOLOWEN AND flying with his angel's wings. He felt so hot and achy all over and sleep held onto him for what felt like days. When he finally opened his eyes, the room was filled with light.

It was daytime. Somehow, he knew it wasn't Tuesday.

With slow, careful movements, he sat up and gazed around the quiet suite.

"Talia?" he called.

Silence.

"Muriel? Kesien? Anahera?"

No response.

His entire body ached as he sat up, head pounding. He was only wearing blue boxer briefs.

He took his time crawling out of bed and standing up, holding onto the bed, his bare feet cold against the marble floors.

The room smelled like lemons and his coconut shampoo. He fumbled for a pair of grey boxer briefs out of the armoire and held onto the walls as he made his way to the bathroom for a nice, long shower. He glanced at his right hand. The wound in the center of his palm had scabbed over.

It was healing. That meant the tether was really gone. He felt overwhelmed with relief.

He took a nice, long shower, shaved, and dressed in jeans, a Pearl Jam T-shirt, and his Navy blue hoodie and dropped down on the couch. Great. The suite was empty for the first time since he and Talia had gotten here—and she was gone, too.

And he didn't even have his phone to keep him company.

Talia was probably doing an interview. It was after eleven A.M. though. Maybe she'd gone down to lunch and was hanging out with Izzy?

It was almost one o'clock when Talia hurried into the suite, smiling when she found him on the couch.

"You're finally up," she cried and rushed over to the couch.

She threw her arms around his neck and kissed him hard on the lips.

"Hey, babe," he said. "Was wondering why you and the squad vanished on me."

"The squad's here," she said. "Just on the roof at the moment. Muriel?" she called.

Muriel blinked through the ceiling and landed beside the glass coffee table. "Hey, Talia," she said. "I was still watching over Jack through the ceilings."

So, he hadn't been alone after all. He sighed. Just as well Talia wasn't here.

"I think I got a pretty good night's sleep last night," he said, turning back to Talia. "So, I'll be fine by Thursday. And just in time for Friday's elimination round."

Muriel chuckled and Talia just smiled at him.

"What?" he asked, frowning.

Talia laid her hand against his cheek. "It is Thursday, lover," she said.

"What? It's Thursday?"

She nodded. "You had a high fever all day Tuesday and Wednesday. It finally broke late last night. Berith said you'd be fine though."

He squinted at her. "Berith was here again?"

"I called her down yesterday and she said you'd be fine today," said Talia, ruffling his hair. "And just in time for your afternoon interviews."

That second challenge seemed like a lifetime away now. He had to think back to everything they did.

"Hope I can remember everything," he said, shaking his head.

"You will," said Talia. "We have our couple's interview first. I asked them to schedule your individual interview as late as possible today."

He took hold of her hands and kissed her fingers. "You're the best, babe," he said. "Wonder how we did at this challenge?"

Talia tossed her head back, laughing, that raven black hair falling in waves across her shoulders.

"I think Steve felt a little insulted when I turned our tablet computer in on Monday. He seemed really surprised that we'd already finished. Izzy and Rachel were surprised, too. Everything just sort of fell in place for us this time."

He nodded. "Sure did. For once. And we even had to deal with Abaddon and Lucifer again."

"I guess we'll just find out what happens tomorrow," said Talia.

"Any word from Azrael on the Abaddon situation yet?"

She shook her head. "Nothing yet. Azrael said that Pravuil had a tiny piece of information that had sparked another investigation into the archive. We'll just hope that he finds something. Otherwise, you'll have to return to the Heavens with me until we figure out how to deal with Abaddon."

Another temporary situation. He just wanted to have his own place. Whether it was here on earth or somewhere in Angel-land, he didn't care as long as it wasn't temporary. He'd been in temporary digs since he'd been fired from *SanFran Confidential* and Rachel walked out on him. He wanted his own place. Just him and Talia.

"I really need some time to find us a place to live, babe," he said and laid his hand against her hair, stroking, tangling his fingers in her long, shiny locks. "Some alone time, just you and me, is what I want."

"Same, Jack," she said and laid her head on his shoulder. "I know things have been chaos for you since I fell out of the sky and into your arms."

"Way before that," he said with a smirk and winked at her. "It started that day in Studio 22 and has never been the same since."

She sat up, grinning at him as she started tickling his sides. "Are you insinuating that I'm trouble?"

He started laughing. "Not insinuating," he said with a hard laugh. "Stating a fact, my angel of death fiancée. You are trouble AND chaos…and the best thing that's ever happened to me."

"And you, Jack Casey," Talia said with intense grey eyes and that teasing smile. "Are trouble, chaos, and reckless abandon. All rolled into the most stunningly handsome being I've ever encountered— angel, demon, or human."

"Even Lucifer?" he asked.

She smacked his shoulder with her hand. "Especially Lucifer, smart guy."

"How about Armand Gianni?"

She grabbed him by his hoodie and pressed her forehead against his. "Now, you know that I never had eyes for anyone but you. And I tried so hard not to fall for you. So hard. But I couldn't help myself. I fell for you that very first day you stood under those hot set lights with all those people surrounding you."

"Why?" he asked, suddenly serious.

He'd always wondered why she'd fallen for him that day. It had been a really bad day and he'd just lost the last acting job—a cameo on his old show—that anyone in Hollywood had been willing to offer him. He'd woken up drunk and strung out on flake. And he'd looked it that day, too.

"Why?" she repeated, staring at him like he'd just run into a wall. "Because you were so hot that you took my breath away, Jack! I was stunned at how beautiful you were—those sizzling light green eyes, your lean body, and that sexy smirk. But there you stood, surrounded by people. Entertainment business people, fans, and other admirers. And in the middle of all that, you looked so lonely. Vulnerable. Tired of pretense. Hungry for something deep and real. Just like I was."

He kissed her lips. "You got all that from my standing under those lights?"

"I am an angel of death, Jack," she said. "I was able to sense all of that."

He shook his head. "So, you knew all of that and you still found me attractive?"

It surprised him that she'd found his weakness attractive. What had she called it? Vulnerable?

"Intoxicatingly attractive," she replied. "Jack, you made my halo spin faster and my wings shudder. I couldn't get you out of my thoughts from that moment on. Ask Muriel if you don't believe me."

Muriel blinked her head and shoulders through the ceiling. "You called?"

Talia nodded at her. "Tell Jack how crazy for him I was that very first day."

"Crazy? Jack, she'd lost her angelic mind over you. Tried to convince me and herself for a week or so that she wasn't head over feet for you." She grinned. "Didn't work."

Then she blinked back to the roof.

"See, Jack," said Talia, turning back to him.

He laughed. She was the first woman he'd met that hadn't known who he was or what he'd done wrong over the past few years. She'd looked past all of that and found something worth saving. He still didn't understand what that was, but he was so thankful she had.

He couldn't stand to ever be without her.

"I don't know what that was, but I'm grateful for it." He caressed her cheek with his fingers. "I don't ever want to lose you, Talia. Ever."

Her grey eyes lit up and she kissed him. "Now, you'd better get dressed for our interviews."

He returned her kiss and then rose from the couch to go change into dress clothes for afternoon interviews.

ON FRIDAY, with less than a half hour before sunset, Jack and Talia stood on the patio in each other's arms, drenched in the simulated candlelight from set lights and dozens of lit candles scattered around the patio.

He and Talia stood between Gianni and Izzy to the left and Rachel and Eric to the right as Devin Van Fossen delivered his melodramatic monologues and introduced canned interviews. Devin shifted from camera to camera, announcing flower hunting footage and other clips as he addressed the television audience that had stuck with them through four seasons now.

They were on another five-minute break for commercials, waiting for Devin to announce the fate of one couple. With Steve threatening to bludgeon anyone that disappeared from the patio during commercials.

Still, Jack kept looking around.

At the roof, behind him in the backyard, and around the sides of the chateau. Worried that Abaddon would return for the next round tonight on the live elimination show. This time, they couldn't throw his lost phone through the wards and break through.

Of course, he wouldn't put it past Lucifer or Abaddon to have another trick ready—especially now. Lucifer had to sense that the soul tether had been broken. And he'd be royally pissed about it, too.

Jack wore a deep blue Brioni suit with a tan T-shirt, and black dress shoes. Talia wore a short lavender dress with thin straps and long sleeves. The dress hugged her curves like a Maserati and she made his blood boil in that dress.

Gianni wore a light grey suit, dark blue dress shirt and tie. Izzy wore a short red dress with spaghetti straps. Eric wore a black suit, black dress shirt, and black dress shoes. Rachel wore a pale pink dress with long, sheer sleeves and another pristine pair of matching pumps with those red soles. Did she have a new contract with Lucifer? Or stock in the shoe company?

"And we're back, my royal subjects," Devin said into camera two. He wore a black tailcoat, white tuxedo shirt, black pants, and a gold bowtie. "It's time to find out the first couple that will return next week. Are you ready? Let's look at our scores."

He pulled out a card from a pocket inside his jacket and stared at it for a moment or two. Then he gazed into camera two with a knowing look on his smug face as he circled Gianni and Izzy. Camera one followed him.

"Is it Armand Gianni and Isabella Castilla?" he asked the camera as he kept walking across the patio.

Devin circled around him and Talia next and Talia tightened her hold around his waist.

"Is it fan favorite, Jack Casey and Talia Smith?" Devin asked the camera as he kept moving.

He walked around Rachel and Eric twice. "Or is it Rachel Daniels and Eric Saunders?"

With a slow, deliberate stroll, he moved back toward his blocking mark and stared into camera one's lens again.

"The first couple that will return for the final competition is…"

Cameras two and three moved in, focusing on him and Talia and Rachel and Eric as camera one zoomed in on Izzy and Gianni.

"Jack and Talia!"

Grinning, Jack spun her around and dipped her, kissing her in a long, deep kiss.

"We did it, babe," he whispered in her ear.

"Congratulations, lover," she said with a nod and kissed him again, her arms sliding around his waist.

Devin cast another grim look into the camera. "But my royal subjects, this means that Armand Gianni and Isabella Castilla are in danger of going home tonight."

Izzy looked frightened. Gianni had that cool, Cary Grant silver screen demeanor, crossing his arms and looking cool and unaffected. That was the actor in him, hiding his concern. Jack hoped Gianni and Izzy stayed. He'd love to see them get married on the show almost as much as he wanted to marry Talia on this fourth season of the reality television show.

"And it also means," Devin continued, turning his gaze to camera two, "that Rachel Daniels and Eric Saunders are also in danger of leaving us tonight. Which couple stays and which couple goes? In a moment, after this break, we'll tell you. Stay tuned."

"All right, we're clear!" Steve shouted. "Four minutes forty-eight seconds. Move away from your marks and I hang you by your thumbs from the evergreens. Got it? Nobody move."

Jack turned toward Gianni and gave him the thumb's up. "Good luck, dude," he said. "Hope you and Izzy stay. I've never been to a final without you there, Gianni. Not sure I can do it without you."

Gianni grinned at him. "I hope you'll vehemently protest if I'm not, Jack."

"I sure as hell will protest!"

Izzy smiled at him, but she looked so nervous. And waiting almost five more minutes was torture.

He glanced over at Rachel and Eric. They whispered together and Rachel looked a little frazzled. He hoped it was Gianni and Izzy who stayed.

The minutes ticked down until Steve gave Devin the signal and counted down from ten and the live broadcast continued.

"Welcome back, my royal subjects," said Devin into camera one as he turned his gaze toward the backyard.

All three cameras honed in on him now.

"America, we've reached that final moment in the show where we must bid adieu to one of our couples. Is it Isabella and Armand or Rachel and Eric?" He turned his gaze to camera two. "We're about to find out."

The cameras rolled back, getting a full, patio view of all the reactions.

"And the couple leaving us tonight is…Rachel and Eric. And we're out of time, my royal subjects. Please join us next week for the final competition. After next week, we begin the final challenge of The Royal Wedding Hour. Where you'll finally watch one of the show's favorite couples wed live. On camera. In a live broadcast. You don't want to miss that. Until next time."

"And…we're clear," said Steve, sitting down in a chair, looking relieved and exhausted.

He wore a jean shirt and a grey *Royal Wedding Hour* T-shirt. His hair was in a man bun and he wore gold-framed glasses.

"Good work everyone!" Herb announced, rising from his chair, grey dress pants and light blue dress shirt wrinkled. "Get some sleep and we'll have the wrap-up tomorrow as we go into an orientation for the third challenge. Have a good night."

Jack looked up as Rachel sauntered toward him, heels clicking against the concrete patio. Smiling, tears in her eyes.

Talia bristled, standing her ground as she stood close to him. Not leaving him alone with her for even a moment.

"Jack," she said and reached out to grip his shoulders. "I just wanted to say thank you again."

Her voice was a little shaky, smoky eyeshadow and mascara smudged as tears slipped down her face. He was never sure when she stopped acting and would never trust those tears again.

"You saved me," she said. "And I'll never forget that—or you. I really did love you, you know. Despite everything I did and said to you, I loved you even though I knew I could never keep you because of…the contract. And Lare."

Even now, Rachel Daniels had no idea what love was—or what it even felt like. He wasn't even sure if she'd ever been capable of that kind of deep emotion. She and Laren Dumont were shallow and narcissistic. Qualities he'd never shared or understood—even at his lowest point, addicted to cocaine and losing everything.

"Best of luck to you and Eric," he said with a nod. "Hope this one works out."

"Me, too," she said, that thick auburn hair falling around her shoulders. "To be honest, I hope I never see Lare again."

She was wearing her hair shorter now. She still had a smattering of freckles across her nose, her skin milk-pale, but she'd aged since she'd been in Hell and returned. The lines were a little deeper around her mouth, between her eyebrows, across her forehead. Had he aged like that in Hell? He hadn't noticed any difference in his face, but seeing it in Rachel's expressions startled him.

She reached out and for a moment, laid her hand against his cheek. "You haven't aged a day since I met you, Jack. Stay young and hot, kiddo." She winked at him. "And give 'em Hell for me."

Then she wrapped her arm in Eric's and sauntered off the patio as Izzy rushed over to Talia and hugged her. He felt Gianni tap his shoulder. He turned and shook the taller soap star's hand.

"We made it to another final, Jack," he said with a big grin. "Congratulations."

"You, too, dude," he said and poked Gianni's shoulder with his fist. "Can't think of anyone I'd rather compete against. Or stand up with as my best man."

"Same, Jack," he said, looking all sober and pensive. "We've been through a lot together on this show. A shame one of us will have to go home."

He shook his head. "Either you're my best man or you're getting married, dude, so you're not going home any time soon."

Gianni thought for a moment and then his smile returned. "That's a good point, Jack. And you're in the same boat. Guess we're in this thing to the bitter end then."

He grinned. "Just the way I like it."

Gianni turned to Talia and hugged her.

As Jack watched them celebrate and chatter away, he felt... unsettled. Felt sudden, heavy darkness at the edge of wards.

He gazed out across the chateau's dusky backyard, feeling a presence in the dark that made the hair on the back of his neck stand up.

Abaddon was out there again. Waiting. Waiting for one of them to screw up and step outside the seraphim wards.

But behind Abaddon was Lucifer. Seething with rage at being tethered in Hell. Blinded by revenge and ready to pour it all out on him.

Somehow, he and Talia had to end this standoff with Abaddon and make sure Lucifer didn't break his halo tether. So, the King of Hell didn't come after him with a vengeance bigger than all the Heavens and Hell.

ON SATURDAY, AFTER A QUICK BOXED LUNCH IN THE MARBLE DINING room with the burgundy chairs, Talia fidgeted beside Jack as she waited for the third challenge orientation to begin. She didn't need or want to eat this food, but she always tried to eat a little to keep up appearances. This time, she pushed the food around on the paper plate, hoping no one noticed.

Through some strange anomaly—maybe the rare bond they shared —only Jack could see her wings and halo on earth, so she kept up the illusion that she was human to everyone else. She leaned back in the padded, burgundy chair in dark blue yoga pants, white tennis shoes, and an ice blue tunic.

The smell of mustard from the sandwiches hung in the room along with the scent of oranges from Izzy's peeled orange that set on a white paper towel beside her. And the apple core that Jack had tossed into the small white box in front of him. He used a folded wet-wipe from the included packet and tossed it into the box. It smelled like lemons.

Izzy wore a rust-colored pair of yoga pants and a long-sleeved Navy blue top. Beside her, Armand wore dark blue jeans and a long-sleeved white polo shirt.

Jack seemed distracted this morning, picking at his half-eaten turkey sandwich. He stared out the window at the formal gardens, his face a mix of worry and pensiveness.

He slouched back in his chair, shoving the box away, and stared across the patio toward the ring of evergreens, toward the hidden fountain pool and koi pond. He wore his favorite Navy blue hoodie over a grey Arctic Monkeys T-shirt and those faded Levi's, spinning a spoon on the table as he glanced from the spoon to the window and back again.

He'd been a little distant this morning and she wasn't sure if he still felt weak after breaking the soul tether. Or was it because they were one challenge away from getting married?

Was he getting nervous about that or was this still about Abaddon? They'd tried wards, seraphim powers, and even reasoning with the confused angel-turned-demon. No one in Heaven understood why Abaddon chose to become Lucifer's enforcer while guarding the Gates of Hell's key and waiting to smite the wicked in the end days.

She found it disturbing that no one, not even God's Scribe or the seraphim, knew how to dissuade Abaddon from his current path. She hoped that Pravuil, who had the Maker's ear, would consult with Him about the matter. Down here, they were out of answers and time.

But something was bothering Jack.

She'd tried asking him before Jennifer, Herb, and Steve walked into the dining room and sat down. He said he was fine, just thinking about the next challenge.

Again, he forgot that angels sensed lies from a great distance. She'd just have to wait for him to talk about whatever it was when he was ready. She hoped it wasn't about getting married. That frightened her after his interactions with Rachel yesterday.

Was he still in love with her—deep down? Or did he just miss having a human girlfriend? Maybe that was it? He'd probably had his fill of all the demons and angels that had barged into his life almost a year ago.

Jennifer set her phone down in front of her as she talked about the last challenge. She wore a purple sweatshirt with the show's logo on it, brown slip-ons, and dark jeans. Her hair was in a ponytail and she held her clipboard in her lap under the table.

Herb, the director, sat beside Steve. His balding head looked shiny against his black sweater and jeans. He looked pleased as he glanced at Steve, wearing a red and blue striped button-down shirt, black tennis shoes, and jeans. His hair was loose around his shoulders, beard trimmed close against his face.

"Already down to two couples," said Jennifer as she slid on a pair of tortoiseshell glasses. "Seems so fast this time, but the rest of the show will be dedicated to the actual wedding. So, it may not feel like it, but we're right on schedule."

Jack fidgeted, leaning back in his chair, one hand still spinning that spoon on the table.

Talia wondered if he was getting nervous about being married. It wasn't like they wouldn't have extraordinary challenges as a married couple. Challenges that he still didn't have any resolutions for—like whether she could even stay with him. She knew that was his major worry, but this new brooding behavior was different.

He was quiet. It was a rare thing for Jack to be this quiet. Usually, he was cracking jokes and setting people at ease, not contributing to the silence.

Jennifer smiled and picked up her phone, reading something on the screen. "So, I'm sure you're all wondering about the last competition. This one's called the bride's challenge. And we're going to enlist the help of our at-home audiences in this challenge. It has three parts. The first one is to work with a dress designer to create a one-of-a-kind, storybook bridal gown for the wedding. Our princesses, with their prince charmings' help, will each design a dress that must have one feature chosen by their prince."

"Whoa, seriously?" Jack replied. "I use the show stylists for a reason."

Chuckles erupted through the room.

He motioned at Armand. "Except for Cary Grant here who was born with his own style manual."

"Sorry, Talia," said Armand, shaking his head at Jack. "I hope you don't mind wearing a metal band logo on your gown—that'll be Jack's contribution."

Laughter echoed through the dining room.

Jack nodded. "You think he's kidding."

"Regardless, your prince charming's contribution needs to be a prominent part of the gown," Jennifer continued. "The designers will sketch your dresses and we'll have the audience vote on their favorite gown. Highest scoring couple wins."

Talia heard Jack sigh and spin his spoon again.

"The second part will be a couple's first dance competition. The couple that performs the royal waltz the best earns points. You'll be taught the dance this afternoon and you'll have until Tuesday night to practice. On Wednesday, both couples will be filmed performing their dances."

"Why didn't I accept that invitation for Dancing with the Stars when I had a chance?" Jack replied with the shake of his head.

He got a round of laughter from the crew as well as Armand and Izzy.

"The third part of your score will come from the flowers you selected for the bride's bouquet challenge," Jennifer replied and glanced at her phone screen again. "We're having a florist assemble the flowers you both chose into bridal bouquets. Our home audience will vote for their favorite bouquet. On Thursday, we'll open the voting for favorite dress, favorite couple's dance, and favorite bouquet until Friday at 6:59 P.M. Pacific Coast time."

Jack sat up in his chair. "So, when the live show starts, no one will know who won yet?"

Steve nodded. "That's right, Jack. I'll be working with our IT staff and the auditing firm to gather the scores and see who won. At five minutes 'til eight, I'll hand Devin an envelope with the winning couple's names. He won't even know until that moment who won."

Talia watched Jack exchange a look with Armand and settle back in his chair again, returning to his spoon spinning.

"So, we're letting our audience select their favorites," said Jennifer, pushing her glasses up onto the bridge of her nose. "We're letting our audience select the couple they want to watch get married in a fairytale wedding."

"Seems only fair," said Armand, steepling his fingers. "They've watched us through four seasons of flirting and dating and coupling. It's only fair that they get to choose the one they want to see actually get married."

Jack nodded. "Couldn't agree more," he replied and set down the spoon. "It's their show, not ours. I like that we're letting them choose." He turned to Armand and extended his hand. "Dude, best of luck to you and Izzy. I can't wait to see you two get married."

"Thanks, Jack," said Armand, shaking Jack's hand. "Likewise. I think we've all watched you and Talia with a high degree of enchantment, hoping the two of you would get your happily ever after."

"Talia," said Izzy, leaning toward her. "You're the reason I even applied to appear on the show. I fell in love with you and Jack that very first season." She put her arms around Armand's waist. "And this man."

Armand kissed her.

"Thank you, Izzy," said Talia. "That makes me so happy to hear."

"Appreciate that, Izzy," said Jack, reaching over and taking Talia's hand. "I tried to get her to marry me at the end of The Prince Charming Hour." He gazed back at her, those light green eyes burning right through her heart. "Kind of glad she didn't answer me for a while. Now, I have a shot at giving her the fairytale wedding of her dreams. Probably not the fairytale prince she had in mind when she started this game, but she's stuck with me now."

Talia threw her arms around his neck. "Jack Casey, you take that back!" she cried. "You're everything I've ever wanted. And you were every bit my fairytale prince charming when I saw you. I've never wanted anybody like I wanted you."

She saw the surprise in his eyes. And it made her sad. Rachel Daniels and Laren Dumont had done so much damage to him. It hurt when she realized that he meant most of his self-deprecating humor. He still had no idea how stunningly attractive he was and most of the time, he saw himself as damaged. It made her want to smite Lare and Rachel.

"I'd ask you to marry me all over again, if I could, Talia," he said and kissed her.

"We'll be running footage from past shows," said Herb. "And we'll be replaying your greatest hits as a couple." He pointed at Jack. "Including a bunch of those off-script moments of yours, Jack. The ones that put this show on the map. Don't forget that. That was all you, Jack."

A crooked smile lifted one corner of his mouth and he nodded at her. "They were Talia-inspired, Herb."

"Okay, let me pass out the schedule," said Jennifer as she rose from her chair.

She walked around the table, handing sheets of paper to Talia, Jack, Armand, and Izzy.

"You'll have individual interviews, a couple's interview, and appointments with the dress designer and the dance instructor. It's all there on the schedule, set calls, interviews, stylists, and everything. Any questions?"

She stood beside her chair, studying them, waiting for questions.

Talia glanced at Izzy and Armand. They were silent. Jack seemed more interested in spinning that spoon again than asking any questions.

"Good," said Jennifer. "You'll meet with the dance instructor on the patio right after this meeting. Both couples together. And we'll be filming. See you then!"

Jennifer, Herb, and Steve exited the dining room along with the handful of crew members in the room, including Roy the lead cameraman.

"Looks like we'll be taking dance lessons together," said Armand with a chuckle to Jack. "I actually have some dance experience. In my theatre days."

Jack nodded. "Same. I was in my share of musicals before I got cast on SanFran Confidential."

So, Jack did have dance experience! She felt so relieved. She had none, but she was an angel. Most had built-in grace, even the clumsy ones. She hoped that together, they'd be fine doing a waltz. She sighed. Despite both of them having wings and halos hidden from humankind.

Jack set down his spoon and rose from his chair, waiting for her to stand. When she got to her feet, he slid his hand into hers. She squeezed his hand and followed him out of the dining room, into the hallway.

"Do you want to change before our dance lessons?" he asked as they entered the tall gallery of the entryway.

She shook her head. "I don't need to, do I?"

He smiled. "Yoga pants—probably the perfect choice for dancing," he said. "And smokin' hot in my book."

He always said the right thing and she loved that he found the yoga pants sexy.

"I'll remember that about yoga pants."

"Oh, please do," he said with a smirk. "And feel free to get them in every color. For science."

She leaned up and kissed him. His lips tasted sweet with apples.

"Everything okay?" she asked in a soft voice.

He opened his mouth to reply, but she stopped him.

"And don't forget that I can sense a lie from any distance," she said with a grin.

He closed his mouth, scowling at her. "I'm fine," he snapped. "Just worried about Abaddon."

"No more than usual," she said and ran her fingers through his hair.

He glanced around and then lowered his voice. "I felt him out there last night, Talia."

A cold wind brushed across her skin. "Last night?"

"During the elimination. I felt him just beyond the patio. Waiting." He sighed and looked over his shoulder, making sure no one heard him. "We've got to find a way to handle him. Can't believe that no one in the Heavens has a fix on this dude's issue. Or why he threw in with the poster boy for disgruntled Heavenly servants."

She bowed her head. She knew Jack was frustrated by all of these issues. So was she, but even angels didn't have all the answers. They didn't have access to the Maker like humans with their direct line. And no one wanted to bother God with small issues—like Abaddon. But the angel had gone rogue and since Abaddon only answered to the Maker, dealing with him was beyond even the seraphim.

"Sorry, just feeling out of sorts and frustrated," he said. "No one knows what to do with me up there and we can't get an answer on where we're going to live. And I'm tired of this little bitch hunting me like I'm in season."

She slid her arms around him and held him.

"I know it's all up in the air and then there's your mother. And you had to say goodbye to Rachel yesterday and…"

He pulled away, staring at her with a confused look. "What's Rachel got to do with any of this?"

She held out her hands. "You've seemed a little sad since she left."

"Sad?" he said, brows furrowing. "About Rachel leaving?" Then he laughed, his tone bitter. "I was relieved. Can't stand that horrible perfume she wears or the way she looks at me, like everything's okay between us. It's not. I may have forgiven her, but I'll never forget the hell she put me through. And I'll never trust her again."

So, it wasn't Rachel. It was Abaddon and something else. Something that he didn't want to talk about right now.

"Hey, you coming, Jack?" Armand called as they turned down the hallway headed toward the patio.

"Be there in a moment," he said and his gaze met hers again. "Babe, I just want answers from the dudes upstairs and I want the dudes in the basement to lose my number. That's all."

"I get it," she said and slid her arms around him again, pulling him into a hug. "I want those answers, too. And I'm willing to smite every last one of those basement dwellers."

He kissed her. "Same here," he said. "With every last seraph power I possess. Even if I'm drunk for a week, it'd be worth it."

She laughed and kissed him back. "C'mon," she said. "Dance with me?"

"Until the universe grinds to a halt," he said in a soft voice, the sound warm like hot, melted caramel.

She tugged him toward the hallway and they hurried out the French doors, onto the patio.

Where a tall, graceful woman with auburn hair, a bright smile, and a warm alto voice welcomed them. She looked like she was in her late thirties. She wore a long black skirt and body-hugging pink tank top.

"Good afternoon. I'm Candy Clark, a professor in the dance program at Sonoma State University. And I'm going to teach you how to waltz today."

Talia watched the woman look Jack up and down, smiling. "Jack Casey, right?" she said. "You were fantastic on SanFran Confidential and I loved you as Billy Riggs in You and Me."

"Thanks," he said. "Appreciate that."

"Ever do any dancing, Jack?" Professor Clark asked.

Talia felt annoyed. Like there weren't three other people on the patio.

"Yeah," he said, rubbing his hand against the back of his neck. "Did my share of chorus parts and a few lead roles before I got cast on SanFran Confidential. Did my share of ballroom dancing for a few parts, too."

"Looking forward to seeing those moves," said Professor Clark, smiling at him.

Talia glowered at the woman as she leered at him.

The woman turned her gaze to Armand next and it was Izzy's turn to bristle.

"And you play Dr. Nick Rossi on Crossing Paths," said Professor Clark. "Ever do any dancing?"

Armand nodded, that polite smile on his face, his classic silver screen looks also catching this woman's eye.

"I did a lot of professional theatre before I took the role on Crossing Paths."

"And believe me, it shows, Armand."

Izzy glared at her.

Professor Clark turned around and smiled at Talia now. "Jack's dance partner...lucky you," she said. "Talia Smith, right? Have you done any ballroom dancing?"

"That's me and no, I haven't done any ballroom dancing," said Talia, wanting to smite this woman.

"How about you? Wait, you're Isabella Castilla. You used to do the channel six evening news in San Francisco, didn't you?"

Izzy looked annoyed, but she nodded. "I moved to Los Angeles to be with Armand. My fiancé." She slid her arm in Armand's and gave this woman her most possessive, but pleasant smile.

So, Izzy wanted to smite her, too.

"And I've never done any ballroom dancing either," said Izzy.

"Well, I'm going to teach you a basic waltz box step with natural turns," said the woman as she turned in a circle toward the widest part of the patio. "Okay, I'd like the men on my left, facing their partners on my right."

Jack moved alongside Armand and stood a few feet from Professor Clark. Armand stood to Jack's left. Talia faced Jack. They were about six feet apart.

"Okay, the waltz is a three-beat count. The men will step forward with their left foot and create a box. Step forward with the left foot. Slide right with the right foot and then close with the left foot. Step back with the right foot. Slide open to the left with the left foot and close with the right foot."

She turned around. "Jack, Armand, you try it."

Jack and Armand had no trouble with that step. They both knew it without even looking at their feet.

"Very good, guys!" said Professor Clark, smiling. "Okay, for the women, you'll be facing these handsome men. So, you'll step back with your right foot first. Slide to the left and close with your right foot. Then step forward with your left foot. Slide your right foot to the right and close with the left foot."

Talia had witnessed the birth of the waltz in Bavaria and its renaissance later in Germany. She'd seen it danced for centuries. She just hoped her natural grace would help her get through this challenge.

"Okay, let's have the women try it now. Remember, your man is leading, so you'll step backward. And count the three beats in your head as you step. It'll help as you alternate right foot then left foot."

Talia pulled all those images of mad and carefree waltzes into her head as she stepped back. Right foot, slide with the left. Close right. Step forward left. Slide right. Close. Repeat.

Her feet were light with an angel's buoyancy, the air currents flowing through her celestial body as she floated through the steps. Right. Slide left. Close. Left forward. Slide right. Close.

She remembered a young Amadè Mozart playing the clavier, one of the best keyboardists in Vienna.

When she looked up, Professor Clark was smiling at her. "My word, Talia! That was lovely."

"Thank you," she replied.

"And very nice, Izzy," said the woman, motioning at Izzy who was standing to Talia's right. "You have a natural feel for the rhythm."

Izzy nodded.

"Now," said Professor Clark, holding out her arms. "I want you to try it with your guy. He'll hold your left hand in his right hand and he'll place his left hand on your waist."

Jack grinned as he stepped up and took her left hand in his and lifted it into the air. His left arm slid around her waist. She put her right arm around his waist.

To Talia's right, Armand had Izzy in his arms, ready to waltz.

"Okay, imagine you're at your wedding and they're playing you and your new husband's first song. It's a waltz."

"Ready, babe?" he asked with a wink, that sexy smirk turning up the corners of his mouth.

She nodded and smiled at him. He was adorable in his blue hoodie and faded jeans, those light green eyes scorching her human soul as she gazed into their sparkling depths. She could lose herself in his eyes.

"Right foot to start?" she asked.

"Right then left," he replied. "And I'm sorry if I step on your toes."

He could step on her toes any time.

"Got it."

"And go," said Professor Clark.

Jack was smooth and graceful and she kept up with him, the movements reminding her of turning circles through clouds as she flew beside him.

Even without music, dancing with Jack was magical. She loved feeling his arm around her, his body turning with hers, the fluid motion as they moved together as one. She wanted to melt into his arms and stay there.

"Okay, you two," said Professor Clark, gripping their arms. "You can stop now."

"I could dance with you for the rest of my life, Talia Smith," he said and Talia wanted to melt with him all over again.

"That was lovely. Jack and Armand, have you done a waltz with natural turns?"

Jack nodded. "Many times."

"Yes," said Armand. "Several times."

"So, you both know how to lead your partner into natural turns?" Professor Clark asked.

Jack and Armand nodded.

"Show me," she said.

"Talia, follow my body as we turn," said Jack. "We're going to do quarter turns each time. That's how we'll move across the floor. Does that make sense?"

"We're about to find out," she replied, still gripping his right hand with her left.

He repositioned his arm around her waist.

"We're going to step and turn as we slide that other foot. Ready?"

She nodded.

Together, they took two steps. And stopped.

"Wait, let's try it again," he said and she brought both feet back together.

It took them four or five false starts and then he made the quarter turn. Other foot. Turn and slide. First foot. Turn and slide.

After a few minutes, they were moving across the patio.

Like flying together around the spires of High House. Bank and turn. Cool wind streaming through her hair, across her wing tips, and against her face. The heat of his hand in hers as they somersaulted through clouds and flew low over the meadows.

Armand and Izzy also turned around the patio, slower and still learning. But Izzy picked up everything quickly and with extreme determination. Talia knew that by the time the show was ready to film, she'd be a master at it. She liked that about Izzy.

"All right, I think all four of you have what you need," said Professor Clark as she brushed a lock of auburn hair out of her eyes.

Talia and Jack stopped dancing and moved over to Professor Clark. Jack shook her hand as Armand and Izzy approached.

"Thanks, professor," said Jack. "Appreciate the lesson."

"It was a pleasure to meet you in person, Jack. You're even more gorgeous off camera. Good luck to you and Talia."

She gave Jack a long, lingering look that made Talia's urge to smite the woman return. She turned to Armand and shook his hand.

"Armand, best of luck to you and Izzy. I'll be watching to see how you all do."

Professor Clark said her goodbyes and went back into the chateau, leaving the four of them alone to practice.

Jack grinned at Talia and bowed like a prince. "May I have this dance, Cinderella?"

"This one and all the rest," she said and held out her hand to him.

He kissed her hand and then they were off, twirling across the patio in a waltz that would have made even Mozart smile.

ON MONDAY, TALIA AND JACK ARRIVED IN A SMALL STUDY OFF THE chateau's main living area. Jack was in jeans, white T-shirt, and a grey V-neck sweater. She'd put on a short jean skirt and a red blouse with sheer long sleeves. One of Jack's favorites.

It was a sunny blue and yellow room with a white French-styled desk and bookshelves against one wall. The books were more for decoration than a library, arranged in shades of blue and yellow. The white bookshelves were interspersed with colorful vases, little gold clocks, and small porcelain figures.

The study smelled like one of those room freshening sprays. Fake linen or chemical cotton. It made Talia's nose itch.

In the center of the room was a yellow loveseat and a blue and white overstuffed chair with an antiqued white coffee table with two huge books on it. One was on the history of Santa Rosa and another was about the palace at Versailles. She was at Versailles, like most angels of death, during the French Revolution. A dark and bloody time, like so many in human history.

But angels' history was just as dark and violent, despite some celestials thinking themselves better—and above—most humans. Celestial violence was still violence.

The pages of these large books were filled with color photos. Jack called them coffee table books. Because they sat on a coffee table? And why just coffee? Why not tea or juice or wine? Humans confused her.

In two corners of the room, cameras had been setup. Roy and Rhonda ran the cameras, Steve standing between them with a wireless headset. They all three wore jeans and purple T-shirts with *The Royal Wedding Hour* logo on them. Rhonda's blonde hair was pulled back in a ponytail. Roy's hair was a short steel grey.

When she and Jack walked in, a short, stocky man with grey hair and gold-framed glasses stood up from the blue and white chair and rushed over to them.

"Good afternoon, Talia Smith and Jack Casey," he said in a bright and flowing Italian accent. "It is my sincerest pleasure to meet you. I'm Luca Carini."

"Luca Carini?" Jack replied, his eyes wide as the shorter man gave Jack's hand a boisterous shake with both hands. "Of Carini and Amanté?"

"You know our work, Signor Casey?" The man looked surprised.

Jack nodded. "You made a dress for my ex-girlfriend for the Emmy's one year. It was incredible."

"Ex-girlfriend, Signor Casey? My condolences."

Jack laughed. "Nah, it's all good." He laid his hands on Talia's arms. "Wouldn't have met the love of my life if I hadn't gone through that." He turned to her. "Talia, these guys are absolute wizards! Whatever you can dream up, they can create."

"Remember, Jack, you have to contribute something to the dress, too," she said to him.

"Oh, no worries," he said with a wink. "I will."

That meant he already had something in mind. And she wanted to know what that something was—right now.

"Now then, Signorina Smith, let's sit down and look at some basic dress shapes to start," said Mr. Carini, his dark brown eyes filled with excitement. "And then I want to hear about your dream dress."

She had no idea what her dream dress even looked like in her head. She remembered the night when she thought she'd lost Jack as her match during *The Cinderella Hour*. And Jennifer whisked her away for a makeover and selecting her princess dress. She hadn't liked any of the choices they'd given her until Muriel chose one. Muriel had the fashion sense, not her.

When she married Jack Casey, she wanted him to be blown away when he saw her walk down that aisle toward him. She wanted an ethereal, cloud-like dress that reflected the Heavens and her angelic form. All light and diaphanous layers that fit her body and made her look like she was floating.

She smiled. No—flying.

Silk and sheer layers. White with hints of ice blue. With crystals and pearls that reflected the light. And off-the-shoulder sleeves styled like the blousy, sheer princess sleeves that floated around her shoulders. With those crisscrossed laces in back like an old-style corset.

Mr. Carini motioned them over to the loveseat. She and Jack sat down with her closest to the overstuffed blue and white chair where Mr. Carini had his brown leather briefcase and one of those tablet computers. Did every single human on this planet have at least one of those things?

"Now, then, Signorina Smith," he said and touched the screen. "Tell me how you want the dress to fit you."

He pulled what looked like a pen out of the side of the device and poised it over the top of the screen.

"I don't want one of those huge, wide skirts. I don't want to get lost in the dress. I want it to fit my body, but I do like the long, trailing fabric in back."

Jack was nodding. He apparently didn't like those skirts either.

"Floor length skirt?"

"Yes, definitely," said Talia.

"Describe how you see your dream dress," said Mr. Carini in a wistful voice.

"I'll try," she said, running her fingers through her black hair. "I want it to be...ethereal and timeless. Magical. All light and sheer, delicate floating layers reflecting the light. Like the Heavens. Pure light and crystalline. And I'd like to see some of the sheer layers fade from white to ice blue. But I also want it to have sheer, blousy princess sleeves, but off the shoulder and a sort of crisscrossed, laced-up bodice in back."

"Do you like pearls?" Mr. Carini asked. "Do you want lace?"

"Yes to pearls," she said with a nod. "And no to lace."

"Satin or silk? Tulle or organza?"

"Silk. With some organza."

"What about some of the more ornate appliques added to the layers? Like these."

Mr. Carini flicked pictures across the screen. One had a bodice that looked like it was just crystals and pearls floating on bare skin in a sleeveless bodice.

"Stop!" she said. "I love that," she said and pointed at the bodice. "They look like stars."

"Bene!" he said, smiling. "I'll make note of that."

He flicked through some more dress images until she saw the sheer flowing sleeves that she liked.

"I like those sleeves," she said, pointing.

"Ah," Mr. Carini said with a smile. "Organza trumpet sleeves. Bene."

Mr. Carini flicked image after image across the screen, but she didn't see anything else that caught her eye except for the sheer layer over a pastel blue that faded to white when it reached the waist of the dress.

"I like the sheer fabric over the color fade," said Talia, pointing at the skirt. "And I like that it doesn't look like a hoop skirt."

He wrote a bunch of notes with that pen on the screen. For several minutes, he wrote and wrote. And then he began to sketch images on the screen. He drew shapes and pictures alongside his notes as well.

"I have your measurements from the show's stylists, Signorina Talia," said Mr. Carini with a sharp nod. "You are a beautiful woman and this young man loves you very much. I will create something amazing for both of you." Then he turned to Jack. "And now, Signor Casey. Your contribution to the dress?"

Jack grinned and then gazed at Mr. Carini. "It needs to have wings."

Talia's mouth fell open. "Jack?"

"What kind of wings, Signor Casey?"

"Delicate, sheer angelic wings," he said. "Not overpowering. Just light and celestial wings, almost like they're made of light. Or glass."

Mr. Carini looked up at the ceiling a moment, a hand on his chin. "I like that! It's not a request I've had or even seen on a dress before. Feathered wings, yes, but not wings of light." He started scribbling across the screen with that inkless pen again, fast, furious strokes and then he wrote for a long time.

Talia gave Jack a look that confused him and his enthusiasm deflated.

She already had wings. Why would she want them on her wedding dress? She wasn't sure about this idea, but the dress had to include some contribution from Jack.

"Why did you choose wings, Jack?" she asked, turning toward him.

"Because," he said, staring down at his hands. "Throughout these four seasons, you didn't just teach me to fly. You taught me to soar. I offered you my heart free of charge, Talia. And you accepted all the pieces of my damaged, broken heart and—"

His voice broke and he pulled in a breath, wiping his eyes. Trying again. She reached out and laid her hand against his cheek.

"Go on, lover," she said in a soft voice.

"And...you put it back together. Gave it wings. You were my guardian angel. And you saved me. The one thing I wanted to see when you walk down the aisle...is wings. Because together, our feet will never touch the ground again."

She couldn't speak for a moment. Those words had come straight from his heart and she couldn't have loved him more for saying that. For telling her what those wings on her dress meant to his heart.

He jumped up from the loveseat, his cheeks flushed. "Sorry if I messed up your dress, babe," he said in a sedate voice and shoved his hands in his pockets, turning away. "Cross that off the list, Mr. Carini. I'll come up with something else. Just give me a moment."

"Don't you dare, Jack Casey," she said, sliding to her feet. "Mr. Carini, don't change a thing."

She put her arms around him and held him tight, her eyes growing misty. "You didn't mess up my dress, Jack. And that was the most beautiful reason I can imagine to add wings to my wedding dress. We'll just trust Mr. Carini's vision to make everything delicate and ethereal—like glass. Like you requested."

When she finally let Jack go, she turned to see Mr. Carini grinning at them as he sketched. He'd been inspired by Jack's heartfelt explanation, too.

"I think that's exactly what I needed to hear," said Mr. Carini as he opened his brown leather briefcase that set beside the chair. "Grazie, Signorina Smith and Signor Casey. I'll send my sketches to Jennifer Collins. She'll run them past the two of you for any changes before it gets posted for voting."

Jack turned around, still looking subdued. "Thanks for everything, Mr. Carini," he said. "It's a real honor to have you sketch a dress for Talia."

Mr. Carini reached out and shook Jack's hand and then hers. "I'll have your sketches soon." He hurried out of the room, briefcase in hand.

"And print that," said Steve. He looked at Jack, smiling, and shook his head. "Damn, Jack—Herb's gonna lose his mind when he sees that footage. Beautiful!"

Jack just shrugged, still looking a little embarrassed. But she loved him for being so honest and speaking from his heart like that.

"I love you," she whispered in his ear as she leaned over and kissed him. "And I love the wings."

He gave her a half-hearted look. "You sure. I don't want to ruin your dress, Tal."

"Jack...it will be amazing. I know it will." She nudged his shoulder with hers. "Come on. Let's go practice our waltz."

Nodding, he walked out of the room and into the hallway that led to the back of the chateau. And the patio.

32

Dressed in his blue Brioni suit, black dress shoes, and a white T-shirt, Jack stood at the window of their suite, staring out at the darkness, waiting for Talia to return from viewing her wedding dress sketches. He told her he didn't want to see the dress until their wedding and she understood.

He stared out at the growing twilight that shadowed the dense trees and shrubs at the edge of the chateau's backyard. Feeling Abaddon's heavy, growing presence beyond the patio. Just beyond the seraphim wards.

With something dark and unholy brewing up from Hell—that had Lucifer's hand all over it. They had something planned. Something worse than setting up the soul tether in his lost phone. Much worse.

And for the first time since he'd been dragged off to Hell and escaped, he felt afraid.

Lucifer's retribution was coming. In a form he didn't recognize yet. Something hidden right under his nose that had gone unnoticed. Slipped past the wards and crouched, ready to strike when Abaddon confronted him again.

That eight-foot monstrosity wanted to kill Talia. And him—to take his soul straight to Lucifer for an eternity of torture. Would make a terrible ending to the royal wedding that Talia had dreamed of since they met.

Lucifer was never going to let him marry the woman he loved. And be happy. No, the King of Hell would just let him get close—and think he could marry her.

Somehow though, he had to ensure that at least Talia survived this ugly last gasp of revenge that Lucifer lived for right now—and was using Abaddon to get it.

The thought of losing her forever again made his eyes sting and his heart ache. Even if he managed to survive Abaddon's next assault, he still feared how Heaven would handle his and Talia's situation.

When they took back his halo and wings—and they would—there would be tons of places where he couldn't follow her anymore. Like back up to Heaven. Besides, she was an angel of death. Azrael's best. The archangel's right hand.

They'd never release their best angel of death and let her live a new life with him on earth.

Looked like he'd earned another Hollywood ending. All smoke, mirrors, and CGI. None of it real—or lasting. And he'd be alone again. Empty. Worse—broken and heartsick. *If* he escaped Lucifer and Abaddon.

How could he go on without her? Even the thought broke his heart.

Something red flashed in the distance. His skin began to crawl.

Demon eyes. Hellhounds. Shifting in the shadows. Hanging there in the growing night. Calling out to him, challenging him to come and face them.

Their voices rasped against his ears.

Jack...come out and play, the assassin demons hissed through the silence.

Face me, little human. Abaddon called out in the growing dark. *Stop hiding behind your little death angel's robes and let's end this, Casey. You don't really want to watch me tear her apart right in front of you, do you? Negotiate. While you still can.*

He turned away from the window, shutting out Abaddon and the demonic voices.

Negotiate with demons? Lucifer? The king of manipulation and treachery? That wasn't a negotiation. It was a death sentence. But his options were fading fast. When Heaven took back its wings and halo, he'd be defenseless against these creatures. Lucifer would own his ass —and his soul. And he'd have nothing to bargain with...nothing that Lucifer—or Abaddon—wanted.

At least he had the seraphim powers right now. Failsafed again by Seraphina, but hey, that was better than no powers at all, right? At least for now.

Tonight, he and Talia were scheduled to perform their waltz on camera beneath the stars on the moonlit patio. Right after Armand and Izzy. Voting on the show's website opened tomorrow at noon. Herb had played all the commercial spots for them at lunch and showed them all the announcements and buzz across social media platforms.

The fans loved being able to vote for their favorite couples and be a part of the decision-making process this time around. It had gotten a lot of attention on social media.

He just hoped he'd still be alive—and not back in Hell—by the time they announced the live results on Friday. Regardless of what happened to him, he had to make sure Talia survived Abaddon and any vengeance triggered by Lucifer.

He loved her and he'd protect her with his last breath. She had to survive this fight.

The doors to the suite creaked open. He looked up.

Talia stepped into the suite, dressed in a short, sleeveless midnight blue dress with silver accents that looked like stars across the bodice. That dark blue made her grey eyes so luminous, her smile brighter than today's sunset.

"Jack!" she cried, heels ticking against the marble floors as she rushed over and threw her arms around him. "Oh, Jack—it's just breathtaking! You're right. Mr. Carini is an absolute wizard. He took all our ideas and turned it into a fantasy. I just love it! Especially the wings."

"Really?" he said, smiling, smoothing the hair out of her eyes.

He hadn't ruined her dress. He was so relieved.

"Yes! It's just beautiful! I hope I get to wear it."

He put his arms around her and held her close. "If we don't win, I'll make sure that Mr. Carini makes that dress for you."

She kissed him and he felt his dark mood lighten, but not his worry. Or the burden of facing Abaddon alone if it came down to that. He had to protect the love of his life.

"Ready to dance in the moonlight with me?" he asked and gazed into the deep grey pools of her eyes.

"Forever," she said, leaning up to kiss him.

He didn't know how long forever would last with the demonic threat massing out there. He just hoped he had a little more time than tonight.

HE AND TALIA stepped out into the center of the moonlit patio, cameras and set lights clustered around the rim, a silhouette against the darkness. He felt the demons pressed against the edges of the wards. Waiting.

But the indigo velvet night chirred with crickets and frog peeps, dragonflies thrumming as a cool wind whispered through the trees surrounding the patio. The air smelled sharp with stargazer lilies and soft with dew-covered grass. Rich shadows of evergreens and box hedges stretched across the bubble and flow of fountains just off the patio.

Herb slouched behind his chair, Steve standing beside him, a hand on his headset. Herb wore tan slacks and a tan V-neck sweater over a blue dress shirt. Steve was in jeans and a grey flannel shirt.

"And cue the waltz music," said Steve in a low voice. "Go ahead, Jack and Talia. Whenever you're ready."

A quartet of harp and strings played bright but soothing notes across the patio from the sound system. He didn't recognize the music, but Talia did. Her face lit up as he lifted his right arm and gripped her left hand, sliding his arm around her waist.

"It's Mozart, Waltz in F Major," she said.

"Didn't know you liked classical music," he said as they took their first steps across the patio to warm up.

"I don't," she said. "And I hate harp music, but I helped Mozart cross over. I was with him in his final, dark days."

He was stunned silent, his mouth open. "Wait, you knew Mozart?"

She nodded as he almost tripped over his own feet. "Your halo would spin backward if you knew the famous—and infamous—people I have crossed over."

"Speechless," he said and turned her as she got comfortable with the steps.

It amazed him how light on her feet she was, how graceful and poised. But much of the time, he forgot she was an angel. Until she unfurled those wings. He'd even gotten used to seeing the gold halo revolving around her head. It was subtle, not like the cartoons or Hollywood classic angels. It was like a reflection because angels were all air and light in their celestial forms, but they also had human-like bodies. Which made it easier for them to interact with humans.

He smiled. And love them—like she loved him.

She was so breathtakingly beautiful, black hair in shiny waves, those light grey eyes reflecting the pale gold light of her halo. Shining brighter than the moon's reflection tonight as she stared into his eyes.

He spun her around, turning her around the patio. Her feet mirrored his as they melded with the music and the moonlight, turning and moving as one. He barely felt the ground underneath his feet as their dance became fluid like the stream flowing alongside Eolowen's paths. Like the air currents rushing through the clouds. Like the steady ebb and flow of his breath in the cool air. All he felt was the warmth of her hand against his, the burn of her eyes only for him, and the drift of the melody lilting around him.

"Jack?"

He heard someone call his name, but he was lost in the moment.

"Jack!"

Finally, the music stopped and Steve stood beside him, grinning, a hand on his shoulder as he halted after another turn.

"We're done filming," said Steve, his gaze moving from him to Talia. "Beautiful, guys. Sorry I had to interrupt."

Jack let go of Talia's hand and stepped back, glancing around. Most of the crew had gathered around the edges of the patio. Watching them dance. Including Armand and Izzy. The whole damned cast and crew stood there watching.

Feeling embarrassed, he laid a hand against the back of his neck, rubbing. "Sorry about that," he said in a quiet voice. "Got a little lost in her eyes."

He felt Talia's arms slide around him from behind and hold him close.

Steve turned toward the cameras. "Couldn't tell at all, could you?"

Laughter echoed across the patio.

"All right, that's a wrap!" Herb called from his chair, a smile on his face. "The fans are going to have a tough time voting tomorrow. See you tomorrow at your interviews."

Jack pulled Talia around to his side and put his arms around her. He leaned down.

"What do you say we send the squad on patrol for an hour and head up to the suite?"

She grinned at him. "I'll have to send Muriel on an errand."

"A really long one," he added. "To Malaysia."

She laughed as they headed back inside the chateau.

FRIDAY NIGHT, he and Talia returned to the patio. He wore a charcoal grey suit (another Brioni that he hadn't worn for over two years) and a grey silk T-shirt. Talia wore a short, ice blue strapless dress that shimmered with crystals. She looked like she'd just floated down from the Heavens, halo burning bright, grey eyes shining in the simulated candlelit glow of the patio. For the very last challenge.

Gianni was on his and Talia's left, dressed in a black tailcoat, fuchsia bowtie with a white tuxedo shirt. Beside him, Izzy fidgeted, dressed in a short, sparkly fuchsia gown with spaghetti straps. Devin stood facing them, staring into camera one in his black tailcoat, white tuxedo shirt, and royal purple bowtie. His light brown hair was freshly highlighted and those over-white, vaneered teeth glistened. He held a card in his hand after introducing the couple's interviews as they waited for the canned clips to run and then the commercials. The show had fourteen minutes left.

"Well, Jack," said Gianni, studying him a moment. "It's almost that time. I hope you and Talia win. Izzy and I can't wait to watch you two get married. Talia asked Izzy to be one of her bridesmaids and she was thrilled.

He smiled, remembering Talia asking Muriel to be her maid of honor last night. Muriel was a little overwhelmed and surprised. Her grey eyes got all misty and she headed up to the roof to patrol immediately after that. He chuckled. Wiping back tears.

"Talia and I wish you and Izzy the best, Gianni," he said and extended his hand. "And we hope you win the wedding package and all the fame that comes from it. But you'd better show up as my best man when Talia and I get married."

Gianni shook his hand. "Jack, Hell's demons couldn't keep me from you and Talia's wedding."

Maybe not its demons, but Abaddon and Lucifer were a whole 'nother episode. He hoped they didn't kill him before his wedding. He kept his game face in place.

"Glad to hear that," Jack replied.

"Fifteen seconds," Steve called. "Devin, camera one all the way out."

Devin gave him a thumb's up and turned toward camera one as he stared at his last card. In just a few minutes, Steve would hand him the envelope with the winning couple's name inside.

Talia rubbed her hand down his arm and he turned back to her, kissing her lips.

"Nervous?" she asked.

His heart had begun to race, fingers turning cold. He nodded.

"Haven't been this nervous since The Prince Charming Hour when I asked you to marry me."

She held up her left hand with his ring still on it, telling him she was still at his side. Through her falling from the Heavens, to bringing him back from the dead in the Garden, and fighting Lucifer beside him at the crossroads. Through demons dragging him off to Hell and holding her captive in the Middling's watchtower. Through endless challenges and another two seasons of this reality television show. She'd worn it throughout, loving him despite everything they'd endured together.

"I'm nervous, too," she said in a half-whisper.

"And despite everything we've gone through to stay together, you're still wearing my ring."

She nodded. "Because I love you, Jack Casey. Forever."

He kissed her as Steve counted down the last commercial break and stepped out of camera range, off the patio. Jack's stomach twisted into a knot. Steve was going to retrieve the winning name from the results and hand the envelope to Devin in a minute or so.

"Welcome back, my royal subjects," Devin said into camera one as the show's host strolled across the balcony, moving in between Gianni and Izzy and then him and Talia.

Devin smiled at Izzy and then Talia and turned back to camera one.

"And now, we come to our crowning moment on this show. The announcement of our royal wedding winning couple, chosen by your votes. This season, our fans have chosen the couple they'd most like to see get married in a royal wedding."

Devin pointed toward the black French doors. "Any moment, one of our set coordinators is going to walk through those doors and hand me a sealed envelope with the name of our Royal Wedding Hour winning couple inside."

The show's host turned back around and retraced his path around Jack and Talia and then around Gianni and Izzy. He moved with relaxed, ambling steps.

"We asked our royal subjects to vote for their favorite bridal bouquet, their favorite couple's waltz, and their favorite bride's dress," he said and turned toward camera one again. He held up three fingers to the camera. "Three votes cast for your favorites. The process and its results have been counted and certified by Beddle and Knutson Worldwide Auditing Services."

Jack glanced over his shoulder, past the fountains. Toward the ring of evergreens. Abaddon stood in front of the bay laurel hedges, all eight feet of him. The massive demon glared at him with those glowing red eyes that bore through him like lasers.

"They can't hear me, Jack Casey," Abaddon called out. "Not even your little angel of death beside you. But you can. I'm waiting for you to fight or negotiate."

Jack just stared. He was in a live broadcast. What could he say?

"Retribution is coming," said Abaddon, his voice rumbling through the growing twilight and deepening shadows. "Ready to unleash against all your little angels of death. Even that kind-hearted archangel that likes you. All of them will perish unless you face me. Alone." He pointed a meaty, leathery finger at Talia. "I'll even stop hunting your little protector there if you give yourself up and face me. Or negotiate with Lucifer."

Did Abaddon have the power to destroy Talia and her entire death angel guard? Including Archangel Azrael? He felt sick.

He turned back around after Talia gave him a strange look.

"Think hard about that, little human. Before you reach that point of no return. And have to watch all these angels perish. At my hand."

And then he was gone as Devin's voice crashed back into the foreground again.

"Jack and Talia," said Devin, motioning at them. "I wish you good luck. Armand and Isabella, best of luck to you." The host turned toward camera one again. "America, this had to be a very difficult choice, deciding between our two most popular couples."

The French doors creaked open.

Steve, dressed in a black tailcoat, white tuxedo shirt, and royal purple bowtie stepped through the doorway, a grin on his face. His hair was slicked back off his bearded face as he stepped toward Devin and extended an official-looking, crisp white envelope printed with the show's season four logo in purple. A big purple waxed seal held a wide purple ribbon across the envelope.

Devin moved across the balcony and hit his final mark as Steve backed out of camera range and hurried around the edge of the balcony, back beside Herb. He bent down and whispered in Herb's ear.

Herb's poker face held as he watched the final moments of the final live elimination show. Steve gave Devin a thumb's up.

Then his mother stepped behind the cameras in her black and white attendant's uniform. It felt strange, but his anger had blunted a little since they'd talked. A little.

He turned away, his stomach doing somersaults. Time to share the results.

He stood up straighter and his arms tightened around Talia.

This was it. The moment he found out whether he was getting married now or later. He looked over at Gianni and gave him a sharp nod in support.

"And now, it's time to open the results and share the names of our winning royal couple with America's royal subjects."

Holding the envelope up to the light, Devin slid his index finger under the ribbon and tugged until the wax seal broke. He pulled the purple ribbon away and tore open the envelope's flap.

With thumb and forefinger, Devin slid out a purple card. His fingers shook a little as he opened up the card and read what was inside. A grin touched his face as he looked into the camera.

"My royal subjects, all your votes have been counted. And the winning couple of The Royal Wedding Hour is…"

Jack felt his heart race like an Indy 500 car burning track toward that waving, black checkered flag.

Devin grinned into the camera, watching them squirm.

"It's…Jack and Talia! Congratulations! You're about to be married in the biggest live wedding that television has ever seen!"

My God. It was real. They won. And he was getting married.

Stunned, Jack felt overcome by emotion as Talia threw her arms around him. He kissed her hard on the lips, his whole body shaking.

Then he took her left hand in his and got down on one knee and the patio went deathly quiet.

"Shit, hold cameras—Jack's going off script." Herb said in a soft, anxious voice.

"Hold positions," said Steve. "And keep rolling."

"Talia, I'll never know what made you accept that empty cardboard box from me four seasons ago," he said, squeezing her hand. "When I offered you my heart, you had no idea that beat up cardboard box held all the broken and shattered pieces of my heart in it. And you had no idea how hard it was going to be to put them all back together again."

Her luminous grey eyes grew glassy as she grinned at him.

"And somehow, you put them back together again. Piece by painstaking piece as you watched me search for you, fight for you, and even defend you. And take my last breath for you. No matter what comes next, I just want to thank you for teaching me to fly and for keeping my heart safe in your hands. Because I'll never stop falling in love with you and I'd do every last moment of this over again as long as you're there at the end waiting for me. I love you—now until forever."

He pulled a small, square box out of his suit jacket pocket and opened the lid. Showing her a large, square cut, ice blue aquamarine on a gold band.

"Will you still marry me? After four seasons of putting up with me?"

"Oh, Jack—it's beautiful," she said with a gasp and pulled him to his feet. "Jack Casey, I'd marry you a million times over. Not for fame. Not for money. Because without you, my heart can't beat and my world can't turn. I love you. Now until forever."

He took the ring out of the box and slid it onto her left ring finger, above his dad's wedding ring. Then he got to his feet and wrapped her in his arms, kissing her.

"And we're clear!" Steve cried, grinning. Wiping away a tear. "Jack...you've got our director over here crying."

"I'm not crying," Herb snapped. "You're crying!"

And then Gianni grabbed Jack and hugged him as Izzy hugged Talia.

"I knew when you and Talia got totally lost in that waltz on the patio that this was your wedding, Jack," said Gianni, letting him go. "And I couldn't be happier for you."

"Thanks," he said in a tight voice, choked up and almost unable to talk. "Wanted to give Talia the royal wedding she deserves."

Herb and Steve walked over to him and Gianni as Talia slid her arms around his waist. Gianni pulled Izzy into his arms.

"Well, Armand and Izzy, it's been a pleasure," said Herb, extending his hand.

Jack stepped between them.

"Not so fast, Herb," he replied. "You're looking at my best man and one of Talia's bridesmaids. These two aren't going anywhere."

Herb's eyes got big. "Are you serious? We talked about having previous contestants as part of the wedding party, but decided that wasn't fair to the winning couple."

Talia laughed. "And Mark Banks is Jack's other groomsman."

The biggest grin he'd ever seen stretched across Herb's face. "This is the best news ever! I've got to get publicity on this right away. Tomorrow at one o'clock sharp, we all sit down and plan Jack and Talia's wedding. Armand and Izzy, be there, too. I'll get Banks up here as soon as possible."

And Herb rushed off the patio, Steve in tow.

Devin shook Jack's hand next and then hugged Talia. "Congratulations, Jack and Talia! I'm so happy for you two. I'm thrilled that I get to be a part of it. See you tomorrow. We've got a wedding to plan."

Jack turned to Talia and pulled her into his arms. "Cinderella's finally getting married, babe," he said and kissed her.

"To her Prince Charming," she replied, returning his kiss.

He still felt a little stunned. He was getting married. On live television.

But his excitement faltered at Abaddon's rumbling laughter that echoed across the fountains, around the box hedges, and through the evergreens. The massive demon was calling him out again.

"Time's running out, little human. I will soon break through these wards. And when I do, I will destroy your friends and all those angels. Including your angel of death bride, Jack Casey. Unless you face me."

He was running out of options. Abaddon and Lucifer weren't going to let him get married. But until Abaddon tore through those wards, he still had time. He could still protect Talia—no matter what it cost him.

33

ON SATURDAY, TALIA AND JACK MET WITH THE CREW AND ALL THE
wedding people—including his mother—in the chateau's dining
room. A dozen people wedged around the long, rectangular dining
table in those padded burgundy chairs with another dozen or so
folding chairs scattered around it. Jack's mother was coordinating the
event setup alongside Jennifer and Steve. The room still smelled like
onions and pepperoni from the calzones at lunch.

Talia turned the gold aquamarine engagement ring around and
around her finger, mesmerized by its pale blue shimmer. It was
exquisite and probably cost Jack a lot of money.

Herb, the director looked ecstatic, dressed in grey dress slacks and
grey dress shirt as he talked in a quiet voice to several people seated in
the folding chairs.

*Something, something, marketing. Something, something wedding party.
Publicity. Jack something or other and genius.*

Guess Herb loved Jack's off-script proposal last night almost as
much as she had. Jack's voice had broken a couple of times as he laid
his heart bare to her again. Live. On camera for the world to hear. She
was the luckiest woman and angel in existence because he loved her
so deeply and completely. And he walked his talk. He'd sacrificed

himself for her more times than she could count, so she knew that he'd meant every word.

And she loved him for that.

Mr. Carini was there with his incredible sketches of her fairytale wedding dress. And so was Muriel, looking human in a short jean skirt and grey sweater, her wings and halo hidden from everyone else in the room—except Jack.

Jack sat between Talia and Armand, looking distracted as he twisted the zipper pull on his Navy blue hoodie, right leg propped on his left. He wore another faded pair of Levi's and a grey Henley, his light blond hair looking sexy and a little windblown. But worry burned in those pale green eyes, churning with all the other emotions she'd suddenly seen there in the last twenty-four hours.

Was it his mother's presence? Or something darker? She remembered the expression on his face yesterday as they waited on the patio for Devin to read the results. He saw something out in the chateau's dusky backyard shadows. She'd asked him a couple of times about it, but he just smiled and deflected her questions.

A lot of the pre-wedding planning had already been done through show challenges. And before they'd even begun filming—blood tests, birth certificates, and wedding licenses. She had to enlist the help of God's Scribe with all of those items before she and Jack ever left Heaven. Pravuil had given her all the identification pieces, paperwork, and documents she needed. They'd even elected to have a civil servant for their ceremony. Jack wasn't religious, especially after everything he'd seen and endured. He'd lived through Hell and even experienced a sliver of Heaven.

For a lot of the wedding's minor details, she and Jack had already made choices before filming or during the actual challenges. Like choosing their cake flavors and wines for the reception. They also got to choose the courses for a sit-down dinner at the rehearsal and after the wedding. The flowers were chosen and so was her dress. She grinned. Her ethereal Cinderella wedding gown—with wings—that would leave Jack speechless. Mr. Carini just needed to get measurements for Muriel's and Izzy's ice blue bridesmaid dresses.

For the men, Jack chose something called an Italian morning coat in a soft, gorgeous grey with a double-breasted silk vest in a lighter grey, and an ice blue ascot which pleased Mr. Carini who would fit Jack, Armand, and Mark when he got here from Los Angeles. She couldn't wait to see Jack in this wedding suit, looking like her Prince Charming.

Their rings were simple gold bands and she liked their sleek simplicity. They reminded her of halos. The band would look perfect with the large aquamarine engagement ring he'd given her. But she wouldn't ever take off the silver band he'd given her. The show had already taken a bunch of pictures of the rings.

"Okay, I think that's everything except the vows," said Jennifer, glancing at an assistant who sat behind her, typing notes on a laptop computer.

Jennifer had on a thin burgundy cardigan over a black top and black pants. She wore a pair of black glasses. They slid down the bridge of her nose as she glanced at the tall, skinny young assistant with clipper-cut black hair and gold framed glasses on his nose as he typed on the laptop.

"Talia," Jennifer said, turning around. "You and Jack need to write your vows and turn them in to me by next Friday."

Jack's face darkened. "For approval?"

He didn't like that at all.

Jennifer shook her head. "Not for approval. Just need to fit the live ceremony and taped footage into forty-eight minutes. So, we just need to attach an allotted time to that part as we make sure we fit everything else into our time slot. We have to account for everything spoken. And the officiate for your ceremony needs to know what you're each going to say."

Talia reached over and rubbed his knee. He laid his hand on top of hers and squeezed.

"Fair enough," Jack said and glanced at her. "Talia and I will write them and turn them in separately. I don't want to know what she's going to say until the actual ceremony."

She and Jack had talked about the vows and they both agreed they wanted that part to be a surprise.

"That's perfect," said Jennifer. "Thank you." A smile touched her face as she turned back around. "Oh, forgot to tell you, Jack and Talia. Apparently, that emerald cut aquamarine you gave Talia has caused an uptick of ring sales across the country."

One corner of Jack's mouth lifted. "Wish I'd bought stock."

Jennifer laughed. "You caused quite a stir behind the cameras and in front of them last night with that off-script proposal, Jack. It's all people are talking about today in entertainment news."

He glanced at her and she smiled, reaching out and caressing his cheek. "I'll never stop talking about it either."

"Thanks, babe," he said.

"And now, I'll turn it over to Herb," said Jennifer, sitting down.

Herb lingered a moment beside the people in the chairs and returned his attention to the table as he stood where Jennifer had been.

"All right, crew," Herb began, hands against the table as he leaned toward everyone gathered around the table. "We have two weeks to put together this wedding for a live broadcast. We have to turn that hidden fountain venue into Cinderella's enchanted courtyard and outfit our wedding party in Carini and Amanté threads." He held out his hand and motioned Jack's mother to the table.

He stiffened, letting his right foot slide to the floor as he sat up straight. Staring at her with an emotionless expression. Talia didn't know if he was putting up a front or if he'd just gotten numb to seeing her now.

Jack's mother had on a flowing leopard print blouse over black pants and she wore red glasses, her hair in that sleek, black-cherry bob.

"As my son has so graciously agreed, I will be coordinating the wedding alongside set coordinators, Jennifer Collins and Steve Kosinski. So, check with me about third party vendor arrangements like flowers, catering, and clothing. Check with Jennifer about ceremony and logistics. If its infrastructure, check with Steve." She smiled. "And if you're not sure, check with Jennifer. She's in charge."

With that, Jack's mother sat down and Steve got up from his chair and stood beside Herb. He had on jeans and a purple T-shirt with the show's logo.

"All right, as Jack's mother indicated," said Steve, gazing around the table. "I'm handling infrastructure—and filming the lead up to the live ceremony show. Devin over there will be doing a lot of roving reporter stuff as he walks the grounds and interviews crew and our wedding party during preparations. If you're out of your suite, you're fair game for the cameras, so don't forget that."

"Where will the wedding be held?" Armand asked.

Steve grinned. "I'm glad you asked that Armand. Jack and Talia found the secret fountain pool, so the wedding will be held at sunset at the secret fountain in the back of the chateau. From there, the wedding party will walk back to the patio and inside to this large dining room where we'll have the reception. All the furniture will be removed and staged for the reception which will all be a surprise for our bride and groom."

"Do Banks and I get to make Jack falling-down drunk at a bachelor party before the big day?" Armand asked as the room broke into laughter.

Including Jack who reached over and patted Armand on the shoulder.

"What's a best man good for if he can't get the groom drunk before the wedding?"

"I promise to look the other way on that part," said Jennifer.

"And I'm sure I can misplace a few bottles for the occasion," said Jack's mother.

Even Jack chuckled at her comment.

"I like her," said Armand, motioning at Jack's mother.

Jack seemed unaffected by Armand's comment.

"And that's all from me," said Steve. "Jennifer?"

"Talia, Muriel, and Izzy, dresses will be ready by the end of the week, so we'll film the fittings then."

Muriel's eyes got wide. "Film?"

Jennifer smiled. "Welcome to Hollywood, Muriel."

Jack laughed out loud which made Talia laugh, too. Muriel looked uneasy now.

"Okay, everyone," said Jennifer, cradling her clipboard against her chest. "We'll talk about the rehearsal parts next week. Until then, remember you're on camera."

Talia walked with Jack and Muriel out of the dining room and back to the suite. To meet Azrael. Who had news from God's Scribe about Abaddon.

BY THE TIME they got to the suite, Azrael was there pacing, hands behind his back, charcoal grey robes fluttering and soot-grey wings twitching. His silver-black hair looked windblown and he looked anxious.

"Talia!" he cried, moving toward her and Muriel as Jack closed the door behind them.

Something was wrong. It set her on edge.

"What's wrong, sir?" she asked.

He took her by the shoulders, his wings extending, red-gold halo turning faster.

"Lucifer's been busy since we tethered his halo to Hell," said the archangel. He let her go and motioned at Jack. "Even before you and Jack returned to earth, Lucifer was busy setting up transfer points."

Jack frowned and stepped beside her. "Transfer points?"

Azrael nodded, motioning toward the back of the chateau. "He's used his sparse resources to his advantage, allowing him to transfer himself from demon to demon, testing the limits of his halo tether. He had them stationed across this vineyard before the vineyards were warded, allowing him to hop across demons and take control. Which lets him be present in your world, Jack. And a terrible danger to you."

Talia gasped and grabbed hold of Jack, holding him close.

"Pravuil thinks that Lucifer has also used this technique to gain control of Abaddon. But he has a plan."

Jack glared at the windows. "So, the times that I've encountered Abaddon out there, I was really talking to that little bitch, Lucifer?"

Azrael nodded. "He found a way to strike back at you, Jack and he's taking full advantage of it."

"Then we have to find a way to shut down all these demons and send his consciousness back to Hell. And to do that, we have to beat Abaddon in a fight."

"Afraid so, Jack," said the archangel. "Wish I had better news."

"So do I," Jack replied, his expression darkening. "Didn't you say Pravuil had a plan?"

Azrael nodded, hands on his hips as he paced through the suite. By now, her squad had blinked into the room and had crowded around the archangel.

"Let's hear it," said Jack, standing in front of the archangel.

Azrael glanced at Talia, still looking concerned. "Pravuil said that to dislodge Abaddon from Lucifer's control, we have to get through to God's Destroyer of the Wicked."

Jack shook his head. "Nothing gets through to that creature. We've tried over and over. Nothing gets through except violence. And he can't be killed, so stalemate."

"Pravuil says the same thing, Jack. But this time, he has a plan. I know we forbid you to use it, but you'll have to use omnificence without Lucifer knowing it."

"Me?" Jack replied, laying his hand against his chest.

Azrael nodded.

"Why not me?" Talia asked, stepping forward. "I'm the angel of death here. I was built for this power, not Jack."

When Azrael sighed, she already knew the answer. It was the seraphim powers. He needed both. Why hadn't she drawn those powers out of the healing stone instead of Jack!

"With the seraphim powers," said Azrael, "Jack will be able to break Lucifer's connection to Abaddon. By being in two places at once—in Abaddon's consciousness and outside of it—Jack can convince to

Abaddon to break free of Lucifer's control and sever their link. Pravuil said that Abaddon willingly allowed Lucifer control because he's angry at the world and angry at Heaven. And he's sworn to kill you, too, Talia."

Talia was angry at Heaven, too. "So, Heaven is expecting Jack to confront both of them alone as he presents himself to Lucifer and Abaddon simultaneously?"

"Yes, Talia, that's the plan," said Azrael, crossing his arms against his chest. "Breaking Lucifer's control will at least halt Abaddon's murderous quest to end both of you."

"Then what about my staying with Jack?" Talia demanded, hands on her hips. "And what happens with Jack's wings?"

"I should have an answer about staying with Jack shortly, Talia," said Azrael, beginning to pace again. "And about Jack's wings…"

He stammered and then shook his head.

"What about them, sir?" Talia asked, feeling queasy at his avoidance of her questions.

"They uh…can't be removed," he said in a small, tight voice.

"What?" Jack cried. "What do you mean they can't be removed?"

A heavy sigh escaped from Azrael's lips as he fixed Jack with his gaze. "Jack…if we remove them, we turn you into a fallen angel."

"Which means?" Jack asked, his voice rising.

"Worst case scenario: you fall to Hell," said Azrael.

Jack's face turned pale.

"Best case scenario: you're banned from the Heavens for eternity."

Jack's eyes got wide. "Even after I die?"

Azrael cleared his throat. "Yes. If you died, you'd be banned from Heaven. And that's why we can't take your wings. Which brings up one more issue."

"There's more?" Jack said, his voice rising.

He looked sick.

"Yes. Jack—you aren't uh…aging—anymore."

Jack looked stunned, his gaze falling away from Azrael as he turned toward the windows.

"What does that even mean?" Jack said in a quiet voice.

"We don't exactly have a precedent for this situation, Jack," said the archangel. "Until we find a way to put you back to your completely mortal human form, we can't take away your wings. We don't exactly know what you are now, Jack. You're one of a kind."

He shook his head. "I don't even know what to say about that."

Azrael sighed. "Neither do we, Jack. And we apologize profusely for this oversight. But the good news is that you and Talia should be able to remain together like this, following her up to Heaven and still living together on earth."

"If Lucifer doesn't manage to drag me back to Hell," Jack said with an angry voice. "Or end me."

"Yes, exactly," said Azrael.

"So, we can still get married?" Talia asked, holding her breath as she waited for Azrael's response.

"Yes, of course." The archangel smiled at her. "Marry this man, Talia. The seraphim are in agreement on that one."

Talia rushed over to Jack and threw her arms around him. At last, the seraphim had responded. She'd have married him anyway, but having their agreement made things easier.

Jack enfolded her in his arms, holding her tight against his chest. "Looks like I've gotta get past Luci one more time."

"We get married first and then we face him," she said against Jack's ear. "Together."

His face had a distant, emotionless expression that unsettled her.

"First, the ceremony and then we fight Luci and Aby together," he replied. "Got it."

There was something in his tone, in his eyes that frightened her. She used her angel senses on him, feeling for the lie, but not even a shadow or a ripple appeared. She held him tight. It was the first time since they'd left Heaven that she'd felt afraid for him. And right now, she was scared to death.

34

For almost two weeks, Jack went through the motions of rehearsals and preparations, acting his way through it all. His heart hurt. Talia didn't quite understand that he was Heaven's sacrificial lamb. But that point had been made crystal clear in Azrael's explanation.

He paced the patio, grey hoodie unzipped, faded jeans swishing against the warm breeze as sunlight streamed through the afternoon clouds. He gazed across the backyard. To the ring of evergreens. Where Steve's set crew had already installed lighting and seating and whatever magical wedding sets they'd created for his and Talia's wedding. He couldn't see what they'd done, but he knew it would be amazing. For Talia and for the audience.

For him, he'd been shot with a strong dose of ugly reality. And it was a fatal wound.

Heaven didn't know what to do with him since he'd contained Lucifer's threat against Heaven, but now, they needed a human sacrifice to stop Abaddon. And his price of admission was getting dragged back to Hell to be Lucifer's punching bag for eternity.

Problem solved.

That's why they told Talia she could marry him. They knew he wouldn't survive an encounter with Abaddon AND Lucifer—even with the seraphim powers. That's why they wanted him to face Abaddon and Lucifer alone. So, their top angel of death didn't get caught in the crossfire. And they could dispose of the abomination that they'd created when they gave him wings and a halo. Tucked away from sight in eternal torment. In Hell.

He couldn't tell Talia any of this. He couldn't break her heart. He had to face Abaddon and Lucifer alone. Save her from a horrible fate. Maybe the seraphim could erase his memory from her consciousness?

So, his absence wouldn't hurt her so much. Because this time, he wouldn't escape Lucifer.

All week, Abaddon—Lucifer—had been calling out to him from the dark. He didn't want to leave Talia at the altar, but he felt Lucifer's control growing. Demons had been popping up in the chateau all week.

They weren't attacking him yet. They were conduits to Lucifer. A show of power. A means of taunting him into this fight to save Talia. He could be in several places at once with the omnificence power, but he couldn't stay there 24/7 to protect Talia.

And Lucifer knew it.

Lucifer meant to show him that one little falter on his part would result in Talia's destruction. Despite Talia's rare powers, Abaddon couldn't be killed.

No, Lucifer had them painted into a corner this time. And the only way to save Talia was to play the good little human sacrifice like Heaven wanted.

That's why he'd offered Lucifer a deal. Yesterday.

He'd offered Abaddon his life in exchange for Talia's. And he planned to renege on it. He'd fight dirty if that's what it took. After all, there'd been no signatures or handshakes.

If Lucifer got hold of him, he'd claim Jack's resurrect power. And that rare angel power would break his halo tether.

Wasn't Heaven forgetting that?

"Nervous, Jack? Tonight's the night."

Startled, he whirled around.

Gianni stood beside him, dressed in jeans and a yellow polo shirt.

"Getting there," he said, forcing a smile.

Couldn't let Gianni know how lost he felt.

"I'll bet you've thought about this day a lot over the seasons, haven't you?"

He nodded. He'd dreamed of this day since he'd offered Talia his heart. Never dreaming that the best night of his life would end with the very worst day. But he had no choice.

Either he faced Lucifer again or the spineless prick would ambush the love of his life—and her death angel guard. And destroy them all, including Berith and Talia's archangel boss. He would protect her at all costs. Azrael said he wasn't aging anymore, but he could still die— as whatever human-angel hybrid he'd become.

"It's all I've ever wanted, Gianni. A life with her. I love her to my last breath."

Gianni smiled and squeezed his shoulder. "Well, dreams do come true, Jack. You and Talia have earned this happily ever after. Everybody deserves to be loved, Jack—even you. I know you think that sometimes you don't deserve it, but trust me, you do. And I'm honored to stand up as your best man and witness it."

"Thanks for everything," he said and hugged the taller actor. "I mean it. I wouldn't be a breath away from this moment without you."

"Glad I could help make it happen," said Gianni.

"Thanks for being there for Talia, too," he replied. "I know you're someone she can turn to no matter what happens."

"Of course," said Gianni. "Always." The soap star squinted at him for a moment. "Everything all right, Jack?"

He nodded. "Yep," he said, turning up his acting an extra notch. "I'm marrying the love of my life in a few hours. Best night of my life."

Live. On a major broadcast. With Lucifer, Abaddon, and a shitload of demons gunning for him. That he had to face alone.

At last, Gianni's smile returned. "I'll see you downstairs in the study soon. Mr. Carini just arrived with our suits and the dresses. Talia, Izzy, and Muriel are in the downstairs bathroom with the stylists and makeup artists already. Getting their hair done and all that."

He couldn't help but smile, remembering how jaw-droppingly beautiful Talia had been when she stood on the palace balcony stage in makeup and her princess dress. He'd never seen anyone so beautiful in his entire life. And he wanted to live through this fight so desperately to stand at that altar and marry her.

But Azrael's words haunted him. He was Heaven's sacrificial lamb. And the only way to erase Heaven's mistake was by letting them all kill each other. And burn in Hell. Either way, he wouldn't get his happily ever after with Talia.

And it made him sick inside.

"Can't wait to see her walking down that aisle to spend the rest of her life with me," he said, choking up.

He'd give anything to reach that moment. To slide that gold wedding band onto her finger and tell her how he'd be with her forever. And mean it.

But he was lost now.

Already doomed to be Lucifer's eternal chew toy again. His only other choice led to Abaddon destroying Talia. He had nothing left to bargain with.

"I'll see you inside soon, Jack," said Gianni and squeezed his shoulder.

The tall soap star sauntered across the patio in his best Cary Grant gait and went inside the chateau. Leaving Jack alone.

Scritch of claws echoed across the patio.

Jack turned.

A red-eyed, leathery skinned demon stood on the patio. Leering at him.

"It's time, Jack," it said in a raspy, scratchy voice. "Deal's been made and I did promise to spare Talia on her big day—if you gave yourself up. A shame she'll be left at the altar, but at least she'll still be in existence. Something you won't appreciate for yourself because I'll be torturing you for eternity. But at least your great love will be spared. Isn't that what you want, Jack?"

Jack glared into the demon's glowing red eyes. "Yes, that was the deal I proposed."

"I do love it when you propose, Jack," said the demon. "So romantic in the glow of Hellfires as I contemplate disemboweling you daily."

"Hell brings out the romantic in me," said Jack with a sneer. "What can I say? Makes me lightheaded as I walk around and tear the limbs off your demons. Luci hates me, he hates me not. He hates me—"

"Shut up, Jack. It's time."

The demon motioned him toward the ring of evergreens.

Sighing, Jack stepped off the concrete patio into the grass. He moved under the shade of tall cypress trees that lined both sides of the huge backyard, past the pool, and over the bay laurel hedges. Into the thick grove of spruce trees. Where no one could see him face Abaddon—and Lucifer—through this demon.

Even as he stepped around the evergreen trees, he felt Abaddon on the other side. His ashen white, leathery skin looked almost translucent as he towered above some of the evergreens that formed an almost fairy ring between the yard and the hidden garden.

He winced, his chest aching. Where he would have married Talia in a couple of hours.

"All right, Jack. Submit to my control. Now. And we'll get this over with."

Wow, just like that. Luci was more desperate than he'd realized. Good.

He lifted his hand against his side, calling up the omnificence power, focusing it on this little clearing. On Abaddon and Lucifer controlling this demon.

With a deep breath, he felt the river of power flood through his body. He focused it down. Onto Abaddon and Lucifer's demon.

And he was moving through the shadows—part of him—sliding toward Abaddon.

He had to distract Lucifer. Stall him.

"How do I know you'll keep your word about sparing Talia?" he demanded.

The words came out at a distance as he moved through the

omnificence power's currents and the shadows to stand in front of Abaddon.

"You're letting him control you. Use you. Why?" he asked Abaddon.

"What else have I to do." Abaddon's gruff, deep voice echoed in his head. "God has forsaken me. Left me for eons in Hell, stuck guarding a gate that no one has ever tried to open. And still, I wait for Him to send me to smite the Wicked. And His enduring silence has broken me at last."

Jack frowned. "So, because God's ghosting you, you've decided to tear up anything and everything in your path like an angry toddler? Dude. Seriously?"

Abaddon was silent as he sat down under the evergreens and leaned against the tree trunks.

"Jack, how many times must I prove my overwhelming strength to you?" the demon said to him.

Just once, Luci. Like when you attacked Heaven and failed. He did his best to hold in his response. Unhinging Lucifer before he freed Abaddon wasn't a good plan at the moment though.

"I just want to know that she's gonna be safe. That's all. A little reassurance. Surely, even you, Luci, can understand that."

"All right," said the demon with a sigh. "Let's go through this again. I'll try to use short sentences and small words this time, so you can keep up. Jack."

In his ethereal form, Jack crossed his arms and glared at Abaddon. *Did all these fallen angels have Daddy issues?* Abaddon felt forgotten and useless. He was like a border collie without a job, chewing up sofas and breaking shit. Called the planet. Hoping to get Dad's attention even for his bad behavior.

Then he remembered Gianni just saying to him that everybody deserved to be loved.

Even Abaddon. If he showed Aby here a little bromance, maybe he'd get him on his side and off Lucifer's demolition team?

He knelt in front of the hulking big angel-turned-demon. "Abaddon, look. I get it. You're stuck in a dead-end job and corporate doesn't know you exist. But getting HR involved isn't going to help your case. Neither is breaking up the company assets. Like earth —and me."

Abaddon's red eyes narrowed and he sat up, his big leathery face about two inches from Jack's.

"You have no concept of eternity, human. And the monotony of waiting centuries—millennia—for a promise that was never fulfilled!"

"I get it," said Jack, laying a hand on Abaddon's ashen white, muscular shoulder. "You were supposed to have the chance to smite humanity and instead, you got nothing. No one to talk to but Luci— that would break anybody. But Luci doesn't want to help you. He wants to use you to get back at God, but dude, trust me, it's never worked for Luci. That's why he's tethered in his playpen without his toys. But you're not. You've got the key and you can go or do whatever you want until that smiting job opens up. Why spend it in Hell?"

"Enough stalling, Jack!" the demon shouted, lunging at his body.

Jack fell backward into the tangle of pine needles on the ground, the demon sitting on his chest.

"What stalling?" Jack replied, holding out his hands. "You haven't shown me anything yet. Haven't given me the slightest reassurance that Talia will survive this stalemate."

The demon's lip curled into a snarl. "What do you call that glimpse of the future, Jack?"

"Fiction," Jack snapped. "That isn't reassurance. That's just some pretty pictures you conjured up. You could show me anything right now." He glared at the demon. "I want assurances that she'll be safe, Luci. Without that reassurance, I won't give you control of anything."

When Jack gazed through the eyes of his ethereal form again, Abaddon towered over him.

Shit. He couldn't fight them both.

"Where would I go?" Abaddon asked.

"Dude," said Jack's ethereal form. "You're so focused on the wicked that you don't know what the good looks like. Dad's gonna blow a gasket if He sends you to smite the wicked and you just smite everybody. Learn about humans. Figure out which one's are worth saving. And have some fun instead of just sitting in Hell listening to Luci's glory days stories." He lowered his voice to a whisper. "Because there aren't any."

"But what would I do?"

"Dude, see the Creation. Go to the beach. Watch the Northern Lights. Hell, run with bulls! Fall in love. Exhaust all the possibilities before you just give up everything to Luci's spoiled, greedy ass. I mean look at you, bro. You used to be an angel. And now you look like some demon on 'roids. Stretch those wings. Find that halo. And use them. Before Lucifer puts you in Hell as a throw rug for eternity."

"It's too late for that," said Abaddon, his deep, rumbling voice sad now. "My wings have dried up and blown away. And my halo has gone dark."

"Nah," said Jack, reaching up to the hulking demon.

He summoned the seraphim powers within him and touched Abaddon's rough, scaly forehead. Releasing a spark of white light that pulsed across his face, down his neck, and over his shoulders.

Red, leathery hands closed around his neck, choking his physical body.

"Whatever you're doing, stop it!" the demon shouted at him. "Right now, Jack. I will end you. Right here. Right now."

Jack struggled against the demon. Using the seraphim power while using the omnificence power had decimated him.

He gritted his teeth and pushed his left hand against the demon's shoulder. Summoning a murder marble.

Reaching up, he shoved it in the demon's mouth.

Three, two, one. Boom!

The demon exploded in a red spray all over the ring of evergreens. And him.

A white flash of light startled him. Blinded him. He covered his eyes as they began to tear up and hurt.

When the bright light vanished, Abaddon towered over him still, surrounded in a bright white aura.

He groaned. Trying to lift his right hand. Couldn't.

Dammit. Lucifer would be back in minutes with another demon

under his control, one he'd hidden around the vineyard before the wards had been placed. And now, Abaddon wanted to grind his face into the sharp, pungent pine nettles clinging to his body.

Or control Abaddon—and grind him into the dust.

"Dude, everybody deserves to be loved—even you," he said, remembering Gianni's words to him only moments ago. "Go out there and find it."

The flutter of wings startled him as pearl white wings unfurled in the white light. Abaddon leaned down, extending his hand. An ethereal, angelic hand.

Jack hesitated a moment and then grabbed hold. He'd used the seraphim powers to heal Abaddon's wings and reignite his halo while controlling omnificence to be in two places at once. And then summoned a murder marble on top of all that.

It was too much. He was done. He couldn't move.

"You freed me, Jack Casey," said Abaddon, his voice rich, lyrical, and baritone deep as he pulled Jack to his feet. "From the downward spiral that Lucifer manipulated. And fed on. I'll return to Heaven. Spend some time in the archive before I set out on this adventure you suggested."

As the light dimmed, Abaddon glowed with the light of his previous angelic form. Hazy image of wheaten hair, soft blue eyes, pearly white wings, and a halo of white-gold light.

"Chicks dig wings," Jack said in a quiet voice. "If they see your angel form, they'll lose their minds. And tell Pravuil I said hi."

"I will, little human," he said. "Now, go—before Lucifer returns with more demons."

He tried to move. Couldn't. Then he felt Abaddon's white light touch him.

"That should get you back inside. And it should slow down the after effects, too."

So, he wouldn't look drunk off his ass when he and Talia walked down the aisle. He grinned. He'd reneged on a deal with Lucifer—and lived.

With wings stretched wide, Abaddon flew out of the ring of

evergreens and disappeared in a flash of light. In moments, Jack was bathed in cool shadows again.

He put one foot in front of the other, feeling dizzy and weak, until he reached the patio. He pushed hard to get to those French doors and managed to pull one open, getting inside. Taking a deep breath, he turned toward the study. He made it inside and over to the yellow loveseat before he crashed headfirst into the arm as darkness spun around him.

35

Jack awoke to someone shaking his arm. He pulled his face up from the pillow, looking into Gianni's kind brown, Cary Grant eyes.

"Jack, get dressed. Now. Or we'll be late."

Gianni was already dressed in tailored grey pants and white shirt. For the wedding. His wedding!

Stumbling up from the sofa, he almost fell to his knees, shaky and running on empty. The power drunk was close, but Abaddon's power was holding it back. He felt grateful as he dragged himself over to the rack of clothes and found the suit bag with his name on it.

Gianni helped him get the grey morning suit out of the bag. He kicked off his loafers and snaked off his jeans, hoodie, and T-shirt, tossing them across the clothes rack. Peeling off his white socks, he grabbed the grey dress socks out of the shiny black shoes with his name on them, size eleven.

He pulled on the socks and pants. From the bag, he grabbed the crisp white, silk dress shirt. Using his angel powers on the clothes, he slid his arms into the sleeves and his wings passed through the fabric, every movement painful. His fingers flew across the buttons, fastening them up to the collar.

Grabbing hold of the clothes rack, he waited out a wave of

dizziness and pulled on the silk, double-breasted vest, buttoning it. Then he pulled on the long, grey morning coat. The last thing he put on was the pale blue ascot and then the dress shoes.

By then, Amber the stylist, a stocky, fortyish woman with red hair and a bright smile, had arrived.

"Sit down, Jack," she said and pulled over a wooden chair from the roll top desk against the bookshelves.

He sat down as she raked a comb through his light blond hair.

"Pine nettles?" she asked, plucking a couple from his bangs.

He just shrugged. "I walked through the evergreens on my way inside."

Gianni chuckled. "Where were you?"

"That ring of evergreens in the back of the chateau," said Jack.

Fighting the King of Hell and God's Destroyer while trying not to die or be dragged off to Hell. Why do you ask?

After Amber had fixed his hair and his ascot and then straightened his haphazard button job, he and Gianni walked out of the study to the entryway. Where Banks stood in his groomsman's grey morning suit.

"Jack!" he cried, rushing up and hugging him. "How you been, man?"

"Banks, glad you made it," he said as the shorter, light brown-haired actor let him go.

"Wouldn't miss it," he said. "Bet you never thought you'd ever get to this moment, did you?"

He shook his head, smiling. He thought he'd be on his way to Hell right now as Lucifer's chew toy. Somehow, he'd freed Abaddon and double-crossed Lucifer. Again. And survived. He bet Heaven was pissed that they still had this abomination on their hands. Azrael would be surprised to see him.

Together, he and his groomsmen posed for a bazillion pictures and then walked across the patio toward the secret garden with its fountain pool.

As he passed the evergreens, he caught sight of a white stone, castle-like tower platform that had been setup for the ceremony. A long, ice blue runner ran between two rows of white chairs on either side of the little round fountain with its koi pond sputtering away in the cool, late day air.

A grey-haired, fifty-something woman in a black pant suit stood beside the tower stage as the camera crews assembled and the set crew adjusted the lights. When the woman saw him, she moved toward him.

"Are you Jack Casey?" she asked.

He nodded. "That's me."

"I'm Samantha Martinelli and I was hired by the show to officiate the wedding."

"Glad to meet you," he said and shook her hand.

"I've got yours and Talia's vows. After the ceremony and filming is over, I'll need you, Talia, and your two witnesses to sign the marriage certificate and you'll be all set."

A string quartet had setup beside the chairs and began tuning their instruments as his mother and her crew setup pale blue urns of Talia's favorite flowers along the aisle leading up to the castle tower altar. Steve's crew pulled wires overhead, moving white and pale blue fabric streamers across the aisle, creating a canopy and arches, framing the aisle. That lit up with little twinkling lights that shimmered like stars overhead.

Another army of set crew poured onto the set, placing what seemed like a million flameless white candles along the aisle and around the altar.

His mother moved toward him. She paused in front of him a moment and then reached out and hugged him, surprising him.

"All right, Jack, Armand, Mark—places at the altar. Look for your marks just like in rehearsal. Good luck, Jack. Can't believe my baby's finally getting married. The last one."

He nodded and said thanks, unsure how he felt about her change of heart.

He wandered over to altar and took his place on his purple square, Gianni then Banks beside him as the crew set out more urns of flowers around them. The spicy scent of stargazer lilies carried on the breeze, softening his nerves.

Gianni leaned toward his ear. "I've got the ring, in case you're wondering."

Jack exhaled a sharp breath. "Thank you. I forgot to even ask."

Gianni smiled and patted him on the shoulder. "You'll do fine. You got the girl. This is finally your happily ever after, Jack. Savor it."

He grinned. At last, he would.

He'd just lived through that encounter with Lucifer and Abaddon. He wouldn't let anything else stop him from marrying Talia.

Then Herb took his place in the director's chair behind the cameras as Devin moved in front, walking the live broadcast audience through the wedding ceremony.

Jack's heart began to pound so fast he thought he was having a heart attack. He looked up as the quartet began to play background music. And grinned.

Azrael, Berith, and Talia's entire guard floated in the skies above the little hidden garden, the fountain's soothing burble floating above the sounds of harp and cello. He'd never seen so many smiles on angels of death before, including Azrael.

Now, all he needed was the woman of his dreams to marry him.

As the sun hung low against the tree line, the set lights flicked on, illuminating the set in a wash of candlelight. And starlight overhead.

His heart raced faster when the quartet began to play Mozart's *Waltz in F Major*. That was the opening cue. His hands began to tremble.

The ceremony was starting.

Izzy appeared first on the aisle, beautiful in a strapless ice blue dress with sheer princess sleeves that hung past her elbows. She took measured steps, holding a small bouquet of stargazer lilies, pale pink English roses, blue hydrangeas, and lavender.

She grinned at Gianni and then smiled at Jack as she took her place across from Banks.

He held his breath as Muriel stepped out with her bouquet, wearing the same strapless ice blue dress with the sheer princess sleeves. She was gorgeous, big light grey eyes shining against the sunset, silky dark brown hair pulled back and piled loose on top of her head.

She grinned at Jack as she stepped onto the castle altar and pecked his cheek. Then she took her place across from Gianni.

When the quartet began to play Pachelbel's *Canon in D*, Jack's heart skipped a beat. Talia's entrance cue.

Someone scattered pale pink rose petals down the starlight aisle.

He held his breath as Talia stepped out from behind the ice blue fabric streamers, a huge bouquet of purple hydrangeas, pale pink English roses, lavender, and stargazer lilies in her hands.

She was a vision rivaling the clouds and the sunset. Her luminous grey eyes burned in the growing twilight. For a moment, he couldn't breathe, his heart slamming against his ribs. He'd loved her from the first moment he saw her that hot August day in Studio 22. One of the best days of his life.

Diaphanous sheer layers of organza and white silk floated around her and streamed behind her in a long train, the white silk fading to an ice blue. Along the skirt that hugged her curves. The bodice was nothing but sheer fabric covered in crystals and pearls that formed a heart shape bodice. It fell into ethereal layers of sheer fabric around her bare shoulders and cascading into translucent princess sleeves that sparkled with more crystals and glistening pearls.

At her shoulders, a pair of sheer gossamer wings sparkled and caught the golden candlelight, holding it around her. Like her halo.

He struggled to pull in a breath as she walked down the aisle toward him, the music swelling.

When she finally reached him, his eyes welled with moisture.

"You're the most beautiful woman I've ever seen, Talia," he said in a quiet, unsteady voice, overcome with her beauty and grace.

"And I'm yours forever," she said, taking hold of his hand.

He was shaking as they turned toward the officiate behind a gold, metal podium draped in hydrangeas and pink roses.

This was it. Finally. His and Talia's happily ever after.

He'd survived Heaven and Hell to get here. And he couldn't wait to get started on the rest of their lives together. Wherever that took them.

"Jack," Talia whispered. "Herb asked me about the honeymoon."

He hadn't even thought that far ahead yet.

"We'll talk about it at the reception," he whispered.

"The network wants to film it," Talia whispered back to him. "But he has to know right away."

Film it? No way!

"Forget it," he said, smiling at the official as she addressed the audience and then him and Talia. "Only room for you and me in this honeymoon. And our bedroom."

"A marriage is a sacred bond between a man and a woman," said the officiate, smiling as the cameras moved in close. "One no one may put asunder."

Hope she told Lucifer that.

"Gianni and Izzy are going to get married here tomorrow," Talia whispered. "They're filming it. They want to send the four of us on a royal honeymoon, Jack. They have to know right away though."

Dammit! He was tired of having a crowd in his bedroom! He wanted Talia all to himself.

"Talia Smith, do you take Jack to be your lawfully wedded husband? To have and to hold, to love and respect, in sickness and in health from this day forward?"

Her smile lit her face as she reached up to touch his face. "I do," she said.

Holding his left hand, Talia took Jack's wedding band from Muriel and slid the gold wedding band onto his ring finger. "Now until forever."

Something scritched and whined behind him. And his skin began to crawl. He glanced over his shoulder.

Behind the chairs and the urns of flowers crouched a legion of demons.

Hellhounds. Shadow panther assassin demons. And an assortment of greater demons. He glanced around for the seraphim wards.

The altar was warded, but a big gap had broken the ward in half between the altar and the chateau. Had Luci and his demons finally broken through one of the seraphim wards?

Muriel stared at him with a mixture of composure and *Holy shit, what did you do, Jack?*

He sighed. Guess that meant Luci had figured out that he'd reneged on their deal.

If he and Talia lived through this ceremony, there'd be one Hell of a reception waiting for them. And they'd spend their honeymoon being hunted.

"The show promised to send us someplace outside of California," she whispered.

Hell was definitely a neighborhood south of Los Angeles.

He glanced up at the sky, seeing Azrael and the guard dropping into phalanx formations.

This was going to get ugly fast.

"Jackson Seeger Casey, do you take Talia to be your lawfully wedded wife? To have and to hold, to love and respect, in sickness and in health from this day forward?"

"Jackson?" Gianni said with a chuckle. "Seeger?" He handed him Talia's wedding band.

"Dad loved Jackson Browne and Bob Seeger—so sue me," Jack said in a sharp whisper.

He held it in his shaking hand as he took Talia's left hand in his.

"I do," he said. "To my last breath. Now until forever."

He slid the ring onto her finger on top of the aquamarine engagement ring. Her eyes filled with tears.

Those eyes would be glowing gold—and furious—when she saw those demons behind them, ready to smite them with every last one of her angel of death powers.

And him when she found out what he'd done.

"Where they trying to send us?" Jack whispered.

"Washington State—to some islands," she answered, gripping his hands in hers.

He held her hands tighter. Islands. Isolated. Easily warded. Might buy them time to shut down Luci's demons? Talia was going to kill him when she found out he'd made a deal—and then broken it—with Lucifer.

Again, he glanced over his shoulder. Shit! Another legion of hellhounds and assassin demons.

"If anyone shows just cause why these two should not be married, speak now or forever hold your peace."

Shit! Lucifer better keep his demon mouth shut.

Talia glanced at him, apprehension in her eyes. He cringed, expecting something to crash through the evergreens or drop from the sky.

But the only sound above the silence was the scritching of hellhound claws above the burble of the fountain.

"I now pronounce you husband and wife," said the official, holding out her arms. "Jack, you may kiss your bride. Talia, you may kiss your groom."

Grinning, he dipped Talia and kissed her with every ounce of strength he had left. She kissed him back hard, her face wet with tears.

Abaddon's angel powers were still holding back the tide of the power drunk hovering in the wings. His wings. He was already spent. He couldn't fight anymore demons tonight, but it looked like he'd have to or he and Talia wouldn't make it back to the chateau in one piece.

He stood her back on her feet and laid his hand against her face. God, she was the most beautiful thing he'd ever seen and she was now his wife. He couldn't help but grin and kiss her again.

"America, I'm delighted to present Mr. and Mrs. Jack and Talia Casey," said the official, motioning for them to turn and face their audience.

And the cameras.

"Before we turn around," he whispered in Talia's ear. "I have good news and bad news."

Her brow shadowed as she stared at him in surprise. He kissed her hand as they began to turn around and face the cameras.

"Good news is we're going to Washington State on our honeymoon," he said, making her grin.

"You'll do the new show?" she cried and he nodded. "What's the bad news?"

He slammed his game face in place. "Lucifer crashed the wedding and we're surrounded by demons," he whispered as they turned toward the cameras. "Not my fault. Mostly."

"Mostly?" she hissed as she came face-to-face with legions of demons surrounding the altar. "Jack Casey, what did you do?"

He smiled his best smile for the cameras. "Tell you later, Mrs. Casey," he whispered and waved at the cameras. "After I wake up from the worst power drunk of my life."

No releasing doves or throwing rose petals at this wedding. Just Holy fire and murder marbles. He had a reception—and a honeymoon —to attend. And Lucifer and his demons weren't on the guest list.

He called up a handful of murder marbles. Time to get this party started.

The End of THE ROYAL WEDDING HOUR: A Game of Lost Souls, Book
Seven
The story continues in...

THE HEAVENLY HONEYMOON HOUR: *A Game of Lost Souls*, Book
Eight
Coming Soon!

NOVELS BY LISA SILVERTHORNE

Standalones:
ISABEL'S TEARS
REDISCOVERY
LANDFALL
PACIFIC BLUE TATTOO

Haunted Portraits series:
BEAUTY: CAPTURED AND FRAMED

A Game of Lost Souls series:
THE CINDERELLA HOUR
THE PRINCE CHARMING HOUR
THE EVER AFTER HOUR
THE FALLEN HEARTS SEASON
THE RISING SPIRITS SEASON
THE ETERNAL SOULS SEASON
THE ROYAL WEDDING HOUR

True Purple series:
RECOMBINANT, Book 1

COMING SOON!

A Game of Lost Souls series:
The Heavenly Honeymoon Hour, Book Eight
The Divine Newlyweds Show, Book Nine
The Celestial Couples Show, Book Ten
The Enochian Apocalypse Show, Book Eleven

Haunted Portraits series:
Monster, Loose and Unhinged, Book Two
Harmony: Recaptured and Under Glass,
Book Three

True Purple series:
Helix, Book 2
Splice, Book 3
Cipher, Book 4

ABOUT THE AUTHOR

LISA SILVERTHORNE has published thirteen novels and more than 100 short stories and novelettes in many genres. Her short fiction has appeared in professional publications that include: DAW Books, Roc Books, *Pulphouse Magazine, Fiction River,* Wildside Press, and Prime Books. She lives in Las Vegas, Nevada.

Before you go, you are invited to please leave a **review of this book**!

Reviews are a wonderful way to help an author. They are also an exciting opportunity to share your honest thoughts with other readers, so **please post yours,** in as many places as possible!

Thanks for reading! We appreciate your support!